Here's a State of Things

Bernard Lockett

Published by

MELROSE BOOKS

An Imprint of Melrose Press Limited
St Thomas Place, Ely
Cambridgeshire
CB7 4GG, UK
www.melrosebooks.com

FIRST EDITION

Copyright © Bernard Lockett 2007

The Author asserts his moral right to
be identified as the author of this work

Cover designed by Bryan Carpenter

ISBN 978 1 905226 96 2

Printed and bound in Great Britain by:
Cromwell Press, Aintree Avenue, White Horse Business Park,
Trowbridge, Wiltshire, BA14 0XB, UK

Dedication

This book is published 25 years after the final performance of the original D'Oyly Carte Opera Company.

The Company is remembered for their 107-year history in performing the works of Gilbert and Sullivan and for their place in the musical theatrical heritage of Great Britain, all to the delight of so many audiences both at home and abroad.

Acknowledgements

I thank most warmly and sincerely my publisher, Melrose Books, and their entire marvellous team for all the valuable, efficient and dedicated work throughout every aspect of the publishing process.

My most grateful and heartfelt thanks to my dear wife, Lea, for her forever wonderful inspiration and encouragement.

Table of Contents

Chapter 1
"In a contemplative fashion..."

The exuberant and excited bustle of the streets of London that night was so typical and like so many other Saturday nights both before and after that late February evening in 1982. This was that in-between time of the winter when early evening is not so black dark but neither does it yet show any true signs of the anticipated flickering spring. The sky hung in a pleasant kind of night blue and to the west there was still showing a tinge of red glow to the far sky as the departing winter sun gave up on its strenuous efforts of the day, at that very moment benefiting the rocks and distant horizons of the Cornish headlands with still a deal more natural light than at the same moment on those London streets.

But what was lost in light from the sky above was more than made up for on those very streets by not only the array of the extensive street lighting itself but also by the brilliant glow of countless light displays from the inviting shop windows, the floodlighting of the many buildings and not least by the house lights and advertising slogans of the numerous theatres lining the various streets. The theatres stood in equal thrill, waiting for the pinnacle of their week's activity – the Saturday night crowds, their audience. If there were ever to be one night in the week when even the most fledgling show would deem to succeed, then surely such a Saturday night audience was assured and

1

theatrical managers could at least sleep more easily for that one night. Satisfaction was then all around.

Even at this relatively early time of the evening, the streets contained a vibrant mixture of massive crowds. People laden with extensive bags as shoppers prepared to head for the station and their journey home, their Saturday's activities by then successfully completed, mingled on the street with more crowds as they came out into the winter's night from the warmth and probably happy escapism of their Saturday afternoon's matinee performances. The fact that their show was over did not dim their excitement because, still tightly clutching their programmes and the remains of the interval chocolates, they still had their happy memories which they would make to last not just for that evening but for the time ahead as well. If all that wasn't enough to make the pavements groan with this inflicted capacity, then still more people were beginning to flood onto the streets as they come into town early on that Saturday evening with an excited anticipation for their own night ahead.

The busyness of the pavements was equally reflected in the roads as the buses, taxis and cars too all did their valued bit to both deliver and collect the crowds. The more people there were, the more congested the pavement, then the appeal of seemingly available street space drew more crowds onto the street itself, spilling off the pavement and onto the street as they rushed along, much to the dismay of the vehicle drivers as they struggled to cope not only with the traffic flows but also with countless sets of feet and swinging bags spilling onto and across the roads as well. But Saturday night would simply not be Saturday night without such mayhem and it was this that gave the ritual a sense of ordinariness, almost a tradition that was as much expected and, who knows, would have been sorely missed by those in town for the night were it not like that. After all, it all added to the occasion, with its sense of activity and drama – people would say "I was there!" and probably with a sense of satisfaction at having been a part of the scene.

Whether it was Piccadilly itself, Oxford Street, Regent Street, Covent Garden or the Strand, then the scene was remarkably the same, a uniform throng. A thrill cast virtually over the entire crowds, whether it was satisfaction with the day spent for those departing the town or the sheer anticipation of the evening to come for those lucky enough to be arriving.

* * * *

Away to the east of the city centre, some six miles off in Stratford where the various roads from north-east Essex and the inner suburbs joined with the route in from Romford and Ilford, all coming together at a very grand junction, a great and masterly circle in which Stratford Church stood proudly in the middle so ably positioned to survey all that was going on around, here more traffic was coming together. Most of these cars themselves had one plan – to continue to head westwards along one route towards Bow, Whitechapel, the City, all with the sole aim of heading to the West End, beckoning enticingly beyond. For most the excitement of the evening was beginning and a Saturday night was already well underway to bring a well-deserved change into the usual weekly routine.

Rupert Moore checked his side-view mirror as he positioned the car to swing right around the circle and to join into the flow of traffic joining from Romford Road to his left. It was clear and in only a matter of seconds the car moved forward before becoming stationary, for a few seconds only, at the red lights beyond the church before once again moving off with the ever-increasing traffic flow that was moving westwards.

"We're in good time," he said as the car clock showed 5.10pm. That was good, he thought to himself before adding "it should not take much more than thirty/forty minutes from here and we'll be in good time – just right in fact," he continued, "to be looking for a parking place just after six which allows us to be on a yellow line twenty minutes before the allowed time of 6.30pm," he concluded with a sense of satisfaction. It was all said and indicated with a sense of military precision that befitted Rupert's plan of campaign for the evening which had begun with the ever so precise departure from home in Westcliff, close to Southend-on-Sea, some 35 miles back eastwards in Essex, at 4pm. The "just-in-case" factor had been diligently built in to the itinerary but so far there had been no need to cover for any unexpected eventualities and the carefully prepared arrangements had worked to an exemplary satisfaction. As with the car's engine, the journey was purring along very smoothly and without problem.

"That's good, Rupert," his grandmother, Alice Harding, commented as the pair headed westwards along their chosen route. Despite being then aged 94, Alice remained a vibrant and, fortunately, most healthy person. She viewed with excitement the prospect of a night out in London with as much enthusiasm as anyone half her age, not to say even a quarter of her age, would have done. The prospect of the approaching West End lights and all that the evening would entail gave her an inner sense of innocent real well being. They had known about the forthcoming evening for over six weeks and as much as Rupert, Alice had been virtually ticking off the days to the very night itself. It was known that the event of the night would come even some months before, but both Rupert and his grandmother also knew that many others would want to go, so much so that it was advertised that there was to be a ballot for tickets.

Rupert had applied.

Following the initial satisfaction of having sent the letter away, it was with a sense of a very dry mouth that the postman's visit was anticipated on those days immediately after applying, by both of them, especially on a Saturday morning when Rupert too was at home when the postman came. Otherwise, it was Alice alone, after Rupert had set off for work on weekdays, with the immediate ordeal of anticipating the mail as it was, some ten days after applying, in the middle of January. Alice recognised Rupert's handwriting on the self-addressed envelope that she held in her hand following the postman's call. Defying her age, and not needing them for anything other than close work and reading, she put her glasses on to see whether there were any give away signs within the envelope – perhaps some tickets – no, that would not have been possible, they had only applied and hadn't sent any money at that stage. No, the news, one way or other, was contained within the sticky confines of the envelope. Alice was proper, brought up by her parents in a Victorian way, to be respectful and decent – the thought of opening the envelope did not even cross her mind. She went through the hall and to the phone, checked the note-pad and dialled the number to Rupert's office in the City of London.

"Is that you, Rupert?" she asked as she heard his voice at the other end of the line.

"Yes, Nan, is everything alright?" Rupert replied, for the moment not connecting why on earth his grandmother should be calling to him so soon after his arrival at work and therefore somehow fearing the worst.

"Yes, everything's fine here," Alice replied. "The thing is," she continued, "I am holding your self-addressed envelope here in my hand – it's come!"

"Open it, then," Rupert, almost uncharacteristically answered, addressing his grandmother without any of the usual niceties. There was a momentary silence on the line that Rupert found almost unbearable and in the ensuing very few seconds he felt his mouth drying and his hands clutching the phone in an almost vice-like grip, with knuckles whitening as a result.

"Well," he continued when the line seemed then to be quiet for endless minutes as he willed earnestly for an answer.

"I've got the letter open and am just reading it – it's certainly from the theatre and on their headed paper," Alice advised. "Yes!"

"Yes, what does it say?" Rupert found it hard to contain himself.

"Oh, dear, Rupert dear, it's fine," his grandmother advised with an obvious thrill in her voice. "We've been lucky in the ballot, we got it, we're in!"

"Are you sure?" Rupert asked, hardly being able to believe the information that he was hearing down the phone from his grandmother.

"Of course I'm sure, I might be old but I haven't completely lost it yet you know!" his grandmother rather cheekily answered and with a mild sense of reprimand in her voice. "It says in the letter that we have been 'awarded two seats in the ballot' and it goes on further to say 'that the seats allocated are Stalls Row H, numbers 3 + 4'. We have one week from yesterday's date to post in our cheque or …"

"Or?" Rupert anxiously asked, fearing that there would then be some kind of horrible term that would completely take away the success of the occasion.

"It says that we can also come to the theatre and collect the tickets from the box office," Alice replied.

"I'll go this evening, after work and before I come home!" Rupert answered, in a fluster and with a sense of determination that having come this far, they were certainly not now going to miss out, adding "better to be sure".

"Rather be sure than sorry!" his grandmother mused in reply, both smiling to herself at the thought of Rupert's anxiousness but also backing up his comments. In reality, though, she equally quietly realised that she was also rather excited just as much as her grandson.

"One thing, though," Rupert began to add, "Row H in the stalls is a bit far back and seats 3 + 4 are rather more to the side than I would wish. I wonder whether…"

"Don't even begin to think of it!" Alice cautioned. "Just think ourselves lucky that we have got any seats at all so let's leave it at that and make do."

"Yes, I suppose that you are right. OK, Nan, so that's settled – I'll go to the theatre when I leave here but I'll be home later than usual - with our tickets clutched in my rather sweaty hands." Rupert at least acknowledge in a rare show of his character self-assessment, his tendency to get just a bit over excited and in equally over-control mode at red letter events in his rather controlled, low-key and well organised life. And this, indeed, was a red letter event.

"Good. Bye love, see you this evening. Perhaps I should get a police escort arranged to get you home safely from the station with your valued package," his grandmother cheekily added with a distinct chuckle in her voice. "Only joking – and I'm thrilled too," Alice said in conclusion of the phone call.

"Bye, Nan," Rupert replied.

Rupert duly finished work that day very promptly at 5.15pm, having really only done the barest minimum at his desk as he could hardly keep his mind off his mission for the early evening. Leaving the office with a brisk pace and only a cursory "Night" to others leaving the building, he was just 25 minutes later at the theatre's box office. Getting there he was not alone and indeed some tens of people had arrived on a similar mission all, like Rupert, clutching their valuable letters in their hands. Rupert felt that he was then amongst like-minded and almost 'friends', not having to feel strange or embarrassed about his obsession or passion. Like the rest in the queue, Rupert merely gave a weak smile and acknowledgement to others around but very little was said as steadily the line moved forward to the box-office window, cheque books at the ready. Although it seemed much longer, the whole transaction took no longer than about half an hour and Rupert was once again back to the tube and retracing his steps eastwards, back to the City and to Fenchurch Street for the train home to Westcliff.

During the journey of 50 minutes, Rupert could not even bring himself to read the "Evening Standard" or his book. He could barely take his eyes off his prized envelope and the tickets contained therein. He felt a sense of pleasure and fulfilment at his success, not just for himself but for his beloved grandmother too. This was his family, almost his only real family. After all, even though he was 37, it was his choice, that he always acknowledged, not to seek to get married or even to set up his own life. He really did want to make his home just for his grandmother and himself, feeling the overpowering need to look after her now that she had nobody else. She had been a widow then for over 12 years and even though she had come from a large family of a total of nine brothers and sisters, typical of late Victorian times, they had all by then died and apart from Rupert, Alice was very much alone in the world. Even her circle of once many friends had by that time dwindled to a virtual less than handful of no more than casual acquaintances. In his task, Rupert felt that what he was then doing was very much reciprocating what his grandmother had done so many years ago in looking after Rupert when his own mother had died and his father had virtually abandoned any family values. For this he felt an even greater sense of duty as his grandmother got older. But it was not at all one-sided. It was a very cosseted life too for him. Even though she was by then 94 years old, his grandmother did virtually everything at home, the cleaning and washing, albeit with the help of any modern aids that Rupert could buy. And every night, when Rupert returned home from his clerical job with a shipping company in the heart of the City of London, he could be sure that a hot and delicious meal would be waiting for him in a warm and welcoming home. Yes, he felt contentment in his life and was supremely happy with his home life – he wanted no more although many others, especially the few colleagues at work with whom he ever discussed any smallest aspect of his very personal private life, did find the arrangement rather strange and probably even felt sorry for Rupert.

"I am so glad about this," Rupert thought to himself as for the umpteenth time during the train journey he sat mesmerised by the envelope with the much valued and prized tickets that he had in his possession. The very thought that they were going to be able to attend, actually to be there at the theatre on the very night when the very final performance given by the original D'Oyly Carte Opera Company was to take place. Yes, a very sad occasion, especially so for real Gilbert and Sullivan enthusiasts like both Rupert and his grandmother, but then, further in his thoughts, Rupert consoled himself by realising that the event was going to take place anyway so is was surely better to be there, at the theatre, to be part of it, rather than not there at all! And, who knows, Rupert continued to think, or force himself to believe, perhaps there will be a last minute reprieve, the Arts Council or some other arts organisation or benefactor, who will not allow the company to close and a life-saving line will be given. Rupert knew precisely what he would have done if he had the money but such was the fantasies that only the wildest of dreams were made of!

In a more down to earth mode, Rupert's reflections continued to be positive. He convinced himself there was surely to be a saving grace to the situation of imminent company closure. And what better place for such an announcement than at the performance itself – and they would be there to witness the revival as well as saying 'Thanks' for the past 107 years of dedicated performances. It was not going to be an evening to be sad, rather one to anticipate the joyous revival of the Company and the continuation of the only right and proper interpretation of the works of Gilbert and Sullivan!

"No, of course not! It was what Mr. Gilbert – sorry, Sir William – would have wanted!" This time, Rupert muttered the words rather too much aloud, the more to give conviction to his thoughts. So much so that the other passengers still left in that part of the train momentarily glanced up from their papers to stare towards Rupert who, rather embarrassed by his outburst, reddened and smiled nervously before he too immersed himself in his still unopened paper, taking refuge from the situation that he had just created. His fellow passengers equally resumed their reading, having supposedly satisfied themselves that their travel companion was not as completely alarming, or mad, as would have first appeared.

Rupert thought on.

He smiled again to himself, this time using the camouflage of his trusted Evening Standard to contain his inward delight and expressions. He knew too just how important it was for his grandmother to be able to attend the performance. As his own love of Gilbert and Sullivan had developed over his 37 years, from first of all hearing his grandparents and even others in his family singing the pieces, his grandfather when he was alive playing on the piano in the lounge at home, a scene then reminiscent of late Victorian or Edwardian evenings rather than the latter half of the 20th Century, Rupert had become a true G&S enthusiast. Not a 'fan', which didn't seem the right sort of word at all when talking about Victorian musical theatre, but rather a dedicated enthusiast. This he further nurtured during his school years by appearing in several school productions and no doubt torturing his critical family as a result of the cringingly bad renditions.

Then there were the D'Oyly Carte 'proper' performances themselves, a virtual 'must' to attend whenever and wherever possible. Rupert kept a record of where and when and whilst he was sure always to attend the traditional yearly London season over Christmas and the following winter months – even going once per week so as to pick up everything in the repertory for that particular season – and if it did get too much for his grandmother, and sometimes it did, if only occasionally, then he made sure to go on his own, straight from work and at the same time make some savings by choosing to sit in the 'gods'. And if he couldn't see or hear everything, by then it hardly mattered as he knew the plot and words by heart! It was a case of being there and being able to indulge in his one and only true hobby. "It really doesn't matter, matter, matter" – his mind rang with the words from the 'Ruddigore' patter song, a sure sign of his total involvement as his thoughts took further hold of him on that journey home.

He had even had the opportunity in his later working years, with his car and well organised and positioned holidays, to see D'Oyly Carte perform in towns and cities in the country. It was not just by chance that Rupert found himself in Inverness at the very time the company were appearing at the Eden Court Theatre, nor that his journey home 'happened' to take him via Stirling when the company were there too! Other similar 'miracles' had occurred and the icing on the cake really came when the company began to include the Cliffs Pavilion in Southend in their tours itinerary. That, for Rupert, really was bliss. He could even be at the theatre in his home town on the Sunday morning when the big lorries arrived to deliver the sets and the costumes from the previous town. The ticket prices were also less in Southend and although it meant for a very quick dash home from work and crossed fingers that the train would run to time, Rupert and his grandmother could be in the audience several times during the season of visits. Then if all that was not enough to fulfil his enthusiasm, Rupert had an enviable collection of all the recordings which he could play endlessly, for both his own and his grandmother's benefit, during the times of the year without any chance of live performances.

Rupert thought of the importance of his passion for his grandmother equally as much as well. He recalled that she had been born on 6 November 1888, just one month and three days after the first performance of 'Yeoman of the Guard'. She had been a year old by the time of 'Gondoliers' and so it had gone on, all as a child of the latter years of the Gilbert and Sullivan partnership. Her own family had been equally enthusiastic and she had told Rupert how her father and mother had attended some of the first performances. They had seen the very first company and it was with an obvious thanks to his great-grandparents that Rupert acknowledged that his own calling had been smitten.

"Now, Alice," Rupert began before realising that he was once again talking aloud! He checked himself, before continuing his thoughts. "Now, Alice, my dear grandmother, you will be attending the 1982 last night." Not a real 'last night' – how, so much, he wanted to deaden the impact of the words; the 'gala' night seemed to be the perfect substitute that allowed his mind to rest more easily. "We will be attending the Gala Night." With that comforting thought, Rupert allowed himself to relax for the remainder of that journey home.

"I still cannot really believe it," Alice enthused when Rupert finally arrived home, still flushed and excited. As if by inner perception aided by a thorough feeling about her grandson's mind, she concluded by re-iterating Rupert's own words. We will be at the Last Night Gala!"

Chapter 2
"I have a song to sing, O"

Rupert's timing proved to be perfect, almost as befits and giving justice to a military operation, as he and his grandmother in the car swung round Aldwych and into the Strand. It was coming up to 6.10pm and therefore just the right moment to find a parking place on a single yellow line, sure in the knowledge that with the 20 minutes grace, the car could be left safe and in order for the remainder of the evening. It wasn't just a pedantic attention to detail for Rupert but rather he wanted everything to really work well to his plan and especially that they could park as close as possible to the theatre for his grandmother to be able to comfortably walk. Sometimes Alice's liveliness and general vitality made it easy for Rupert to almost forget his grandmother's advanced age but inwardly he more than realised that any distance walking would so easily tire her. He didn't want that to happen before the theatre had even begun.

In the final moments of the drive, the sense of the coming occasion cast a silence within the car that for most of the journey from Westcliff had been a centre of constant sayings and expressions of thoughts and feelings both for the evening ahead and about the sights and scenes of the places which the pair drove through and which Alice had known all her life. Here it wasn't a case of Alice having sombre reflections such as "it was better then" but more a sense of "I remember it like" and more often than not saying "I like that better now!" But with a fusion of mind that was totally appropriate for two people whose very life was entwined both at home and in their chosen theatrical appreciation, both Rupert and Alice had the same silent inner feelings as the car neared the end of its journey and made a slow progress in the traffic along the Strand. The sight of the approaching Adelphi Theatre, with its brilliant floodlit house lights and billboards proudly displaying that the D'Oyly Carte Opera Company in Gilbert and Sullivan Operas was appearing at that very theatre, brought everything so very much into an immediate reality.

In the long history of Gilbert and Sullivan, the very Strand was truly the absolute centre of that special world for which they both, especially Rupert, felt very much a part. Just to their left as they drove slowly along was the Savoy Theatre itself and even though not the first place to have staged productions, it was where the original company had opened the theatre as brand new in 1881 and had staged all the First Nights of the Operas from 'Iolanthe' onwards. The Savoy was in every sense the spiritual home of the operas and the theatre had been so often the scene of performances over the immediate past years too, including the company's very own Centenary Galas in 1975. To add to the occasion, on the other side of the Strand, in Southampton Street, was the very birthplace, in 1836, of W.S. Gilbert himself. The original impresario, the theatrical genius behind the Gilbert and Sullivan partnership, Richard D'Oyly Carte, had lived in Adelphi Terrace overlooking the Embankment, just parallel to the Strand. These very thoughts emotionally flooded Rupert's mind and he somehow felt overwhelmed in a sense of history that was only suddenly broken when his grandmother, herself in similar reflective mood, said:

"Rupert, dear, it is so appropriate that we should be going to this Last Night in this very street!"

"Nan, that's right, I was thinking just the very same at this very moment," Rupert replied, deciding to let his grandmother's reference to 'Last Night' pass without comment. "And what's more, you know another thing, the Gaiety Theatre is where it all began in 1871..."

"'Thespis' you mean?". Alice's brain was fortunately as still as bright as a button.

"Yes, Nan, that was what I was thinking, although it's never strictly considered anymore as the start as it really was, because it was never a success and hardly played or referred to since," Rupert answered, before continuing, "that was at the Gaiety Theatre which used to be on the corner of Wellington Street and Catherine Street, just at the back of the Strand over there," he said, whilst pointing with his free left hand over his shoulder to his right as he continued to grip the driving wheel with his other hand and keep the car on track to negotiate the traffic. "Of course, tonight, we are going to the Adelphi Theatre where 'Cox and Box' was given in 1867 – so it is all so very appropriate, everything about this evening in this very place."

Rupert was in an encyclopaedic mode which Alice, whilst very slightly appreciating his obvious enthusiasm and interest, sometimes found just a little over-trying and so interjected "For it all to end," not intending to be sharp but rather to be reflective in the situation.

"No, Nan, not to end." Rupert this time broke into his grandmother's conversation, perhaps rather harshly, which he didn't intend, but equally he had convinced himself that the night would surely herald a new beginning and a magic continuation of the D'Oyly Carte Opera Company. To that ideal he had convinced himself not to accept any other possible version of events, no matter who said it. "It's only the end of the first 107 years and therefore the beginning of the next 107," he stressed, more in an effort to thoroughly convince himself rather than any water-tight held belief. In any challenge in his life, Rupert was not adverse to seeing the clear way forward in some kind of make-believe solution that often would not stand up to reasonable or credible analysis.

Alice knew better than to challenge her grandson's thoughts, especially at times when he was as then in an obsessive mood and she let the statement pass without comment. In her long life she had seen so many things come and go, changes that she would never had believed to be ever possible – both good and bad – and she had long realised that so many things in her life that she had held dear were always so liable to be and become different that she almost felt sanguine to changes as a result. For Alice, she was just so glad to still be alive and in reasonable health and she had long past ceased to become overly concerned about anything that she considered to be lesser issues.

Just beyond the turnoff for the Savoy itself, near to the entrance to the Shell-Mex Building, Rupert found a place to park – on the very Strand itself. "There you are Nan, couldn't be better, just across the road from the Adelphi Theatre - perfect," he said to his grandmother, barely able to hide his sense of satisfaction and self-congratulation to himself that, so far, his campaign of action had worked so well and to precision with such positive result.

"That's good, dear," his grandmother answered. This she really meant and was relieved that there was only a short distance to walk across the road to the theatre itself. Rupert had said that if they were unable to find parking close enough then he would have dropped his grandmother outside the theatre whilst he went off to park elsewhere. This, Alice had not fancied at all and she was very happy that such a happening would not be necessary.

Looking across the road towards the theatre itself, they could see that a large crowd of people were already gathered outside but that the house doors were still closed. It was not an especially cold evening but it was obviously not right to stand in the cold for an old lady, as much as Rupert would have liked to be at the door there and then. Here, again, Rupert's contingency plan came to the fore as he reached behind his seat in the car to recover a strategically placed flask of tea and a packet of sandwiches and cakes which Alice, with equal preciseness, had prepared before their departure from home.

"Tea is served," Alice giggled as Rupert in his sense of excitement grappled with the mugs, dropping one on to the car floor as he released the stopper from the flask. The preparations were very worthwhile as after their journey up from Westcliff, it was a welcome snack that the pair ate as a prelude to the main part of the evening.

"Well, I suppose I can say that I'm having tea and sandwiches by the Savoy if not actually in the Savoy," Alice continued as, with an almost girly impishness, she began to revel in the events of the evening, especially feeling relieved at being so close to the theatre. Rupert, in return, muttered an almost impolite "Umm" as he kept his eyes on the doors of the theatre lest they should be thrown open in the meantime and they couldn't be amongst the first to go in, even though it was still more than an hour before the performance was due to start.

"I think that I can see some television cameras over there," Rupert observed, pointing his hand with a half-eaten sandwich across the street to the direction of the theatre. "They must be going to film the show!"

"Oh, I don't think so," Alice more correctly observed, and remarkably so given her age as opposed to Rupert, "cameras wouldn't be on the street if they were filming the show! No, it's more likely that they are filming the people going in as it's a ..." Alice paused to correct herself, "special performance".

Rupert took up the theme with an equal amount of glee and relish. "Yes, that's right, they will be there ready to announce the reprieve, that the show will go on!"

"Yes, something like that," Alice replied, knowing only too well that it was useless to shatter her grandson's possible illusions at that very moment.

The two finished their picnic and Rupert took the mugs before placing the flask back into the basket on the car floor. Looking once again across the street, he observed the added brilliance, a virtual spotlight on the scene across the road as the lights for the television cameras were switched on and with that, at the same time, the jostle of the crowd as the theatre doors were finally opened.

"They are going in," Rupert shouted whilst at the same time he fumbled with the handle of the car door as he made to get out in such a rush that any casual observer would have thought he was late for the show rather than being there an hour before curtain-up!

"Don't rush, there's masses of time!" Alice commanded, although by that time Rupert was out of the car and had already made his way round to his grandmother's side of the vehicle where he stood with the door already open for her. Alice ignored

Rupert's rash moves as she deliberately pulled her coat on, tidied her hat and scarf, pulled on her gloves and slowly swung her legs around the seat to the open door. Rupert took her hand and supported her under her arm as she equally slowly began to stand on the pavement. For a moment they stood by the car as Alice got her bearings and became used to the night air as opposed to the gentle warmth of the car. Only then did she feel steady enough to move off with a slow but deliberate step. She realised the limitations of her age and the importance of taking things easy. In many ways, Rupert respected that just as much, although at times such as that very moment he so often in his perceived panic almost forgot the situation. They made to move off.

"Haven't you forgotten something?" Alice asked.

"No, I don't think so," Rupert replied as at the same time he fumbled in his coat pocket. "Look, I've got the tickets right here!"

"No, Rupert, not the tickets – I meant that you have forgotten to lock the car," Alice added as she looked quizzically at her grandson whilst at the same time frowning a kind of 'tut-tut' at his display of forgetfulness in his panic to get across the road to the theatre.

In a fumbled motion, Rupert returned to the car door, locked it and then taking his grandmother's arm once more made to cross the road in the direction of the theatre.

By the time that they had reached the outside of the theatre, the crowd already there had begun to go into the foyer. Rupert and his grandmother walked slowly past the television cameras that they noticed were, despite the bright arc lights, not actually filming anything at that moment.

"Shame, I've lost my moment of stardom!" Alice quipped as the reached the door of the theatre. Rupert, impolitely, didn't comment as he was too engrossed in the moment of time.

The foyer was a milling throng of people, most happily chatting, exchanging small talk, many laughing and smiling at recognised acquaintances in what was an obvious close circle of fellow Gilbert and Sullivan acquaintances. For Rupert, a very closed kind of personality, such sociality was not something in which he felt very comfortable and despite his own obvious love of the operas and his following of the performances, he had never ever considered joining a society of fellow enthusiasts. Rupert and his grandmother moved on through the crowd, making for a corner of the foyer that appeared to be less busy and where there was a wall that Alice could lean on whilst they waited. Little was verbally exchanged between the two of them as they just stood, watching and generally taking in the scene, barely being able to accept that they were really part of it. Rupert was very deep in thought as he recalled the time, by then almost 25 years beforehand, when his grandparents had taken him to his very first Gilbert and Sullivan opera – again in London at the old Princes Theatre to see 'Mikado'. Even though he was then only around 12 years old, he remembered so clearly being immediately captivated even in his young years and had been well and truly an enthusiast ever since.

How, he recalled, he had been overawed then as the orchestra had tuned up, the house lights had dimmed and the conductor had entered the orchestra pit to then slowly bow towards the greeting audience before raising his baton, after which the overture began. With the curtain later raising on the make-believe Japanese scene, the chorus with their powerful singing, the main characters with the beautiful costumes, the brilliance of the Mikado himself and the throat curdling in his own main song, the encores and wonderful stage business for the patter song "Here's a how-de-do!". All had contributed to a magnificent evening from which Rupert had embarked on many years of blissful theatrical happiness. The immediate following years soon saw Rupert introducing himself to 10 more of the main operas plus the so-called 'curtain raisers' of 'Cox and Box' and 'Trial by Jury' until his own knowledge of the repertory was complete apart from the lesser-known 'Utopia, Limited', 'Grand Duke', not to say 'Thespis' which was never, well "hardly ever!", talked about. He often thought about what was his very favourite of all the operas but somehow he had never found his real answer to that question, settling instead on the general feeling that the very best was the last one that he had seen! It had been years of absolute pleasure and with a self-inflicted nudge, Rupert told himself it would continue equally into the years ahead.

"What about us going to have a pre-performance drink, an aperitif?" Alice's question broke Rupert from his self-imposed dreaming.

"Yes, fine, why not," he replied, in a rather absentminded way. "We're to be in the stalls and there's a bar there over in the corner which should be fine and you won't have to climb any stairs," he continued, regaining a sense of care. "Let's go now before it all gets too busy and then we will be ready to go and take our seats as soon as they let us in!"

"I think that I should go and powder my nose first!" Alice replied, choosing to be rather delicate when talking about such matters and always realising the propriety of a grandmother and adult grandson relationship. Rupert took her arm as they made their way in the direction of the ladies room. Gently, Rupert let go of his grandmother's arm as he held the door open for her and she went in.

Rupert stood a few yards from the door, at what he considered to be a discreet distance, and waited, his mind soon going once again into deep memories of his experiences of all past performances, of favourite songs and verses from the operas, so much so that he was oblivious to all that was going on around him. In fact he was so deep within his thoughts that he hadn't recognised that already his grandmother had been gone almost 10 minutes. Becoming quickly concerned he looked at his watch – it was already a quarter to seven – where was she? He looked again towards the door that continued to keep opening and shutting as people went both in and out. Still no sign of his grandmother. By then Rupert became really alarmed less something may have happened to her. Had she become suddenly ill, was the strain of the journey, the whole evening, proving to be too much for the old lady? The awful and negative thoughts would not go away as Rupert considered what he should do. He considered approaching the next lady who he saw that was going into the room and asking her to check! He saw a lady making towards the door, herself probably not many years younger than his own grandmother, and immediately made to intercept her.

19

"Excuse me, please," Rupert began before immediately stopping in his tracks as he saw Alice coming towards him from the door. "No, umm, sorry, it doesn't matter," he quickly said to the puzzled lady.

"Where have you been?" Rupert almost cried with relief but his words came over as very cold and demanding.

"Don't be rude!" Alice replied. "You know precisely where I've been and it's not very ladylike to discuss such matters or for gentleman to ask!"

"Sorry," Rupert answered, "it was just that you seemed to have been gone for such a long time that I thought that…"

"I may have passed out!" his grandmother replied almost cheekily whilst accepting her vulnerability. "It was very busy in there and a lady has to be sure to make herself look pretty!" she added with a smile.

"As long as you are alright – let's go and have that drink," Rupert replied, quickly changing the subject.

The bar was already busy when the two entered but Rupert managed to find a small table with two stools in the corner. Sitting his grandmother down, he quickly went to the bar and ordered what he knew was her favourite sherry whilst, what he considered to be rather racy giving that he was later driving, a whisky for himself. What with the significance of the evening and the recent self-imposed fright, he really felt the need of something to steady his nerves and in any case, he told himself, the night was young yet and it would be some hours before they would be back to the car. By the time that he had returned to the table, drinks in hand, he had begun to calm down a little and was more prepared once again to take in the surroundings and to exchange social niceties with his grandmother. Alice, herself, was already beginning to revel in the occasion and thoroughly enjoyed her sherry whilst, at the same time, having a thorough look at everybody else in the bar.

"Isn't that? Oh, what a lovely dress that she's wearing! That coat must have cost a fortune! I used to have a stole like that when I was younger, your grandfather bought it for me from a really nice shop in Bond Street. Can you imagine, me being bought something in Bond Street!" Alice recalled with an obvious glee.

Rupert merely nodded. It wasn't that he was in any way disrespectful towards his grandmother's thoughts but rather that even within his own very small family circle he was not the best equipped for what he considered to be small talk. Rather, he felt, he should be going over and over again with his memories and thoughts of past performances, his favourite singers, various productions – anything to put an even bigger stamp on to the evening. But since he had been talking of little else not only during the drive on the evening but also ever since they knew they would be attending, let alone having also seen once again, for goodness knows how many times, several performances during the very present London season, Alice, whilst herself appreciating the occasion, felt it good for a change to be able to indulge in some of her own fantasies.

Outside the bar, Rupert heard a commotion and quickly realised that the doors to the auditorium itself had been opened and that already some of the audience had begun to file in.

"Quick!" he exclaimed, heart racing at the possibility of missing out on being amongst the first to go in whilst at the same time jumping to his feet, calling out "we must go!"

"Oh, dear, there's no rush, I can see that it's barely seven, a half hour before curtain-up," Alice observed but, knowing her grandson, decided it was best to drink up and prepare to go. Within a matter of seconds they were out of the bar and at the door to the stalls, Rupert holding the tickets for inspection in what by then was a very sweaty hand.

"Thank you, sir," the usher answered, "please take the right hand corridor and your seats are on the side of row H."

"Yes, fine, I know where to go," Rupert answered in a rather unkind fashion that he didn't realise. What he did know though was the directions to their seats, a fact that was engrained upon his mind from the very moment that he had got the tickets and had checked the theatre's seating plan well in advance of that very evening. True, his preferred seats, where countless evenings before had been spent, were always in the front circle and therefore the stalls were a virtual unknown territory, a "strange and undiscovered land" for him that only added to his perceived sense of adventure for which he was well prepared!

A few short steps along the carpeted corridor and they were there! Here again was that wonderful smell of theatre, the rich reds of the seats and matching carpet, the beautiful stage curtain, again in warming reds all the more brilliant with the house lights already trained upon them. Despite his perceived sense of many others having rushed in before them, when Rupert looked around he realised that there were only a mere handful of people already in their seats – Rupert, with satisfaction, acknowledged that they were amongst the first to be in the theatre itself after all; that gave him an extreme sense of satisfaction. As they walked towards their seats, Rupert bought two programmes and noticed the words 'Gala Evening' which precisely settled his own mind for the occasion.

He helped his grandmother to take off her coat and held her seat down before guiding her into the seat. He then removed his own coat and folded them both in perfectly neat fashion under his own seat. Then they were well established and ready to enjoy the immediate atmosphere as the theatre, at that early hour, began to slowly fill up. Alice, too, liked those moments, spending the time 'people watching' as well as having a cursory look at the programme. "Cursory" was not a word that would apply to Rupert's own attention to the programme – it was an immediate in depth study, taking in within a remarkably few minutes a virtual thorough knowledge of what the evening would entail.

"Pieces from every opera!" he exclaimed with glee. "Everything from 'Cox and Box' right through to 'Grand Duke' – that's marvellous!"

"Not 'Thespis'," Alice rather cheekily commented, knowing full well what reaction such a comment would likely bring from her grandson and she was not to be disappointed!

"No, Nan, but then you remember that it's not really talked about anymore," Rupert replied quite seriously and rising all too quickly to Alice's neatly laid bait.

"Really," she replied as she continued to enjoy people watching.

Soon, and once Rupert was fully conversant with the evening's programme, he too joined her in taking in the sights of the then busily filling auditorium. He noted that the atmosphere was not as subdued as would seemingly fit an occasion like a very 'last night' which gave Rupert further proof to his inwardly held notions that something good would come from the evening after all. There was a buzz about the theatre – a general bevy of chatter as people acknowledged those that they knew or merely made comments amongst themselves. The atmosphere was further charged as members of the orchestra began to take their places in the pit to be followed by the first strains of the various musical instruments being tuned, a scene that Rupert and countless others in the theatre that night had seen and heard countless times before. The cacophony of ensuing and unmelodic noise gave the occasion a sense of theatrical normality that in itself further enhanced Rupert's feelings that everything was merely set to go on and on.

He looked at his grandmother who smiled back at him – it was not then an occasion for any exchange of words but rather one in which to sit and take it all in. The irreverent noise from the pit had stopped as the leader stood up, tapped his music stand and charged the orchestra into finally playing as one, in tuneful readiness for the evening ahead.

Rupert looked at his watch – almost 28 minutes past seven and therefore he realised only a mere few moments to go before the overture would begin – but which one would that be? Any of 14 or 15, the programme didn't say so the quandary gave Rupert something to think about in the very few moments before the house lights dimmed and an expectant hush descended upon the whole audience, all chatter then extinguished as eyes turned towards the orchestra pit and the brightly lit stage curtain beyond. Just then, as on so many thousands of other occasions, the conductor came into the pit to be met by a truly thunderous applause from the expectant audience, shouts of "bravo" and cheers to an extent that Rupert felt dampness in his eyes as tears welled up at the enormity of the event as the conductor himself bowed in response. He felt his grandmother's hand reaching over to touch his own hand and he looked at her in a kind and loving way. The performance was about to begin.

But there was no immediate overture. Instead, with the conductor still standing and looking towards the stage, the same position to which all eyes in the house were then fixed, the stage curtains parted just a little to reveal the London Town Cryer.

"Welcome to the very last night of the D'Oyly Carte Opera Company."

* * * *

On a late December night, in 1871 and a 111 years before that very night when Rupert and Alice were amongst the audience in the Adelphi Theatre, Thomas Dobbs was also making his way across the Strand but in the direction of Wellington Street and the stage door of the Gaiety Theatre. He had come from across town, walking from his home in Shoreditch, a reasonably lengthy walk for him but something that he didn't mind at all. Anyway, he had little choice if he was to continue with his job as a stage hand for the new enterprise just started by Mr. W. S. Gilbert and walking cost nothing.

As he told his wife, Nellie, it was "fresh air and exercise and that never 'urt anyone!" adding "You should try it more yourself, always stuck in the 'ouse 'ere or that 'orrible sweaty place where you work!"

"Now listen 'ere, Tom," his wife had replied, "there's not so many jobs around for me as a trained seamstress and we need the money – besides, it's more than 'andy being just round the corner and I'm there and 'ome again, in a jiff – so you go off to your fancy jobs in the 'featre up west and leave me be. You won't moan when you come home and I've got yer tea ready on the table, so get off with you," Nellie said, giving her husband a friendly shove on his shoulder. "Someday, who knows, when there are some little 'uns running around the 'ouse, then maybe I'll have a life of luxury and get all the fresh air I need up in the park."

They both laughed at the very thought before Tom had once again set off for his work, but not before he and Nellie had kissed in the doorway of the little terraced house.

For Tom, though, of course there were plenty of similar stage work jobs in the various music halls throughout London, even ones that were nearer to his home both in Shoreditch and Islington, but somehow ... well somehow Tom liked the thought and was attracted to this new project – to work on and be there for the start of a possible English very own comic opera. In this he wasn't at all pretentious but rather it was a general love of the musical theatre that had begun when his own parents had at first forced him to be a choirboy at his local church. The fact that he had little formal education didn't mean for Tom, as far as his family was concerned, that he should not be given some sort of chance in life. Even though Tom resisted at first, in effect he had little choice and had to do exactly what his parents instructed. It proved to be a good move and before too long, Tom acknowledged a developing liking for the activity and from the church came a love of music outside. Often, Tom stood for many minutes listening to street organs, trying to remember and humming the various tunes he heard. From this came also a liking for the musical theatre, anything really although he couldn't be bothered about the music of Grand Opera, which neither the language nor the tunes he really understood or even bothered about. If it wasn't immediately hummable then it was of no interest to Tom.

He had already heard of the work that Mr. Arthur Sullivan had collaborated with F.C. Burnand on some four years before, in 1867, a piece called 'Cox and Box' which had been given as private performance and later even played at the Adelphi Theatre. Tom had even heard that Mr. Gilbert himself had reviewed the work when working as a journalist on the magazine 'Fun' where he had said: "Mr. Sullivan's music is, in many places, of too high a class for the grotesquely absurd plot to which it is wedded". Nevertheless, Thomas surely hoped that the new venture would still bring an audience with positive critical acclaim.

In the event, it was not to be that Thomas Dobb's hopes were to be happily realised as the opera, 'Thepis', only played for 64 performances. Their collective future didn't look too good and Nellie urged Tom to look for something else.

"Look 'ere, luv," Tom told his wife, "the whole piece was only put together in less than three weeks and we only had the chance for a week's rehearsal. Mr. Gilbert 'imself was not at all happy either with the result. You'll see, it will be better another time!"

"But who pays you, who looks after the 'ouse bills till 'another time? You can't expect me to do everyfink," his wife quizzed him. Nellie had her feet very much on the ground and sometimes her husband's theatrical fantasises really frightened her, so far were they removed from what Nellie saw as the realities of life.

Tom was silent. Somehow he had faith that there was going to be another time. After all, wasn't it so, he frequently told himself, that Mr. Gilbert had already written a number of pieces, his Bab Ballads, he recalled them being titled. Then, Mr. Gilbert knew about the theatre and precisely what he wanted for his stage craft. And of Mr. Sullivan? Well he was already a respected and renowned musician, coming from a musical family.

"Do you know, luv," Tom told his wife, "that Mr. Sullivan, well he's only just turned 30 and he was only eight years old when he wrote his first anthem, 'By the Waters of Babylon'. And, Nellie, well you know the hymn that's just been written, 'Onward Christian Soldiers'!"

His wife nodded, although she was barely taking her husband's words in as she busied herself around their little house. For her, Tom's working world and his enthusiasm for the theatre seemed an age away from her own. She didn't understand it and wasn't really bothered, only concerned that money would continue to come into their home so that one day, well one day perhaps, they could begin a family.

"Well, there you are, Mr. Sullivan wrote that too!" Tom added, enthusiastically, hardly noticing that his wife was not paying too much attention to his sayings.

As the days wore on, though, Tom soon, reluctantly, realised that Nellie was perhaps right after all and he took a job in the local music hall when it became apparent that there was little immediate prospect of there being any further works coming from Mr. Gilbert and Mr. Sullivan. But he kept in close touch with an 'ear to the ground' in his beloved theatrical world and his persistence finally paid off when he heard of a resurrection of the pair's efforts but this time with the involvement of an enlightened theatrical manager, Mr. Richard D'Oyly Carte, and his company playing at the Royalty Theatre. Tom made his way, this time to Dean Street in Soho and to the Royalty Theatre. His efforts were rewarded and he was once again at work on a beloved project.

"And will it be better than last time?" Nellie asked.

"'Course it will, luv. Mr. D'Oyly Carte is already going to play the Offenbach piece, 'La Perichole', at the theatre and he needs a small curtain-raiser to accompany it and, what's more, he has re-introduced Mr. Gilbert and Mr. Sullivan to write and compose the very work! They work perfectly together, Mr. Gilbert with the words and Mr. Sullivan with the music. You know, Mr. Gilbert doesn't even interfere with Mr. Sullivan about the music. In fact he said that he only knows two tunes. One is 'God Save the Queen' and the other isn't!"

"Well as long as you know what yer doing," Nellie added, not really listening to all the detail that her husband told her as once again she got on with her household duties.

"It will be alright, this time I'm sure," Tom tried to reassure his wife. "The piece is to be based on one of Mr. Gilbert's own Ballads and well, Mr. Sullivan is already writing the music and reckons to have it all complete in only three weeks! Mr. D'Oyly Carte has the grand idea of starting English comic opera in a theatre devoted to that alone – you see, that's what I've always believed in too."

"Do what you think right, Tom, but remember, it's me that you will have to answer to, not your Mr. Gilbert or Mr. Sullivan who probably have plenty of other places to make their money. Go, get on with you and leave us be, so at least one of us gets an honest day's work!"

With that exchange, but also after a fond kiss to his wife, Tom once again set off back to his work at the theatre and for what he this time hoped would be for a more secure and permanent employment. As he walked what was becoming for him a well trodden route, his mind filled with some of the tunes that he had heard being rehearsed and he sang quietly to himself:

"Hark, the hour of ten is sounding:

27

Hearts with anxious fears are bounding..."

The rest of the words, for the moment, failed his memory but the tune carried on as he hummed for the remainder of his walk. That was what, he hoped, the audience would do too!

Chapter 3
"All hail great Judge"

Having already enjoyed a couple of excerpts from 'Cox and Box', Rupert and Alice were then revelling in the well-known pieces being that moment performed from 'Trial by Jury'. How they and the whole audience clapped and cheered as one of their favourite performers sang the Judge's song. Even though they had heard it many times before and could quite easily have recited the words just as easily themselves, they listened intently to the song and laughed at the various bits of action and stage business, almost for them as if it was a completely new theatrical experience. But the whole point of their satisfaction was that the work was being performed for them exactly how it should be and how it was meant to be, to a perfect tradition of 107 years:

"For I thought I should never hit on a chance
Of addressing a British Jury –
But I soon got tired of third-class journeys,
And dinners of bread and water;
So I fell in love with a rich attorney's
Elderly, ugly daughter."

The audience, as one, laughed almost as if they had never heard the lines before and greeted the end of the song with wild clapping and cheering, hoping that the conductor might even raise his baton, the traditional, sure and awaited signal that a much wanted encore would be given. This time, though, it was not to be, and if it had, then they would without doubt have been at the theatre all night – which was just what they all wanted anyway!

"Enjoying it, Nan?" asked Rupert, red-faced as befitted the effect of the heat on him, whilst almost brimming over with excitement, in the moments that the clapping of the audience halted any further performance and it was safe to divert the eyes from the stage.

"Of course, love," Alice replied, "and who couldn't enjoy such wonderful music and lovely singing." She squeezed her grandson's hand, knowing just how much he was enthralled by the performances and just how much he was really feeling about this 'last night'. Rupert smiled back at her before all eyes were back to the stage once more as the show continued.

* * * *

Fortunately for Tom, the reaction of the first night audience at the Royalty Theatre on 25 March 1875 was equally enthusiastic. His spirits were lifted and he could go home and tell Nellie of the success although she at first didn't bother to take the news too very much to heart, being rather used to her husband's whims. But even Nellie was forced to accept something good was happening when Tom rushed home just four days later, waving newspaper cuttings at her.

"Look, look here, Nellie," Tom said breathlessly as he virtually charged into the small parlour of their home.

"Goodness, Tom, what is it?" his wife asked, getting rather concerned and agitated at her husband's flushed appearance.

"Nellie, it's what the papers are saying about 'Trial by Jury'. It's good, they like it!" Tom then began to read the extracts. " . . 'a pleasant addition to the bill of fare at Madame Selina Dolaro's pretty theatre in Soho' (The Royalty), and here," he continued, pointing to another piece of paper held in his hand, "'a show with tunes you can whistle'; that's what I always said I wanted from this sort of theatrical piece. And there's more, listen: 'No longer is the theatre regarded as an anti-room to hell'. It's all here," he continued, pushing the papers into Nellie's hand.

She immediately handed them back. "Yes, fine, I'm sure it's good, if you say so and, well, of course I am pleased if it is going to go well but…"

"There's no 'but'," Tom answered, "it's really the very best news and Mr. D'Oyly Carte has said that he would like Mr. Gilbert and Mr. Sullivan to now go ahead and write a full length opera. Just think, Nellie, a real English own comic opera!"

"Oh, I don't know, that sounds a bit fanciful to me. You told me this present piece lasts no more than 40 minutes – well that's a bit different from a full length show," Nellie replied. "Surely, it's early days yet and probably everybody will have forgotten about it in a few weeks and nobody will ever think about these fancy comic opera ideas again. I doubt if it will last!"

"You don't know that!" Tom replied, getting a bit agitated about his wife's dismissive remarks. "In any case, what they are saying is that 'Trial' will succeed where 'Thespis' failed because of the improved skills of both Mr. Gilbert and Mr. Sullivan in musical theatre and especially with Mr. Gilbert's efforts in the drilling of the actors in the way that he wants – and that's where I come in by helping there too," Tom added, proudly.

"No Tom, it's true, I don't know that it won't last, but then neither do you. Either way," Nellie reasoned, "all I worry about is what effect it's going to have on our lives here at home. Keep yer feet firmly on the ground and don't get yer carried away with yer high minded dreams, don't you. Fancy ideas, dreams, well they ain't going to bring home the food are they and it's not right if you expect me to work all hours God gives just so that we can have food on the table!"

"Course not, luv, I don't expect that of you, not for you to have to do all the work," Tom reasoned as he put his hands around his wife. "But wait, you'll see, this is really going to work and well, I'll get really big in the theatre and stage work and, well, Mr. Gilbert will appreciate me, he's real demanding for attention to every bit of stage business and I'm following his every word, he will know that he can rely on me. Even so, when he's not there, and he can't be at the theatre all the time, then I want him to know that I can do everything that he wants and in the way he wants!"

"Well, I certainly hope so – for all our sakes."

"Yes, it'll be fine, it'll be fine," Tom added for reassurance. "These performances are going to be around for a long time to come and then there'll be more, more operas and a full and complete repertory not just in London but throughout the whole country, perhaps even the world. I can see it now!"

"Oh, Tom, come off it, listen to what I've just told to yer, 'cause yer being a bit fanciful. Believe in what you like, but don't get carried away, not in this 'ouse," Nellie declared. "Like I always say, you do what you like and do yer work proper – 'cause I'm pleased when you do something you like and even better if what you say is true…"

"It's all true, luv, I wouldn't lie to you, you know me better than that," Tom reasoned.

"Come 'ere, you silly old fing," Nellie answered, once more clasping Tom close to her, "you do your best, I know that and it's good if that Mr., what's he call himself when he's at 'ome?"

"Mr. Gilbert, Nellie, that's his name, 'blimey, I've told you enough."

"That you have! Anyway, what I was going to say, was just that it is good if this Mr. Gilbert appreciates the work that you do and that you do a good job 'cause that's what will bring the pennies to the 'ouse! But, Tom, just be within reason and don't get ideas above your station, this 'ere fing about more and more shows and, a what do you m'call it, repar…what, eh?"

"Repertory, Nellie, that's the word, you know meaning various works in the programme."

"Whatever. Well, anyway, just keep your 'ead about yer – and, remember, bring 'ome the money for these 'ere bills. That's all I ask and expect!" Nellie exclaimed.

Chapter 4
"Oh joyous boon! Oh mad delight"

Tom was initially kept very busy with the performance of 'Trial', thrilled to be going to Soho and the Royalty Theatre each day, there to interpret Mr. Gilbert's stage instructions and to help with the preparation for each night's show. But despite his obvious thrill at his daily tasks, he grew increasingly concerned when he heard that there was still no immediate prospect of the full-length opera being written as a follow-up. In fact, life was once again very much less secure for him and during the early months of 1876 he had to go back to working in the musical hall so as to keep wages coming in, something that Nellie regarded in an almost understandable "told you so" kind of way.

The atmosphere at home became very tense as a result and Tom felt extremely downcast and unhappy, not least because of his own unfulfilled dreams but also he felt a grave sense of having let his little family down because of what he realised were his own selfish interests. He hated his work when away from what he increasingly saw as "the proper theatre" and also what he regarded as a far more respectable way of making a living. Whatever was the reality of his own comparatively lowly background, he saw no wrong in trying to better himself and striving for a more rewarding working life.

Going to the music hall each day, the place of such wild and raucous behaviour, the constant beer swigging and foul behaviour of the 'audience' ("Audience!. How can I think of them by that name?" Tom frequently thought to himself) became increasingly difficult for Tom who felt totally uncomfortable and out of his own values of life in such an environment, especially after he had tasted what he felt was a better way of working life. He found he had to really force himself to tread the heavy steps to Islington but for that there was immediately no other choice. Food had to be found and bills had to be paid and that could not become just the sole responsibility of his Nellie. Tom could not and would not allow that to be the case.

During his walks, Tom could not help but think longingly and wish again to see Mr. Sullivan entering the orchestra pit, there to nervously bow and then to raise his baton to urge his players as they performed his magical music. Tom sighed and his own steps became more laboured, and even greater force was necessary for him to make on his way, as he had only his happy memories to help him along

"Swiftly fled each honeyed hour
Spent with this unmanly male!
Camberwell became a bower,
Peckham an Arcadian Vale!"

The words from 'Trial by Jury' flooded Tom's mind. He smiled and continued humming to himself other tunes from the opera as a reassurance of what was surely to mean better things to come. It helped him a good deal even if Islington, for Tom, could never be an 'Arcadian Vale'!

If all of that wasn't enough to cause unhappiness in both of their lives, to make matters worse at home, Nellie fell gravely ill in the autumn of the year and it became clear to the pair that any hope of starting a family was not going to be. "Just look after yourself, don't fret," Tom urged of his wife as she lay listless and weak in bed, wracked by fever with Tom dabbing her forehead tenderly. Fortunately, Tom felt, there is some reason in life at that present moment because through his lack of absorbing work, he had plenty of time during the day to look after and nurse Nellie, which he did with relish not only because of his deep love for his wife but also it gave him a sense of immediate purpose, away from his worries about work. How he would have been able to cope if he was hard at work with the new operas, he was barely able to contemplate.

Fortunately Nellie responded by very slowly getting back to health and by the Christmas they could look back to the year with a sense and hope that the next year would be better for them, although because of her illness, or perhaps because she hadn't felt like raising the issue, there had been little talk at home about Tom's theatrical dreams. In that, there seemed so little relevance given how seriously ill Nellie had been. By January, Nellie was able to go back to work at the dress factory and their small lives once again took on a reasonable air of normality even though poor Nellie suffered so much from mixed emotions – sorrowful that they could never have a family of their own but otherwise just simply grateful to be alive, something she felt with even greater emotions as she frequently watched Tom bustling around and making sure all was well for her. It was a time of mixed emotions for Tom too – his beloved Nellie was restored to health but in complete contrast he was more and more unhappy with his work, really hating even worse than ever what he saw as the low and utterly miserable life of the music hall as compared to the new life he had temptingly tasted of the comic opera.

He vowed not to be put off his chosen track and in that he was relieved and grateful for Nellie's full support. He kept in touch with his newfound theatrical mentors, even taking an occasion walk during the day to speak directly with Mr. Gilbert, calling to see him at his home at No. 24, The Boltons, in Kensington, a place where Tom was always so pleased to receive a genuine welcome. The fact that it was such a very long walk for Tom didn't bother him too greatly and he felt better for making the effort and for what he saw as sound steps for securing his future should the operas one day go ahead. That mere thought kept him going as afterwards, leaving Kensington, he had to set off back out of town in the late afternoon, not home to Shoreditch but much worse, north of his own home to what he called "the wretched music hall in Islington". Still, Nellie didn't any more challenge her husband about what he was doing, her own period of ill-health had made her a little more circumspect about her own and her little family's vulnerability and, more to the point, she felt relieved and simply glad to be alive. Indeed, she had reflected that as her own period of illness had shown, they had somehow survived, even if with difficulty, on just one set of wages coming into the home. Christmas had been austere, the worst they had ever experienced in their married years, with little in the way of special food on the table other than a small morsel of cold goose which the lady who ran the clothing factory had sent round to them in an unexpected display of charity. But somehow they had both managed to keep reasonably warm and not too hungry, more delighted than ever to be in each other's company given the year they had endured.

By the early months of 1877, Tom's persistence with his walks to Kensington suddenly seemed to not have been in vain. He was told by Mr. Gilbert himself that a new piece was being planned, the much anticipated full length comic opera based on a story about an entire English village taking doses of a love potion. Tom was thrilled once again, even more so when he heard that in June, Mr. Sullivan had written to Richard D'Oyly Carte to inform him that "Gilbert and myself are quite willing to write a two-act piece for you". What was more, Tom very soon learnt that the terms had been set and agreed: "Payment to us of 200 guineas on delivery of the manuscript, words and music, then six guineas for the run of the piece in London – deducted from the 200 guineas paid in advance so that the additional payment of six guineas per performance will not really commence until about the 33rd or 34th performance".

With absolute relish, Tom was once again pleased to leave the music hall in Islington, with the calls of his workmates ringing in his ears: "Ain't you not just a bit too grand there, Tom, with yer fancy ideas of working in that ere opera place – yer be back, tail between yer legs, don't yer see, and we're all be good enough for yer again". Tom forced a smile and tried not to look back, in fact he hoped that he would not that time have to look back to that place again but… Tom tried not to think about it. Anyway, this time what he was doing was very much with the support of Nellie who felt both relieved and delighted to see how her

husband's spirits were lifted, singing as he bustled around their
tiny house:

"When first my old, old love I knew,
My bosom welled with joy;
My riches at her feet I threw,
I was a love-sick boy!"

"Cor, Tom, how lovely it is to hear you chirping away there,
like on an old cockney sparrow," she called out as Tom prepared
to set off to work. "You've been such an old misery around the
'ouse that it's good to see you smile for a change."

"It's not just been about the work, luvvie," Tom replied. "I've
been so worried and concerned about you – all those weeks of
your illness and well…" Tom fell silent but they both knew what
Tom meant and what thoughts were flooding his mind and
which he just could simply not put into words.

"Come 'ere, you silly old fing," Nellie declared, throwing her
arms around her husband. "You don't have to fink or say fings
like that. Me – I'm fine now, never been better and that should go
for you too, what with the work starting again on what you really
want to do. Go on. Be off with you now and work your 'ardest so
that this is not just one show but the start of 'undereds!"

"I don't know about hundreds, luv, but this time I hope we
have a good run and then, well let's see how more could come
afterwards." If only Tom could at that moment have the foresight
towards the next century then he would have been immediately
reassured!

"You work 'ard and do your bit, and who knows!" Nellie
exclaimed as they kissed in the parlour and Tom finally made
ready to set off. He gave his wife an extra special and loving hug,
feeling his own eyes well up with emotion at what he realised
he could so easily have lost and also how grateful he then felt
for Nellie's almost change of heart and support for him in his
work.

That work was extremely hard and demanding as very slowly
the new piece was rehearsed from scratch with a totally new
company of actor/singers needing to be hired. Mr. Gilbert's

demands were very exacting and this, in turn, was passed down to Tom who soon found the need to be every bit of a perfectionist as he listened to Mr. Gilbert's words so as to be able to interpret the stage commands. Tom was exhausted but at the same time so exhilarated by the challenges which he faced and for which he felt increasingly confident in being able to succeed.

"Do you know, love," he said to Nellie after he had arrived home late in the evening after a long day of rehearsals, "Mr. Gilbert has insisted on disregarding West End favourite actors, or those with grand operatic voices, and concentrating on singers who could act and therefore do justice to his words."

"Really," Nellie answered as she served out the ready stewed beef and vegetables that she had prepared for Tom's meal.

Tom remained enthusiastic and untroubled by his wife's apparent lack of in depth interest about his news, continuing: "Mr. Gilbert, he is in command about the hire of the actors although he does consult Mr. Sullivan about their musical capabilities. I've heard them talking and, do you know, they really mould the cast into what they really want and to the finest detail. We stage crew are already beginning to call it the 'Gilbertian style' – and we are all part of that!" he concluded proudly, as Nellie placed the steaming plate of stew in front of him. For once, Tom was so hungry, that he tackled his meal and ate so intently that he gave no further immediate news of his day's activities!

But what Tom didn't know, and perhaps may have not even believed even if he had known, was that the castings being made and which he so excitedly had been talking about to Nellie, were unwittingly the stereotypes for all the future operas that were still to come – the comedian roles, the contraltos that would in the future include the Katisha's of the G&S world, the beautiful Mables and the aristocratic Don Alhambra.

On the other hand, Rupert and his grandmother, in their place and time enjoying the results of Tom's earlier labours, did know!

As the autumn wore on, Tom's work became even more intent as the first night for the new opera, to be called 'The Sorcerer', loomed. Tom's routine meant an early start each day for his walk to Wych Street, a Victorian backwater and virtual mysterious underworld reached by a dark and dingy approach from the Strand, hardly a place more unprepossessing for what was to be the start of a new musical adventure at the Opera Comique. Once inside the theatre, it didn't matter to Tom as to how the outside world was. He was in a world of theatrical make-believe, immediately transported on stage to an idyllic English village which was called Ploverleigh and its characters of happy villages - Dr. Daly, the vicar, and the village's elderly Baronet, the evocatively named Sir Marmaduke Pointdextre.

"Welcome joy, adieu to sadness." That line, for Tom, said it all and epitomised for him his magic world of not only the theatre, but the whole world of English comic opera. It was only the character of John Wellington Wells and his song's reference to "Number seventy, Simmery Axe!" (St. Mary Axe) that returned his mind to London and an address barely two miles away to the east in the City!

The approaching first night even moved Nellie to a raising excitement! Her own hard life of work and home doings had often made her appear less than fully involved with Tom's working life but slowly, very slowly, she was becoming infected by Tom's thrill and enthusiasm.

"How do you fink it will be, is everyfing alright with all the stage props – all that you have worked on? Then what about the actor's movements, where they are supposed to be, where and 'ow to stand, what they are supposed to do? 'ave you got the directions right, 'ave you done all that Mr. Gilbert wants?" Her questions came thick and fast and even Nellie felt herself surprised as to the extent of the knowledge that she had picked up from Tom – and that she had even understood and remembered!

"I've really studied everything that I've been told and, do you know, Nellie, I really have learnt a lot during the rehearsals, I listened to all that I have been told and look here!" Tom reached into his trouser pocket and pulled out a rough note book, pages turned up and almost falling apart through constant use. "This is what I've done – written everything down so I can be sure to get it right!" he concluded proudly.

"Tom, you really believe in all this stuff, don't you luv," Nellie acknowledged, "and I can see that everyfing is safe in yer 'ands and do you know what Tom, I am really proud of you and if everyone else at the 'featre is as sound and proper as you me luv, then it will surely be a success and who knows … well, who knows indeed," she concluded, giving Tom an affectionate pat to his shoulder. She pulled him closer to her and hugged and kissed him. "There, 'ows that?" she said.

"None of this would have been possible if it wasn't for you," Tom replied as he revelled in his wife's affections and her words of real tributes to his efforts. That he walked that day to work with a greater spring in his step was of no surprise or that he was with extra intent as he went through the day's work leading up to the very final rehearsals and the opening night of 17 November, then less than a week away.

"What would be made of it?" Tom thought "How would the public react, would the thoughts of a home-bred comic opera be well received or would it be compared unfavourably with what was seen always as the ultimate and more sophisticated works from Offenbach and his contemporaries? "Well, it's too late now," Tom realised, "this time next week, well we will surely know and I'll know if I'm going back to the Music Hall!"

Tom didn't immediately have to think about a return to the Music Hall. Fortunately both for him and all concerned, the new work was well received and over the winter the audiences came in healthy numbers. Some concerns, however, filled everybody's minds when by the following spring the Opera Comique was not always full. Tom and his stage colleagues talked amongst themselves and together they realised that it would take more than one work to educate and get the public used to the idea of English comic opera.

Mr. Gilbert had a solution immediately to hand with a brand new plot for a new comic opera that he planned could follow on at the very same theatre before the coming summer. The prospect of the continuing worked thrilled Tom who excitedly told Nellie: "The new work will follow on immediately 'Sorcerer' finishes, so not only do I have to keep the present production going but I'm to work on the new one as well. I've already started and the plot is already outlined and even some of the songs are ready! It's going to be busy and – best of all – there's no going back to the Music Hall for me!" he exclaimed with a pride and satisfaction in his voice.

"Well, not at least for the moment," Nellie cautioned.

"What never, well hardly ever!" Tom replied, grinning, as he remembered a verse from one of the new opera's songs that he had been working on that very day.

Chapter 5

"Fair moon, to thee I sing"

"Everything is being done about the new opera, as always, to be just right! Do you know what, Nellie love, Mr. Gilbert has been down to Portsmouth and on board 'Victory' just to see how it all is, how the sailors are dressed, watching their every movements as they go about their work on deck – getting things right for us as we do the stage movements. Then, he's been to a Navy tailor's in Portsmouth itself just so that he can get the authenticity of the costumes and to make sure everything will be looking good!" Tom was bubbling more than ever with his news to what he hoped was becoming a more involved and interested Nellie. Her frequent reticence to show any in-depth interest or to be more excited about what Tom saw as his exciting new work with the Gilbert and Sullivan operas did cause him slight angst. "Well, you are a dressmaker!" he exclaimed, not in anger but as a statement of reality.

"Seamstress," Nellie interjected.

"Yes, alright, I know that love, but you're in the dress trade and you know how important these things are," Tom continued, trying to induce more interest from his wife, before briefly gathering his thoughts and then voicing what he had been contemplating for a while and waiting for what he saw as the right moment before broaching the subject. "Nellie, there's something that I have been meaning to say to you, rather to suggest to you." He tried to choose his words carefully but, he realised, all too formally and felt ever so slightly embarrassed at his obvious clumsiness, something he invariably did when broaching something important.

Nellie was intrigued as she realised that there must be something of importance coming from Tom because otherwise he would not be so roundabout in his talk, so evasive but rather coming more usually straight to the point. "What is it, Tom?" she asked, curiously.

"I've been wondering, why don't you think about joining us at the theatre, coming to do your dressmaking work there, to even oversee all the work being done with the costumes. Maybe you would get soon to be the chief wardrobe mistress. I can put in a word. We don't really have one as such now and we'll soon need somebody good and, that somebody should be you! It would be fine for you and you being such a good worker and a perfectionist, you would get on so well not only with Mr. Gilbert but with everyone. He would so appreciate your work and you would like that and, what's more, it means we can work together and be more with each other. With my hours getting longer and longer as all the productions work increases, well we'll be together – what do you think? It would be good, it makes sense!" Tom's words tumbled out thick and fast, as befitted his delivery when having something what he saw as important to say. He was virtually unstoppable and Nellie merely waited her chance before even trying to interject, although she was full of respect for Tom's considerations and for his unstoppable enthusiasm.

"Oh, Tom, I don't know about that," were her first words, which as soon as she had said them, she regretted her immediate dismissal and obvious negativity which she did not mean in exactly that way. Rather more to the point was that she hated the thought of making any changes to her regulated life or situations where she knew her place and felt comfortable.

"Please, please, Nellie, don't say 'No'. Why? As I see it, it's the perfect answer and you'll love the life in the theatre – all the people who you will meet and who you will find to be exactly like us – nice and ordinary, good hearted people. Go on, love, say yes!" Tom implored. "Before long we can be humming along with all the tunes together!"

"Maybe sometime, but not now, that's what I 'onestly think," Nellie replied with a determined frown that highlighted her serious consideration. Tom looked crestfallen and Nellie felt very sorry for that because she didn't want to hurt him. "It's not that I don't think that it's a good idea, 'cause I do, I do really, and what's more, I probably would like it – especially to be able to work together," which she said with an honest meaning and in an effort to make amends to her husband for her swift dismissal of the idea. "But … well, what I think is that they 'ave been so good to me at the dressmakers, you know when I was ill, and they do rely on me and expect a lot of me and, well, I couldn't live with myself if I let them down, to do something against them – not, as I say, after they've been so good to me."

"What, love, do you mean with your saying they being good to you? Just bringing round a bit of cold goose at Christmas, that's about all they have been good to you – don't be beholding to them if you've got this chance to better yourself. Opportunities like this, well they don't grow on trees and you must take it when they happen! Besides, they don't treat you that well and they don't think anything more of you for all that you're saying! Come on, love, make this change now – it'll be good for you, good for both of us and good for Mr. Gilbert, Mr. D'Oyly Carte, everyone. They will all love having you and working with us all together," Tom implored. His eyes narrowed and his whole face contorted as he pleaded with his wife for what he saw as a just cause.

But it was to no avail because Nellie's mind was made up and stubbornly she was not to be moved. "No, Tom, you're not right about all they did for me when I was ill, not right at all and I 'fink it bad of you to speak about them the way you 'ave. It wasn't just remembering us at Christmas, as nice and welcomed though as it was, but they kept me job vacant for me – and that's something I really appreciate of 'um. Quite easy it was for 'um just to get someone else in to fill me shoes and to send me away a'packing. But no, they somehow muddled through without me, even though it must have been 'ard for 'um, but they kept me place for me and when I was well, there was my job, just as before, waiting there for me as if I'd never been away ill. I remember that and I am grateful to all of 'um there for that. I am not one now to go and throw mud in their face and be letting them down – I couldn't be living with myself if I done that and I would be thinking about it all the time and a right misery I would be in the featre with that on me mind."

Tom nodded. Although he didn't agree and he so wanted Nellie to be with him, he did realise that her mind was set and there was very little that he would be able to do about it – at least for that time and he would let the issue rest but not forgotten for a more opportune moment, that Tom availed. Besides, Tom thought, the last thing he wanted was to pick a fight with his beloved Nellie and he considered the old maxim – 'least said, soonest mended'.

"Besides," Nellie continued, "I think that it makes sense that we should work in different places and with different employers 'cause none of us knows what is going to 'appen and somehow it makes our money more secure if we are in different places, in case somefink goes wrong. It wasn't that long ago when you 'ad to go back to that music hall work when none of the new bits were coming from your Mr. Gilbert."

Nellie's words came out fast, although with thought even though she forgot herself and proper pronouncing as she got more agitated with the situation. "Sorry, Tom, but that's how I see it." Seeing Tom's frown and sullen look, though, Nellie ended by adding "I'm not saying never, perhaps sometime it would be good, but not now, luv, please see what I say and try to understand, it really is for the best, as I sees it here and now".

"Alright, my love, just for now do what you think is right."

"Thanks for that, Tom," Nellie replied, once again going to her husband's side and cuddling him. "Like I say, this don't mean that I will never do as you are saying and I'm sure I would love it, but … well, let's see how things go and how the life works out for us."

"I think I understand what you say and, well Nellie, it's not the way I see it but I do respect your feelings," Tom added. The fact that he was sadly looking down to the floor, though, showed

45

his disappointment that his idea was not then to be and for what he saw as a great opportunity lost for both of them, especially Nellie. For a few moments little was said between the pair until Tom, realising that perhaps they could return to the idea at a later time, added "Well, Nellie, at least you're not saying 'never' so who knows, another time, eh love, what do you say?", his spirits immediately rising with the mere thought.

"Yes, Tom," Nellie reassured, "we will talk about it and I will 'fink about it another time!" And so, for that moment, the matter was left, which for Tom was probably just as well as there was little else he hated so much in his home life as facing up to and being involved in weighty issues requiring actions and decisions.

Their words, though, did continue to play on Tom continually following their exchange and especially so when he was on his way to and from the theatre each day although the busyness of his work on Gilbert and Sullivan's new piece, 'HMS Pinafore', the long hours and all events leading up to the new production very soon filled his every waking hour and the issue slowly faded from his immediate mind. On the other hand, Nellie was more than aware just how much she had disappointed Tom and, by way of compensation, she made extra sure each day to pose more and more questions to Tom about his work and by so doing, raising her own interest. The fact, probably as much as any behind her decision, was that she somehow still didn't feel comfortable with the thought of Tom's work at the new opera and very much saw opera as something that wasn't for the likes of somebody either in her station or Tom's in what she saw as their own very lowly social position within Victorian life. She admired, even respected, Tom for taking his work so well and for, at least to her, never even questioning whether it was something for him to be doing and she knew that he was comfortable and without any of her qualms. How delighted she felt at the possible ordinariness of it all when one evening as they were talking about their day, or rather Tom was talking about his day as Nellie was well aware there was little about her own day which was ever any different from any other that had either preceded or would succeed it in the foreseeable future, when Tom told her: "Do you know, one of the singers was being really difficult today and Mr. Gilbert, well he just said to her 'Madam, this is not Italian Opera, it is only low burlesque of the worst possible kind!' so she soon got on with what she was told to do!"

"But is it low bur… what-do-ya-ma-call it?" Nellie asked, both at the same time relieved and intrigued at what Tom was telling her.

"Burlesque – that was the word that he used, love," Tom replied.

"Yes, whatever, bur – what-do-ya-ma-call it," Nellie continued, "but you 'ave told me that it's proper."

"Oh it is love, it is, but don't you see, it was just Mr. Gilbert putting one of the singers in their place when she was being over difficult! But the thing is it isn't like the Grand Opera, the Italian kind of things, it is different because it is English comic opera, something really new – witty, melodic, not grand, not posh – just like I've told you!" Tom concluded.

During the evening, Nellie thought a deal about what Tom had told her, feeling immediately far more comfortable in that what Tom was working on was not "too grand nor posh" and as such was more acceptable and altogether more comforting to her thoughts after all. As she lay in bed beside Tom who, as usual, was exhausted after his day and had quickly fallen into a sound sleep and was already quietly snoring in perfect slumber, Nellie relived his comments and vowed that "maybe, just maybe, I will fink about Tom's suggestion and go to get work alongside 'im in the 'featre!" She smiled to herself and with an evident feeling of happiness that such a move would bring to her beloved Tom, Nellie was soon herself in a similar happy repose to that of her husband.

During late April and May of that year, 1878, Tom was working harder than ever with feverish rehearsals, Mr. Gilbert often rushing away from the theatre to re-write pages of script that he felt weren't working on the stage and then it was up to Tom to quickly get acquainted with the revised instructions. At the beginning of May, just three weeks before the opening night, libretto and stage instructions were being constantly altered with Mr. Sullivan still working on the music. One night Tom didn't leave the theatre, utterly exhausted but somehow equally exhilarated, until after 3.30 in the morning, walking home through the dark and gas-lit streets of Victorian London with just some down and outs and ne're-do-wells for company. Tom kept his head down, quickened his pace and talked to no one although being very much aware of who and what was about him all the way back to Shoreditch. Once at home he quickly got undressed and crawled as quietly as possible into bed beside a slumbering Nellie who with an inner sense of comfort at his safe return, put her arm out to him and cuddled beside him.

Nellie tried to be as quiet as possible when she got up to leave for her own work even though Tom was only in a shallow sleep and before she had even left the house, just before seven, he was up and washing at the basin that Nellie had tried to quietly place in the corner of the tiny bedroom, soon to follow her only a few minutes later out of the house and back to Wych Street and the Opera Comique, there to begin another 18-hour session. During that time they had little chance of exchanging anything but a very few words about Tom's days and Nellie could only hope that all was going well although she held deep fears that the constant rehearsals and changes didn't bode too well, refusing to accept Tom's assurances that it was nothing other than Mr. Gilbert being a perfectionist. The pitch of their lives continued right up to opening night, 25 May, when Nellie waited at home, unable to go to sleep or even relax until Tom had arrived home.

"I think it went well, it was well received by the audience, they clapped, they laughed, they called for both Mr. Sullivan and Mr. Gilbert at the end, and yes, we were all very happy but, well, we'll have to see how it goes from now on, also, more immediately what the reviews will say," Tom cautioned. In that, Tom was very alarmed shortly afterwards when the Daily Telegraph commented about "HMS Pinafore – a frothy production soon to subside into nothingness".

It soon looked as if the newspaper may have been right as into June the nightly receipts alarming fell, along with the dwindling audiences. Tom felt a slight sense of uneasiness each night after he left the theatre, sweating as he walked home in the heat of a very early and stifling summer. There was little relief from the heat at home where the clamminess of the mass of back to back little terraced houses and the enclosed streets generated even more heat and with it a sense of perspiring and gasping for air for Tom, Nellie and all residents alike. The stench of the hot London streets added to what was a very difficult time once again for them all.

What with the heat and worries about 'Pinafore' there was little chance of sleep in any case although it was Nellie that reasoned with the situation, saying to Tom: "Look at it this way, luv, who in their right mind would want to go and sit in a blooming 'featre in this ere 'eat? It's bad enough in the 'ouse without going out to the 'featre and paying for it! You'll see, once it's cooler again, they're all be flocking into the 'featre again and all will be well!"

Tom hoped that she was right, saying a quiet "that's it, love" although, in his heart, he couldn't help but reflect on what he had heard and what others in the theatre were saying they had heard about 'Pinafore' – "that Gilbert's mockery of the British system of appointing 'names' to official positions was too hard for many to stomach", "it was poking fun at class distinctions". After all, Tom recalled, in the opera itself, the character the First Lord of the Admiralty, The Rt. Hon. Sir Joseph Porter, K.C.B. himself sang the words:

"Stick close to your desks and never go to sea,

And you all may be Rulers of the Queen's Navee!"-a loaded reference to Mr. W.H. Smith who had landed the top job at the Admiralty.

But he wasn't able to keep his fears from Nellie for long as not much later in that long and hot summer, Tom had to return home to tell her that his salary was to be cut by a third and that every week dismissal notices were placed around the theatre, only to be taken down again as there was another very small, but much welcomed, improvement in takings. Nellie sympathised but couldn't but help feeling relieved that she had earlier stood her ground by staying on at the dress factory rather than joining Tom at the theatre. She didn't say anything about it to Tom, though, realising just how worried he was increasingly becoming.

Bernard Lockett

Again, though, fate was to take an upper hand and it was a very spirited Tom that burst into the terraced house just as Nellie was placing the plates for their tea on the table. "Mr. Sullivan has included a selection of music from 'HMS Pinafore', playing it at the Summer Proms in Covent Garden and they say that it was well received by the audience and already, the takings at our own box office have improved!"

Even better news was immediately to come as a kind of Pinafore mania hit London with the music shops selling around 10,000 copies of the score every day. Each night the Opera Comique was again full, something that Tom never tired from relating in earnest to Nellie on a regular and extremely repetitive basis. Before long, another theatre in London began to start performing what was really an unauthorised production, although it was something beginning to show in a most positive way that audiences were becoming enthusiastic about Gilbert and Sullivan. Very soon, Tom had to join some of the other stage staff and act as Mr. Gilbert's 'sandwich-board' men to patrol the London streets to inform the public that "HMS Pinafore at the Opera Comique was the only authorised production".

Word soon got back to London that performances of the new opera were even being given in America.

"They say that there are eight theatres performing 'Pinafore' in New York but, do you know what Nellie, not one penny comes back to Mr. Gilbert, Mr. Sullivan nor to Mr. D'Oyly Carte, they are all so called pirated versions and that's how it is!" Tom exclaimed in a high degree of vexation to Nellie. "Just imagine how it would be for them, perhaps even all of us, if they and us could benefit from all those audiences."

"I suppose it would," Nellie answered although she realised that she felt totally incapable of really digesting or fully understanding what Tom was telling her.

"Anyway, it's made the three of them," Tom began.

"Three of 'um, who, what do you mean, who are you talking about?" Nellie interjected, in increasing confusion.

"Why, Nellie, Mr. Gilbert, Mr. Sullivan and Mr. D'Oyly Carte – that's who I mean, you should know that by now," Tom replied with a slight degree of exasperation at his wife's lack of understanding. "Anyway, what I was saying, the three of them now realise the international value of what they have produced and there's even talk that they may go to New York to mount our production there!"

"New York, New York, what in 'eavens are yer talking about now, Tom – 'ave you completely lost yer 'ead!" Nellie replied. Her own horizons barely reached as far west as Hyde Park let alone the other side of the Atlantic.

"I'm just telling you how it is, love, that's all. Anyway, I'm not saying that I'm going to New York, nothing like that, but all I'm trying to show you is how everything now seems to be taking off and that's only as benefit for all of us," Tom declared. "And there's more – we've been told that a cable has been sent now to J.C. Williamson Ltd, an Australian theatrical firm, with that an agreement for them to handle our productions there. Just think of that and all!"

But that was all just too much for Nellie to take in and she handled the news in the only way that she knew how – by bustling around the room and cleaning!

The talk, especially about New York, though, was very much on the minds of everybody working at the theatre in London and plans for the London production to open there became even more founded when Mr. D'Oyly Carte himself made a visit to America and returned to tell the assembled London company, Tom included, that "the people had excellent voices... but not the remotest idea how to play the piece. Acting, costumes and timing of the music were too atrociously bad for words to express". There and then it was decided that Gilbert, Sullivan and D'Oyly Carte would all go to New York to mount an authentic production as was then playing in London. Tom felt proud that he was asked to continue to oversee the staging of the London performances in the meantime and he told himself that he wasn't in the least bit sad at not being given the chance of going to America. In his heart, though, that was not strictly true as on one hand part of him would have longed to have gone but on the other hand he knew that it would both be unfair and difficult for him to have been parted from Nellie even though the time away would have been just a matter of months. Nellie for days bore similar concerns that were only lifted when Tom told her the news.

"Well, that's good, Tom, 'aint it, you being given the responsibility of looking after the London production whilst they are all off to America," Nellie said.

"Of course it is love, really good," Tom replied as his eyes cast to the ceiling.

When the three left for America in the autumn of 1879, they went with the goodwill of Tom and all the stage crew and actors still performing in London. What, though, was even more exciting for those left behind was the news that Mr. Gilbert and Mr. Sullivan had in their bags the outline of their next opera!

* * * *

At the Adelphi Theatre in London, some 103 years forward from that time, Rupert and his grandmother Alice were, with the rapturous audience around them, clapping wildly as all their cherished and favourite excerpts from 'HMS Pinafore' concluded with the triumphant sounds of:

"For he himself has said it,
And it's greatly to his credit,
That he is an Englishman!
That he is an Englishman!"

ringing in all their ears.

"Enjoying?" Rupert asked of his grandmother, almost by way of an aside as he could barely take his eyes away from the stage, fearing that there may be some extra bit of stage business or cue from the conductor for an encore, which he would miss.

"Wonderful, of course I am," his grandmother replied. "What's next?"

"Why, 'Pirates of Penzance' of course," Rupert replied, rather unmeaningfully curtly as he remained, as if in a dream world, with his eyes transfixed towards the stage.

Chapter 6

"How beautifully blue the sky, The glass is rising very high"

. As the rapturous applause subsided, the audience, Rupert and Alice included, who as a pair, cast a contented and satisfying glance to each other but did not speak. Looks said it all and words were neither necessary nor called for, as they settled down once more as the orchestra struck up with the beginning of one of the familiar musical introductions from 'The Pirates of Penzance'. As if with a favoured and well respected friend of countless years acquaintance and with a true sense of enchantment, they were all ready and waiting to be happily transported in their sight and minds from the stage of the Adelphi Theatre in London, westwards to a 'Rocky Sea-shore on the Coast of Cornwall'. Awaiting them there was the familiar world of Major-General Stanley, Mabel and his 'bevy of beautiful maidens' who Frederic, the Pirate Apprentice, found them not to sound at all "like Custom House". The world too of Ruth, the aptly 'Pirate Maid of all Work', The Pirate King and the blundering Sergeant of Police, the originator of the "The policeman's lot is not a happy one, Happy One". All of the audience were equally agog once more as they were immersed in their beloved world of Gilbertian characters coming to life before their eyes, bringing with it, at least for that very moment only, the sure feeling that all was very well and right with their world.

For the whole audience, the performance was as it was meant to be, thoroughly authentic, in virtually exactly the same way sung and acted as most of them had seen over their many years of coming to performances given by the D'Oyly Carte Opera Company, a style with which they were happily comfortable and equally respectfully enjoyed. Not only that, for not just Rupert and Alice, but for everybody in the theatre as well, it was a production that was also extremely very well done with perfect timing, stage business, acting and singing in 1980's London just as Mr. Gilbert would have so very carefully instructed a century before. As the ladies of the chorus began to sing "Climbing over rocky mountain", Alice nudged Rupert with a wink. He immediately realised the significance, the particular piece being performed had first been in 'Thespis' and had been resurrected in 'Pirates', in itself quite an unusual happening in the whole range of Gilbert and Sullivan. Rupert smiled towards his grandmother at their private joke although his eyes were not averted from the stage for too long lest anything significant would be missed – and even if it had, then memories of countless similar performances before would have adequately filled the gap. But that was not the real point, it being live theatre, the 'there and now' factor was of prime importance.

Tom, too, could equally have looked forward to that same scene with a sense of perfect satisfaction and wellbeing in his time over a century before. Perhaps, though, he would have equally found it very hard to believe that the work with which he was so enthusiastically involved in the mid-Victorian years in London should still be playing to an equally delighted audience a hundred years later. But then, without the benefit of a suitable potion from the Sorcerer's 'John Wellington Wells', he was unaware but, surely, how he would have loved to know and even to say: "Nellie, can you imagine, what I've been doing, what we have all been doing, we're forging a theatrical tradition that will be respected and will last to delight audiences for years to come!" Further, make-believe would have had him say: "Nellie, an audience in this very part of London, on the Strand itself, still enjoying the works all those years to the future – unbelievable". But, of course, that was mere make-believe!

With such benefit of vision, Tom's daily steps each way between his Shoreditch home and the London theatres would have been very light indeed and with a sure spring.

Immediately, though, there was no such comfort of foresight for Tom. Instead, though, in the late autumn of 1879, he had to concentrate his mind on the work in preparation for the new production as well as to continue to keep HMS Pinafore going smoothly, or rather as Nellie joked with him at home "in ship-shape!". Nellie was very proud, indeed almost both in awe and surprise of herself, to have had the sense to make a relevant joke to Tom to which he reciprocated with quiet admiration for his wife.

There was an added dimension to Tom's working world when it became known that the first performance of the new work, to be called 'Pirates of Penzance', was not to be at their London "home" of the Opera Comique but instead performed by a makeshift first performance at the Bijou Theatre at Paignton in Devon.

"Now, you're telling me that you are 'orf to Devon in the days before Christmas – I won't be 'aving none of that and yer can tell 'em plainly that from me!" Nellie declared incredulously when Tom arrived home to tell her of the plans for the new piece.

"Maybe not me, at least I don't think so," Tom informed. "A touring company will be already in Devon with 'Pinafore' and they will go over to Paignton to give the new show, at least that's how we think it will be."

"Well, you'd better not be going away yourself, that's what I say. I 'ardly see anything of you as it is at 'ome and I'm not certainly going to be left alone at Christmas, that's for sure and you can tell your Mr. Gilbert that – from me!" she re-emphasised. "But what's this all about, why aren't they having the first performance in London, like always – it don't make sense to me," Nellie declared.

"Well, it's like this," Tom began. "You know how Mr. Gilbert, Mr. Sullivan and Mr. D'Oyly Carte are all in New York." Nellie nodded, clearly indicating that she did, in fact, know, once

55

again almost surprising not only herself but Tom too that she had remembered. "Well, they've decided that they are going to premier the opera in New York and so set the copyright in America. So, that's planned to open on the last day of the year and we're to have the very first performance in Paignton, the night before on the 30th. That's about how it is, then we're to have a real London proper first night later on, perhaps next spring!"

"Sounds a bit ups and downs to me," Nellie replied. "If you ask me, seems everyone's getting just a bit mixed up and it's like you've all been spending a bit too long in that make-believe 'featre world of yours!"

"Who knows, perhaps Mr. Gilbert will write his next piece about this very tale!" Tom declared. Nellie just averted her eyes as she, as usual, thought that tidying up the house made all thoroughly better sense.

Tom later heard when he arrived for work at the London theatre that all was not going too well in New York. There, the orchestra had gone on strike with word coming that they considered that the music was not ordinary operetta music but rather grand opera! Arthur Sullivan had said that he "was much flattered by the compliment they have paid to my music but declined to submit to their demands", further indicating that he would play the pianoforte with Alfred Cellier (a friend of Sullivan's since they had met as choristers at the Chapel Royal and who then helped him with the orchestral arrangements) at the harmonium. "My bluff was successful," Sullivan declared when the American orchestra gave in and returned to work. It was all a struggle and the full score for the opera was not finished until 7am on the morning of 28 December, and the overture not completed until the early hours of the opening night, 31 December 1879, at the Fifth Avenue Theatre, New York.

Because of all this, it was a very rough and ready performance indeed that declared the opera open at Paignton on the night before New York, especially as the full score had not even been received in time from America. Although Tom very much liked the build up to, the excitement and atmosphere of the First Night, he was on that occasion very pleased that he was not involved away from home and was instead still busy working with the established 'Pinafore' in London. His sense of well-being was all the more for having had a warm and cosy Christmas at home with Nellie, with wages enough this time to put decent food upon the family table.

During the early days of January, the tones of the cables filtering back to the stage staff in London, though, showed that despite the chaotic beginning, 'Pirates' had been well received in New York, with Mr. Sullivan soon cabling to declare "immense business in New York. Our plan is now to take the opera to Chicago, Cincinnati, St. Louis – may even go across to San Francisco as there is money to be made there!" Tom heard the news with mouth wide open but immediately decided that at least for the moment that it was probably best not to tell that news to Nellie! He did, though, allow himself a wry smile, not just at the knowledge as to how well things were going, but also with the thought of what could maybe happen someday to their small, organised lives in Shoreditch!

Later news, though, he did pass on to Nellie. "Mr. Gilbert, in New York, tells us that they are all going to 'polite parties, just like those in Kensington!'"

"You don't say," Nellie replied, her eyes becoming wide open, similarly her mouth, as she was told the news. But having heard it, she made no comment because the news was of a world that she felt no part of and had no idea about.

For Tom, though, it was totally different as he continued to find himself almost revelling in news from America that was soon related, as if by magical practice, to the London stage crew by the theatre manager as soon as yet another cable was to hand. It was soon such common practice that Tom was almost blasé about the modern communications development and found that he hardly stopped to think anything special about it. They heard how the threesome were feted wherever they went and how both Mr. Sullivan and Mr. D'Oyly Carte loved the social spotlight whilst Mr. Gilbert was showing signs of increasing irritation with the number of social gatherings. Much amusement was felt in London with the news that at a party a few evenings before, Mr. Gilbert had been asked: "Do tell me, what is 'Baytch' (Bach) doing now – is he still composing?" to which Mr. Gilbert had replied "Well, no madam – just now, as a matter of fact, Bach is by way of decomposing".

By the early spring of 1880, Tom and the team in London were thrilled with the news that at long last a date had been set for the opening of 'Pirates of Penzance' officially in London, their minds being concentrated and their eyes set to the coming 3rd April at the Opera Comique. Truthfully, Tom was not alone in feeling just a little down at heart, almost outcast, at being left out of all the events that they had heard about in America. For the London team, it felt as if they were being left out of a family party, so much they looked upon the new works as their own and they were envious at what had been going on over the other side of the Atlantic. Then for Tom, part of him really wished that he could have gone with the team but in his heart he also knew that it would have caused enormous problems at home with Nellie, especially as it was only a relatively short time since she had been so ill. The news of the London opening was just what they all needed and spirits were well and truly lifted even though Tom, at least, could not dispel the thought that the work was not for something completely new anymore and it was, for him, just carrying on with something that others had already begun.

However, Tom soon realised that it was a great help for them all with so much groundwork having been done and that he had the benefit of being home not so late in the evening, something which was an almost luxury.

"Ain't you so busy no more?" Nellie asked as, for the third or fourth night running, Tom came through the door just after nine in the evening.

"No, it's much less work this time," Tom replied, "we've got the American performances to pick up from, it's not like just starting from the beginning. I like it better like we did with the earlier pieces, 'Trial' or 'Sorcerer', not to say 'Pinafore' it's more exciting, more satisfying being at it from the start and straight from the newly written page!"

Nellie listened. But Tom was silent as he reflected further. His quietened demeanour caused Nellie to feel a chill of disquiet shivering down her back. "You're not going to suddenly tell me that you're fed up, oh, surely not Tom what with all the business we 'ad with you in the first place to get this 'ere job, those music 'all days, with you mopping around with yer 'ead 'anging down as if the weight of this 'ere world was on yer shoulders!" With her concern and excitement of speech, in her usual way, Nellie had by that time dropped enough 'h's' to litter the gutters of all the streets in Shoreditch even though she had been trying so very much, with Tom's well-meant tuition, to be more careful.

"No, it's not like that, it's just – well, one of those things," Tom replied, anxious not to cause his wife any further distress. "All it is love, I just liked it best when we being in from the very start, you know, with Mr. Gilbert and Mr. Sullivan coming to the stage with the pages, still with almost wet ink, in their hands."

"That's you all over, you 'ave to be at the front, get yerself involved and, well if you don't, then yer like me mother's old cat what 'as lost 'er cream!" Nellie exclaimed. But, as was so often the case, she was exactly right and Tom really had felt lost, so much less involved, just because he wasn't in at the beginning.

Fortunately, it didn't take many days back at the theatre for the old magic to once again have the positive effect on Tom and the thrill leading up to the opening night finally dispelled his moods and he cheered up as a result. Again, he strode confidently onto the stage where, from Mr. Gilbert's notes, he checked all the props and backdrops to make perfectly sure that here really was "A Rocky Sea-shore on the Coast of Cornwall".

The orchestra in their rehearsals soon instilled into Tom the wealth of attractive music that once again Mr. Sullivan had composed and although he was no musician, admitting to himself only that "I like a really good tune, one that I can remember and hum", Tom could also understand, or at least thought he could, why the musicians in America had likened the music to grand opera. From the opening chorus of "Pour, oh pour the pirate sherry", the Pirate King's rousing song, "... And live and die a Pirate King.", Mabel's sweet "Poor wandering one!", the very clever "Yes, I am a Major-General!", the Sergeant's "Tarantara's" and to Mabel and Frederick's beautiful duet of "Stay, Frederick, stay!" "Nay, Mabel, nay!", the music was not only superb but also soon passed Tom's test of being beautifully easy for him to hum. Then, even though Tom didn't want to admit to himself that he felt very proud with the stage settings, he was impressed and none more so than at final rehearsal as the stage was filled and he saw for the first time the ladies' chorus, their beautiful dresses for which a newspaper critic in America had already declared "old fashioned English as if out of a Gainsborough picture".

"This is the place where my Nellie should be and is going to be!" Tom avowed with sincerity. And in that thought he knew that he was perfectly right and not only that Nellie would do good work that would be in the spotlight on stage night after night for all to see, but he also felt that the theatre life would be a far better place for her to be than the awful dress factory. It would be a matter of time, Tom knew that, but he knew that he would pick the right moment and would not let the issue drop until he had achieved his ambition – Nellie and him together at work and at home.

Business continued to be good at the theatre throughout the whole of 1880 and with it a growing feeling of confidence began not only to felt by Tom, but indeed the whole of the London crew plus other colleagues that were in the touring company, by then spending most of their time in various theatres throughout the length and breadth of the country. For Tom, it really meant that for the very first time he felt a sense of security at his work and the dread of a possible return for him to what he considered to be the very bleak world of the music hall began to finally drain from his thoughts. "After all," he told himself, "even if there were no more new operas now, we have behind us already three full length ones, already proven to be good, that could continue to play and I've been in from the start and would surely be relied upon to help in any re-runs!" But there was more to Tom's confidence. With the on-going work came the surety of the weekly wage and the chance for Tom and Nellie to spend a small amount of money on some much needed furnishings for their small home.

"C'or, Tom, yer making me feel like I'm living in me own little palace!" Nellie declared, her words almost causing Tom's eyes to well up and moisten, so thrilled he felt at causing his beloved wife so much pleasure.

But it was in no way one-sided, most certainly not. Because of Nellie's work at the dress factory, their clothing had never been too much of a problem as Nellie worked wonders with the various 'cast-off's' and remnants that always, legitimately, ended up discarded on the factory floor, all finding their way to make respectable clothes for Tom to not have to feel either out of place nor inferior at his work. And Nellie equally made sure that she looked her best for 'walking-out, which for her meant whenever she went out of the front door. "We might be poor and 'aving it 'ard, but we don't's want the 'ole world to sees it or knows it!" she frequently declared. They both had their standards and that was something in which neither was to fail.

And for that reason, Tom also knew they could do better and one day they would do just that – when Nellie came to work with him in the theatre. But once again, he felt he should leave the issue just a little longer.

Chapter 7

"If you walk down Piccadilly with a poppy or a lily in your mediaeval hand"

The performances of 'Pirates' continued to draw full audiences to the satisfaction not only of the writer, composer and theatrical manager but also to Tom and his team of fellow workers who especially grew in confidence about their job prospects and for the positive outlook for all with which they were involved. For them all it was nothing less than the introduction of a very special brand of English comic opera, already proven to be not only of a localised attraction for Victorian London society, but also for vast audiences in theatres up and down the country, not to say already being performed with huge success in America, Canada and Australia. For Tom personally it was even more profound. For him, it wasn't anymore just a case of his getting on with the job at his place of work but rather a true awakening of his enthusiasm and the beginnings of a steady but growing understanding of all that was going on in the musical theatre. 'Musical theatre', a term so very dear to Tom's ears as opposed to 'music hall', for that was a part of his working life that he sincerely hoped was well and truly behind him.

Whilst he had never before been a musical person in the sense of either enjoying or even understanding symphony concerts or grand opera, neither had it even been in his social class or aspirations to even attend such events, he easily found just how much the new pieces from Gilbert and Sullivan were to his liking. For him it meant everything that was to his preferences – catchy music with tunes that he could remember, delightful songs, fine acting and stage business, the excellent costumes and, whilst he was loathe to actually show off, he felt immensely proud of the stage settings and just how good everything was to look at – so idyllic yet also exquisite. Very much something he never failed to appreciate whenever he stalked away to the back of the darkened theatre to cast his eyes towards the stage and to all that was invariably busily going on. He felt very satisfied indeed, sometimes almost overcome at what had so far been achieved and his own part in it, however small that he often felt it really was – and that especially sent a quiver down his back. And to top it all, Tom never failed to feel a sense of thrill in his walks through London when he heard people in the street whistling and humming the growingly familiar tunes that were increasingly becoming played by a variety of musicians and organ-grinders in the street to a general public appeal. People, too, were picking up the catchy phrases from the pieces with passers-by on street corners saying to each other "What never?" to the reply "Well, hardly ever!" Always, Tom smiled and felt an over-demanding urge to intervene and to tell of his own involvement in the works – but his naturally modest disposition overcame any such uninvited intervention.

Tom had been used to the idea that with a new production underway and with it receiving a positive response from the audience, he found himself full of expectation, with a growing anticipation of what might then become the next opera. This time, though, even Tom was not fully prepared to hear so early during the summer of 1880 that Mr. Gilbert had already presented to Mr. Sullivan, much to the delight of Mr. D'Oyly Carte, thrilled at the prospect of his growing company and with it, his overall theatrical standing and business, the outline and basic dialogue for a new piece. Rumour and stories filtered through to Tom and the stage crew that for the new piece, Mr. Gilbert had chosen the very topical aesthetic craze that was so rife in Victorian London at that time, the so called "greenery-gallery" fashions and affectations so epitomised by Oscar Wilde, then aged 25 years.

On hearing the news, Tom at first scratched his head and was the first to admit that it all sounded just a little bit strange and very uninteresting to him, simply it was something that he did not understand in the least. It was from a world that was somehow there, or rather, so he thought, but one of which he had no part. He had loved the setting of the Court of Law in 'Trial', respected the English village scenes so well depicted in 'Sorcerer' and had so happily understood and could identify with the navy storyline of 'Pinafore', or the Cornish and virtual swashbuckling scenes of 'Pirates'. But as far as the new piece was concerned, with all that he had heard, well that was something quite different. He mentioned that there was to be a new work at home, only briefly, to Nellie and was more than relieved when she asked no questions nor posed any form of enquiry about the piece.

Of altogether greater significance, though, for Tom and everybody came at the same time and this time, it was something for which he was able to rush home and inform Nellie, time and time again, until she even had to beg him:

"Tom, me love, I've 'eard this all before, so many times that here's me 'finking that you must believe that I am 'ard of 'earing or somefink, when you goes on and on saying this same bit of news over and over again!"

"'Of course, I don't think that," Tom answered, ever so slightly taken aback and unable to understand his wife's irritation. "Don't you see, love, this makes all the difference for us, my future more assured with Mr. Gilbert, Mr. Sullivan and Mr. D'Oyly Carte, this big investment in the new operas and the prospect for all the work to continue!"

"It's just bricks and buildings! All this far-fetched talk of sometime later there even being a big fancy 'otel – well that's really pie-in-the-sky! Anyway, that will never be for the likes of us," Nellie replied.

"Oh, no, love, you are wrong there," Tom answered, becoming all together more serious and with a deeply frowned expression on his face at his wife's lack of serious interest and rapid dismissal to his news. "Firstly, they are building a brand new theatre which they say will be the finest in the whole of London and just you think, Nellie, that will be the place where I will be working and, soon, hopefully…" Tom stopped himself just in time, realising that the moment was not right for him to raise, yet again, his so long-held dream and sure aim of having Nellie work beside him in the theatre. He blushed before continuing. "That's the whole point. Yes I know that there's talk of a big and fancy hotel but that's for something way ahead in the future, after the theatre has been built. No, Nellie, I'm only thinking about the excitement of being involved in the new theatre and how that will be for us, em, me, I mean!"

Nellie seemed to be unaware of Tom's slip of the tongue and if she was, then she chose not to refer to it. "I can see and understand how the new 'featre delights you and all that, but all I am saying, well, it's another world and like I'm always saying to you, it's only right and proper that you keeps yer feet very much on the ground!" Seeing Tom's somewhat sullen expression, Nellie felt guilty that her words were a little unkind, even harsh, almost a put-down to Tom on something that he obviously felt about deeply and, in any case, Nellie only too well realised that it was his very work that brought in their money and ensured food was on the table, something that she could never do alone from her small wages at the dress factory. Turning to Tom, she softened her expression and put her arms around him. "Where did you say the new 'featre is to be?" she asked, with a revived interest.

Even though Tom had told her endlessly, he didn't get angry. Rather the opposite, as he smiled to his wife, very delighted with her show of interest. He reciprocated her hug by placing his own arms closely around her. "It's going to be almost in the same vicinity of where we are now with the Opera Comique - by the Strand and on a site overlooking the Thames at the Victoria Embankment. That's the place where it's going to be, just a stone's cast away from our present place," he declared.

"… like an 'ome from 'ome!" Nellie replied, laughing.

"Yes, that's it love, just like that!" Tom replied reflectively, knowing indeed just how much he wanted the new theatre to be like a "home from home" for both of them even if the time still wasn't ripe for further broaching the subject.

Any further thoughts on that particular subject were soon cast aside as Tom set to work very hard on the new opera, especially so when he was told that the plan was to open in the following April, barely more than a year following the London opening of 'Pirates'. It was a very hectic pace indeed, even more so when Tom still felt a lack of empathy with the subject and frequently found he didn't really understand either the significance or the dramatic line of what he was being asked to do and work upon. Tom wasn't one to pose questions, he still felt that was not for someone in his position, and merely buckled down to do all that he was being asked but this time it was so much more difficult for him through the lack of understanding of the subject, besides it being one with which he could not identify. Quietly, he even acknowledged to himself that he was rather glad that Nellie wasn't beside him working in the theatre as he dreaded to wonder what she would have made of the storyline of the new opera. "Probably would have gone at me for forcing her to come here," he thought, with a certain amount of genuine despair.

Some talk amongst the stage crew did little to allay his fears, only increasing his immediate concerns. He felt even more alarmed and unsure of himself when the stage manager explained to the whole crew: "Mr. Gilbert has written the new piece as a target against affectation and that's why for the opening scene we will have the love-sick maidens in the opening scenes dressed in Liberty fabrics – it's a kind of skit upon the contemporary art of the Pre-Raphaelites!"

Tom recoiled, the words almost floating senselessly over his head. He simply had no idea what all this was about, nor even began to understand what he was being told. More each day, he found that he had, with much effort, to really concentrate extra hard to make any sense of what he had to do and what was required of him for his preparatory work. Only when they began some work with the stage setting itself and with it the movements required for a little later on in the First Act, did he then begin to feel something as part of him in the new work. Then he worked on the opening men's chorus, a brassy rendering.

"The soldiers of our Queen
Are linked in friendly tether."

For Tom, suddenly, like an aspiration, this was immediately more like it, similar to the rousing Sailor's chorus of 'Pinafore' or the swashbuckling 'Pirates'. With a more relaxed smile he once again he immediately warmed to the tasks in hand, even more so when it was explained that the chorus would be resplendent in the red and blacks of the Dragoon Guards. At first he failed to recognise the significance of it all, the link between the aesthetic affections, the almost, to him, unreal make-believe of the love-sick maidens as opposed to the tough, military and real world of the Guards, how through it all Gilbert was virtually poking fun at a fad as compared to an honourable tradition. But very slowly, and by purposefully listening to every stage direction, to his colleagues, and very much to Mr. Gilbert's readings, then the piece began to make some kind of sense to Tom and he found himself gradually warming to the new opera.

The work for everybody was hard and although Mr. Gilbert had the narrative written, and from that for Tom a start could be made on the stage directions, the completion of the new opera was frequently held up by Mr. Sullivan being late with the music. The frantic mood affected everybody, with rehearsals in the theatre each morning to be followed by Mr. Sullivan then rushing to his home in Victoria Street to set to and compose another song or to work on some other aspects of the music. Often, it would be as late as eight in the evening when Mr. Sullivan eventually returned to the theatre with some more of the completed score and rehearsals would once again resume in earnest.

Tom, like all the rest of his colleagues, would not finally get home until well after midnight, and then in the knowledge that he would have to be back at the theatre by 10am sharp the next morning. At least though, although Tom didn't fully appreciate the fact, he would be at home for bed whilst for Mr. Sullivan, it was home in the early hours for more work on the music. "Second tenor song and sketched out overture. Finished all scoring of the opera – to bed at 5.30am," he wrote.

Just like all times of production, especially when leading up to the first night, the pace was relentless with Tom's life revolving around endless hours at the theatre or walking to and from home with barely a few hours sleep and scarce little time with Nellie other than crawling in quietly to their bed in the late hours, only to rush around in the mornings as they both prepared for their daily toils. Through his tiredness, though, Tom almost felt himself lucky as compared to the performers themselves who had enormous difficulties in learning their roles with everything happening with the music so late and so much ever closer to the opening night. Frequently, Tom wondered just how it was ever possible that somehow the performance came together at all but miraculously it did with the huge efforts and attention to perfection, firstly from Mr. Gilbert himself and the directions meticulously handed down. Whilst he didn't modestly like to admit to it, it was even down to Tom's delicate interpretation of the stage instructions.

The rising excitement for the new production, which by then everyone had been told was to be entitled 'Patience', fed through the whole company and even by then Tom's original qualms had been dispelled as he was more and more immersed in the new work. How, by then, he loved the opening chorus: "Twenty love-sick maidens we," later the chorus of the ladies "In a doleful train", to be interweaved with the Dragoons' "Now is not this ridiculous – and is not this preposterous?" to be followed by the Colonel's "When I first put this uniform on", with sheer bravado and pomposity. By then, too, Tom felt the significance of the comparison to the so-called "Fleshy Poet", Bunthorne, and his cleverly versed opening song "Am I alone and unobserved? – I am!"

As often as he could, Tom found himself spending as much time as possible in the wings, not only because he needed to be there frequently to control the stage settings and also to be sure all was in place, but also because he found he was becoming increasingly captivated by the music and the songs of the new opera. Gilbert's creation of the 'Idyllic Poet', Archibald Grosvenor with his song 'A magnet hung in a hardware shop'. The chorus of a 'Silver Churn!',the song of Patience herself,

'Love is a plaintive song, sung by a suffering maid'. He would gently hum along quietly to himself the duet from the two poets, Bunthorne and Grosvenor:

"When I go out of door,
Of damozels a score
(All sighing and burning,
And clinging and yearning)
Will follow me as before."

Tom even found that he was able to pick up the rhythm of the music more and more and his toes almost began to tap along in time – for that he very quietly smiled to himself, thinking "who would have thought that of me, Tom from Shoreditch, Nellie's Tom!" But then, exactly in the same way that it manifested itself for Tom, that was in general the very key to the success of the new works – something with which so many people from various walks of life and social structures felt that they could identify with and enjoy, exactly why on opening night, and all following nights, the balcony would be as full as the best stalls seats. One day for sure Tom knew that he would get Nellie to enjoy it too and this thought gave him a happy and satisfying glow as he got on with the variety of tasks necessary as preparations for the new opera were finalised in the immediate hectic hours.

Opening night and the sense of the occasion was equally as significant for Tom and the theatre crew, let alone the singers but also for the gathering and highly expectant audience too. In all, an excited hubbub filled the Opera Comique, perhaps touched with a slight tinge of sadness for the Opening Night of 'Patience' when all realised that the occasion was the last first night in the old theatre with the anticipated move to the new theatre very much in everybody's mind. It was pure nostalgia because nobody really liked the old theatre; working conditions could not have been more dingily Victorian and it was cramped, dusty, very smelly – all very unprepossessing. As countenance to that, though, it had been for over four years their home and the scene of three already successful opening nights. Besides, Tom hardly knew anything very much better, either in the awful old music halls where he had worked and, although he would not readily admit it, his own home was equally not very much different; cold, grim and austere despite both of their efforts to make the place as cosy and comfortable as possible.

To befit the last time in the old theatre, the First Night of 'Patience', on 23 April 1881, was a magnificent success with a total of eight encores being given by the delighted musicians and singers to the equally delighted audience. Tom watched from the wings as much as he could when his time wasn't needed, which was very rarely, working on the many stage and prop duties that were his charge. Even Mr. Gilbert and Mr. Sullivan allowed themselves a contented smile whilst Mr. D'Oyly Carte, the earnest theatrical and company manager that he was, thought satisfyingly about the mounting receipts and takings that were anticipated from the box office.

At large, throughout London, there was always growing excitement at the prospect of another Gilbert and Sullivan opera being produced. Much was done by all concerned, both at the theatre and in the production generally, to keep details of the new piece as secret as possible before curtain up, which only added to the sense of excitement and occasion. The company's previous experiences of the works being performed unauthorised, especially in America and for which neither the authors nor the theatre ever received any royalty monies, added a sense of urgency to the secrecy. For Tom, the fact that he so often told Nellie about the new works didn't concern him because he knew that it was not her style to gossip about his work. Neither would it be of interest, he had to admit, to the sort of people that Nellie met in going about her daily life. Besides, Tom thought his wife probably only listened to him out of a sense of duty to her husband rather than either being especially interested or really understanding what she was being told. Tom smiled to himself within his thoughts, realising that whatever she might be, Nellie was his very special and loving wife who, above everything else, he really adored like nothing else in his life. Even the theatre, he avowed, took second place to that.

It was the early hours of the morning when Tom finally reached home. Nellie, as usual, had already gone to bed and was in a kind of restless slumber as Tom crawled into the bed as quietly as possible so as not to disturb her. She was aware, though, and in a kind of in-between sleep and half-awake kind of way, put her arm out towards Tom who moved lovingly towards her. "Was it good, everyfink go well?" she half-asked but was once again in sleep almost before Tom replied, "Yes, my love, it was a magnificent night". Tom's mind was still racing from the events of the night and it was rather many hours before he too was able to join his wife in some kind of rather restless repose.

They talked briefly the next morning as they both bustled for the start of their respective days and Tom told Nellie that he had to leave even a bit earlier to go to Bond Street.

"What are yer going off to the likes of Bond Street for?" she asked.

"They've asked me to go early to that music publishers, Chappells, to help out. They expect there to be a queue of vans outside from first thing to pick up the newly-published music of the opera. They say that it was busy enough before and now will be more so as the work gets more and more popular," Tom added, with a sense of real pride raising in his chest.

"Well, that's good then, in'it – but just you be careful – I don't want you to be getting any high-minded ideas from the likes of those what go to Bond Street," Nellie replied as she made a final and swift rush about the room to be sure that all was a tidy and spic and span as possible for the day before they both kissed each other at the doorstep as they each made about for the duties of their days – Nellie heading off eastwards for the relatively short walk to the clothes factory and Tom heading in the opposite direction, first to the shop of the music publisher and then back to the theatre, "up-west". There could hardly have been a greater contrast between their two directions.

Tom glanced back to see Nellie hurrying along the grimy and congested street. "One day," he repeated over and over to himself, "one day, my Nellie, we'll be going this way together, to our work in the theatre, just you see my dear girl!"

Chapter 8
"When I first put this uniform on"

Throughout the summer of 1881, with the continued successful playing of 'Patience' to enthusiastic and packed houses, for Tom and everybody else in the theatre each passing day meant only one thing – getting ever closer to the opening of and the consequent move to the new theatre, with all the excitement and anticipation which that entailed. With the new production no more than a bare few months old, there was never any question that there would be a new opera ready to open the new theatre and that indeed 'Patience' would be the debut piece for the new building. Tom was not alone in being rather grateful for that, being well aware of the work needed for the move let alone having a new opera to prepare for production at the same time.

Each day during that summer as Tom made his way along the Strand, he was intent on frequently diverting from his path for a quick look at the steadily growing building on the south side of the street, there overlooking the Victoria Embankment. As they had all been told from the start of the new project, this was indeed to be something very special, a theatre of which the whole of London could be proud, as Tom could see on his frequent visits. The chosen site was close to the Savoy Chapel and on a site where formerly had stood the Savoy Place, the former homes of John of Gaunt and the Dukes of Lancaster. Mr. D'Oyly Carte had told the whole company that he had chosen "the ancient name of the 'Savoy' as an appropriate title for the new theatre".

Later, Tom joined his colleagues on the stage of the old Opera Comique and together they heard more details of what was to become their new theatrical home. The "oohs" and "aahs" and other gasps swept around the stage as incredible detail after incredible detail was made known to the assembled actors and stage workers. With amazement, long after the news was first given to them, each and everyone repeated the news between themselves. For both the teller and listener, it was like something new or unknown: "the theatre is to be large and commodious"; "they say it will seat 1,292 persons"; "did you hear that the enterprise of Messrs. Siemens Brothers Company has enabled Mr. D'Oyly Carte to experiment with exhibiting electric light in the theatre"; "they say that there will be 1,200 individual lights, that's one light almost for every person and that the power to generate sufficient current for them is obtained from large steam-engines giving about 120 horse-power!"; "they say that the new light is not only used in the auditorium part of the theatre, but on the stage, for the footlights, side and top lights". That particular news, Tom could barely begin to believe, so used was he to working in the grim, dismal, foul air and heat of the gas-lit stage and theatres.

"That don't seem right to me, not at all – won't it all catch fire?" Nellie exclaimed as Tom had tried to tell her about the coming of the electric lights in the theatre, in a way as best he could but with difficulty when he could barely understand what he secretly regarded as new-fangled developments in any case. "Don't you be standing too close to them there 'fings – I don't want yer going up in a puff of smoke!" Nellie warned with a growing sense of increasing alarm at the barely believable news that her husband was telling her.

"It must be alright," Tom reassured her but not altogether with too much conviction. "Besides, they say that the electric lights will also be for the comfort of the performers by placing the lights in dressing rooms too. Now, they wouldn't do that if it wasn't safe now, would they? There would be no company left!" he added, as much as to convince himself as well as Nellie.

73

"So that means, don't it, that where you work, on the stage and at the sides, that you'll have these new electric fings as well, all around yer. Oh, Tom, just you be careful," Nellie warned, her eyes blinking with her obvious concerns.

"Of course, love, I'll not do anything daft and, anyhow, do you really think that Mr. D'Oyly Carte would be spending all that money on the new theatre just to have it burnt down as soon as it is built – no, of course he wouldn't," Tom replied although he still had his reservations. He was more than pleased when Nellie changed the subject completely and more mundane issues of their regulated lives were then discussed.

The impending move to the new theatre caused even more repercussions for Tom and his stage colleagues than he ever at first thought. The brighter lighting from the electricity at the Savoy meant that all the scenery had to be repainted to appear clean and fresh. Then, with the larger stage at the new theatre, Mr. Gilbert wanted the whole production to be mounted anew. Tom immediately regretted his initial thoughts that his working life would be easier without work on a new opera because what he was then having to do really added up to the same thing with the same amount of toil anyway.

In early October the whole company – Mr. D'Oyly Carte's Opera Company – moved to the Savoy in readiness for the new opening night of 10 October 1881. Tom's initial qualms about the electric lights were soon quelled as he marvelled at the warmth and brilliance of his new working surroundings and the ease in which everybody took to the invention. At the final rehearsal on 9 October, Tom once again took himself to the back of the theatre, this time keeping his eyes tightly closed at the moment when he turned to look back towards the stage. Slowly, he opened his eyes and could hardly believe the brilliance of the scene before him, seeing for the first time, from a distance, the sheer splendour of the costumes and stage setting. He had to stifle the gasp of amazement rising in his throat as he felt the tears of joy with which he could no longer hold back. He felt himself shaking with excitement and needed to take hold of the back of a stalls seat to steady himself. For several moments he just stood and stared before realising that his tears were no longer just expressions of immediate joy but also rather ones of sadness that Nellie was not there beside him to witness the scene. "But I can do something about that," he cried as wiping his cheeks, he very slowly made his way back through the auditorium and towards the brightly-lit stage.

If anything, for once it was not the opera on the next night that was the centre of attraction, perhaps understandable in that 'Patience' was already known, very popular with the London audiences and had already been running for almost six months. This time, though, it was either the theatre itself or the electric lighting that not only shared centre stage but was in every way the principle star attractions. Tom tried to take everything in with an almost encyclopaedic memory so that he could relate the scene to Nellie the moment he arrived home, tired but jubilant after another night in the Victorian world of Gilbert, Sullivan and D'Oyly Carte.

"When the curtain fell, Mr. D'Oyly Carte came onto the stage to thunderous applause and do you know what Nellie?" Tom asked.

"Course I don't know what 'appened, I wasn't there, was I!" Nellie exclaimed, somewhat exasperated. "It's you who are me eyes and ears so, go on with you, be telling me!"

"Yes, of course, love. Well, Mr. D'Oyly Carte came on the stage and he was carrying in his hand a brilliant and glowing electric lamp. The audience gasped and a strange and almost mystical hush came over the whole theatre so that you could almost hear a pin drop," Tom continued with added rigour as he noticed that he had Nellie's almost divine attention as he could see from her ever widening eyes. "Next, he, Mr. D'Oyly Carte, I mean, he placed a piece of muslin around the lamp, next he took a hammer and with it he smashed the lamp which, naturally, then was extinguished." Nellie looked on with an even more amazed expression, so much so that she did not say anything. Tom continued: "He then he held up the muslin to show the audience and all saw that the muslin was indeed unburned, no marks at all and the whole audience went absolutely wild. Mr. D'Oyly Carte bowed and then he left the stage but the cheers went on and on, they were all so enthusiastic, that he had to

75

come back to the stage – twice he came back, like two encores as if he was appearing as the lead in the opera himself!" Tom concluded with as much excitement as those who had been at the scene that he was describing. "It was truly fantastic!"

There was some silence for a moment between them as Nellie struggled to take in and make any sense of what Tom had been telling her, before she replied, rather quietly, "that must have been some evening for yer".

"It was, love, it really was," Tom replied, his eyes still wide with excitement from all that he had experienced. "And there's more, the theatre itself, it is so beautiful, they say that it is the most handsome theatre in the whole of Europe, a right and proper home for English light opera!"

"Well, that's alright for them that can afford to go," Nellie reflected, "but it surely don't mean much for the likes of you, do it?"

"Oh, Nellie, love, it does mean a lot for me, emh us, too, you just don't realise," Tom replied rather indignantly before he bit his tongue and continued. "It means a far better place for me and all the company to work and perform. No more do I have to be in that foul air of the old places, all that gas fumes, the heat, the smells, the dark, damp and dingy rooms, the dull stage, breathing in all that muck the whole and every night! You see, love, we are all set to benefit and Mr. D'Oyly Carte hasn't only just done what he has done for the audiences, but it's also for all us of too, all involved in the operas!"

"If you says so, then I believe you, 'though fousands probably wouldn't," Nellie replied rather dismissively to what Tom had told her.

"There's something else you should know, Nellie," Tom continued, with even more rising excitement and almost uncontrolled enthusiasm, "when you say it's not for us – well remember that I told you that lots of poorer people come to see the Gilbert and Sullivan pieces and they go to the gallery, just like at the music hall, and you've been there! Even for them, Mr. D'Oyly Carte has made sure that the Savoy will be a better place too – he's introduced a queue system for the cheaper seats to do away with the awful rush and scrum like mayhem that came whenever the old theatre's doors were opened with everybody rushing to get a seat. Well, now that's no more!" Tom added, his chest rising with pride.

"Well, if that's right, well, that's good then, aint it?" Nellie answered.

"Of course it is, love. One day, you'll see for yourself," Tom replied but even then decided that once again the time was not ripe to broach the subject of Nellie coming to work with him. The fact that he wondered if that time would ever be right was the only thing that caused him any upset as he and Nellie had a hot drink together and gradually prepared for bed, knowing that for both of them the following day would be another of immense toil, even though far more rewarding for Tom than it would be for Nellie.

The Savoy had barely been open for a fortnight or so, playing to even larger and enthusiastic audiences as befitted the larger theatre, when one evening, the stage manager, Fred Dean, called Tom over as he was helping to prepare the set for the coming performance.

"Tom," he called, "let's be having you over here a minute!"

Startled, Tom went over to his boss immediately, with a slight sinking feeling in the pit of his stomach lest there should be something that he had done wrong, some piece of stage equipment out of place – or something even much worse that he hardly dared to contemplate. The stage manager, noticing the fears in Tom's face and already being aware just how good and sincere worker Tom was, kindly and quickly spoke to allay his colleague's very obvious concerns. "It's nothing to be worrying yourself about, quite the opposite!" he declared. Tom's spirits immediately lifted and he allowed a relieved half smile to appear on his face.

"Mr. Gilbert, well he notices your work, he knows you are good and reliable and also how you have been with us now through thick and thin – really from the start too, when you went a looking him up those years back," Fred said with a comforting smile. His words caused a glimpse of embarrassment on Tom's face. "Well, it's like this here – Mr. Gilbert wants you to be having a couple of tickets so that you can see the performance for yourselves, amongst the audience in the theatre! There you are, take them, it's his acknowledgement and it'll give you the chance of taking that lovely wife of yours, well, you're always talking about her, of taking her out and bringing her to the theatre. She must be sick and tired of you going on about it all the time, so now she can see for herself," he concluded with a smile as he handed the tickets to a startled Tom.

"Thank you, Mr. Dean," Tom began to reply before the stage manager interrupted him, raising his hand.

"It's not me you should be thanking, I'm only the one who's passing on the message, like I say, it's Mr. Gilbert that has given them to you, they're from him!" Fred Dean replied. "But anyway, I'll be letting him know just how pleased you are in case it's some while before you gets the chance of saying so yourself."

"Righty-ho," Tom answered, "but thanks to Mr. Gilbert and thanks to you, of course," Tom added.

"What for?"

"Thanks for everything, thanks for everything," Tom added for emphasis, as he quickly moved away, daring not to look back to the spot where he had stood a moment before with Fred Dean and busied himself with his stage duties, very pleased to be once again getting on with his work. Only when he was later alone did Tom take a moment to have a quick glance at the tickets, noting that they were rather good ones, not the very best, but still centre circle. He smiled to himself at the very thought that he would soon be going to the opera with Nellie on his arm!

That night, Tom could barely make his steps home fast enough as he rushed to tell the news to a very startled Nellie who, on hearing, was unable to immediately steady herself so she took refuge in the safety of the chair by the fireplace and the warmth of the still glowing embers of the fire on a cool late October evening.

"What, me, go to the opera, go up west in London, go to the 'featre!" she gasped, with an air of total disbelief.

"Why not, why ever not!" Tom exclaimed. He grabbled in his jacket pocket and

pulled out the pair of tickets that were fast becoming rather rumpled, so many times had he already looked at them, over and over again, on the way home. "Look, love, look at these tickets in my hand, they're for us, given to us, look for yourself!" Tom showed his prized pieces of paper to his wife and noticed her look of sheer amazement, almost confusion, at the situation he presented. Tom, too, realised that he was in a state of almost animation at what he saw as the unexpected fortune then cast upon his small family.

"But that's not for the likes of us – er – me! For you, wot, that's different, it's where you work, but me, no, no, never, there's no place for me to be, not up London with all them in society. Besides, they're all laugh at me, sneer at me, make me look and feel cheap – well, there's nothing wrong in that 'cause that's what I am – just everyone and everyfink to their own place and station!" Nellie was once again gabbling, almost unstoppably so, but it was more than that, more with a sense of real fear about the situation with which she was being faced.

"Love levels all rank," Tom thought aloud as he recalled a line from 'Pinafore' that he felt was just right for their situation, something that he would like to have believed in but secretly knew not to be the real case.

"What's that yer say?" Nellie asked

"Nothing, love, nothing really," Tom replied as he once more gathered his thoughts before he continued. "Nellie, don't you see, it's these tickets here, well, they are an honour being bestowed on us," he continued, rather over grandly and not in anyway really helping his wife to come to terms with the invite. "Mr. Gilbert has given us the tickets, he almost gave them personally but via Fred Dean, the stage manager. If we don't go, especially if you don't come, well that's rather like an insult! His declaration was met with a stony silence in the room as Nellie buried her face even more into the chair as she sought the greater security that her own fireside offered.

The silence that then enveloped the whole room was of a virtual total deafness, the only discernable sound being that of the ticking of an overly loud clock on the mantelpiece above the fire, the fire to which both Tom and Nellie were staring in a concentrated stance. Tom was quite bereft as to knowing what to do then or how to break the situation so he did what he was best at in such a demanding situation – nothing and kept quiet. So it was in the room for what seemed an interminable number of minutes.

"It's like biting the 'and what feeds yer!" Nellie's words finally broke the silence.

Tom could scarcely believe the words that his wife was saying. "What do you say, Nellie, please say it again?" he asked.

"I'm saying, it's like biting the 'and what feeds yer – that's what would come from me attitude by demonstrating about going out with you to the 'featre. I sees it, I do really, and then I finks about it and I finks just 'ow would it look to your Mr. Gilbert, not to say your very boss, that stage manager what passed them tickets over to yer, if I says 'no, I'm not coming'. It'll be a right and proper insult, that it would! Alright, I've thought about it, in me own way just ere now and I'm finking – right you are, Nellie, get yerself together and make a do, no matter what I really finks. I will come with you! I'll see fer meself just what all this 'ere nonsense is about in this 'ere 'featre world of yours and what keeps yer away from 'ome for all the hours what God sends!"

For Tom, her words were like magic to him. He knelt down on the floor beside Nellie's chair and took first her hands, then her arms until he held her whole body firmly clasped to him. Overjoyed, he said: "Thank you, thank you my darling Nellie, for saying what you have just said and for agreeing that we do this together. You won't regret it, not at all and then going the once, you'll be wanting to keep going back for more and more, that I promise you!" He thought for a moment before continuing, this time ever so gently and with sincere feeling, "And I will be the proudest man in the whole of London to have you on my arm and be able to show you, my own very dear wife, to the people at the theatre – everybody, the audience, the stage crew, the actors, as I say, I mean everybody!" and with the closing words he hugged his wife the more, if that was possible.

"Oh, go on, ere's listening to yer," Nellie answered, with a nervous, almost embarrassed laugh. "You'll be 'aving me fink I'm some kind of princess or somefink with all this kind of talk! I'm me and that's that – all the toffs up there can make of me what they like!" She fell silent for a moment, staring once again, very much in deep contemplation, into the fireplace which by that time of night was then barely more than a distant, feeble glow with a similar pitiful warmth. "But goodness at all knows what I'm going to wear!" she concluded.

"Nellie, Nellie dear!" Tom exclaimed, "you're a seamstress, what to wear is the very last of your problems! You will look the part, you will knock them all cold and look what you are, my lovely girl! Besides, we're not so badly off now with our regular wages and you've never allowed me to spend anything extra on you so, my girl, now's the time and I'll make sure you get something nice. Besides, it's about time that sweatshop place of your work gave you a little something anyway." As usual, Tom found it hard to hold back the contempt at what he genuinely felt was the way that the dress factory treated Nellie, more so when he was so intent that she should one day come to work in the theatre where he knew for sure that she would be better treated.

In the immediate following times, Tom could scarcely believe it as he made his regular way to and from the Savoy that in less than two weeks, then only one week, then only a handful of days, he would be on the same journey with Nellie by his side.

There had been little further talked about the coming event at home, not that Tom hadn't wanted to each and every hour of the time he was there, but he understood that it was still a difficult situation for Nellie to face and he realised that she needed her own time to prepare in the way that only she knew how. What he did notice, with a very obvious and glowing sense of pride, though was Nellie's home activities with dress-making and the very obvious preparations that she was making for the night out, then just three days away. For them both, it was more than just an all too infrequent night out together, it was an event and for Tom alone, almost the only weekday evening in which he hadn't been working for he couldn't remember how long.

How proud Tom felt when, with Nellie on his arm, they closed their front door and took for the first time together the very familiar steps for Tom westwards. Nellie, Tom thought, looked a real picture to him in the feathery hat that she had made, then a long black frock coat over a long black skirt with a high necked frilled blouse where, in pride of place, was the broach that Tom had carefully purchased for her, albeit from a secondhand stall in Holborn, but still from the jewellery quarter itself which was what really mattered, as a very special gift to mark the occasion.

"You look a picture, love," Tom almost purred to his wife as they made their way along the, for him, familiar streets.

"And you don't look too bad yerself!" Nellie replied as she squeezed his hand in a loving grip. "We look quite the proper 'featre-goers, you in your smart jacket, nice hard collar, that 'ere cravat neatly tied-up all crisp and proper.

As they walked along Bishopsgate, Tom's attention was for a brief moment diverted from his wife as he looked up and down the street. "What yer doing?" she asked.

"You'll soon see," Tom replied. He already had his hand raised and within a second Nellie was stunned as a hackney carriage drew up beside them, with the horse, as Tom thought, almost standing to attention. "Me-lady, your carriage awaits," Tom declared with glee as he held his arm out for Nellie and helped her into the waiting carriage. "Savoy Theatre, if you please," Tom instructed the driver, with as much poise as he could muster and they were off.

For Nellie, it was totally overwhelming and she remembered very little of the journey as they passed the Bank, on beyond St. Paul's Cathedral, up Fleet Street then along to Aldwych before finally reaching the Strand itself where, she gasped aloud at seeing the approaching Savoy Theatre and the mingling crowds outside. There, she barely registered the billboards announcing that Mr. D'Oyly Carte's Opera Company were performing 'Patience', or that other signs said "House Full". As if in a trance, Nellie found herself whisked in to the reasonable warmth of the theatre from the cold October night; she realised that an attendant was asking for her coat and somehow she remained composed enough to hand it over; she tried to recall what she saw around her as Tom led her up the stairs to the circle and to their seats which she somehow noticed were just a couple of rows away from the front. What, though, she did notice, was what to her was an unaccustomed blaze of light everywhere she looked – around her in the auditorium, in the corridors leading into the place and vividly towards the stage itself. It was to that point that she found her eyes diverted with the gathering activity in the pit as the orchestra, in their crisp black evening suits, white shirts and black bow-ties, began tuning-up. She was aware of Tom chatting helpfully away, virtually all the time, explaining this and that, with diligence explaining everything, but she was hardly able to take it all in as she looked around. She surprised herself that she in fact felt not to be out of place, even managing to smile and acknowledge those around her as they passed by saying "excuse me, please" to take their seats. Tom held her hand all the time but, still so amazingly for her, she felt no longer afraid nor vulnerable in the situation, such a magical world she then found herself to be in. Soon Nellie was aware that the bright lights had somehow dimmed but in their place the area towards the stage was brighter and she noticed that a man with a monocle who was standing before the orchestra had then turned towards the audience to acknowledge the crescendo of applause and cheering that was coming from all around her – from the circle, from below in the stalls and from the very heights of the theatre that Tom had said was the gallery. "It's Mr. Sullivan," Tom quietly said to her.

Nellie was amazed at the immediate silence that then followed, replaced very soon by the sounds of what even to her was the most melodious music that she had ever heard, being drawn from the orchestra as if by magic by the command and diligent conducting of Mr. Sullivan. She was immediately captivated and remained so when after the overture the curtain rose upon the scene 'Exterior of Castle Bunthorne, with the entrance to the Castle by draw-bridge over the moat' she noted from the programme which Tom had bought and given to her and which she kept firmly held in her gloved hand. Her expert dress-making eye noted the beautiful costumes of the Rapturous Maidens as they began singing their opening chorus 'Twenty love-sick maidens we'. Then the following song from Patience herself 'I cannot tell what this love may be' melodiously cast upon her ears. How she almost jumped out of her seat as the orchestra changed its tempo and with an increased rousing sound began the introduction for the entry of the Dragoon Guards, Tom's favourite song when he first heard the new opera, 'The soldiers of our Queen'. She watched all so intently, glancing only occasionally to Tom, who continued to lovingly hold her hand, so as not to miss anything on the stage before her.

The Colonel launched into his own song, 'If you want a receipt for that popular mystery' sung with such speed, yet meticulous diction, that she heard and understood every word. She laughed, along with the rest of the audience, at the acting and the comedy of the two poets, Bunthorne and Grosvenor, then became almost overwhelmed as the whole stage was a mass of singers, a virtual extravaganza of beautiful costumes and light as the orchestra led the chorus in the finale of the First Act, 'Let the merry cymbals sound'.

The curtain fell to thunderous applause which seemed to Nellie as if it would never subside, indeed that the whole new theatre was deemed soon to collapse under the cheers and stamping of feet coming from the gallery above. She was so involved in what was all around her that she hardly realised that Tom had said three times to her "Well, how is it, are you enjoying…"

"Tom, oh Tom," Nellie began, "I never in me wildest dreams 'fought it was going to be like this! I can't believe it, and do you know, for once I'm just lost for me words, I'm so overcome!"

"Not too overcome that we can't go and have an interval drink, I hope," Tom smiled, as he gave his wife his arm to help her from the seat. Nellie must have been overcome because she didn't even question her husband but merely yet meekly rose from her seat and with his guidance followed him to the back of the circle, along a short corridor there to a brightly lit and very busy bar. Quickly, Tom brought to her not only a very delicate glass filled with what looked like some very dark, almost ruby liquid, but also he had in his other hand a plate with some pieces of her very favourite pork pie.

"What's this 'ere?" she asked, "you trying to get me squiffy in public, Tom Dobbs!"

"Its just a small sherry, for you, the real star of the show this evening!" Tom replied with real affection.

"Oh, Tom, you makes me feel like a princess, you's really do!" Nellie declared.

They ate their pie and sipped their sherry, neither of them feeling the least bit strange in their unaccustomed surroundings, as much for Tom to be 'front of house'. Tom was so delighted as Nellie told him how much she was enjoying the opera, the whole evening and everything that she was experiencing. "I never, ever, 'fought it would be like this," she repeated over and over again. "All this time, when yer being going on and on about your work, I 'fought you were 'aving a turn and just didn't take notice of 'yer! But now, now I sees it for what it is and do you know what?" Tom shook his head. "Well," Nellie continued, "I don't feel a bit out of place with the likes of these people, they are all liking the music just like what I – and you – are!"

"And that, my dearest, is exactly why the Gilbert and Sullivan operas, English comic operas, are becoming so popular," Tom declared with pride. "Folk in the best seats in the stalls, the London society, like it every bit as much, thinking it every bit for them as do ordinary day folk like us, who sit up there in the balcony – here's where the grand opera and music hall well and truly mix!"

Nellie listened and nodded to acknowledge what Tom had told her, before adding:

"Well, we're not sitting in the balcony – so we must be society!" Nellie giggled. "I hope the sherry's not getting to me!"

Tom laughed. "You're fine, and what's more, you're enjoying yourself!"

"Yes, Tom, I really am," Nellie replied, quite seriously but very sincerely as they finished their interval refreshments before making their way back to their seats, Nellie making sure she smiled as demurely as she could to all the other people that they passed. "You're beginning to like this, girl, ain't you," she said very quietly to herself with an obvious sense of self-satisfaction.

Back in the auditorium there was once again an excited air of expectation from the whole audience, not least Nellie, as the house lights dimmed, Mr. Sullivan rejoined his orchestra in the pit and the curtain rose upon Act 2. Immediately, Nellie became thoroughly immersed in all that was going on. The Lady Jane's plaintive song 'Silvered is the raven hair', to be followed by Grosvenor's witty song 'A magnet hung in a hardware shop', Patience herself again with 'Love is a plaintive song', the fabulous trio of the Duke, Colonel and Major with their 'You hold yourself like this' accompanied by screaming laughter from the audience. All too soon for Nellie, everybody else too, the finale came and for that night the magical world of the Gilbert and Sullivan opera again came to a close as the curtain fell and the whole house erupted with such noise that Nellie had never heard before. She found herself clapping, stamping her feet, cheering until she was so hoarse that she could not utter a single extra sound.

"I just don't want to go 'ome," Nellie sighed as they made ready to finally leave the theatre as it became evident that after the seventh occasion of calls, the curtain was not going to raise again that night, despite how much the audience seemed to demand.

"We, don't have to go home, not for a while, at least," Tom answered. "I want to take you back stage. I would like that for you and we should go and say 'thank-you' to Mr. Dean who passed the tickets over to us. Besides, I want to show you off to everybody, let them all see my darling wife that I run home to each night!" Tom was surprised, indeed almost flabbergasted, when Nellie made no protest to his suggestion as he had expected her to say "Oh no, not me" but she didn't.

They collected their coats, Nellie tidied herself, especially her hat, and pulling her coat around her, made her way with Tom down to the now empty stalls and through a door at the side which led them to the less opulent, but still well-lit and quite warm, backstage world of the Savoy.

"Isn't that?" Nellie asked Tom as the singer that she already recognised as Patience herself, Miss Leonora Braham, passed them by, nodding a friendly "hello". She felt then her own knees quiver as next, the very singer she recognised still dressed in the costume of Archibald Grosvenor himself, Mr. Rutland Barrington, called out "Tom, hello, what an evening off for you to-night!" and then quickly passed before Tom could do more than say a very quiet "yes, right, umh". With Nellie on his arm, they moved to the wings of the stage where Tom saw the stage manager, Fred Dean, busily checking all was well before he too would be able to leave for the night.

"Tom, there you are, we've missed you here tonight – we all so rely on you. And this, well this must be your wife that you are always telling us about!" Fred Dean smiled and came over to Nellie and before she knew it, placed a kind kiss on each of her cheeks.

"Please to meet you, I'm sure," Nellie replied, quite overcome at the genuineness and friendly reception with which she was being shown.

"Well, my dear, what do you think, did you enjoy your evening, the opera, and what do you thinks about your Tom's work." Fred Dean spoke with an obvious warmth and kindness that Nellie found very hard to take in, given how she was normally used to being treated in a place of work.

Tom spoke for her, noticing how she had immediately become lost for words. "It's been a really wonderful evening, Mr. Dean, for both of us. Me to see the opera, for the first time really, as part of the audience and to experience and see for myself just how they all like it so much. Then for Nellie, well she . . ."

"It's alright, Tom," Nellie intervened, recovering her being, "I can say, Mr. Dean, that's it's been one of the most wonderful evenings in me life! Never in me wildest thoughts did I even believe this Gilbert and Sullivan opera 'fings what Tom is forever going on about at 'ome, never did I 'fink it would be as good and wonderful as what I've seen 'ere to-night and what I've 'eard with me own ears!"

"And that's praise indeed! I'm glad to hear it, truly I am," Fred Dean replied "and what's more we'll be letting Mr. Gilbert know what you have said and I am sure he will be as pleased as I am!"

"Ooh, really!" Nellie exclaimed, "but thanks, really, it was marvellous and now, well I'm quite smitten with it all, that I am!" Nellie's words were like magic to Tom's ears and he winked quickly to Mr. Dean.

"Well, you know, we can always do something about that," the stage manager replied. "Tom's always telling me about the good work you do at the dress factory and, well, we need that kind of real good dress-making here at the Savoy, especially when we all expect there to be new pieces coming from Mr. Gilbert and Mr. Sullivan all the time." He saw Nellie's glazed expression and immediately sought to re-assure: "Don't say anything now, but think about it, do!"

"Thank you Mr. Dean, you never know," Nellie, replied, as Tom's mouth fell open in amazement at what was fast becoming a truly memorable day.

The bustle around the stage suddenly quietened, making them aware that many had left the theatre, their day's work once again successfully completed. Tom and Nellie took their leave of Fred Dean but not before he had said once again in Nellie's ear, much to Tom's barely concealed delight, "nice to meet you, love, don't forget what I said to you, think about coming here to work, be sure". They left the theatre with the words ringing in their ears but Nellie also with the events of the whole evening as a perfect picture within her memory.

With the house lights of the theatre dimming, Nellie looked back at the Savoy as, for only the second time in her whole life, she once again sat in the hackney carriage as the horse reared his head and made steps eastwards back along the Strand. She clutched Tom's arm and somehow they both knew that a defining moment in their lives had occurred that night.

* * * *

The night, by contrast, was still young for Rupert and Alice, some 100 years and four months later, very much in the vicinity of the Strand at the Adelphi Theatre, as they enjoyed the closing moments of the excerpts from 'Patience'. For them, the night was by no means over as Rupert calculated that, with 'Cox and Box', they had so far seen excerpts from only six of the operas. "Eight more to go!" he said to himself with obvious satisfaction, "hardly halfway with, some will say, the best still to come!"

With applause so similar in its enthusiasm to that Tom and Nellie had experienced all those years before, Rupert, sitting beside his grandmother, Alice, settled down once again, their eyes too fixed towards the stage in readiness for the next piece to be performed. Whatever maybe the final outcome for the evening, there was still much to be enjoyed.

Chapter 9
"When Britain really ruled the waves"

The mighty and stirring chorus of 'Loudly let the trumpet bray! – Tantantara!', the rousing march and entry of the Procession of Peers in 'Iolanthe', reverberated in magnificent tone from the stage of the Adelphi Theatre on that February evening in 1982. Although Rupert and Alice had heard it countless times before, more than enough for each of them to know every word, every stage movement, it somehow made no dent in their very obvious enjoyment of what was happening on the stage before their very eyes, as equally in raptures then as if they had never seen it at any time before. But now on what was an auspicious occasion, still one that Rupert could not even come to terms with, it was even more magnificent than ever as the chorus and orchestra were accompanied by the trumpeters of the Grenadier Guards, themselves in their red tunics and black bearskins.

With the closing of the final chorus 'Tantantara! Zting! Boom!' the theatre erupted once again, for the countless time already that evening, in tumultuous applause from every part of the near hysterical house. "That was just fantastic!" Rupert exclaimed, his eyes welling up and his face reddened from the sheer thrill of it all. "That's one of my favourite pieces and this is really my most favourite of all the operas!"

"You say that about every song, about every opera, you daft thing," Alice replied to her grandson, not maliciously and with a very obvious wink in her eye. Rupert just nodded and realised there was a good deal of truth in what his grandmother had said! Still, with the applause subsiding and once again there appearing little chance of an encore because if there had been then the evening would go on for ever – Rupert felt "and what was wrong with that" – his attention was once again returned to the stage as further action began. "I'll really have to make my mind up about what really is my favourite, I suppose, but now's not the time for that," he thought as the show was again underway.

* * * *

Not more than a few hundred yards from the very site of the Adelphi Theatre, on the other side of the Strand and just over a hundred years earlier to that night, towards the end of the year, 1881, Tom did not then have the problem of wondering which of 14 operas was his favourite. There were still only a total of six pieces then written and he was still working on the nightly performances of the fifth of the main pieces, not counting 'Cox and Box'. Besides, Tom in any case had much more on his mind, something no less than the fulfilment of his long ambition – ever since he first began work on 'Trial by Jury' in 1875 – that of having Nellie work beside him at the Savoy.

Ever since the night, just two months previously, when he had taken her to a performance of 'Patience', his hopes of achieving his ambition had been significantly raised. As much as he wanted to, Tom realised there was little point in trying to rush or over influence his wife; rather to let matters take their natural course when he had waited so long anyway. Nellie's words, "you never know", were at least some comfort to his aspiration.

These desires received very much a helping hand in the weeks running up to Christmas when Nellie had been forced to work extra long hours at the dress factory and for which she received no acknowledgement or even "a little something extra" with her wages. Worse, she had been called into work even on 26 December and throughout the week leading up to New Year. "I can't be 'aving too much more of this," she cried to

Tom, "especially when they don't fink no more of me for all I'm doing – not even so much as a 'fanks or a bit more money in me pocket. I'm sure it didn't use to be like this and I felt I was worth something at one time, no more I'm not!"

Tom listened and tried to offer words of support to his wife, realising that she was then becoming so tired and distressed that he began to fear once more for her health and well being. Just the night before New Year's Eve he got home from the theatre a little after eleven to find Nellie already in bed and, worse still, crying fitfully to herself.

As Tom rushed to her side she turned to look at him and he could see, even in the dim candlelight, that her face and eyes were swollen with the tears and she sobbed to him. "It's too much, all of this work, the conditions, the place, what's expected of me and for what I don't get an extra penny. Sorry, Tom, but you must let yer brother know they can't come 'ere for the New Year, I not up to it and I've said the same fing to me sister today. She understood so surely yer Albert will as well".

"Course I'll do that, first thing in the morning, they'll understand," Tom replied quietly as he sat on the bed, his arms cuddling his wife. "Just look after yourself, we don't want you getting ill again and ... well let's talk about it when you've had a good night's sleep, but we'll not let this get you down – I won't allow it," he stressed.

Nellie replied with a very quiet "thank you, luv", as she turned in the bed and soon fell to sleep with Tom continuing to sit beside her, gently caressing and cuddling her soon sleeping form.

The next day, on the way to work, after making sure Nellie was comfortable and warm in bed, he called to the dress factory and told them his wife wouldn't be in to work that day. "That's most inconvenient!" he was told in most uncertain terms by the supervisor to which Tom replied a curt "well, she's not well and that's that!" "Just make sure that she finds herself in here first thing on New Year's Day – or else!" was the closing command that rang in his ears as he walked away.

Next he went by way of Stepney, eastwards and completely off track from the Savoy, to call quickly at his brother Albert's house, there to tell his sister-in-law, Nancy, that their planned evening was not to take place. Nancy understood and said that she would go over to see Nellie during the day and that pleased Tom greatly and eased his mind as he once again headed westwards and to his work at the Savoy.

By the time that he got home that evening, quite early for him at around nine as Fred Dean had told him to get off home quickly when he knew that Nellie was ill. He was immediately relieved to see his wife already seeming much better.

"I feel likes me oldself!" Nellie exclaimed, "and what was nice you know is when Nancy called round and stayed to make me some soup – and I didn't 'arf enjoy it. Then no sooner that than me own sister, Maud, came round with that cake," she smiled, pointing to the mighty fruit and flour concoction sitting in pride of place on the mantle shelf. "So yer sees, I ain't 'ad such a bad day."

Tom was very glad how the family had rallied round. He almost didn't want to bring up about his own visit to Nellie's dress factory but decided to tell her. "That don't surprise me at all, that 'ow they are these days, just like the sweatshop what you always calls it!" Nellie answered. At that, Tom let the matters rest for the evening, wanting his wife to get her strength back and also for them to be able to enjoy New Year's Eve comfortably together at home.

In Tom's very limited and for him relatively orderly life, there could have hardly been a year of greater excitement and change than he and Nellie were about to experience as they sat cuddled together on the last night of 1881. On top of the offerings that they had at home from their family, Tom had also, extravagantly for him, bought some cooked ham from the market at Spitafields and that went nicely with the soup they had and a few extra potatoes and pickles. They tucked in with relish and looked forward to the extra cakes and buns. In pride of place, though, on the hearth was the small bottle of whisky that Tom had saved since before Christmas when he had been given it as a thank you from no less than Mr. Gilbert.

"Nobody's ever given us a work present like that before!" Nellie had exclaimed when he had proudly brought it home, carefully clutching it wrapped in newspaper under his arm.

They sat happily together sitting snuggled on cushions on the floor enjoying the warmth and glow of the burning embers from the fireplace before them.

"'appy, Tom, love?" Nellie asked.

"Course I am, dear Nellie! What more could a man want than to be how we are at this moment, beside my beloved and in the secure comfort of home," Tom replied with an air of contentment.

"It's not much of a 'ome," Nellie reflected as she stared into the fire. "True, it's a roof over our 'eads," she continued, looking above her to the darkened ceiling. "It's not even much of a roof at that really, is it?" to which they both laughed. After a few thoughtful moments, Nellie continued. "We 'aint got no fine fings, nothing fine like what yer see everyday at the Savoy! Then our money is about enough to stop us ending up in the poor 'ouse and that's not yer fault, it's more mine really as I finks about it and finks about how little I get for me wages when I work between 12 and 15 hours every day at the factory." She sighed and looked even more deeply into the fire as, with an inner sense, Tom let his wife gather her thoughts.

"Tom, I've been finking, that I 'ave," Nellie began to speak once again. "Yer right, yer been right all along about me and the dress factory – what yer told me about earlier today only just strengthens me mind. I've made me New Year's Resolution – I'm going to leave that factory and I am going to come to work with you at the Savoy – that's if they'll 'ave me!"

"Nellie, my lovely Nellie!" Tom exclaimed, clutching his wife even more closely if that were possible, "of course they will have you – you know what Mr. Dean said!"

Nellie nodded.

"Well, he wants you almost as much as I do!" Tom continued. "You won't regret it, not at all, and this will be a proper new beginning for both of us to be together at work and at home and it won't matter how long the days are because we'll both have each other and nothing will put us asunder! You know it's what I've always wanted and what I honestly think will be good for you – and me. What has finally made you come to the decision, I would just like to know, if you don't mind telling me now?"

"It's everyfink really, Tom, everyfink since I went with you that night to the Savoy and saw for meself. Oh I know that the night in the 'featre, with all the wealthy people and all that, well, that's a dream world, and I'm not on some cloud there way up in the sky with me dreams! Nellie exclaimed. "I know's that it will be different with the stage and backroom work but it doesn't matter. I likes the 'featre world what I saw when you took me backstage. Then, how the Savoy was, all that bright light, the warmth, the sheer pleasure of it all when I compares it to the grime and drudgery of me Shoreditch dress factory, let alone this 'ouse! But what it was, more than anything, was yer Mr. Dean saying to me as if he means it that I should come to work there. Yer know, Tom, nobody as me bosses as ever said that sort of fing to me – not ever and that's what set me a thinking." Nellie sighed, although more of a kind of contented sigh as she looked first at Tom and then cast her eyes once more towards the fire.

"Another 'fing," Nellie continued, "somehow, I now feels more confident about us 'aving all our eggs in one basket, both relying on our wages from the same workplace, now I've seen for meself what this Gilbert and Sullivan is all about, 'ow it seems to be popular, with everybody, not just society but the likes of us too, then more pieces may also perhaps be likely if what you 'ears is true?"

Tom nodded but otherwise felt it best not to interrupt his wife.

"Then today about the factory, what they said, then all the extra work with no fanks over the past days, well that's a finally tipped the balance for me, that it surely 'as! Oh, I've not forgotten about 'ow they were that Christmas years back when I was ill, I was grateful for that, truly I was, but they're not the same now!" Nellie sighed and snuggled up even more closely in to Tom's arms.

For long, Tom and Nellie embraced and said nothing. The situation called for no words. But what the situation did call for was the most happy thoughts and feelings which they both had as they heard the church clock strike twelve midnight. With due ceremony, still not speaking, Tom unscrewed his prized bottle of whisky, poured two glasses and handed one to Nellie.

"Happy New Year, my love!" There was no call for anything else to be said.

"And to you," Nellie replied as they snuggled further and most contentedly into each other's arms. Long after they had finished their amber nectar, they continued to lay together still in each other's arms for much of the night beside the fire which, by morning, gave little more than a softened glow.

On the first day of the new year, Tom at first worried when he woke that it had all been a dream as he symbolically pinched himself and tried to dispel the fears that Nellie would change her mind. The coldness of the room added to his worries as he, with vigour, rubbed himself to restore some semblance of warmth to his being. He need not have worried because as he soon realised the mere fact that she had been called into work on New Year's Day ensured that was to be no going back upon Nellie's decision. Tom was charged the very next day when he went back to the Savoy of asking Mr. Dean if Nellie could be considered for a job.

"Tom, Tom, you know that you don't even have to ask me that – one word, two really. Yes, yes!" Fred Dean replied. "I've even taken the liberty of saying as much to Florrie Parker, the wardrobe mistress. She'll be really delighted when we can tell her now that your Nellie wants to come, especially as she's been getting more and more worried about all the work here, all that's demanded of her and her team. Mr. Gilbert will be happy about it too – we all know what a stickler he is for detail and how he's always looking for the best of workmanship – your Nellie will certainly do that! I say again, yes, yes, and be sure you run home tonight and tell that dear wife of yours exactly just that! "

Fred immediately led Tom off to the crowded wardrobe room were Florrie was busily working. The stage manager immediately gabbled the news to an obviously work-stressed wardrobe mistress who kept bobbing to and fro between the rows and rows of stage costumes. She stopped her duties for only the briefest of moments to say "Thanks for that, thanks for that" before turning to Tom and saying in the same frame of tone that Fred had used a moment earlier. "Just you tell that wife of yours that I'm waiting here with open arms for her – not to say a worthy supply of pins and needles!"

With such ease it was all set with everybody happy all round. What was more, Tom was able to tell Nellie that she would come into the theatre, immediately to the position of assistant wardrobe mistress, second only to Florrie herself.

"There you are, love – a boss already!" Tom declared happily to his wife when he got home to tell her the exciting news.

"Cor, blimey!" was just the only exclamation that Nellie could make in reply to the news that her husband had given her.

"I'll be having to bow to you at work, keep touching my cap, that's how it seems to me by the way that everything is going!" Tom said, laughing and also making sure to duck from the fast moving fist that his wife was playfully directing to his shoulder.

With an ever gathering pace, by the first week of January Nellie resigned from the dress factory. "They didn't even 'ave the decent behaviour to ask me to stay on – let alone to even say 'fanks for everyfink what you've done for us – none of that! As for a few extra pennies in me pocket as an acknowledgement – well, there weren't any!" she bemoaned, sighing to herself.

So Tom, in complete fulfilment of his long held dream, at last had a companion as he set off each morning to the Savoy – his wife Nellie on is arm. That morning, they even celebrated by taking the horse-drawn omnibus from the Bank to the Strand so that Nellie wouldn't arrive tired from her walk on her first day as senior assistant wardrobe mistress in Mr. D'Oyly Carte's Opera Company at the Savoy!

In 1882 their joint life in the theatre had well and truly begun.

As if in celebration of Nellie's arrival, word soon spread around the Savoy that Mr. Gilbert had already submitted the plot idea for a new opera to Mr. Sullivan. Fred Dean told Tom that he understood the piece would include such characters as Lord Chancellor, Peers, Fairies, adding that it appeared to be very funny but was still at that time an outline and rather vague. They all then heard that Mr. Gilbert was working hard on the libretto that would bring fairyland to Westminster and make fun of the sacred subject of British politics.

"Every bill and every measure
That may gratify his pleasure
Though your fury it arises
Shall be passed by both your Houses"

Worse was to come!

"You shall sit, if he sees reason
Through the grouse and salmon season!"

To Tom, the words were a little above his head but he took his cue from Fred Dean who seemed to recite the pieces and laugh with unreserved mirth and heartiness. For Nellie, she was happy enough to hear that a new work was being prepared, the news giving her the confidence that she had made the right decision to come to work at the theatre.

Whatever, she was supremely happy and didn't regret her move to the new job. In many ways, though positively, it was a totally strange work environment for her. It took her ages to learn to address the wardrobe mistress as 'Florrie' rather than for ever saying 'Miss' or 'Miss Parker' as had always been the way in her old job at the dress factory, that is assuming she had been allowed to speak out of turn to any of her superiors. Equally, she found it very hard, although gratifying, to be given praise for her work, to be often thanked for what she was doing and to top it all she found it hard to get used to there being laughter in the workplace. Her only regret was not having agreed with Tom's frequent request that she should have come to the theatre to work earlier. Happily, then, she got on with her duties and even found she was picking up the tunes, humming to herself the music that she often heard drifting up from the orchestra pit itself as intensive rehearsals continued around her. But the biggest delight of all – that was to see Tom many times each day as either he rushed to the wardrobe room to collect some stage items he needed or she went down to the stage itself to deliver something that she had been working on.

One day she could barely contain herself and had to rush down to the stage to see Tom in the early afternoon.

"Tom, Tom!" she cried as she rushed across to the corner of the stage where Tom was working. "You will never guess what has just 'appened!"

Tom could see as he looked at his wife that whatever the news, then it couldn't have possibly have been anything bad, she was too radiant and obviously excited for that.

"It's Mr. Gilbert 'imself," Nellie continued, "he came into the wardrobe room and came over to me special he did."

Tom smiled towards his wife.

"Then he says to me, 'Welcome to the Savoy Mrs. Dobbs – I've heard much about you and I am very pleased that you should be working for us here along with that excellent husband of yours!' That he did, Tom, 'onest, he said every one of them very words to me as God is me witness!" Nellie concluded, with a contented sigh and only then allowing a broad smile to spread across her face.

"There you are, love, I've told you how it is here and what you say doesn't surprise me one bit," Tom replied, smiling himself just as much as his wife. "I'm glad, especially that they all appreciate you too – it's what you deserve – so well done!"

They enjoyed a concluding moment together at the side of the stage, kissed each other and with a cheery "bye" both immediately got back to their work, each with a warm and very happy feeling within their hearts.

All at the theatre had become well used to Mr. Gilbert's earnest attention to every detail so none felt surprised when Fred Dean called all the stage crew together. "Mr. Gilbert has had one of these new contraptions called a 'telephone' installed at his home and then one installed here at this very theatre, right by the prompt entrance. So now he will be able to hear the very performance, as it happens, at home in his study each night. That'll keep us all very much on our toes!" Fred declared.

Through the hot summer of 1882, 'Patience' continued to do well. Fred told Tom that they were taking £250 for each night's performance. Steadily, the rehearsal work for the new piece was introduced and rumours abounded that it would be set to open in the coming early winter. Nellie was charged with helping to prepare the new costumes which, as she took every opportunity to frequently tell Tom, would be more beautiful, more special than had ever been seen before.

As was usual, Mr. Sullivan was once again late with the music for the new piece but, as was equally normal, that did not prevent the general rehearsals or the stage and wardrobe preparations from going ahead in frenzied activity. With the performances of 'Patience' still occupying the Savoy each evening, all were called to the theatre for 10am each morning for several hours of new rehearsals which were carried out in the same meticulous way as they had all become so used to by then. Nellie came down to the stage area with some costumes and was standing by the side of Tom when they both overheard Mr. Gilbert in the full throws of rehearsal.

"We've been over this 20 times at least". So said George Grossmith, who was by then already established as one of the leading singers of the company.

"What's that I hear, Mr. Grossmith?" Mr. Gilbert asked.

"Oh, er, I was just saying, Mr. Gilbert, that I've rehearsed this confounded business until I feel a proper fool," the singer replied.

"Hmph – now we can talk on equal terms!" Mr. Gilbert replied as the assembled stage crew and singers continued to look on.

"I beg your pardon," Mr. Grossmith said.

"I accept your apology," came back Mr. Gilbert's reply.

Tom and Nellie smiled to each other and then immediately got back to their individual duties as rehearsals continued without any further interruptions. Even though 'Patience' continued to perform to packed houses, rumours soon abounded that the new piece was likely to be opening the coming November, giving an added dimension of urgency to all of their work.

As Mr. Sullivan delivered the music, the new piece came immediately together. It was again the time when everybody in the theatre dropped the word 'piece' in favour of the more appropriate term 'opera'. This time, Tom revelled in having

Nellie frequently at his side as together they both had the opportunity of seeing the various scenes coming to reality before their very eyes. They saw the fairies and their opening choruses, were introduced to a fairy then called 'Perola', the Fairy Queen herself, then to 'Strephon', an Arcadian Shepherd who was only "half a fairy"! Virtually the whole crew stopped work as the rousing music heralding the entry of the Peers themselves flooded magnificently throughout every part of the theatre. As if that was not enough, later at the final rehearsal the chorus was preceded by no less than the Band of the Grenadier Guards.

Tom and Nellie could hardly take in the overwhelming sight before their eyes. "This is unbelievable," Tom said, with his emotions causing his cheeks to be wet from the tears flowing uncontrollably down his face.

Nellie's emotions had also got the better of her and all that she could do by way of reply was to grab her husband's hand ever more tightly. Tom was too intent on what he saw and heard on the stage to react in anyway to the pressure that he only very distantly felt in his hand, blood drained from his wife's ever tightening grip.

"Can you imagine how the audience will react to this when they see and hear this magnificent chorus!" Tom exclaimed. "It will be a near crescendo of applause, that it will, and the whole theatre roof will lift off! And the beautiful costumes, all that done with your own fair hand," he concluded as he turned to his wife.

"Not too bad, are they!" Nellie replied modestly. But she knew that it was very much more than that. With dedication she had worked with Florrie on the costumes for the Peer's chorus. Together they had produced the cloaks of light blues, crimsons with rich purple, ermine and velvet for the Knights of the Garter, Bath and Thistle, George and Star of India. They had worked long hours but she could see at that moment just how much it had been worth it. She felt very proud and wished inwardly that she could have taken one of the cloaks to show then all back at the old dress factory, a place that she was pleased was then becoming no more than a distant, bad memory.

"All of London will receive this by storm," Tom exclaimed. "And after that, America, Australia, who knows wherever. Maybe we are all now involved in something that will set finally in place English comic opera that will be left here and popular long after you and me have gone!"

"I don't know yet about that, Tom, but who knows," Nellie replied. "I don't yet understand it all but I agree with yer, in me limited way, I can see for meself and it is good, that I grant yer!"

Tom was excited, very naturally, and at that time he couldn't know, other than in his dreams, how he and Nellie were involved in what was to become a beloved English musical theatre tradition. Nor could he have possibly known either that a hundred years forward from that very time, and only a few hundred yards away on the opposite side of the Strand, the likes of Rupert and his grandmother, along with the whole audience, had just enjoyed the very same chorus, performed in much the same way, dressed in costumes faithfully reproduced from those that Nellie and Florrie had studiously prepared. Had such forward perception been possible, then Tom and Nellie's thrill and excitement would have no doubt been many times greater.

They listened intently as the character, one of the Lords, Lord Mountararat, sang before them in rehearsal:

"When Britain really ruled the waves –
(In good Queen Bess's time)"

to conclude with a topical satirical flourish:

"And while the House of Peers withholds
Its legislative hand,
And noble statesmen do not itch
To interfere in matters which
They do not understand,
As bright will shine Great Britain's rays
As in King George's glorious days!"

Again, first Tom, then Nellie, took the cue from Fred Dean and all laughed heartily at the rehearsal of the opening scene of Act 2, set in Palace Yard, Westminster to a backdrop of Westminster Hall, as the sentry, Private Willis, sang:

"When in that House M.P.'s divide,
If they've the brain and cerebellum too,
They've got to leave that brain outside
And vote just as their leaders tell 'em to."

Before concluding his song:

"That every boy and every gal
That's born into the world alive
Is either a little Liberal
Or else a little Conservative!
Fal lal la!"

When George Grossmith came again to the stage in his role as Lord Chancellor, in resplendent wig and gown that Nellie herself had proudly crafted, it was with amazement at the sheer length and complicated verse that Tom heard him sing from his second act song, he assumed without error as Fred Dean, avidly following from the prompt book clutched in his hand, didn't stop him:
"When you're lying awake with a dismal headache and repose is taboo'd by anxiety" to conclude:

"But the darkness has passed, and it's daylight at last, and the night has been long – ditto ditto my song – and thank goodness they're both of them over!"
Through all the twists and turns of the plot, the highly topical references, the whole theatrical crew soon saw, as the company launched into the rehearsal of the last scene, that all was to end in a highly satisfying Gilbertian way:
"Every one is now a fairy!" and:

"We will arrange

Happy exchange –
House of Peers for House of Peris!"

To top it all, making every use of the new electricity at the Savoy, the fairies had electric lights in their own headdresses.

Tom and Nellie were together at the side of the stage as all the singers came away from the last rehearsal, all in elated spirits and thrilled by the result of everybody's efforts. Fred Dean, however, asked everybody to remain for a moment, indicating that he had an announcement that he had to make.

"Throughout the rehearsals we have been using the name 'Perola' for our new opera. Well, this has been 'cause we've been trying to deceive the music pirates and I'm now to tell you that the opera is, in fact, to be called 'Iolanthe'. So, ladies and gentlemen, all you have to remember is tomorrow, at the first night, to sing and say 'Iolanthe' when otherwise you've sang 'Perola' – simple really!" he concluded.

Fred Dean's announcement caused a deal of consternation amongst the company as they left the stage, so much so that Mr. Sullivan himself called out:

"Never mind, so long as you sing the music – use any name that happens to occur to you! Nobody in the audience will be any the wiser, except Mr. Gilbert – and he won't be there!"

Tom, on hearing, realised that it was very true that Mr. Gilbert would not be present for the next night's first performance – he never attended the first night, always leaving the theatre at the start of the overture. They all understood that he then prowled up and down the adjacent Thames Embankment only to return to the theatre just in time for the final curtain.

All first nights were special for Tom, none more so far than that of 'Iolanthe' on 25 November 1882, the first time when he stood at the sides of the stage with Nellie by his side, virtually for the whole performance except for frequent moments when each was attending separately to their various duties. Together, they took every opportunity possible not only of enjoying the new opera but also to peer whenever possible towards the auditorium itself. It wasn't new for Tom, but Nellie found herself both tingling and gasping at the finery that she saw before her eyes. At the very start of the evening and also before the curtain fell at the end of Act One, before they were again both heavily involved in all the work to prepare the costumes and the stage with the new scenery for Act Two, they had a few moments together, in the wings.

"'ave you seen all them beautiful dresses and clothes that the audience are wearing?" Nellie gasped, her eyes wide open in sheer amazement. "I've never seen such a sparkle of diamonds, nor so many starched dress shirts that the men have got, or 'ow they all turn to look at each other, suppose to gossip about it an' all!"

"I've seen it, and this time is no different from the past. You see, a Gilbert and Sullivan first night is a society social occasion," Tom replied, imparting the knowledge as if being a theatrical professional of years standing. "You see, m'love, in the house tonight, in the stalls and the first circle, you know where we sat, are the leaders of fashion, literature, politics, the law, science, arts and business, the tops of society," he concluded, satisfied with himself that he had remembered all that he had heard Fred Dean saying!

"Cor," was the limit of Nellie's reply.

"But that isn't everything," Tom continued. "Up there, up in the gallery." He stopped for a moment, touching Nellie's arm, guiding it and casting his eyes whilst pointing to the distant top of the theatre. "Up there, you've got the normal people, like us, from the same working areas of London like us, we call them 'the galleryites'. They're not any special people, normal working folk, saving their every penny so that they can come here. That's the wonder of all of this as I've told to you – these operas are as much liked and loved by all walks of society and that's something that's never been in the likes of London theatre before! Didn't you hear them all singing choruses from the earlier operas, up there, before tonight's performance begun? Nellie, this is a theatrical revolution, no less!" The words were not all Tom's, mostly he was repeating exactly what Fred Dean had told to him although he agreed with it in every way and believed in it as well.

Once again, Nellie said little but merely nodded silently towards her husband. She thought a lot, though, and just like so often before in this new life to which she had entered, Nellie found herself completely overwhelmed by the occasion. But she was happy, especially to be with her Tom and to her that was everything.

Finally, the performance was over and Tom and Nellie were at the side of the stage just as Mr. Gilbert rushed in from his evening walking the Embankment, quickly handling his hat and cape to one of the stage hands before rushing on stage to take his curtain call alongside the delighted Mr. Sullivan who came up from the orchestra pit where he had been conducting the whole evening. Nobody present in the theatre could have had any doubt that the evening had been a complete success as the audience erupted in cheers and shouts to demand curtain call after curtain call. Almost as if with a degree of embarrassment, the writer and composer shyly took their bows and shook hands before they finally left the stage with the audience becoming more and more hoarse.

The stage and wardrobe crews, the members of the orchestra, the singers themselves mingled in groups about the stage, in the wings and in all corridors of the theatre for some time after the curtain had finally come down. The evening had, for all of them, been one of such high emotions and excitement that it took many moments for any semblance of normality to return. Both Tom and Nellie were similarly affected by the thrill of the evening although they both still had much work to do – Tom with the stage sets and preparing all for the next day; Nellie, with bundles of costumes to collect and sort also for the next performance.

It was with those thrills, plus the music and melodies of the evening still ringing in their ears, when well after midnight they were both finally able to leave the theatre, their duties successfully completed. The dark and quietened streets through which they walked immediately after leaving the area around the Strand and the Savoy Theatre itself were somehow in pleasant contrast to the light and the sounds of the evening. So much so that they walked, holding each other's hands, in silence at first and it was not until they walked by the Bank of England itself, into a very dark and almost gloomy Threadneedle Street, that Nellie uttered the first words of the walk home.

"Thanks, Tom, thanks from the bottom of me 'eart, that through you, I've been brought into this working world of the 'featre!" She paused for a moment before continuing. "Me only regret is that I didn't come sooner – but I've only got meself to blame for that, not you!"

Tom clutched his wife closer and said nothing for a few seconds. "It's me who should really be saying 'Thanks' – and that's to you, m'dear, firstly for you being you and secondly, yes, for agreeing to coming with me to work!" A church clock, probably, Tom thought, from nearby Bishopsgate, struck one o'clock. "What sort of life for us together would it be anyway if it was just me working all these hours, getting home in the early hours and going out again just after eight!"

"Well, that's 'ow it was!" Nellie reasoned.

"True. That makes me even more glad that it's changed now," Tom replied as once again they both sunk more into thought as they finalised their walk home to a very dark and dingy Shoreditch, where crying cats and various ner'do wells were their only company.

"What a contrast to me day life," Nellie thought as they entered their tiny home and closed the door. But for the moment, she was too tired to think further as both she and Tom prepared for bed as quickly as possible. Neither was either warm or comfortable again until they were cuddled together with the sheets pulled up as close as possible around them.

Even though Nellie quickly fell in sleep, Tom's mind was still racing from the events of the night and it was long before his heavy eyes finally closed, as he tossed and turned in bed. Just then, the Lord Chancellor's song from earlier in the evening seemed so entirely appropriate:

"For your brain is on fire – the bedclothes conspire of usual slumber

to plunder you:

First your counterpane goes, and uncovers your toes, and your

Sheet slips demurely from under you…"

Chapter 10

"And, isn't your life extremely flat
With nothing whatever to grumble at!"

The happiness that Nellie felt for her work was not matched by her increasing dismay that she felt about her home. No doubt her eyes had been opened by her new life in the theatre and for the first time she had something on which to compare her two environments. She fully realised that when she worked in the dress factory, then her day was one of total grime, of filth and general grubbiness wherever she looked in her world that consisted of a few local streets in a not especially nice part of London. But now that she spent almost half of her day working at the Savoy, then Shoreditch simply could not compare. The difference was so great that she lost much of her usual heart, spirit and dedication in trying to make something of their little home, which no matter how she tried, could never be made to look clean. They had already lived there for twelve years, having moved from her parent's home in Tottenham a year after they had been married in 1869. For both her and Tom there had only ever been two areas of London where they had ever lived and that had been their very limited world. Now she felt tired and dispirited about the place they both called home, and an area which held no family ties in any case.

"Ugh, this 'ouse!" Nellie bemoaned to Tom one Sunday not long after the opening night of 'Iolanthe'. "It don't matter what I do, 'ow 'ard I try, I can never get anyfink clean and no sooner 'as I done it and it all looks as black and as grimy as before!"

Tom, who was busily mending his favourite armchair by the fire, stopped what he was doing and looked over to his wife. "You do your best, don't fret so, but we know that we can never make anything special of this place – it's impossible – all the cleaning in the world can never make any difference to this grimy street!"

"That's exactly what I mean!" Nellie exclaimed, brushing the hair out of her eyes and then rubbing her hands over her becoming increasingly dirty pinafore. "And what really gets to me is that we pay 15 shillings in rent for this place every week and we might just as well live in the coal depot! We can't go on like this Tom and, well besides, we're becoming respectable now, ain't we, and Shoreditch, well it surely ain't the place for us anymore!"

"Nellie Dobbs – not even a year in the theatre and you're getting some high falutting ideas!" Tom exclaimed and immediately laughed when he saw how his remark which he saw as nothing more than a harmless joke had caused his wife to look so dismayed.

"No, it ain't like that, you knows me better than that, Tom!" she replied, just a little crestfallen. "It's just, well, I fink it's time we tried to better ourselves, especially now that we both have good work at the 'featre and things look good. What do you think, Tom – we could afford it couldn't we, at least work it out and see what we could do, won't yer?"

"Of course, I reckon we could probably pay around double what we do now without being in the workhouse! If that is what you want and . . ." Tom thought for a moment before continuing. "I can see how you feel and, well yes, me too I suppose, although I don't think so much about the home as you do, but, yes, why not! The time is right, what with Mr. Dean telling me that I am going to be promoted come January to assistant stage manager, no less, and with it I'll get an increase to four pounds and 15 shillings a week."

"And I've got good money, three pounds five shillings a week, nearly double what I got at the dress factory!" Nellie interjected.

"Course you have, love, so together we're not too badly off, I suppose, but with hardly anything put aside, well, at least not yet although we will," Tom reassured. Nellie. "This has already been a year of change for us, with you coming to work with me, so let's really do something to make it a notable year – let's do as you say, let's move!"

"What's more, let's be sure to be out and in a new place by Christmas, so there's no going back on our words!" By then Nellie was getting very excited at the thought. "We only have to give a week's notice to the landlord – so there ain't nothing stopping us!"

"Having some other place else to live – that's what's stopping us!" Tom replied.

"Well, look 'ere Tom, stop mending that chair of yours and let's get out of the 'ouse this afternoon when we both have got the day off, and let's start looking – no time like the present!" Nellie insisted.

Tom immediately realised that any further remedial work to his faithful armchair was not then going to happen as he followed his wife to get changed into their 'Sunday Best' for an initial trip out, there to begin a house hunt. It was not a successful afternoon and nothing much was discovered on that day. Neither did they much like what they saw in the immediate area or in neighbouring Hackney, all looking as equally grimy as their own street in Shoreditch. But during the coming week at work Tom asked for Fred Dean's advice as Nellie did exactly the same with Florrie Parker. After all the help that they had received, they talked of little else other than their pending moving plans during their journeys to and from work. The next Sunday, Tom and Nellie, again very much dressed in their 'Sunday Best', set off early in the morning to head south of the Thames, almost a foreign territory for them both and a virtual voyage of adventure, there to head to Peckham, an area where by hardly any coincidence, both Fred Dean and his wife, Rose, and Florrie Parker and her sister, Lillian, lived not many streets apart.

Before long, they had seen two places which they liked, one especially that was quite near to the railway station and was not too close as to be "indecent" as Nellie put it, to either of their two bosses. Even though both had asked them to call by, they decided not to infringe on that occasion but instead to "keep their place", as Nellie put it. The chance of a possible new home excited them and they talked of little else as they journeyed home, heading north once more across the Thames and back to Shoreditch.

"It'll make a perfect little 'ouse for us," Nellie enthused. "Two little rooms downstairs and a small scullery, a nice bedroom upstairs and even a little boxroom besides, almost another bedroom really. And, well, I never did, even a small bathroom with water pipes and all!"

"We'll like the area too, won't we?" Tom asked, to which Nellie, still very much deep in thoughts, nodded in reply. "It's so much cleaner than where we are now, plus Mr. Dean told how it's nice to be near some parks and the big park only a couple of miles along the road at Greenwich – we'll be getting some fresh air in our lungs after all the years of the grime!"

"Pinch me, Tom 'less it's all some kind of dream."

It's no dream, love," Tom replied, "and as soon as we can we'll make it reality!"

On Monday, Tom asked Fred Dean if it was possible for a couple of hours off from work that week to which he was informed that he should go that very afternoon to be sure he could secure the house upon which they had so much set their hearts. After telling Nellie that he could go, Tom rushed off and well before curtain up that evening was back at the Savoy. Respectfully, he first saw Fred Dean before immediately rushing up to the wardrobe room where he found Nellie busy making repairs to a Peer's coronet for that night's performance.

"How appropriate, Nellie, love, my Lady Dobbs!" he exclaimed, giving his wife a symbolic cardboard key that he had found amongst the stage props.

"You got it for us!" Nellie cried, hardly able to control the tears of joy welling up in her eyes.

"That I have, love, and what's more we can move in any time after next Monday. It'll cost us one pound 15 shillings a week, more than double what we are paying now, but it'll be alright and I've signed the lease for six months – so we've got to afford it now!" Tom said with a delighted air, which he thought befitted a rise coming to their social station.

"And that's better than the week arrangement that we have now – when the landlord could 'ave us thrown out any time he 'finks fit!" Nellie replied.

"Yes, it most certainly is," Tom agreed. "So, it means we'll make the move before Christmas and that's everything complete for this to be a special year for us both. "Peckham an Arcadian Vale" as the song goes in 'Trial by Jury' . . . ."

"Tripping hither, tripping thither,
Nobody knows why or whither;
We must now be taking wing
To another fairy ring!"

Nellie replied, by singing to Tom from 'Iolanthe'. He hugged her dearly, hardly able to contain his overwhelming sense of happiness, not only about their impending home move but also how he immediately realised that Nellie too was then becoming increasingly as besotted as he had already become with the works of Gilbert and Sullivan, works that now meant so much and were so significant to both of their lives.

Tom and Nellie were extremely grateful that without question, or them even having to ask, they were both told by their respective bosses that they could have three whole days off the following week to make their move. Fred Dean did more – he arranged that a carrier who they used for shifting big scenery to their warehouse would be sent to Shoreditch to effect their move to Peckham. "Mr. Gilbert has told me you're not to pay for it either!" Fred said to a delighted Tom.

In the days leading up to Christmas, with the move successfully completed, Tom and Nellie joined, as Tom called them, "others of those riding up the ladder of social acceptability" in taking the train from Peckham each morning and home again each night, using in London the convenient station at Blackfriars where it was for them only a 10-minute walk to their place of work at the Savoy.

In early 1883, even though 'Iolanthe' played to delighted and packed houses, because the whole company had become so used to the idea of a new piece to be produced regularly, there were some initial concerns when no word immediately came about the next production. Their fears were, however, quelled when news came on 8 February that a new agreement for five years had been signed by Mr. Gilbert, Mr. Sullivan and Mr. D'Oyly Carte. It also ensured that for a similar period, Mr. D'Oyly Carte's Opera Company, Tom and Nellie's very employers, had the licence to perform all the operas already composed, or to be composed, by Gilbert and Sullivan at the Savoy Theatre.

"At least our own rent's secure!" Nellie observed to Tom with obvious relief, a feeling that Tom entirely reciprocated.

Another cause for celebration came in May 1883 when Arthur Sullivan was knighted at Windsor on the 22nd of that month. Tom felt it rather sad that Mr. Gilbert had not been similarly acknowledged although Fred Dean had reminded him "Sir Arthur Sullivan has composed many works other then the operas. You know, the Symphonies, the Overture 'Di Ballo', then there's all the choral music, the hymns like 'Onward, Christian Soldiers!' and the Christmas hymn 'It came upon the Midnight clear', then his work with the Leeds Music Festival. It's a big musical commitment to the life of our country!"

As the summer progressed, with Tom and Nellie well settled in at Peckham and also able to enjoy on their rare days off, the open spaces of Greenwich Park to which Tom had long craved, the news for which the whole company had been waiting was finally announced. Mr. Gilbert had submitted the idea for a plot, for a new opera, based on women's emancipation or, as he put it, "a respectable version of 'The Princess' by Lord Tennyson," the Poet Laureate of the time. Soon, Tom heard that the new piece was going to have three acts, a first for any of the operas, which he realised would involve more complicated scene changes and stage work. He was also told that the libretto had been written in blank verse. That meant very little to Tom who merely nodded at the information.

Rehearsals began in earnest during the last weeks of the old year, in readiness for a proposed opening night in early January 1884. The almost fantasy sets of a Pavilion in King Hildebrand's Palace for Act One, the Gardens of Castle Adamant for Act Two and the Courtyard of Castle Adamant for Act Three all caused Tom and his team a deal of hard work. When he bemoaned the fact to Nellie, she quickly told him in no uncertain terms that she too had an equal deal to do with all the new costumes. "Soldiers, Courtiers, Girl Graduates, Daughter of the Plough, and that's just the chorus, not to say for all the Principals, they're 12 of them as well!"

"I'm sure I'm no ascetic; I'm as pleasant as can be;
You'll always find me ready with a crushing repartee,
I've an irritating chuckle, I've a celebrated sneer,
I've an entertaining snigger, I've a fascinating leer."

… as the words were rehearsed by George Grosssmith, on stage in his role of King Gama in the coming new opera. To some, Tom included, it was an amusing song but others saw an altogether deeper significance, more that Mr. Gilbert was writing of himself rather than of a created character.

The whole company were becoming by then rather into the pattern of nightly performances of an existing opera, then 'Iolanthe', whilst mornings and afternoons were spent preparing for the new piece. It also came as no surprise to the singers and musicians that Sir Arthur Sullivan was late with the music, not something that particularly affected Tom or Nellie, both of whom could get on with their various tasks without interruption. At these times, they saw a lot of each other during the day as Nellie frequently came down to the stage for dress fittings or to bring more costumes to be left ready in the wings. Tom was always ready and waiting for such moments and at the very least they managed a quick wink or an exchange of blown kisses between each other.

"Perhaps if you address the lady
Most politely, most politely –
Flatter and impress the lady,
Most politely, most politely –
Humbly beg and humbly sue –
She may deign to look at you,
But your doing you must do
Most politely, most politely"

The song from the new opera Tom found very apt and he committed it to memory in readiness to pass on to Nellie when he next saw her at the side of the stage.

"Oh, you!" Nellie giggled as turning a shade of bright crimson, she rushed back to the wardrobe room.

With Florrie's help, she soon got her own back as rehearsals continued and learnt an appropriate response:

"Mighty maiden with a mission –
Paragon of common sense;
Running font of erudition –
Miracle of eloquence!"

… which she sung, or rather recited in a kind of melodic way, to Tom on the next occasion she came to the stage. He loved it and spoke of nothing else when they were together on the train home to Peckham late that evening.

Nellie's sister Maud, with her husband and two small children, Tom's brother Albert and his wife Nancy, all spent the Christmas with them at Peckham. Fred Dean with his wife, Rose, were invited to a tea that Nellie had long and lovingly prepared. She had also asked her own boss, Florrie Parker and her sister Lillian as well, making a very crowded home, but an extremely happy and good natured gathering. Tom had forgotten just how good his brother was at playing the piano and it was almost an alternative, although small and scaled down, D'Oyly Carte Opera Company that night in Peckham as they sang their favourite choruses from all of the operas. Fred ended the evening by his own rendition of the Sergeant's song from 'Pirates of Penzance'.

"When the foreman bares his steel,"

to which all the rest sang the hearty reply – "Tarantara! tarantara!" – with both gusto and uncontrolled hilarity all round.

The holiday was but a short, although, very happy one and with the first night planned for the coming 5th of January, it was an extremely busy week running up to the New Year and the immediate days thereafter.

"'Princess Ida', that's a beautiful name isn't it?" Nellie said to Tom when the name of the new opera was finally announced, to which Tom agreed.

The frantic rehearsals just four days before opening night went off reasonably well but still the music wasn't finally completed for two songs. Sir Arthur worked on it through the night, coming in for the final rehearsal the next day, obviously both very tired and ill. The whole crew were alarmed when Sir Arthur collapsed during the evening. A cab was called and he went home to rest, then the next morning, on the day of the first night, it took a strong hypodermic injection to ease the pain from a recurring kidney problem. At the theatre he was given a strong black coffee to help keep him awake before he finally entered the orchestra pit at ten past eight on the evening of 5 January, 1884. The sense and thrill of the occasion immediately revived him as the performance of the new Gilbert and Sullivan opera, 'Princess Ida', begun.

Nellie joined Tom in the wings as the chorus and whole company sang the finale:

"It were profanity
For poor humanity
To treat as vanity
The sway of Love.
In no locality
Or principality
In our mortality
Its sway above!"

The curtain fell to thunderous applause. For once, Mr. Gilbert had not spent the evening walking The Embankment but rather had been instead in the green room reading a paper and trying very hard to look unconcerned. He came very quickly to the stage as soon as he knew the performance to be over to join Sir Arthur Sullivan on stage for their customary bow. After only a couple of curtain calls, Sir Arthur fainted, the pressures of the past days and his ill health having finally got the better of him. The composer's collapse caused consternation amongst the whole company which was only eased when news came after a couple of days, by way of a doctor's bulletin, that Sir Arthur "is on the whole, much better".

Again they had all achieved a brilliant success, although the review posted by a Yorkshire critic was perhaps of some concern:

"Ah like t'music well enough; it's full of toones as ah can whistle. But t'words sounds too much like Shakespeare for t'likes of me to understand!"

Far more positive though, and to Tom and Nellie's delight, Fred Dean called them to the stage, along with Florrie, to read them a report from the January edition of the paper, 'Theatre':

"'The three sets are amongst the most beautiful pictures ever exhibited upon any stage. The graduate robes and Amazonian armour must be seen to be properly appreciated, the former are gravely gorgeous, the latter indescribably brilliant and splendid'. And that, Mr. D'Oyly Carte and Mr. Gilbert has asked me to say, is all thanks to all of your work – well done!" Fred concluded with smiles and handshakes all round.

At the very same time, unbeknown to any of those then gathered on stage at The Savoy, some correspondence was passing between the composer and the theatrical manager that could have the most grave consequences for all of them. Sir Arthur had written to Richard D'Oyly Carte at the end of January saying he would write no more of the comic operas and as much as he tried, the theatre manager could not then persuade the composer otherwise.

For both Tom and Nellie, with all of their stage colleagues, it was perhaps well that for the moment they were unaware of the potential difficulties they could face. But they lived in false security only for three months as by the spring the nightly takings for 'Princess Ida' were dwindling. Tom could tell from the wings that the theatre was not always full and even though he at first tried to dismiss Nellie's fears, he too was soon to worry. For the first time for almost seven years and even more so since Nellie had joined him in the theatre just two years earlier, Tom began to have fears for both of their wages, so much so that in the early spring days, neither felt like going to Greenwich Park on their days off. Then, to add to the growing sense of possible crisis, the clerk at the box office had the task of phoning the result of each evening's takings direct to Mr. Gilbert, using an elaborate code system so as to avoid eavesdropping on the telephone.

It was a most upsetting and distressing time. Richard D'Oyly Carte pressed for a new piece to be written only once again to be rebuffed by Sir Arthur Sullivan who initially replied:

"With 'Princess Ida' I have come to the end of my tether – the end of my capacity in that class of piece." Word of the exchange soon reached Tom and his stage colleagues who received the news in a state of gathering gloom. As try as he might to be cheerful with Nellie, she knew from her own conversations with Florrie that all at The Savoy was far from good.

"What are we going to do?" she pleaded with Tom, "What's going to 'appen if there will be no more new operas?"

"Come, Nellie, don't fret yourself just yet. Even if there wasn't one more new piece, well then there are seven already produced, plus the two 'curtain-raiser' pieces, so that's enough to keep us going – then there are the touring productions, it'll be alright, you see," Tom said as reassuringly as he could, although deep down in his heart he didn't feel nearly as confident.

Nellie wasn't for fooling either. "It's not that easy, Tom, and you know it!" she replied. "When an opera is revived, then all the stage work, all the costumes, are all ready and apart from a bit of patching for wear and tear, then there ain't so much to do. Miss Parker and a girl could easily cope – where would that leave me?"

"It won't come to that, you'll see," Tom replied although he turned away from his wife so as not to betray his very real concerns.

Later the same day, Fred Dean told Tom that Mr. Gilbert had submitted to Sir Arthur ideas for a new piece based on his favourite "magic lozenge" plot, already quite abhorrent to the composer who had replied "it is going back to the elements of topsy-turveydom which I hoped we had now done with".

Fred Dean himself was also by then becoming increasingly concerned. The last thing he wanted was to have to dismiss good colleagues that had over the years become a very good stage team but.... The news continued to get worse when he was told by Mr. D'Oyly Carte that Mr. Gilbert had written to Sir Arthur, who had somehow had a slight change of heart about his comic opera work, to say "I cannot consent to construct another plot for the next opera". To that the reply had come from the composer: "The tone of your letter convinces me that your decision is final and therefore further discussion is useless. I regret it very much".

The atmosphere throughout the theatre was grim indeed, with both singers and stage crew frequently gathered in small groups discussing the growing situation with grave expressions and bowed heads. In that, Tom tried to remain as positive as he could which in the circumstances seemed most unreasonable. He tried hard to be over cheerful with Nellie but there was little to disguise the fact that the potential situation was indeed serious and with grave implications for their small family.

It was finally announced that 'Princess Ida' was to close after a run of 246 performances. This, for a Gilbert and Sullivan opera, was a dismal result, as all at The Savoy only too well realised. 'Patience' had an initial performance run of 578 and 'Iolanthe' 398, not to say the original 'HMS Pinafore' with a grand total of 700. With no new piece available to replace it, Tom, clutching at straws, took great delight when he heard that in place of 'Princess Ida',for the first time at the Savoy, performances of 'The Sorcerer' and 'Trial by Jury' were to be given.

Excitedly, he said to Nellie: "There you are, what did I tell you. Because it's never been performed here, like when they transferred 'Patience', all the scenery has got to be redone and the costumes upgraded too – it'll be alright."

Bernard Lockett

"It's only got to be done the once, a make-up and repair job – it ain't like 'aving a completely new opera, so don't go and get yerself carried away!" Nellie warned, she thought with good reason.

Tom didn't really know what to think. What he didn't want to think though, or even contemplate, was perhaps that they were all witnessing the end of a great musical partnership.

* * * *

Rupert and Alice, at the Adelphi Theatre on that night of 27 February 1982, had, as the curtain fell on the last of the extracts from 'Princess Ida', so far that evening enjoyed over and over again some of their favourite songs and pieces from nine of the operas. True, there were only excerpts and Rupert for one would have wished for more, often regretting that a special favourite song had not been included. But it was an evening to treasure nevertheless. It was as well for them that they had the opportunity of an interval to gather their thoughts, reflect on what they had so far seen, to anticipate what was hopefully still to come, even to relax for a moment from what Rupert saw as the high drama of the occasion. The highly-charged emotions of the evening, especially for Rupert, meant that he made no suggestion to his grandmother that they should leave their seats for an interval refreshment but rather settle to tackle the chocolates they had brought with them, there to continue to savour the atmosphere within the auditorium.

Rupert noticed his grandmother dabbing her eye. "Is everything alright Nan, you don't feel ill do you?" he asked with concern, momentarily forgetting his own worries about what the future might hold for his beloved Gilbert and Sullivan.

"Yes, it's alright, love, I'm fine," Alice reassured. "But I feel quite overwhelmed, more than I ever thought that I would. It's been such a wonderful evening and it's brought back so many happy memories from all the past years that I have so enjoyed the operas – a lifetime for me, really."

"Well, naturally, Nan," Rupert interrupted, "after all, when you were a child growing up, some of the operas were still being written. For you, the operas were the popular music of your day, no less!"

"That's right! And it reminds me," Alice continued, "how as a young child I used to gather on a Sunday evening, with my brothers and sisters – all eight of us - in the front parlour at our house in Tottenham with my father sat at the piano and my mother standing beside him, turning the pages of the music and both singing, all the popular songs from Gilbert and Sullivan. I grew up with it and I was probably not much older than eight when I was taken to The Savoy, just across the road from here, to see my very first opera. Next I saw a performance when the company was on tour, at the old Hackney Empire, not so far from our home then." She reminisced and sighed but with a contented smile. "Yes, this music has really been a very happy part of my life – so wonderful!"

Although Rupert had heard the story countless times before, he listened once again intently, conjuring up in his mind how it must have been to be part of the audience in those late Victorian times. The mere thought once again sent a shiver of delight down his back. How so very much he wished that if only he could have been there for the very beginning of it all, being involved as the operas became reality, witnessing their very birth. He thought further, about actually attending the original productions, even perhaps being at the glamorous first nights, the social occasions. All but a dream – he realised that he had been born around 70 years too late! How much better it would have been to be there at the beginning rather than at the end! The end! The mere phrase meant that the shiver down his back was immediately changed to one of immense fright! But now, what now? That thought returned him to reality and to the very evening and the performance they were witnessing.

Alice continued: "So you see, Rupert, whilst I've been enjoying the first half, thrilled to bits, I've been reflecting too. I've been thinking too about what may happen now, if this will really be the last night, although I sincerely hope not! Whilst it won't mean so much for me, I've had my time and I won't be around for long any more to see what happens anyway."

Rupert looked immediately concerned at his grandmother's words, his face noticeably whitening at her statement.

"Don't be silly," Alice insisted, seeing her grandson's reaction. "I am only stating facts, facing a reality. I'm not infallible and I've had a long life, I can't go on for ever. None of us do that – it's nature! No, what I'm saying is that I've so enjoyed and am thankful for the part that both Gilbert and Sullivan, indeed this very company, have played in my life and, yes, naturally I hope that it carries on so that others can enjoy as I have done. Everybody should be able to continue to enjoy the operas! And, do you know what gives me so much pleasure?"

"What is that, Nan?" Rupert asked, growing increasingly concerned and uncomfortable, with a slight sickening feeling as a result of the tone of the conversation.

"That, Rupert, is to see just how much you appreciate and so thoroughly enjoy the operas – not just as much but even more than me, if only possible!"

"I do, I do!" Rupert interjected.

"Don't I know it!" Alice laughed in the endearing way that meant so much to Rupert. "To me, I see it as a continuation of everything that I've experienced from my very youngest days and that makes me feel good. No, of course, I hope that they go on and on and that younger people of today can enjoy what I, and you, have for so long." Alice reflected a moment further before finally collecting her thoughts and making herself more comfortable in her seat. "Enough of this! Let's now settle to enjoy what I hope will be an equally wonderful second half of the evening!"

"Especially with an announcement that the company will continue to perform – to go on and on!" Rupert added, although increasingly without conviction.

"Let's hope so too!" Alice added.

"It must surely come – after all the company have approached the Arts Council for the financial support that they so badly need – and deserve! Imagine, that for over a hundred years they have performed the works of Gilbert and Sullivan without ever receiving a penny of Arts support – touring the country so that all can enjoy, year in year out with a full orchestra, chorus, principal singers, the lot! This is our musical heritage that must continue!" Rupert emphasised, getting even more worked up and carried away in the passion of the words he was saying. "When you see what wonderful quality of performances that they still give and have always given – take just this evening for example – then something must be done – it must! Isn't that what the Arts Council is for? They would happily donate our money, tax payers' money, for some horrible piece of abstract art in some gallery, but this, something that thousands and thousands enjoy – well that's another story!"

So intense and involved Rupert was with his statement that by the time he had finished, his knuckles were white from grabbing the seat. Alice was quietly glad that their immediate neighbours had all left their seats for the interval. Although she appreciated her grandson's enthusiasm, she could not help but find some of his passion just a trifle overbearing so she simply replied with an agreeing but un-involving nod.

Even though in 1982, Rupert, like the whole house that evening at the Adelphi Theatre, enjoyed the performance with a noticeable tinge of sadness as to what may be, they all collectively shared a benefit over Tom and Nellie, then almost a hundred years earlier who were both worrying for their own working future. If it were only possible, Rupert could have reassured Tom that the operas on which Tom, Nellie and so many others had worked were indeed to last and to continue to delight audiences for a century. Not only that but, Rupert could have also told Tom that the D'Oyly Carte Opera Company itself played all that time apart from a short period in London in the early 20th Century and the interruption of some of the war years. Tom and Nellie would have also taken enormous comfort to know that the company of which they were the founding part had played not just in London, also at times again at the Savoy itself, but throughout the country with regular tours to America and Canada, even also to Australia and New Zealand.

With benefit of foresight, Tom and Nellie would have enjoyed a happier summer than they did in 1884. But for that to have been possible, for Rupert to have been able to tell Tom, then nothing short of Mr. Gilbert's much vaunted "magic lozenge" plot would have been necessary – and that was not forthcoming!

Chapter 11
"A source of innocent merriment! Of innocent merriment"

The increasingly excited noise and bustle of activity around them quickly made Rupert and Alice aware that the auditorium was once again filling as people returned from their various interval activities. It was a fortunate cue for Rupert to speak more quietly, or even to become suddenly silent as he watched the mingling multitudes, some acknowledging each other and chatting whilst others were just making their way to their seats.

"Probably known each other for years, even met at Gilbert and Sullivan performances and have met regularly ever since in this kind of rather wonderful club-like atmosphere," Alice commented as she too busied herself watching the increasing activity. "And very nice it is too for people to meet up like that, especially when they are all as friends enjoying the performance together, probably reminiscing like us as well!"

"And wondering about the future, too!" Rupert replied.

"I am sure that's so. You - I mean we - aren't the only enthusiasts around as tonight surely shows!" Alice answered, remembering again not to let Rupert think that it was a problem about which she cared less.

Their conversation was immediately interrupted by a general gasp from the whole audience around them, all of whom almost as one in unison got to their feet. Rupert quickly did the same and stood first, helping his grandmother also to stand although still not for the moment sure as to the reason why. He saw that everybody was looking towards the stage box and then a crescendo of clapping and cheering broke out. Only then could Rupert and Alice see why.

In the box, then standing and acknowledging the cheers, was Dame Bridget D'Oyly Carte, the grand-daughter of the company founder, Richard D'Oyly Carte, who herself had been controlling the company for then 34 years, since 1948.

"How must she feel tonight!" Alice exclaimed as she wiped not just a tear, but an almost torrent of tears, from her eye. "All those years of hard, dedicated and selfless effort, all for a company that has been in control of the same family, her family, for over a hundred years – it's a crying shame that the future has come to this! When I've said to you that I've been in my thoughts, reminiscing, what then must it be like for her! It's awful, so really sad!" Alice's comments were by than as charged with emotion as her grandson's had been earlier, belying her earlier comments otherwise.

All that Rupert could say in reply was "I know, yes".

It seemed that nothing could stop the audience from their cheering and applauding that continued for countless moments in a charged sense of unremitting euphoria. Rupert and Alice understood why, especially that emotions were so poignantly bubbling over. There before them all was the tangible link through the theatrical family of D'Oyly Carte right back almost to the very start, nothing less than through most of the whole 107-year history of Gilbert and Sullivan.

At last, though, it was obvious that the theatre manager had the answer as to how once more to control the audience's enthusiasm – the house lights were dimmed and the bright spotlights were once again trained upon the stage curtain. Rupert signalled his grandmother that it was time again to sit down and he held her seat whilst with the other hand he gently assisted her to sit down whilst she still dabbed her eyes. Apart from a few others who refused to budge, most of the house took the cue to also sit down and again cast their eyes away from the box and towards the stage. Once more the conductor entered the pit and this time the cheering and clapping, as raucous as ever, was directed to him, as he turned to face the audience and to acknowledge the warmth of their heartfelt appreciation. That very important lady in the stage box could once more retreat, most probably, as Alice had been doing for the whole evening, into her own quiet thoughts and memories on what was a very emotionally charged and special night.

The conductor raised his baton and the second half of the evening began.

* * * *

Tom and Nellie, indeed none of their colleagues in the then Mr. D'Oyly Carte's Opera Company, could have possibly known in 1884 the significance for them all of a huge Japanese sword, decorating a wall in Mr. Gilbert's study, suddenly falling to the floor with a huge clatter in the writer's presence. The happening soon suggested a broad idea that immediately then turned Mr. Gilbert's mind to a Japanese Exhibition that had recently opened in London, where he had also seen Japanese men and women, dressed in their exotic robes, walking in Knightsbridge.

Unknown then to Tom and Nellie, Mr. Gilbert's quill pen was once again hovering over a blank sheet of paper – a new piece was in the very early stages of planning. In his mind he saw again the big Japanese sword but this time as carried across the shoulders of a diminutive Japanese Executioner. He envisaged a chorus of Nobles, Guards, Coolies and Schoolgirls. With other thoughts duly collected, including some more outline principal character sketches, Mr. Gilbert wrote immediately to Sir Arthur Sullivan – the planned work was to result in the opera destined to be the most popular of all.

"If you want to know who we are,
We are gentlemen of Japan:
On many a vase and jar –
On many a screen and fan,

We figure in lively paint:
Our attitude's queer and quaint –
You're wrong if you think it ain't, oh!"

The news that a new work was in progress, although at first without detail, reached Tom, Nellie and the whole company at a crucial time as they prepared for the revival of 'Sorcerer' and 'Trial' which, exactly as Nellie had predicted, caused only a limited amount of work activity for them all. As always, Fred Dean was first to hear and he in turn quickly told Tom who immediately scampered upstairs to the wardrobe room, as he was wont to do whenever there was something to tell or to talk about and for which he felt his worth as a messenger.

"Nellie, Nellie!" Tom exclaimed as he entered the room, even then so much less than its usual hive of activity because of them only working on a ready production, just as Nellie had feared. "I've just heard, Mr. Dean has told me, Mr. Gilbert is writing a new piece!"

Florrie Parker who was preparing, rather just brushing in an over meticulous way, the barrister wigs for the coming evening performance of 'Trial by Jury', immediately stopped what she was doing and made her way across the room to where Tom was standing beside Nellie. "What's this you've heard, Tom, we're the last to know anything here, only if some costume doesn't fit, or a hat appears ill-finished, then they're at us like all life depends on it!" Florrie exclaimed.

"I don't know much really," Tom replied, just a trifle embarrassed that he alone should be the bearer of such important news although as yet without much detail. "All I know is that it's true, there's a new piece already underway – well more than that really, plot, story everything like that!" The latter was not strictly true as Tom had not been told anything other than "work in progress". In his enthusiasm Tom had rather exaggerated in his role as news reporter, but the story was right in spirit and it immediately lifted the gloom that had already descended upon the wardrobe department over fears for the future.

Just a couple of days passed before once again Tom received further news from Fred Dean, just as he was clearing up the stage and settings from the evening's performance of 'Sorcerer', news that was far more explicit than that given a few days before. This occasion he didn't have time to run off to Nellie but at least they had plenty to talk about as they walked to Blackfriars and then took the train home to Peckham.

"It's going to be a Japanese subject then, the new opera!" Tom excited exclaimed to a rather bemused Nellie.

"Cor!" Nellie exclaimed, "what the 'ell do I know about anyfink Japanese? Not to say costumes! I ain't too sure about that – are you sure you got it right, Tom, not just imagining them fings just 'cause you want an 'appy ending!"

"No, oh no, Nellie, Mr. Dean has told me just before we left the theatre tonight. Both Sir Arthur and Mr. Gilbert are now working on the new opera. He told me it's to include Japanese characters but – as he put it to me and I wrote it down." Tom fumbled in his jacket pocket before he retrieved the paper with his precious notes. "Yes, this is it," he declared and immediately began to relate to Nellie, "Japanese characters but recognisable as grotesquely and easily familiar English figures".

"Do what!" Nellie incredulously replied.

"Japanese characters but recog . . . . ." Tom began, immediately to be stopped by Nellie raising her gloved hand.

"I 'eard you the first time!" Nellie responded, "but lord knows I ain't any idea about what yer saying or what it all means, you might as well be talking in Japanese yerself for all that I knows!"

"I think it will all make sense. Mr Dean has told me about the Japanese Exhibition in London, so that will be where the idea comes from," Tom advised a little pompously as if he were the very authority on the news.

"Well, one fing I knows, or at least I fink I do, is that them folk wear very funny clothes, and I don't have much idea about any of it meself," Nellie replied.

"It's geisha girls dressed in kimonos," Tom interjected, still anxious to impart further the information he had just gained from his boss.

"Whatever!" Nellie replied. "I knew what I was a doing with the costumes for 'Iolanthe' – the peer's robes, the fairy dresses

– even 'Princess Ida', the costumes weren't too bad although not easy. But Japan, I don't know much about that and it really worries me!"

"You know Mr. Gilbert and how he attends to all the details, very careful he is too. Well that's how it will be with the costumes for the new opera and he'll be telling you what and how he wants it," Tom assured.

"Let's 'ope so, but it'll be Miss Parker who he tells it to, not me!" Nellie responded and then immediately decided to spend the remainder of the journey home on the train flicking through a paper she had been given by Florrie Parker. But deep down inside she felt very pleased, both pleased and relieved indeed that a new opera was already underway. She knew also that her reaction towards Tom had all been a bit of an act and she fully realised her professionalism as a dressmaker and seamstress would mean she could make almost anything provided she got some guidance in the first place. No girl, she sighed to herself, you don't even need too much guidance, just a bit of thought and concentration! In her contentment she smiled to herself and quietly placed her hand on Tom's lap as they continued the train ride home.

Naturally, Tom's assurances about costume guidance proved to be perfectly right. A geisha girl was brought from the Japanese Exhibition by Mr. Gilbert to the Savoy, not only so that the costume could be examined by Florrie Parker and Nellie, but also so that the cast could be taught proper Japanese deportment. Fabrics of pure Japanese silk were ordered from Liberty's in Regent Street for the chorus whilst the dresses to be worn by the principals were to be genuine and original Japanese ones. Nellie was immediately thrilled by the work that would have to be done and despite what she had said to Tom, quickly responded to the tasks before her in making the kimonos and gowns, even helping in all the accompanying fans and exotic headdresses with relish.

"You're a sure treasure!" Florrie Parker said one morning to Nellie when she presented another set of costumes for the wardrobe mistress' inspection. "I would say that these are even better than the ones worn by the Japanese lady that Mr. Gilbert

129

brought to the theatre! And don't you worry, I'll be letting Mr. Gilbert know – and he'll see for himself – just what a wonderful standard of dress work that he gets from you! If the whole company is going to be dressed like this, then this opera will look very special indeed! All I can say Nellie, dear, is this is wonderful, one done and only another 23 to do!" She chuckled as a rather embarrassed Nellie mumbled a swift "thank you" before going back to get on with her work. In her all working years at the dress factory, nobody had ever made appreciative comments to her, taking everything for granted. Nellie still found it very hard either to believe or understand that such remarks could indeed be said to her even though she knew her worth. She did not know how to react.

"Now," Florrie continued, "we have to start work on the costume for the main character himself, they call him 'Mikado' which, or so they tell me, is like an emperor! They'll be a gold embroidered robe which is to be a faithful replica of the ancient official costume of a Japanese monarch. So we can say that whilst we made the robes for the members of the House of Lords for 'Iolanthe', now we've moved up a peg to royalty, even if of a far eastern nature!"

Nellie gasped and held her hand to her mouth in a sense of amazement at what she had been told.

"That's how it is!" Florrie continued, "we'll have plenty to do my dear girl, but it will all be something that we can both be very proud of! You can imagine just how it will be on the opening night, when the audience see it and word sweeps round the whole of London!"

Nellie was almost speechless at what the wardrobe mistress had told her. She merely nodded and smiled before quietly making her way back to carry on with the multitude of tasks before her. If anything, she could not help but feel a kind of nervous embarrassment at the realisation that her dress work had already been seen, and would continue to be seen, by so many thousands of people.

"And they'll be society people too, won't they, Tom!" Nellie asked her husband.

"Too right, my love," Tom replied and gave Nellie an encouraging hug. "Another thing, your name's in the programmes for all to see, under Miss Parker – so there you are!" Tom emphasised. The mere thought sent shivers down Nellie's back, so she hurried away to seek the security of her wardrobe room.

"Three little maids from school are we,
Pert as a school-girl well can be,
Filled to the brim with girlish glee,
Three little maids from school!"

The three sisters, the wards of Ko-Ko, were singing in rehearsal for Act One. The delightful music wafted up from the stage. It helped Nellie overcome her nervousness about herself and what she had realised and been told about the importance of her work. Indeed, the music gave her a satisfying inspirational spirit, so much that she even found herself picking up the melody and humming to herself as she once again busied herself with her work. Inwardly, she smiled to herself again and not for the first time said a silent prayer of thanks to her Tom that he had been so persuasive in getting her to join him at the Savoy.

It was soon apparent to all in the theatre as rehearsals became more intense, that the new opera did indeed display English characters in a far eastern setting, a Japanese camouflage for Mr. Gilbert's sharpest satire. At least that was what Mr. Dean told Tom and he felt in no position to question the advice!

Together as they busied themselves with others in the stage crew with stage directions and preparations at rehearsals, they listened with a developing ear to the perfect characterisations opening up before them:

Rutland Barrington, as Pooh-Bah, the Lord High Everything Else, rehearsing his own lines: "… as First Lord of the Treasury, I could propose a special vote that could cover all expenses, if it were not that, as Leader of the Opposition, it would be my duty to resist it, tooth and nail. Or, as Paymaster-General, I could so cook the accounts that, as Lord High Auditor, I should never discover the fraud."

They listened intently as George Grosssmith rehearsed his role as 'Ko-Ko', Lord High Executioner of Titipu, and sang his "Little List" of things that "never would be missed", nothing more than a catalogue of some of the features of English life in the mid-1880s:

"And Children who are up in dates, and floor you with 'em flat –

All persons who in shaking hands, shake hands with you like THAT."

To continue:

"Then the idiot who praises, with enthusiastic tone,
All centuries but this, and every country but his own;
And the lady from the provinces, who dresses like a guy,
And who 'doesn't think she waltzes,
but would rather like to try';
And that singular anomaly, ..."

It was all a little above Tom and again he took the cue to laugh from Fred Dean whose shoulders were continually shaking with his thorough enjoyment of the piece.

"It's all so very topical, so very relevant to our day," Fred commented to Tom who was just happy to accept what he was told and to answer with a rather meek "right you are, Mr. Dean".

"I only hopes that Mr. Gilbert has got it right and that there won't be too many howls of protest from those kind of people that have been referred to on that 'Little List' song!" Fred Dean concluded.

"Or, Mr. Dean, more likely protests from those that were left out from the list, now that's more the thing!" Tom declared in such a rare show of perceiving the situation that Fred Dean was momentarily taken aback by his accurate observation.

The company learnt that the first night for the new opera was planned for the coming March, 1885, just nine months from the time that the sword fell from the wall in Mr. Gilbert's study. That meant nothing short of feverish activity in every corner of the Savoy – with Nellie's costume making, Florrie's overseeing efforts, the whole theatrical crew and especially Fred Dean with Tom's assistance with all the stage work, not to say with the musicians and singers themselves. Everybody tasked with the new work during full days whilst spending each evening in performance of 'Sorcerer' and 'Trial'.

Each night as they made their way home, sometimes with Florrie Parker travelling with them on the same train although never Fred Dean who no matter how decent he was as a boss to Tom somehow didn't then want the social line to be too readily extended, they were mostly too tired for extended conversation.

"Alright, Miss Parker?" Tom might ask Florrie, out of politeness rather than wishing to engage in too much conversation.

"Thank you for asking, Tom," Florrie would reply, "just quite tired after our day, isn't that how we both feel, eh Nellie?"

"Oh, yes, Miss Parker, just like you say," Nellie would reply as she felt her eyelids heavily falling and sleep virtually descending.

Tom was the perfect gentleman in the circumstances and furthered no form of communication. What he did do, though, was to be very much on guard so as not to fall to sleep. He looked over the two dozing ladies beside him, smiled, leant his arm inside Nellie's coat and kept watch over his charges, daring never to sleep in case they missed their station at Peckham, then to be transported by the train to the far flung realms of darkest South London, perhaps a 'foreign outpost' for them, somewhere like Crystal Palace, late at night. Tom never failed in his devoted duty and the three would safely alight at Peckham Station and then walk, still quietly, together, often taking Florrie Parker to her home first, before retracing their steps just a few streets to their own front door. Only then did Tom let himself succumb with just a bare few moments elapsing before both he and Nellie had quickly undressed and made ready for bed. Tom's sleep was immediate, Nellie perhaps following just a few moments afterwards as her train snooze had invariably slightly refreshed her. But not for Tom any reflections back to 'Iolanthe' and the Chancellor's Nightmare song "When you're lying awake with a dismal headache"!

133

"14 March!" Mr. Dean declared to his assembled stage crew, Tom included. "That's the date set for the opening night of the new opera, 'The Mikado', of course here at the Savoy."

An approaching opening night always brought with it both rising excitement and a deal of nervousness amongst the whole company. Even though it was to be only 14 months since the opening of 'Princess Ida', it had been a long time for all concerned given the less than immediate success of that last opera. On top of that had been the alarms and pressures, so epitomised and felt by Tom and Nellie, as to whether there would be any new works that created an unusually stressed atmosphere within the company at the Savoy. That wasn't helped either by one or two articles in the press which seemed to suggest that Gilbert and Sullivan as a partnership might be played out, one even asking was "their vein of genius exhausted?"

Sir Arthur Sullivan, of the partnership, was always the one to be somehow more at ease, more controlled, but as Fred Dean said frequently to Tom, "it's not Sir Arthur who controls anything that goes on up here on the stage, it's Mr. Gilbert – he's the one that matters most to the likes of us! And Mr. Gilbert, well he gets increasingly on edge, almost to the point of on-going nervousness as a first night looms!"

Whatever he felt within himself, and indeed Tom had often his fears that he was always sure not to allow Nellie to notice, he did contain himself within his work, always keeping his head down and doing whatever duties were required of him. By 1885, Tom was not only approaching his 40th birthday, a milestone for anybody, but also he had already been involved in the works of Gilbert and Sullivan for over 14 years if counting the early work for 'Thespis', or at least permanently for 10 years since 'Trial'. He was someone with a growing and recognised skill of experience who could be relied upon and trusted. Fred Dean knew that precisely and so involved Tom in all parts of the production and entrusted him with a steadily growing amount of work, knowing that he would get a job well done and, what was more, that it would be done exactly to Mr. Gilbert's wishes.

"These are Mr. Gilbert's written instructions, I can leave them with you and you'll just get on with it, won't you, Tom," Fred Dean would usually say.

There was never any question with Tom's reply. "Certainly, Mr. Dean, yes!"

As the final rehearsals for 'Mikado' came, even Tom's patience was sometimes just a little tried by Mr. Gilbert.

"I just hope everything is going to be alright with the new opera," Tom exclaimed to Nellie. "Mr. Gilbert, well he's so especially anxious and fussy this time, really on edge. Yesterday, he told us that he's decided to cut one of the main songs of the Mikado himself from Act 2 – it's the one that goes tum, tum, tum, 'My object all sublime, I shall achieve in time…'". Tom stopped for a moment, admitting to himself that his own version of the song was something less than convincing and that by trying to sing it then probably Nellie would agree that it should be cut from the scene! "Mr. Richard Temple, you know who is playing the role of Mikado…"

"Course I know it's Mr. Temple, I've only been making 'is costume!" Nellie intervened.

"Anyway," Tom continued, unabashed by his wife's interruption, "Mr. Temple, he was naturally upset about it, but he's a gentleman, so didn't seem to want to make any kind of fuss about it. Today the choristers, all of them, objected to the cut and so went to see Mr. Gilbert! They pleaded with Mr. Gilbert to re-instate the song and, do you know what?"

"Tell me, Tom!" Nellie responded, getting just a little exasperated at the length of Tom's story, especially as she was busy herself.

"Well, Mr. Gilbert, he agreed and the song is now back in the opera and will be performed by Mr. Temple on the opening night," Tom advised, satisfied with himself at having finally delivered the story.

The whole day of the first night – 14 March 1885 – passed in a whirl for Tom, Nellie and the whole company. Stage scenery was set up, dismantled and re-set on stage until everything was perfect. And to look back to the stage from the back of the stalls, Tom soon realised that it was indeed perfect. Act One was set as the courtyard of Ko-Ko's, the exquisitely-written character, the Lord High Executioner of Titipu, Official Residence; Act Two as Ko-Ko's Garden. Tom felt very good about all that he saw although naturally he had never seen the real thing, and felt that they had faithfully reproduced all that could be expected of a Japanese theme with sliding screens, distant orchards, a quaint bridge and stream.

Tom's obvious satisfaction was equally shared by Nellie as she, with Florrie for probably the 20th time, first set out and then fitted the singers with their costumes, both handling the delicate fabrics with so much, almost fond, care. Nellie ensured that all costumes were correctly distributed to everybody's dressing room, made sure that final fittings were in order, that costume changes were in place and ready for the performance. All around her, many of the cast, even in the last moments before curtain up, were still practising their hand movements with the fans, remembering exactly what had been instructed by both Mr. Gilbert and the Japanese lady brought in to help. Like the well drilled team that they were, nothing was left to chance.

As the house began to fill for what was obviously going to be another society occasion of a Gilbert and Sullivan first night, the gathering excitement from the auditorium, the rising level of chatter as many of the audience recognised and acknowledged those it deemed right to so do. In complete contrast came the singing, once again, of choruses from earlier G&S operas, sung by the lower classes filling the gallery. All the sounds were part and parcel of the occasion, showing the wide appreciation of the operas across all facets of society. "Making the English musical theatre respectable again", that was how Fred Dean had put it to Tom and he could see how that observation was apt. That rising level of anticipation coming from the audience both thrilled and infected the whole company.

"The Duke and Duchess of Edinburgh are to be in the audience tonight," an excited Tom declared to Nellie on one of their frequent encounters as they rushed about their duties either on the stage itself or in the overwhelmed wardrobe room.

"Will we see them?" Nellie asked as she touched her own hair as if, in a dream, making ready to be presented herself.

"No, love, of course not, well not unless we get a chance to peak through to the audience from the sides of the curtain sometime," Tom declared. "That's if any of us have got any time to do anything tonight other than concentrate on the work!"

The next Tom heard, from the side of the stage, was the deafening roar from the auditorium, a noise so overwhelming that it carried itself upstairs to Nellie in the wardrobe room. Both knew that it meant only one thing – Sir Arthur had entered the orchestra pit. The early drum beat within the overture signalled that the first night of 'Mikado' was underway.

"Good luck," Nellie said to herself, taking a moment to stop work and to cross her fingers. In his part of the theatre, simultaneously, Tom reciprocated his wife's actions in precisely the same way, as the growingly familiar strains of the overture filled the whole theatre, front and back stage.

It was soon apparent to the whole house, except, that is, for Mr. Gilbert who by then was once again prowling the streets of London, that the new opera was being not just well, but ecstatically received.

'Ko-Ko's' "Little List" song was a perfect success and for three times Tom, and everybody, heard the song "Three little maids from school are we," as Sir Arthur bowed to the demands of the house and gave the piece a treble encore, the three singers – Miss Leonora Braham, Miss Jessie Bond, Miss Sybil Grey – themselves all completely overwhelmed and giggling with excitement when they finally left the stage.

"There really are just 'three little maids', isn't that so, Tom?" Fred Dean commented as he watched them go off to the wings for some costume adjustment, ever attended by the faithful and dedicated Nellie.

"Surely are," Tom replied, "and they, like all of us, must be very happy with the reception that the whole evening is getting so far." Fred nodded in acknowledgement as they were both, again, too busy for words.

In contrast to the rousing cheers for the trio's song, there was a complete hush over the whole house as Miss Rosina Brandram, who had appeared at the Savoy as a principal in all of the original productions, in her role as 'Katisha', the so-called 'elderly Lady in love with Nanki-Poo', the son of the Mikado although disguised as a wandering minstrel, sang her deeply moving song:

"The hour of gladness
Is dead and gone;
In silent sadness
I live alone!
The hope I cherished
All lifeless lies
And all has perished
Save love, which never dies!"

"That's where Mr. Gilbert – of course Sir Arthur too, with the music – they get it just right – making the audience roar with laughter and cheers the one minute, only then to have a really moving and calming piece of singing the next!" Fred rightly declared, as was befit to his own knowledgeable authority on the operas. Tom's quick reply of "That's right, Mr. Dean," was just as much because there was no time for discussion rather than Tom's inability for once to understand.

And so to the finale of Act One, "Ye torrents roar!", and to the curtain then coming down to such a roar that again Tom felt sure the roof of the theatre would lift off.

"Did you see them, have you had a chance?" an excited Nellie asked Tom as she managed to get a quick moment to come down to the stage area, Nellie clearing some costumes from the first act and making ready new ones for the coming act.

"Who, Love?" Tom replied, barely concentrating as he and his stage crew colleagues were busy making their own scene changes for Act Two.

"Why, the Duke and Duchess of Edinburgh, of course!" Nellie replied, just a little indignantly.

"No, no, sorry love," Tom answered, "there hasn't really been much time for a peek – but why don't you come down to the wings yourself later in Act Two when you're not so busy with no more costumes to make ready!"

"I'll do just that – if yer wants somefink doing properly, then do's it yerself!" Nellie exclaimed but with a knowing wink to Tom that she was only playfully teasing.

"Braid the raven hair –
Weave the supple tress –
Deck the maiden fair
In her loveliness –"

The ladies chorus once again filled the theatre and Act Two was underway.

Again, the appreciative and highly enthusiastic audience left no doubt as to how they were receiving the new opera as their cheers greeted virtually every song and stage business.

"The sun, whose rays
Are all ablaze
With ever-living glory,"

Then followed by the delightful madrigal, beautifully sung by Mr. Durward Lely, as 'Nanki-Poo' and Miss Leonora Braham as 'Yum-Yum', the two aspiring lovers:

"Brightly dawns our wedding day;
Joyous hour, we give thee greeting!"

Tom and Fred Dean winked to each other as they heard Mr. Temple, as the Mikado himself, launch into his own principal song:

"A more humane Mikado never
Did in Japan exist,
To nobody second,
I'm certainly reckoned
A true philanthropist"

Then to conclude:

"My object all sublime
I shall achieve in time
To let the punishment fit the crime –
The punishment fit the crime;"

"There you are," Fred Dean declared to Tom, "that's the song that Mr. Gilbert first cut out just the other night until the chorus suggested otherwise! And listen to how the whole house has roared its approval! Won't Mr. Gilbert be pleased that he listened to the chorus pleas!"

"Well yes," Tom replied, "Mr. Gilbert will be pleased…"

"Maybe, well rather, will be – but since he's not here then somebody will have to tell him, won't they?" the stage manager replied.

"Expect you can do that, Mr. Dean, can't you?" Tom answered, swerving to miss Fred Dean's approaching fist, playfully meant, as they again both busied themselves on more scene preparations. "Sir Arthur will get to him long before I ever will!" came the reply from the stage manager.

"The flowers that bloom in the spring,
Tra la,
Breathe promise of merry sunshine."

Again that evening, Tom, as everybody, heard the piece sung three times to satisfy the audience's demands for ongoing encores, only later for the house once again to become ever so quiet, listening intently, as Ko-Ko sang to Katisha:

"On a tree by a river a little tom-tit
Sang 'Willow, titwillow, titwillow!'
And I said to him, 'Dicky-bird, why do you sit
Singing 'Willow, titwillow, titwillow'?
'Is it weakness of intellect, birdie?' I cried,
'Or a rather tough worm in your little inside?'
With a shake of his poor little head, he replied,
'Oh, willow, titwillow, titwillow!'"

Tom felt Nellie's head resting on his shoulder as they both stood in the wings, listening, as George Grossmith, acting Ko-Ko sang the song.

"A'int that just beautiful," Nellie sighed, "no matter 'ow many times I 'ear it, I always want to cry, it's so very lover-ly!" Tom smiled towards his wife but said nothing. Actually he turned slightly away from Nellie – his own eyes were rather moist.

Soon, though, the audience reactions swung the other way as both Ko-Ko and Katisha began to sing the more rousing:

"There is beauty in the bellow of the blast,
There is grandeur in the growling of the gale."
And:

"There is beauty in extreme old age –
Do you fancy you are elderly enough?"

To happily conclude:

"If that is so,
Sing derry down derry!
It's evident, very,
Our tastes are one!
Away we'll go,
And merrily marry,
Nor tardily tarry,
Till day is done!"

The song concluded to, as everybody that evening was expecting once again, thunderous applause.

Nellie was once again beside Tom, standing in the wings but still unable to identity the Duke and Duchess of Edinburgh through the side curtain, at the end of the opera to witness the rousing finale:

"Then let the throng
Our joy advance,
With laughing song

141

And merry dance,
With joyous shout and ringing cheer,
Inaugurate our new career!"

"You're humming, love!" Tom declared to his wife, "you are really picking up on all of this now, who would ever have thought it!"

"Watch yerself, Tom Dobbs!" Nellie exclaimed, "we're both of us in the 'featre world now, it' not just yer anymore!" Tom and Nellie both embraced at the side of the stage, an embrace that said it all – both their personal happiness as a couple and their joint happiness about their work at the Savoy.

Their moment of reflection at the side of the stage was all but brief with the coming end of the evening. As Sir Arthur finally lowered his baton, the cheers rang through the whole theatre, so much so that the tremendous reception meant only one thing – the 'Mikado' was a fabulous success. Mr. Gilbert had again timed his evening perfectly and rushed back into the theatre from The Embankment to join Sir Arthur and the whole company of singers in taking curtain calls. He did not have to ask how everything had gone, the sounds from the auditorium told him all. Later, though, he did let it be known of his fears, saying, "What I suffered during those hours, no man can tell. Agony and apprehension possessed me".

By the time everything was finished after the show and as much as possible was made ready for the next day, it was close to midnight when Tom and Nellie were ready to finally leave the Savoy. They left the stage door with Florrie Parker and, most unusually, even Fred Dean was beside them, something that Tom hadn't immediately noticed until Nellie touched him on his shoulder and nodded in the stage manager's direction, also rising her eyebrows at the same time.

"You don't mind if I join you?" Fred Dean asked to be replied to with a polite smile from his three colleagues. "But we're not walking to Blackfriars, it's too late for that, we're taking a cab, and all the way to Peckham too!" he declared as he escorted his colleagues to the waiting vehicle. "Mr. Gilbert's instructions, that everybody, chorus, singers, stage and wardrobe, all must go home by cab tonight!"

"And thanks to Mr. Gilbert for that!" Tom declared as he quickly set himself up as representative for the three, very appreciative, travellers.

The next day, Tom and Nellie were back at the Savoy mid-morning and with the whole company, wallowed in the glow of the glittering first night. Everybody had been pleased with the performance and there hadn't been any hitch, not even for Fred Dean and his discerning eye. Seeing Nellie with Tom, he even called out to her – "well, my Nellie, you can be surely proud of all those most beautiful costumes!"

"Thank you, Mr. Dean," Nellie replied to the compliment, wishing very much that she had in her hand one of the chorus' fans to hide her modest embarrassment. She beat a hasty retreat to the safety of her wardrobe room.

Within days, the company gathered on stage to hear Mr. Dean tell them of the critical acclaim that 'The Mikado' had received, in certain backing of the audience's reaction not only on opening night but on all the immediate following few nights too.

"It says here," Fred Dean announced, holding up a copy of 'The Theatre' of 1 April, "musical jewels of great price, all aglow with the lustre of pure and luminous genius'. Another paper has made the very cryptic comment that Sir Arthur, Mr. Gilbert and our own Mr. D'Oyly Carte are 'monarchs of all they Savoy' – that's a play on words, you understand!" Fred Dean emphasised, Tom thought it was said just for his benefit.

Both the daily receipts and forward bookings for the new opera were so healthy that any concerns for the continuing success of Gilbert and Sullivan were no longer relevant. That meant for the whole company, Tom and Nellie included, that they could, perhaps for the very first time, at least for Nellie, really relax in their work without the fear of any threatening theatre closures, and so enjoy even more each day. For Tom, any thoughts and memories of his dreaded music hall days were then confined very much to the back of his mind.

Once again, word soon passed around of more company overseas tours, first to Holland and Germany with the new

'Mikado' but also with 'HMS Pinafore' and 'Patience as well. For Tom and Nellie, it meant one thing – even more work preparing for the tours with scenery and all the extra costumes needed whilst productions continued not only at the Savoy but in the D'Oyly Carte touring companies travelling all the time to theatres in the length and breadth of Britain. There was never any question that either Tom or Nellie should travel with any of the touring companies, something that despite the possible appeal, didn't really bother either of them. Their own personal horizons were perfectly limited, with the own home move to South London just a couple of years earlier more than enough to fulfil any imminent travel ambitions. Besides, what they both found the most satisfying was the identical word that they received from their respective bosses, Fred Dean and Florrie Parker, that they were "too valuable to us here at the Savoy, for us to let you gad about!".

But the statement was in so many ways true. Even when some of the company left for America in readiness for the opening night of 'The Mikado' at the Fifth Avenue Theatre, New York, on 19 August 1885, Mr. Gilbert himself remained at home, to frequently drop into the Savoy to check up on company discipline to the performance, something too that kept Fred Dean very much on his toes. And if Fred was kept aware and on his toes, then Tom was also very much as well!

"That stage screen is in precisely the same place as last night, isn't it Tom?" the stage manager asked.

"Yes, Mr. Dean, I measured it up myself," Tom replied.

"Right you are, my good man," his boss replied, satisfied as he then turned his attention to the next detail.

Tom was at the side of the stage one day when Mr. Gilbert was once again in the theatre, and overheard one of the writer's disciplined commands, to the singer, already himself a company member for many years and having a major role in the operas since 'Sorcerer'.

"I am told, Mr. Grossmith, that in last night's performance, when you were kneeling before the Mikado, that Miss Bond gave you a push and you rolled completely over on the floor."

"Yes, you see, I, in my interpretation of 'Ko-Ko' . . . . ." the singer began, only to be interrupted by Mr. Gilbert:

"Whatever your interpretation, please omit that in future," came the reply.

"Certainly, if you wish, but I got a big laugh by it!"

"So you would if you sat on a pork pie!" Mr Gilbert answered and so ended the conversation!

Tom chuckled to himself as he kept busy. It was common knowledge amongst all the company that whilst Mr. Gilbert and even Sir Arthur Sullivan too, were strict disciplinarians, they were aware of the necessary standards and all only had to look to the successes of the operas and the performances to see that it all worked. Then, if that wasn't enough, there was always Mr. D'Oyly Carte himself to keep all aspects of the theatre in tight control.

"Yes, it's a well ordered and very proper world," Tom said to Nellie when he got a chance later that day to relate the incident.

"And that ain't any bad fing," his wife replied, "I just wish that we 'ad the likes of Mr. Gilbert at 'ome to keep you in check as well!"

* * * *

Across the Strand, at the Adelphi Theatre, almost 97 years after the opening of 'The Mikado', Rupert and his grandmother, Alice, had savoured, as always, the excerpts presented that evening from the same opera. Throughout the Gilbert and Sullivan world, the opera remained in many people's hearts as the best, certainly the most popular. For once, though, Rupert did not say to his grandmother that it was his own favourite, even if, for the moment, he really thought it was anyway! In so many ways, the performance, singing and delivery that very evening had been a faithful re-enactment of all previous performances over the years, so much so that even Mr. Gilbert would have probably been more than satisfied. Without doubt, Tom and Mr. Dean would have appreciated the stage setting as Nellie and Miss Parker would have been as delighted at the recreation of their original dresses, fans and headgear.

One thing, though, that would not have been recognised, was the slight changes made to Ko-Ko's song, "Little List". Often, over the years, topical references had been added to those "that never would be missed". On that night, 27 February 1982, the inclusion of a reference to the "Arts Council", the villains of the peace that night, was cheeringly received by the audience of the D'Oyly Carte Opera Company enthusiasts, in the much the same way that reference to "European-Unionists" had been on the "List" in the early 1970's. But it was all done in perfect character and the more appreciated for that.

With the conclusion of 'The Mikado', Rupert well realised that the evening was over half completed, with still no mention made about the future of the company. His remorse cast a depression over the immediate moments of the evening that he found himself clapping the end of the excerpts from his present favourite opera, in a hypnotic, virtual robot-type fashion. He felt so deep and down in his thoughts that he hardly heard his grandmother saying to him "Now it's the beginning of the next opera – that must surely be your favourite!"

Chapter 12
"For duty, duty must be done;
The rule applies to everyone."

London, not to say throughout the country as well as virtually the whole English speaking world, continued to be 'Mikado' mad for all of 1885 and into 1886, with the music heard as much from barrel organs on street corners as in the theatre itself. Music sheets were bought in abundance for the songs to be sung by friends and families gathered round the piano at home, be it in the best houses of Kensington or Yorkshire, the growing middle class suburbs of any of the major cities around the country or in the poorer districts of London's East End or Lancashire. In London society, it was a talking point to be asked whether you had yet seen the new Gilbert and Sullivan opera or, if not, how long were you having to wait before being able to get a seat. There was equally as much enthusiastic interest amongst the lower classes that ensured an overwhelming demand for the gallery seats at every performance. The virtual mania and abounding appetite for the operas bought nothing but delight to the whole company at the Savoy.

That delight was equally felt by Tom and Nellie, both of whom revelled "most politely" in their involvement in the productions and, what was more, both were told of their worth time and time again, much to their personal delight. For some while, Tom had appreciated just how much Fred Dean left him in charge of many of the stage activities and knew confidently that he could be charged to do a job well done. It was the same too with Nellie as Florrie Parker relied on her to an equal degree although it took Nellie far longer than Tom to become accustomed to praise, especially to be told as much.

The successes of the operas meant also that productions were mounted not just in America but also in Australia, New Zealand and in South America at Buenos Aires, Montevideo, Valparaiso and Lima. The news thrilled all the company back home at the Savoy and with so many productions on the go, with so much being prepared in readiness for various tours, all were kept more than busy, too busy for anyone to even begin to think of when a new opera might be written although all expected a new piece to come as a matter of course at some time.

Sir Arthur Sullivan was writing the music for his setting of Longfellow's 'Golden Legend' that he intended to be performed at the Leeds Festival in October 1886. Tom asked Fred Dean, although not any more with concern in view of the successes of all the productions then being mounted, if that meant there might not be any immediate new Gilbert and Sullivan pieces.

"Not at all, Tom," the stage manager advised. "In fact, Mr. Gilbert has told me that he has a piece already prepared – just awaiting for Sir Arthur to have the time to consider it."

"Can you say, if I may ask, at this time if you know how the piece will be?" Tom asked of his boss.

"Course you can ask, Tom, you're not just anybody, you're, together with your Nellie, amongst our most important members of the team, after all!" Fred declared. "As I understand it, Mr. Gilbert has written a kind of operatic version of the old fashioned blood and thunder kind of stage melodrama."

"That sounds as if it'll mean plenty of stage work, that's for sure," Tom considered, "we'll be kept busy then!"

"Just like always!" Fred Dean replied, with a smile and a friendly pat on the back to Tom.

As Mr. Gilbert had indeed told Fred Dean, there was to be no question that the writer would rest for too long before starting on the next piece, no matter how much success 'The Mikado' was enjoying. In fact, Mr. Gilbert let Fred Dean know that he was becoming increasingly anxious that it was Sir Arthur, because of his many involvements, who was holding up the new work. Mr. Gilbert read to the stage manager the letter that he had sent to Sir Arthur Sullivan. "I congratulate you heartily on the success of the Cantata – I don't expect you will want to turn to our work at once without immediate rest, but if you do I can come up any day and go through the manuscript with you!"

"The trouble is," Fred Dean relayed to Tom, "that Sir Arthur has been busy, not just with the work for Leeds Festival, but also 'cause the composer, Franz Liszt, has been visiting London and Sir Arthur has had to entertain him at a round of functions."

"Well, that's surely an honour for Sir Arthur, isn't it Mr. Dean?" Tom observed.

"It is indeed – and it only goes to show in what high regard Sir Arthur is held, a sort of musical figurehead here in England. Still, that doesn't help Mr. Gilbert with his quest to get on with the new opera! But we've seen it all before, we get to know just how the two of them work, and it will all come out right in the end, it always does!" the stage manager assured, to which Tom nodded his agreement.

In his customary way, at the first opportunity Tom conveyed the news to Nellie.

"Frankly, Tom, Miss Parker and me are up to our bloomin' necks in kimonos, fans, robes and all manner of whatya-me-call-its for all these touring productions of 'Mikado' that me hopes that Sir Arthur will be kept busy entertaining all the composers from wherever, be they dead or alive, for as long as he wants to and for many months to come!" Nellie declared, barely taking the time to lift her eyes from her mountain of needlework.

"That's what you say, now," Tom answered, "but before you know it, you be looking forward to getting your hands on doing some new costumes for whatever the new opera will be, I know you!" Nellie chuckled, realising just how accurate her husband's comments were as she thought to herself that her husband knew her far better than she often gave him credit for!

Tom and Nellie thoroughly enjoyed their year of 1886. The security of their joint work and regular wages ensured they could make some purchases for their home in Peckham which they both acknowledged was becoming, as a result, more like the 'Arcadian Vale' depicted in 'Trial by Jury' 11 years before. It meant, too, that with happy heart they could frequent Greenwich Park on summer Sunday afternoons, to walk arm in arm in total contentment, enjoying the fresh air and the sights of London, across the river beyond. A sight, too, that they realised was to a distant, although not seen, Shoreditch, a symbolic life from which they had both moved on. It was, too, a contentment made even more by hearing passers-by humming and singing pieces from not only 'The Mikado' but from many of the earlier Gilbert and Sullivan operas as well. But Sundays were very much for themselves, their valued private moments enjoyed in each other's company. They felt no urge whatsoever to announce to passers-by what they both knew was their very personal and valued involvement in the operas.

Being so refreshed from a late summer Sunday, Tom and Nellie returned to the Savoy on the following Monday morning, to be met just inside the stage door by a very excited Fred Dean, a piece of paper waving from his hand.

"Morning Tom, Nellie – well, here it is, the word from Mr. Gilbert about the new piece. It's to be called 'Ruddygore'. Sir Arthur has managed at last to give some of his time already and, well, now – we're off!"

"That's good news, Mr. Dean," Tom replied in his rather understated way as his wife, by his side, nodded in agreement.

Just before they parted for that moment to begin their various duties for the day, though, Nellie did take the chance to ask Tom "'ere, Tom, that wasn't your Mr. Dean swearing was it, that's so unlike 'im, real gentleman that I always fink he is?"

"No, my love, of course not, no it was Mr. Dean telling us what the name is for the new opera. 'Ruddygore', that's the name," Tom emphasised.

"Well, that sounds pretty strange to my ears," Nellie replied, "and I ain't too sure what the folk will make of that! Still, that's not for me to worry about, not for now anyway. I'm back to Japan, so to speak, and that'll continue to keep me busy for time enough!" With that, Nellie kissed Tom – their individual working days had begun.

The original news about the new opera was right – it was to be a true Victorian melodrama, with all the complicated stage production work that it entailed. Tom's days were no more spent on just tidying up the running production of 'Mikado', although the strict demands of not only Mr. Gilbert but also Fred Dean and the whole company meant that the ongoing production could not be simply ignored – that would both never do nor would it have been something that Tom would have wanted. So it was once again that the working days became long with concentrated time in the mornings and afternoons on the new opera, with the late afternoon and evening on 'Mikado'. Tom was glad about that because the growing long run of the opera had meant he had a very personal liking and regard for it and wanted to hang on to his involvement with the opera for as long as possible.

One aspect about the new piece was easier, though. When Tom heard that the setting was to be Cornwall, his mind raced back the few years to 'Pirates of Penzance' although he was then still unsure of exactly what Mr. Gilbert might have had in mind. Nellie was pleased too, as she put it to Tom. "It's been sort of fun doing all the fancy costumes for Japan but it's all been way above me 'ead. Well, Cornwall, that's somehow different, more natural, more like our own, although I ain't ever been there, naturally – I'll like that, much more easy!"

Nellie's initial calmness was very soon shattered when the final details of the costume requirements became known. There was to be no easy way of using the ideas from 'Pirates' and with Mr. Gilbert's attention to every detail, they should have realised that in any case. Florrie Parker went though the plans with Nellie at the first opportunity.

"For the men's chorus we're going to have to make uniforms of 20 British regiments dating back to 1810 and then, I'm told, when we've finished, they've to be inspected by Sir Arthur Herbert for accuracy!" the wardrobe mistress announced.

"Sir Arfur who?" Nellie responded.

"Sorry, dear," Florrie replied, "it's Sir Arthur Herbert, the Deputy Quartermaster of the British Army, no less, he's to check our work, for our accuracy!"

151

"Blimey, Miss Parker!" Nellie replied, regretting immediately that she hadn't checked herself before allowing the exclamation. Florrie let the comment pass without issue – she felt exactly the same herself although she thought she might have put it differently!

"Well, that's Mr. Gilbert and we should all by now be getting used to his demands for accuracy. But we'll cope, I've every confidence in that, especially in you my dear, then when the first night comes it will be just like always, the whole of London, then later the world, will marvel at it all!"

"Let's 'ope so, Miss Parker, we'll do our bests, sure we will." With her usual reassuring comment, Nellie settled back to her immediate far eastern work and a dedicated hush of activity descended again on the wardrobe room.

On stage, Tom scratched his head, copying the very same action that he saw Fred Dean do just a few moments before as befitted the complex nature of the situation in which they found themselves. They both looked again at the stage instructions given to them. "Tom, this is going to be very hard," the stage manager declared, "somehow we have got to be able to bring to life the portraits of the Ancestors in this scene in Act Two – anybody would think that we are supposed to be as clever as Mr. John Wellington Wells from 'Sorcerer'!"

Ignoring the stage manager's last comment, Tom instead asked: "Will that mean Mr. Dean that we'll have to have the portrait pictures actually move and . . .?"

"Absolutely, Tom – the portraits will move, the pictures to slide away, and then the chorus, coming to life so to speak, before the audience's very eyes will emerge from the space and step forward, down onto the stage," Fred Dean advised, scratching his head and frowning.

"Oh goodness!" Tom replied, using a word more considered than that his wife had uttered to Miss Parker, upstairs, just a few moments earlier. "We'll have to make sure it's all done as quietly as possible otherwise the whole theatre will be alive with creaking portraits, not to say we have to make sure of sturdy construction of the gallery wall otherwise…"

This time it was Fred Dean who interrupted with the obvious "We'll have the whole bloo . ." Fred stopped to check himself. "We will have all the gentlemen of the chorus falling on to the stage, Tom!"

The implication of the scene caused them both to stand quietly, in deep thought, for many moments. They paced the stage together, pushed settings against the wall, stamped around, before after many hours of trial and effort, with the help of the whole stage team, they managed to build a secure stage set.

"There," Fred Dean declared, "that'll never fall down, no matter if the whole British Army comes though the portraits!"

"That's so, Mr. Dean," Tom replied, "but there's still something that really worries me about this scene."

"What's that, Tom?" Fred Dean replied, just a little agitated that all issues might not have yet been dealt with.

"Well, looking at the stage instructions Mr. Dean," Tom began, glancing to the notes in his hand, "the stage is to be dark when the portraits come alive, so everybody's going to have to be really well drilled and to know what they're doing!"

"And that, my dear Tom, is where I know that I can rely upon you!" Fred Dean replied, patting his colleague on his shoulder. Tom smiled with a degree of embarrassment and continued scratching his head. "But it is a point and I've been told that Sir Arthur will be having a special glass tube baton that'll contain a platinum wire which will glow a dull red – then the chorus will be able on the darkened stage to see Sir Arthur's beat and signal for their entry – nothing left to chance, you see!" Fred Dean concluded with a smile.

"Painted emblems of a race,
All accurst in days of yore,
Each from his accustomed place
Steps into the world once more!"

Tom and Fred watched as the pictures upon the darkened stage slid ever so silently aside as the chorus of Ancestors, perfectly drilled and instructed, stepped carefully from the frames and so to the stage:

"Baronet of Ruddygore,
Last of our accursed line,
Down upon the oaken floor –
Down upon those knees of thine."

Fred Dean patted Tom satisfyingly on his back. "You're a wonder Tom, that went so very well, without a hitch I must say. I hardly heard any sound of the picture frames moving, neither did I see a single wobble of the gallery wall whatsoever. All the singers knew perfectly what they were doing too! Well done, lad!"

"Thank you, Mr. Dean," was all that Tom replied, preferring to get on with his work rather than spend time on receiving acknowledgements. One thing, especially, he did appreciate, though, was how even at being over 40, the stage manager often called him 'lad'. As Nellie told him, it was more likely that it made Fred Dean feel good as he was only a couple of years older than Tom anyway!

But Tom and Fred Dean still had to hold their breath as their trials were not yet over.

"Painted emblems of a race,
All accurst in days of yore,
Each to his accustomed place
Steps unwillingly once more!"

The final singing of the chorus that signalled for the whole delicate operation to be performed in reverse – the Ancestors steeping once again back within the picture frames and, in darkness, the pictures sliding back into place. Only then did Tom and Fred let out a collective sigh of relief, although both acknowledged that this was something now set to happen night after night. What was more, Fred Dean dared not even then to begin to think of touring productions that might need to be mounted as well – but Tom did and he felt distinctly apprehensive.

If the Picture Gallery of Ruddygore Castle in Act Two was a problem to set, at least Tom and his stage team knew that Act One, by comparison, was not nearly as difficult. The requirement was to create a Cornish fishing village, to be called 'Rederring', "an apt Gilbertian name", as Tom was informed. There were to be stone houses, cottages, a well, street scene and a distant sea – by no means simple but, as Mr. Dean assured, "at least we don't have to have anything that needs to move nor all sorts of people needing to step through the walls!"

"Fair is Rose as the bright May-day;
Soft is Rose as the warm west-wind;
Sweet is Rose as the new-mown hay –
Rose is the queen of maiden-kind!"

Tom heard the lady's chorus, the so called "professional bridesmaids and villagers" in rehearsal for the opening of Act One. He was then aware as once more, George Grossmith, ready again to create another of Gilbert's main comedy characters in the same way that he had done in every previous opera since 'Sorcerer', was at the side of the stage awaiting his own entry as Robin Oakapple in the new opera.

"I know a youth who loves a little maid –
(Hey, but his face is a sight for to see!)
Silent is he, for he's modest and afraid –
(Hey, but he's timid as a youth can be!)"

As he heard the final chorus of "poor little man, poor little maid", Tom felt that there surely was to be another Gilbertian phrase that would be taken up on every street corner in just the same way as "what never, well hardly ever!" had been when 'HMS Pinafore' had been first produced nearly nine years before.

Into the new year,1887, 'The Mikado' continued to play right up until 19 January when the original production closed, still in triumph, at its 672nd performance. The whole company then had just three days to make the final preparations for the first night of 'Ruddygore' set for 22 January. In those three days, the gallery scene from Act Two was rehearsed over and over again and even during the afternoon of the opening night itself, the whole team were still making sure that all the scene changes would run smoothly. Both Tom and Fred Dean, more than at any opening night before, felt a greater sense of apprehension, almost to the point of sickness and nervous sensations in both of their stomachs.

Nellie and Florrie Parker had no similar qualms. All their military costumes had received the seal of approval from Sir Arthur Herbert and they both felt very pleased with the beautiful dresses for the bridesmaids and villagers. Nellie, though was well aware of Tom's concerns and made sure each time that she went down to the stage area with costumes to prepare for the coming performance, that she took a moment to give Tom an encouraging hug.

"Stop worrying and making yerself ill!" she said to Tom. "'ow long 'ave you been in the 'featre now and the music 'all before that?"

"It's been 12 years now that I've been mostly full time with Mr. D'Oyly Carte," Tom replied.

"Well, that's what I mean – you're a professional in all of this and yer knows what yer doing – away with yer and settle then!" Nellie commanded, although playfully as she slapped her husband on his back.

22 January 1887 – the first night of 'Ruddygore' at the Savoy and the usual sense of occasion both front of house and back stage where Tom and Nellie were both caught up in all the manic activity necessary prior to curtain up, an activity carried out with dedication and precision.

"Tom, have you 'ad a chance to peak through to the audience yet, anyone special in, do you know?" Nellie asked as she set some bridesmaids costumes down in the stage wings.

"They say, as always, that the theatre is packed with the usual cream of society – then to hear them singing up in the gallery you would think it was another performance of 'The Mikado', so much have they been going through all their favourite songs with relish!" Tom answered. "But one thing Mr. Dean did tell me, and that alarms me, is that Lord and Lady Randolph Churchill are in the stalls and were overheard to whisper that they considered the title of the new opera 'was not quite nice'".

"And that don't altogether surprise me," Nellie replied. "You know what I said the very first time when I 'eard Mr. Dean tell us the name – I 'fought he was swearing, d'you remember?"

"I do that, Nellie, but – well, let's see. I'm sure of one thing and that is our folk in the gallery won't be too bothered – in fact they most probably like the name," Tom said, with a wry smile as the pair continued their duties in readiness for the opening.

Any qualms and uneasiness were soon cast aside when Sir Arthur Sullivan once again made his first night entrance to the orchestra pit, welcomed by a rapturous applause that only subsided when he finally signalled the start of the overture. The audience listened intensively and at the end gave their roar of approval before settling down, full of expectation, for the First Act.

"I shipped, d'ye see, in a Revenue sloop,
And, off Cape Finistere,
A merchantman we see,
A Frenchman, going free,
So we made for the bold Mounseer,
D'ye see?

Jauntily, Durward Lely, as 'Richard Dauntless', sang his entry song with the closing line:

"We were hardy British tars
Who had pity on a poor Parley-voo,
D'ye see?
Who had pity on a poor Parley-voo!"

The final verse caused rapturous cheers, especially from the gallery, even more so when the singer finished by dancing the sailor's hornpipe, something that he had himself suggested to Mr. Gilbert who immediately agreed that the dance should be included to the routine.

For the remainder of the First Act, the response from the audience continued to be largely enthusiastic although if on occasions somewhat muted. Both Fred Dean and Tom felt that it was generally less well received than previous operas with there certainly being fewer demands for encores. Those fewer demands kept Tom and all the stage crew very much on their toes as when an expected encore didn't happen, they all had to make sure that the next singers were ready to immediately continue the performance. Come the interval, all the stage crew had only one thing on their mind – the coming, almost dreaded, gallery scene in Act Two and whether everything would go to their well-drilled and rehearsed plan.

"Good luck, Tom, I've got me fingers crossed," Nellie whispered both lovingly and with concern as she passed through the wings in the interval. Tom's mouth was so dry, his hands so sweaty, that he had no more ability other than to nod to his wife. What he did do, though, was to think to himself that his theatre career of 15 years could so easily be brought to an abrupt end that very evening!

As the moment came in Act Two, when the stage darkened and a discernable expectant hush descended upon the whole house as they wondered what possible scene may then be unfolding before them, Tom could barely summon up the courage to even look towards the stage. Both he and Fred Dean saw the members of the men's chorus, so very quietly, lining up behind the gallery screen in still and perfect order, remaining unseen by the audience and waiting for the picture frames to slide away. Fred then gave the cue for the scene change – the picture frames moved as silently as their meticulous rehearsal had intended, the chorus members stepped through the vacant frames and towards the stage to a discernable gasp from the audience. Fred and Tom breathed a sigh of relief. "Now, Tom, all we have to do is to get it all to happen in reverse, only then can we relax!" The stage manager spoke softly but Tom was still too apprehensive, still full of foreboding, to make any reply.

Then Richard Temple, by then a worthy veteran of many Gilbert and Sullivan new productions, this time playing the Twenty-First Baronet – Sir Roderick Murgatroyd – himself stepped through the picture frame and with a mighty swing of his cloak captivated the audience with his opening song;

"When the night wind howls in the chimney cowls, and the bat in the moonlight flies,

And inky clouds, like funeral shrouds, sail over the midnight skies

Then this is the spectres' holiday – then is the ghosts' high noon!"

The chorus reply of:

"Ha! Ha!
Then is the ghosts' high noon!"

came with such verve and gusto that the whole theatre seemed to shake, such a crescendo of sound that Tom feared the stage set would collapse. All was well! For a moment of brief relaxation, he almost forgot that the scene with the chorus stepping back into the picture frames was then about to happen. Again, though, all went to order and for the very first time during the evening, Fred Dean and Tom felt that they could safely relax.

Even though Fred and Tom felt better, there was nevertheless a sense that within the auditorium, the audience were somehow becoming a little restless, even disinterested in what was going on before them on the stage. "It's not quite right, Tom!" Fred Dean observed quietly, "it's as if they've lost interest, that the performance may be dragging a bit. It's certainly not the same atmosphere as what we are used to!" a statement to which Tom could only agree.

At curtain fall, there were cheers and clapping enough within the theatre but as Sir Arthur and Mr. Gilbert came on to take their customary bow, some from the gallery were heard to shout "take it away – give us back The Mikado!" Whatever Tom may have thought about the galleryites' acceptance of the name didn't then seem to reach as far as their appreciation of the whole opera!

There was no doubt amongst the company that the night had been the least successful of any so far and it was of little surprise when Fred Dean announced that Sir Arthur and Mr. Gilbert were to meet immediately the next day for an inquest about the new opera. With that news ringing in their ears, the whole company experienced a most subdued and dispirited end to the first night. Tom and Nellie felt especially downcast, Tom because of all the hard work that had gone into Act Two and during which, despite all their earlier fears, the scene change had gone off like clockwork; and Nellie, because she felt that there had been far too little appreciative comment about the British Regimental uniforms, or the beautiful bridesmaids dresses that both she and Miss Parker had painstakingly prepared and for which they felt so justifiably proud. Although they had what was then becoming the traditional after the performance first night cab ride home with their bosses, for once none felt very much like talking. Tom frowned and scratched his eyes just as soon after that he had seen Fred Dean do the same thing. Nellie and Florrie Parker fiddled with the buttons on their coats, otherwise only the sounds from the passing street scene interrupted the silence. It was to be only their beds at their respective homes which finally were able to offer them sole safe refuge that night.

The meeting with the composer and writer immediately brought about some remodelling of Act Two where it was considered, as Fred Dean had observed, that the end had dragged somewhat. "More work for us on stage, Tom, but at least the gallery scene remains as is!" Fred Dean declared. The major change was that the opera title was to become 'Ruddigore' in response to the bad feeling about the spelling of the original name. "Told you!" Nellie said to Tom. Mr. Gilbert, though, thought that the opera should be re-titled 'Kensington Gore; or not so good as The Mikado'!

Critical reaction, too, was mixed. Many thought that the solemnity of the ghostly music in Act Two was too much of a contrast to the "bright and cheery demeanour of the First Act". Another said "The new opera has a number of perceived musical gems and the aria 'Ghosts high noon' was worthy of grand opera at its best." "There you are, Tom," Fred Dean observed, "positive mentioning of our gallery scene, and another paper has paid high regard to our stage setting!" Naturally, Tom was very pleased to hear the news too although he would have been more delighted if there had been more critical approval about the costumes that he could have rushed to tell Nellie about, to give her one of her charming embarrassed thrills.

Despite the whole company's initial disappointments following the less than successful first night, with it's new and more acceptable name, 'Ruddigore', the opera did settle down with both full nightly audiences plus reasonable forward bookings. There was no doubting that the opera was more controversial than anything before, despite the previous operas often making highly pointed comments about the English establishment. Now, there always seemed to be some negative comment that came to the company's ears. One such article came from the Paris 'Figaro' which Fred Dean read one morning to the assembled company. "I suppose it was to be expected, but what this French newspaper is saying about our new piece is that Richard Dauntless' 'Parlez-voo' song is an insult to the French navy and the French nation. Ah well, so be it, I suppose," Fred reflected.

A little later, the stage manager once again called the company together. "You all need a smile, what with all this unaccustomed less than good issues we've had to deal with the new opera, so I thought you may like to hear this little story that Mr. Gilbert told me – he said I could tell you! It goes something like this:

"Friend to Mr. Gilbert. 'How is Bloodygore going on?'

Mr. Gilbert, well he replies. 'It isn't Bloodygore, it's Ruddigore'.

Then the friend says. 'Oh, it's the same thing'.

And Mr Gilbert answers. 'Is it? Then I suppose you'll take it if I say I admire your ruddy countenance, I mean I like your bloody cheek!' I think I got it right!" Fred concluded. By then he was laughing and the assembled company took their cue and responded likewise, as they returned to their work.

The gallery scene continued to work smoothly at each following performance without mishap although Tom felt very apprehensive at what might happen when the production went on tour. Then there would be an almost different theatre each week, most with far less proper facilities than those found at The Savoy.

"Well, that ain't your problem, is it Tom?" Nellie observed, "your job is 'ere in London and your not-a-going to get gadding

161

about the country, at least not without me, just to see 'ow your pictures are doing up there on them gallery walls!" Tom smiled to his wife and he knew he agreed with her comments, liking both being always with Nellie and his London life, at the very centre of the productions, too much. He realised that he didn't want to get himself involved with any of the touring companies other than to make the initial preparations.

**   *   *   ***

Rupert liked 'Ruddigore' – but then he liked every Gilbert and Sullivan opera so perhaps his critique was not too important. Perhaps, what was more valid was the fact that during the excerpts given on the special performance that evening in February 1982 at the Adelphi Theatre, he did, for once, not whisper to his grandmother, "this is my favourite!"

He was aware through all his years of patronising the D'Oyly Carte Opera Company's performances that the opera wasn't ever performed so often as most of the other more popular ones. Once he had read that in 1937, 50 years after the opera's original production, the 'Manchester Guardian' had written that they thought it "incomprehensible that Ruddigore should ever have been considered less attractive than the other comic operas in the Savoy series. The libretto gives us Gilbert at his wittiest and in the music we hear Sullivan not only in his most tuneful vein, but also as master of more subtle rhythms then he commands elsewhere."

Rupert's thoughts at the moment when the curtain came down after the last piece from 'Ruddigore' was that the evening was already more than half over, more nearly two-thirds. The words of 'Robin Oakapple' in 'Ruddigore', "My eyes are fully open to my awful situation", seemed both apt and confusing to Rupert. They reflected very much on the state of affairs affecting the D'Oyly Carte Opera Company, perhaps the whole world of Gilbert and Sullivan. Rupert knew that only too well. But he was confused because he still felt a 'John Wellington Wells' like character would somehow come before them on the stage to perform a miracle. The mixed reactions gave him an even more anxious feeling in the pit of his stomach, so much so that he found himself clapping almost robot-like and not so really taking in what was happening around him. Alice, his grandmother, noticed his rather distant look and said softly: "There's plenty more to come – it's not over yet!"

"I hope you're right, Nan," Rupert whispered

"Of course," Alice replied, more with a sense of trying to cheer her up grandson rather than with any real conviction. "You'll see – we've just seen pieces from 'Ruddigore' and as the words of the song go, 'it doesn't matter, matter, matter'!"

"Oh, but Nan, it does matter, it matters very much indeed," Rupert replied indignantly.

"Oh, I know that, love, I was only trying to cheer you up," Alice replied, realising that there was no point to further the conversation. She was very pleased to see that the spotlights were once again trained on the curtain and that the performance was about to continue. "What's next, love?" she asked.

Chapter 13
"Gallant pikemen, valiant sworders!"

On a warm late summers day in September 1887, Tom and Nellie, with their fellow D'Oyly Carte Company colleagues, were enjoying what had become a grand tradition for the whole company – be it from the young call boy, not long out of school, or one of the long serving company principal singers like Mr. George Grossmith – the summer river picnic. It was a special highlight of their year that Tom and Nellie especially looked forward to, a relaxing day and for them a rare day not to be spent at The Savoy – not that they didn't enjoy their work, far from it, but a day in the fresh air with their colleagues, really a close family for them, was something to be savoured and enjoyed.

Just as for anytime but even more so on that special day, Tom felt immensely proud of Nellie, ever delighted that she was by his side. "May I say, my love, you look yourself an absolute picture," he declared, acknowledging the exquisite floral summer hat adorned with flowers that she was wearing, together with a beautiful creamy frock coat and elegant, long matching skirt. As always for Nellie, in pride of place, at the neck of her frilly blouse, peaking out at the top of her coat, was the treasured broach that Tom had bought for her on that so important night for both of them when she had been to The Savoy for the first time ever, by then nearly six years before, to see 'Patience'. What a significant night it had turned out to be for their small family.

It was the night that had forever changed their lives, all for the better. First, the new work for Nellie in the theatre, meaning they could always be together each and every day and lastly for them both to have the chance of a better home with the move to the more fashionable suburb of Peckham, away from the grime of Shoreditch.

Tom always joked that for Nellie, the broach was nothing less than the magic teapot from 'Sorcerer', capable of doing so many things whenever she rubbed it. Not only did Nellie adore the broach, she equally realised the significance it had played in both of their lives and for that she would be for always grateful. With her floral parasol shading her eyes from the sun, she looked up towards Tom with a very happy and contented smile. "And you don't look so bad yerself, either, in yer striped blazer and boater!" she said, a remark which caused Tom enormous self-conscious embarrassment.

"Well, love, I couldn't ask for a better clothes maker," Tom quickly answered in an attempt to hide his blushes. "It's down to you, Miss Parker and the team to make sure we all look good for the day – as always, you've done us proud!"

"We sail the ocean blue,
And our saucy ship's a beauty!"

Tom and Nellie looked across the river as one of the other three river steamers, also full of company members, drew close to them, everybody singing happily the opening chorus from 'Pinafore'. Not to be outdone, all in their own boat immediately sung in reply:

"Hail, men-o'-war's men – safeguards of your nation",

to the great hilarity of all aboard. Together, all the boats in unison, sang the rousing chorus of 'That he is an Englishman', the beautiful sounds of all their voices carrying across the Thames towards the woods at Cliveden which they were just approaching. Very soon, on shore, other people who were enjoying their own day by the river, recognised the approaching vessels as carrying no less than Mr. D'Oyly Carte's Opera Company and spontaneous cheers broke out from the spectators along the river banks. When onlookers next recognised no less than Sir Arthur Sullivan in one boat, Mr. Gilbert in the next and Mr. D'Oyly Carte in the third, the reception became even more enthusiastic and boisterous. The whole company responded by first waving to the onlookers and then giving a further impromptu chorus from another of the operas, this time 'Iolanthe':

"Tripping hither, tripping thither,
Nobody knows why or wither;
But you've summoned us, and so,
Enter all the little fairies
To their usual tripping measure!
To oblige you all our care is –
Tell us, pray, what is your pleasure!"

"Nellie, that was beautiful, you singing there," Tom declared. "When you get fed up with dressmaking then I'm sure the chorus will be waiting for you!" Silently, Tom thought how his wife had by then so easily picked up so many of the tunes and songs from the operas in complete contrast to what she had said those years before.

"Get orf with yer!" Nellie replied, giving a friendly shove to Tom who almost lost his footing on the deck if he had not immediately been able to grab the side rail. "Don't yer let Miss Parker be 'earing you say any of that 'cause she'll be looking for someone else to assist her!"

By then, all three steamers had come together by the riverbank to allow all to scramble ashore and head to the shade of the woods to begin their picnic – salmon, lobster, salads, pigeon pies – all catered for by Mr. D'Oyly Carte. To accompany the meal, there could be only one song for the whole company to sing – from 'Princess Ida':

"Merrily ring the luncheon bell!
Here in meadow of asphodel,
Feast we body and mind as well,
So merrily ring the luncheon bell!"

The yearly picnic day was always the occasion on which all the D'Oyly Carte Company could reflect upon their very obvious successes with Gilbert and Sullivan operas, themselves nothing less than a new musical form of a series of homespun English comic operas. The company's delight, too, reflected what was in effect the high summer of the Victorian era, especially so in the year of Queen Victoria's Golden Jubilee. The feeling of well-being was not just reflected within Tom and Nellie, or even the whole company, but also in the country at large.

As the sun finally began to set, giving way to a brilliant moonlit sky filled with a galaxy of stars, almost symbolically like the three riverboats themselves with their precious passengers, they sailed for home, the wicker picnic baskets all empty. The whole company were tired but happy from their refreshing day. Not too tired, though, for another song from 'Pinafore':

"Fair moon, to thee I sing,
Bright regent of the heavens,
Say, why is everything
Either at sixes or at sevens?"

Tom laughed to Nellie and said "That's the first time I've heard that sung as a chorus, it's usually just for Captain Corcoran to sing as a solo".

"All right, clever!" Nellie replied, "just 'cause I wasn't even in the company for 'Pinafore' don't means that yer 'ave to show off!"

"Sorry, love . . . .," Tom began to reply as Nellie immediately interrupted him.

"Yer silly old fing, I was just pulling yer leg!" she declared to which they both collapsed in laughter.

"Your Nellie and my Tom seem to be enjoying themselves!" Fred Dean said to Florrie Parker who responded with a happy smile herself. Before they had a chance for any further conversation, Rutland Barrington, himself another leading singer from the company, called all together and began to sing from 'Mikado', in his much cherished role of 'Pooh-Bah'.

"I am so proud
If I allowed,
My family pride
To be my guide"

He was then joined with the whole company singing in chorus. As the three boats made their way along the river, the music and singing still happily continuing, further large groups of onlookers stood at the different locks that the boats passed through. There they cheered the impromptu concerts being performed by the company from the Savoy Theatre, like a private, albeit mighty, front parlour around the piano sing-a-long that so many people themselves enjoyed

The amiable and happy tone of the day displayed that this time there were few concerns felt by any of the company that no new opera was so far being prepared. It also showed that despite their collective earlier misgivings at the end of the first night of 'Ruddigore', the opera was still continuing to perform at the Savoy to more than adequate houses, although nobody expected it to be in anyway as long a run as 'Mikado'. Even so, nobody doubted that in time there would be another new opera but if that proved not to be the case, all realised that there had by then already been nine full length and successful operas, especially 'The Mikado' which was then still creating a world mania. As Tom said to Nellie, there was doubtless enough potential for revivals to keep everybody busy, not just at the Savoy but in British and overseas tours equally as well.

"I am now over 40, you're just a year away from that yourself, so I don't think either of us have got much to worry about for our working lives," he said, perhaps a little ungallantly to his wife as they travelled home from the theatre one evening.

Nellie thought for a moment, decided to ignore the reference to her approaching 40th birthday the next year, and simply replied "I ain't worried, Tom, not this time".

At the turn of the year, into 1888, it was finally announced that 'Ruddigore' was to close, after a run of 288 performances, almost only a third of 'Mikado'. The opera was to be replaced by a revival of 'HMS Pinafore'.

"There you are, love, you said on the picnic last year that you weren't at the theatre for the original 'Pinafore' so here's your chance now!" Tom declared to his wife. "Now you can set your hands to all the navy uniforms and more lovely dresses for 'Sir Joseph Porter's sisters, cousins and aunts'!"

"I shall look forward to that!" Nellie replied with a wide smile. "It'll be nice for me to set to work on all the operas before 'Iolanthe'. I've talked about 'em all with Miss Parker and I would love to do it."

"Well, don't get too set on those tasks because I somehow think there will be a completely new opera before too long – Sir Arthur and Mr. Gilbert will see to that," Tom affirmed.

Tom felt surprised at just how busy they all were with their work for the revival of 'HMS Pinafore'. "It's just like we are rehearsing for a completely new opera all over again," he declared to Fred Dean as they both worked on the set as the singers went through their parts before them.

"Well you know how it is," the stage manager replied, "Mr. Gilbert is always a thorough professional and dedicated director in all that he produces and it isn't any different with a revival. Anyway, Tom, as hard to believe as it is, do you know that it's now 10 years since the very first production of 'Pinafore' – for many of the younger members of the company it is like a new piece altogether."

"That's true, Mr. Dean," Tom replied, "so much 'as happened that I almost have forgotten that myself."

"Of course you have, Tom, you, like me, are so much part and parcel of the furnishings of this place!" Fred Dean answered with a smile, before he next added in a more serious vein. "One thing I have noticed, though, is that Sir Arthur and Mr. Gilbert are not talking much to each other, they haven't hardly exchanged any words during the whole time we've been rehearsing."

"I have noticed that, Mr. Dean, but then, it's sometimes like that, isn't it?" Tom reasoned.

"Yes, I suppose so, but we'll have to see. Anyway, we've more than enough to do here without any of that to worry about!"

Whilst the atmosphere amongst the company at the Savoy was confident, many music critics were beginning to voice their concerns that perhaps there were to be no more new Gilbert and Sullivan operas. One day, Fred Dean took the opportunity, when the whole company were gathered on stage, Florrie Parker and Nellie attending to costumes there as well, to talk to everybody.

"Just as we've got a moment, I won't keep you too long," Fred began. "I thought you may like to hear this article from the 'Times' – I'll read a piece to you." Fred cleared his throat, almost as theatrically as many of the assembled singers would do themselves. "Here it is then. 'The middle classes and even the working classes which had no opportunity of appreciating either art or music fifty years ago, cannot now complain that these wholesome enjoyments are monopolised by fashionable aristocracy. W.S. Gilbert and Sir Arthur Sullivan have been notably connected with the spreading of these wholesome enjoyments.' There, what more could we ask, what more for an appreciation of what we, everyone of us, has so far achieved in our work with these English comic operas."

A chorus of "hear, hear" and "bravo" rang around the stage. Tom put his arms around Nellie, some tears welling up in both their eyes at the evident acknowledgement of all their work that Fred had read to them. As they once more dispersed to carry on with their various activities, Tom said to Nellie "and all that Mr. Dean has said is exactly what we have always said, and felt amongst ourselves!"

"What exactly do yer mean?" Nellie asked.

"Well, you know, that each night when we peek through to the audience, we see the society people in the stalls and circle, then folk like us, up there in the gallery," Tom declared, his eyes looking and his hands pointing to the very top of the then silent auditorium. "It's everybody, no matter from what background, all like the operas and that's what makes it all so special, a kind of social change, no less. Another thing, it's special not only for now, but who knows, perhaps for years to come!" The mere thought sent a shiver down his back, a sensation reciprocated and felt by his wife.

"Oh, that makes me feel kind of strange, that 'ere we are the two of us, both doing somefink – like what did you say?"

"A social change, no less," Tom re-affirmed to his wife.

"If you says so, right!" Nellie replied. "But whatever, it makes yer fink too if, as you says yerself, that may be 'ere around for some time in the future too!"

"Well, who knows," Tom sighed.

And of course he didn't know, nor did anybody that day at the theatre. They couldn't possibly have known that all their work which they had themselves begun on the first productions was something that would continue to be performed by the very same company in a reflective traditional way, dedicated to Mr. Gilbert's original stage directions and Sir Arthur's musical notes, then for another 92 years forward. Neither did they know that someone born in that very year, at Tottenham in North London, Alice Harding, had enjoyed all of the Gilbert and Sullivan operas and, like many, many thousands of others, had seen them all performed in 20th Century years at the very same theatre, even if not on the same stage, upon which they were then standing. It was impossible that they could foresee that Alice Harding was herself still enjoying a D'Oyly Carte performance 92 years later, just across the Strand from where they were. Perhaps they would not have believed that in those forward 20th Century years, new devotees to the operas, like Rupert Moore, would be attracted to the works, every bit as enthusiastically as their own first night audiences. If all that was too much to envisage, then the fact that the company for which they all worked, the D'Oyly Carte Opera Company, would continue as virtual custodians of the works, to perform not only to achieve their own centenary but to add a further seven years as well.

No, such vision wasn't possible for them or anybody, that day on the stage as they dispersed from Fred Dean's announcement. Had such vision been possible, then the shivers that both Tom and Nellie felt down their backs would doubtless have been even more sensational.

Soon it became known in the theatre that Mr. Gilbert had once again submitted an idea of his becoming infamous magic lozenge plot but was very promptly dismissed by Sir Arthur. That news didn't surprise the company but, as Fred Dean said,"At least it shows once again the pair are giving some consideration to a new opera, even if they don't agree on the plot!"

171

Once more, as had happened when a Japanese sword had fallen from the wall in Mr. Gilbert's study to be the cue for 'Mikado', again a happening then unknown to those at the Savoy was occurring a few miles away – on a railway station. There, Mr. Gilbert saw an advertisement for the Tower Furnishing Company, depicting the Tower of London. Later, Mr. Gilbert told Fred Dean that he thought that a beefeater would make a good picturesque central figure for another opera and that a wonderful title would be 'The Tower of London'. The writer's words soon became common knowledge around the company as the stage manager was ever prone to pass on, in a well meant and nicest possible way, any tips or gossip he had heard!

Later, further news was received at the theatre that Mr. Gilbert had decided to set the new opera in Tudor times and as a romantic and dramatic piece – "no topsy-turveydom nor fairies". "Sir Arthur will be pleased to hear about that!" Fred Dean commented to Tom who smiled at the thought. The news that a new opera was being written caused excitement generally, especially from some of the press who had doubted there would ever be another work.

"Hey, Tom, look what it says here, in the 'Sporting Times' no less," Fred declared, holding up the paper as Tom came across the stage to where he was standing. "Here it says 'a real comic opera, dealing with neither topsy-turveydom nor fairies' – that was how Mr. Gilbert put it, wasn't it?" Tom nodded. "It goes on: 'A genuine dramatic story would be a greater novelty and a more splendid success than anything we are at all likely to see during the present dramatic season.' There – doesn't that sound good, what say you, Tom my lad!"

"Certainly, Mr. Dean, yes," Tom replied, inwardly delighted at the prospect of a new opera soon to be able to work upon.

In his time honoured way, within moments Tom was upstairs in the wardrobe room, delivering the news to Nellie and an equally attentive Florrie Parker.

"I quite fancy meself making beefeater costumes," Nellie exclaimed, to which the wardrobe mistress nodded her agreement, adding "the gentlemen of the chorus will look most 'andsome!" Tom purposefully didn't respond to her remark.

Even in the early days of the new opera's preparation, it soon became apparent that the new piece would be a much grander Gilbert and Sullivan opera, quite unlike anything that had preceded it. For the first time, Mr. Gilbert was not tilting at any British institution, or, as Fred Dean put it, "no 'little-lists' this time!" They then heard that one of the main characters, 'Jack Point', was to be a strolling jester who would loose the sweetheart of his life, 'Elsie Maynard' to one 'Colonel Fairfax' who was himself imprisoned in the Tower of London.

"Don't that sound awfully sad," Nellie said to Tom, when she heard, whilst dabbing her eye with her handkerchief. "Now you've told me that, I fink that I'll be crying all the time as I makes the costumes!"

"You, silly," Tom responded, "it's only a story and you mustn't get yourself in a state!"

"Ah, away with yer Tom Dobbs, don't yer being so bloomin' 'eartless. I fink it sounds an 'eart warming story and I'm sure it will be very loverly. Don't you know 'ow it all ends?" Tom shook his head. "Well, yer better 'urry up and jolly well find out now that you've only told me 'arf the story – I won't sleep a wink until I founds out!" Nellie demanded.

Unfortunately for Nellie it was to be sometime before any further details about the new opera became known to any of the company as both writer and composer continued to slowly finish the work. Instead, after the revival of 'Pinafore', further revivals of 'Pirates of Penzance', yet another of the earlier operas new to Nellie, and the immensely popular 'Mikado' were performed at the Savoy. It was enough to keep the company very busy indeed, so much so that Nellie almost forgot that she was awaiting news of how the storyline of the new opera would end. Further delays to the new piece occurred when Sir Arthur suffered a return of ill health and decided that he would go off to Monte Carlo for recuperation.

Without an immediate prospect of the new opera, further concerns, especially for the theatre manager, Richard D'Oyly Carte, came with the news that a musical play entitled 'Dorothy', written by Alfred Cellier, had opened at the Gaiety Theatre.

"Well I never!" Fred Dean declared to Tom, "if that isn't a coincidence. You remember the Gaiety Theatre, don't you Tom?"

"Course I do, Mr. Dean, way back in 1871 – it was where I first came to you to begin work on the very first Gilbert and Sullivan piece, 'Thespis'," Tom replied. "What do they say about the 'Dorothy'?"

"Well, quite good I believe. But it's very obviously exploiting the very successful field of our own operas here at the Savoy," Fred Dean answered. "You can be sure of one thing – Mr. D'Oyly Carte will now, more than ever, be pressing for the new opera to get finished as soon as possible. He won't want another theatre getting ahead and producing similar styles as us here!"

The news from the Gaiety did much to ensure that Mr. Gilbert and Sir Arthur diligently got on with completing their new opera. Fred told Tom that Mr. Gilbert was himself walking around the Tower of London day after day to fully absorb the atmosphere.

"The screw may twist and the rack may turn,
And men may bleed and men may burn,
O'er London town and its golden hoard
I keep my silent watch and ward!"

Fred Dean read from Act One and realised what Mr. Gilbert had told him. "Mr. Gilbert has written truly in the spirit of the Tudor poets, quite unlike any of the words we've heard in any of the previous operas," he told Tom, who nodded his agreement.

"Mr. Dean, do you know how it all ends yet?" Tom asked anxiously, realising that Nellie would want to know.

"As a matter of fact, I think I do," Fred Dean answered. "It seems that at the end, Jack Point, the jester, well he falls insensible at the feet of his girl, Elsie, who has by then married Colonel Fairfax. I don't think yet whether Mr. Gilbert has decided if it is to be just a swoon or even that the jester dies from a broken heart."

"I can hardly believe that, Mr. Dean," Tom declared, "before this, all the operas have been cheerful and finished on a very happy ending."

"Well, this is supposed to be different – I even understand that the opening of Act One is with a solo as opposed to the usual rousing chorus. We'll soon find out once the rehearsals get underway," Fred advised. "One other thing is certainly different though, Tom!" Tom looked quizzical as the stage manager continued. "This time we're to have the same scene – Tower Green itself - for both the two Acts. At least for us we only need to bother about a bit of tidying up during the interval instead of the usual frantic scene changes – time for a mug of tea!"

Tom laughed. "It'll be an easier opera to take on tour," he suggested.

"You're right there, Tom," Fred replied. "But, do you know, it all sounds so very different from anything before, far more serious, that I just wonder how the devoted audiences will take to it – but, like I said earlier, we'll just have to see."

At least, after waiting for so long, Tom had at last the news to tell Nellie about the ending of the new opera.

"There yer are, Tom," Nellie cried, again dabbing her eye and blowing her nose, "I fought it would be very sad and I was right!" She thought more for a moment and continued, more composed, even smiling. "You would 'ave fought that Mr. Gilbert would 'ave written a more comical piece for me 40th birfday year!"

"Away with you, Nellie!" Tom laughed. "You really had me taken in for a moment."

"No, I do find it sad Tom, that I really do and I fink 'cause of that it will be appreciated by many in our audiences, all what like a more human story."

"I was wondering," Tom began, although he should have said more correctly, 'Mr Dean was wondering', "that because it sounds far more serious than any of the other operas, whether our usual audience will like it so much."

"Well, that ain't for worrying here and now – time will tell yer!" Nellie replied.

It wasn't just Tom, Nellie, or Fred Dean that were beginning to become worried about the more serious tone of the new opera as rehearsal work became more advanced. Even Mr. Gilbert himself occasionally felt some unease and the fact that he was suffering from gout at the same time hardly helped his feelings. The original title of 'Tower of London' then became instead 'The Tower Warden' only then to be changed yet again to 'The Beefeater'. Mr. Gilbert advised Sir Arthur and the whole assembled company: "I am more than convinced that this should be the name for the new piece. It is a good, sturdy, solid name, conjuring up picturesque associations."

From Act One, all heard in rehearsal the trio:

"Temptation, oh, temptation,
Were we, I pray, intended,
To shun, whate'er our station,
Your fascination splendid;"

Then from Act Two, Colonel Fairfax himself with three other principals singing:

"Strange adventure! Maiden wedded
To a groom she's never seen –
Never, never, never seen!
Groom about to be beheaded,
In an hour on Tower Green!"

Then, Jack Point:

"When a jester
Is outwitted,
Feelings fester
Heart is lead!
Food for fishes,
Only fitted,
Jester wishes
He was dead."

Then it wasn't just Nellie alone with tears in their eyes. The whole company stood, head bowed, listening intently to all that was being rehearsed. Many were very obviously moved and it came as no surprise when they heard that Sir Arthur was very pleased that the new piece had all of the human elements that he had long craved for in their works. It was also very evident that the writer and composer had captured the Tudor spirit of the piece both in their words and music, "Gilbert's more severe words being matched by the beauty and harmony of Sir Arthur Sullivan's music". Anyway, that was what Fred Dean told Tom and he was perfectly happy, as ever, to accept what his stage manager told him as being right!

"What did I tell 'yer Tom!, Nellie exclaimed, "there's plenty of folk that are wanting a 'uman story, somefink very touching, kind of 'eart warming really even if the end is sad – but that's life ain't it?." This time it was Tom who had to reply that everyone would have to wait and see.

Yet again there was a change to the new opera's name whilst rehearsals were in the final stages. Whilst it had happened with 'Iolanthe' for special reasons to avoid any possible copying of the work, with the new opera so many changes only added to the singers' and theatrical people's long felt superstitions that the new work was somehow doomed even before the first night. Nellie's words "I don't 'old with any of that kind of talk!" went a long way to reassure Tom, though. "In any case," Nellie added, "I fink that the title, 'Yeomen of the Guard', is very good and proper!"

Tom noticed that George Grossmith, who was to play the part of the jester, 'Jack Point' and who would once more be inaugurating a major role in a Gilbert and Sullivan opera, was going through his lines at the side of the stage but his opening song was still without music. "What's that about, Mr. Dean," he asked.

"Do you know what, Tom, Sir Arthur has told Mr. Gilbert that he is stumped over the music for that particular song," Fred Dean answered. "Well, Sir Arthur wrote to him because, apparently, Mr. Gilbert had often said that he has an old tune in his head when he's writing the lyrics. And that was just how it was this time too. Mr. Gilbert has just told Sir Arthur that he had in mind an old Cornish carol – 'Come and I will sing to you' – now, I've been told, he's even hummed the shanty to Sir Arthur who's now about to finish the music for the song."

Within a couple of days, George Grossmith was able to complete his rehearsal properly once the music was finally ready. The accompanist at the theatre rehearsal was a young man, new to the Savoy company – Henry Wood.

"I have a song to sing, O!

It is sung to the moon
By a love-lorn loon,
Who fled from the mocking throng, O!"

The reprise of the song, coming right at the very end of the opera, everybody knew would be the very heart-rending and extremely sad finale. Naturally all singers were on stage, but the rest of the company, Tom with his arms around Nellie, Fred Dean standing beside Florrie Parker, were all quietly standing in the wings, many with their heads bowed, some, Nellie and Florrie included, with handkerchiefs at the ready:

"It is the song of a merryman, moping mum,
Whose soul was sad, and whose glance was glum,
Who sipped no sup, and who craved no crumb,
As he sighed for the love of a ladye!"

The jester fell to the stage, insensible, at the end of the song, the stage directions still left open as to whether the jester had died or collapsed through sadness.

The ladies of the company gathered in the wings let out an audible and collective gasp, Nellie probably the loudest although she had known from Tom what to expect. Tom squeezed his wife lovingly as she turned to him, saying "I don't think I have ever seen anything so moving, so beautifully done," she said tearfully. "And if that's 'ow it's going to be on the night, then methinks we will have another enormous success at the Savoy!"

"I hope that you are right," answered Tom who still felt grave doubts that the faithful audiences would take to the more serious piece, or, more likely, whether he himself could take to it. Would it be too much like grand opera for the gallerites? Equally, would the society people of the stalls perhaps be unwilling for a Gilbert and Sullivan opera that wasn't entirely of fun and rousing choruses. What if the audience were unsure about the ending, whether the jester had died? A death in a Gilbert and Sullivan opera! No, Tom was sure that wasn't possible and probably would not be accepted by many in the audience. Then, he realised that even though at the very last minute one song had been cut out, the remaining first four songs of the new opera were in the range of tearful, serious and sentimental, far removed from what audiences had so far come to expect. Time will tell, Tom sighed and thought to himself as he once again busied himself with some props at the side of the stage.

In his further thoughts, though, as he worked, Tom was sure of one thing – once again, Nellie and Florrie Parker had created an incredible range of beautiful stage costumes. The chorus of Yeomen of the Guard in Beefeater dress looked spectacular and, as always, were a meticulously drilled team upon the stage, very worthy of attending the Ceremony of the Keys anytime, he further concluded with a very satisfying and contented smile. Then the spirit of Tudor England that had been captured in the dresses and clothes for all the citizens – again Tom felt immensely proud of his Nellie. Yes! Whatever his misgivings, then all of this would make sure that the audiences would take the new opera to their hearts!

But the misgivings were not so easily dismissed as that, as Tom discerned from the thoughts and mumblings from very many of his colleagues that he heard over the following few days. Many felt as ill at ease as Tom did during the last couple of rehearsals prior to the opening night and for very similar reasons. He even noticed that Mr. Gilbert himself was very edgy and Fred Dean told him that might be because he was suffering from gout – although the stage manager added, more aptly, "but I know that he is worried about the serious tone of the opera and that he feels he may have over done the tragic element".

During this time, as a very welcome antidote to his qualms, he was especially glad to listen to Nellie who remained very relaxed and as calm about the new opera as he felt nervous.

"I told, yer and as it 'appens, I believe it is what many will fink, this new piece is kind of human, so very beautiful words when you really listen to 'em, words with real meaning and depth," Nellie declared. "I don't know much about music meself, but the melodies what I 'ear from this opera are all so very 'armonious, so really beautiful. No, Tom, I says it again, it's a piece with meaning, real depth and I fink it will be well received, all the more because of that!"

The high drama of a first night felt by all in the company was even more charged on 3 October 1888 as they prepared for the curtain to rise on 'Yeomen of the Guard'. As Tom and Fred Dean made the final stage preparations, the singer Jessie Bond, herself having already been a principal in the company for 10 years since first appearing in 'HMS Pinafore', who was playing the character Phoebe, came to sit in her position on the stage. Fred nudged Tom and said, quietly, "this time, it's very difficult for Miss Bond, to be alone on the stage when the curtain goes up and that's when the audience are all expecting a rousing opening chorus – we've never had a solo singer for the very beginning ever before – so much depends on her and she must be feeling it!"

"That's exactly what I've been thinking, too," Tom replied.

And it wasn't just Fred Dean and Tom voicing similar feelings. Within moments they were soon joined on stage by Mr. Gilbert, himself very obviously in an equally nervous state. "Is everything alright?" they heard him ask Miss Bond, time and time again, the last time even after Sir Arthur had entered the orchestra pit, to the usual thunderous applause, and the overture had begun beyond the still closed curtain – a curtain still protecting the performers from the ordeals of a first night. As Mr. Gilbert again asked the question, the pair at the side of the stage heard Miss Bond reply "Please go Mr. Gilbert, please go!" Mr. Gilbert did as he was requested but not before kissing Miss Bond, again wishing her well. Tom and Fred Dean exchanged glances and next saw Mr. Gilbert leave the theatre, not to return until he knew the performance would be over. In fact, as he later told Fred Dean, he had spent his evening at the Drury Lane Theatre seeing a production called 'The Armada'.

"When maiden loves, she sits and sighs,
She wanders to and fro;
Unbidden tear-drops fill her eyes,
And to all questions she replies
With a sad 'heigho!'"

And so to conclude the second and last verse of the solo and opening song:

"'Tis but a foolish sigh – 'Ah me!'
Born but to droop and die – 'Ah me!'
Yet all the sense
Of eloquence
Lies hidden in a maid's 'Ah me!'"

As the song finished, the audience clapped and shouted their appreciation. Tom looked towards Fred Dean and smiled; Nellie was also by then in the wings preparing to inspect the chorus' costumes before they made their own entry. She smiled and winked a kind of "told you so" to Tom who reciprocated by blowing a kiss towards his wife. In a far lighter mood because of the initial response, he then busied himself with his stage duties, all carried out to ongoing cheers and enthusiastic applause from the auditorium after every song, every piece of action and stage business. "What did I tell you?" he finally said to his wife when he caught up with her during the interval, "it's all going very well indeed – there was never any need to worry!" "Ouch," he concluded, responding to Nellie giving him a friendly kick in the ankle!

Once Mr. Gilbert returned to the theatre in time for final curtain, despite the original misgivings of which there had been many in the company, Tom included, there was no doubt whatsoever that the new opera had been enthusiastically received. Tom was very relieved to hear once again the cheering from all parts of the theatre – from the society people in the stalls up to what Tom and Nellie considered to be "their own folk" in the gallery - as the writer joined Sir Arthur on stage and took several curtain calls, although there could have been even more had the pair not decided to take their leave of the stage.

Everyone's initial thrills at the Savoy only went to be further confirmed in the following days as press reaction followed, all very agreeably positive. Fred Dean told the company that "the notices have been very gratifying". He then held up a copy of 'The Theatre' and said: "I'll just read this one line from the review – they say – 'consider the music to be of a higher form than hitherto'. So, ladies and gentlemen, I would suggest that says it all and we can now relax and prepare ourselves for what I hope, am sure, will be a good run for 'Yeomen'."

And that was precisely what happened. Again, Tom, Nellie, indeed, the whole company, settled down early in 1889 to the regular pattern of an established new opera at the Savoy and to the preparation of touring productions. All was very well within the world of Gilbert and Sullivan.

* * * *

"You know, Nan, that really has got to be my favourite," Rupert declared as he, along with the whole overwhelmed house, clapped vigorously at the end of the selections of songs and music from 'Yeomen of the Guard'. Alice Harding did nothing but smile towards her grandson. It was already rather a long evening which, whilst she was enjoying it immensely, she felt it would be just a little too tiring to challenge Rupert about whether or what was his favourite opera!

"It's always been so special, this one, something about it, more in-depth, a more feasible story line perhaps, you know the kind of drama that you often experience with proper opera – not to say that Gilbert and Sullivan is not proper! Then the music, some of the best of Sullivan and I've always reckoned the overture to be the most wonderful of any of the works, so powerful – just like an imagery of the Tower of London itself! I like, too, the solo song to open the First Act, then that always compares to later in the same Act when the chorus of Yeomen enter, both vigorous and thrilling, before the next thing when we have the jester and his mindful song."

Rupert collected his thoughts, and his breath – but not for too long! "Another thing, there's so much feeling that comes through the whole opera, a kind of pent up emotion rising, and that's underlined continually by the music! Yes, in many ways, this must surely be my favourite," Rupert declared, by then very red in the face and with droplets of sweat appearing on his brow.

Alice decided that it was probably best just to listen and to smile occasionally. The last thing that she wanted to do was to dampen her grandson's happiness but, at the same time she was beginning to dread just what would happen if by the end of the evening, by then not so long away, there was no announcement of whether the D'Oyly Carte Opera Company was going to continue. The thought of that situation and how to deal with it made her feel distinctly uneasy. She was almost glad that Rupert was taking the opportunity to carry on talking whilst they waited for the next part of the evening to continue.

"There's another reason why I think that I may like this best of all."

Still Alice just nodded and smiled towards her grandson.

"That's because I always remember just how marvellous it was when performances of 'Yeomen' were given during the summer in the very moat at the Tower of London – we were there – in 1962 and 1966 – that was it, wasn't it?" Rupert answered his own question before Alice, even if she had especially wanted, had a chance! "Yes, they were the years, during the City of London Festivals. Marvellous occasions, even if it was outdoors but what could be nicer on a glorious summers evening! I remember gazing across to the Tower itself as the principals sang the words:

"Groom about to be beheaded
In an hour on Tower Green!
Tower, Tower, Tower Green!"

The air was still, even for the moment, no sounds of birds, traffic noises, not even, for once, any planes flying overhead, nothing - the words rang out – and like I say, that very actual backdrop – it was just magic – a moment of life to forever savour! I'm sure neither Gilbert nor Sullivan, or anybody of their time, would have ever thought of the opera being performed at its very location – magnificent!" Rupert's eyes closed for a fraction of a second as he once again recalled those moments going back some 20 years.

Alice thought too about what he had said and knew also the poignancy of it all. She remembered as well her own visits to the Tower of London and how, despite the chill of a supposed summer's evening, how seeing the opera actually performed on site had equally captivated her as well. But that was just one of many, many memories for her that she had experienced of Gilbert and Sullivan operas during her long life and which had always meant so incredibly much to her, whether at home or in the theatre. And unlike so very many other things in life, they had been only the most happiest of memories. She sighed.

Both Rupert and Alice were shaken from their collective memories as the house lights again dimmed and the conductor appeared in the pit to the becoming customary round of cheering, clapping and by then also, feet stumping – so much so Alice that was pleased they were sitting in the stalls – unless, she quickly reminded herself, the circle might fall on top of them!

"I'm glad they're going to play this selection now!" Rupert declared as he turned once more towards the stage, his whole face full of expectation.

"So am I," Alice replied, "I expect it's your favourite!" She simply could not resist adding that with a kind of cheeky smile but Rupert was too intent just then on what might happen to rise to his grandmother's wry, but well-meaning, bait!

Chapter 14
"Take a pair of sparkling eyes"

Nellie entered into her 41st year in supremely happy spirits. Domestic happiness was assured and was never in question then nor ever had been – that was something for which she felt especially fortunate and forever grateful. Work, on the other hand, had been a different matter during her life, a source of frequent misery and hardship until she had come to the theatre. Increasingly now, Florrie Parker gave her more and more responsibility in the wardrobe department and heaped nothing but generous praise on all of her efforts, so much so that Nellie had by then almost forgotten her previous hard and unhappy working years in the East End dress factory. That her working life was so equitable was matched perfectly by her home life away from the theatre. She positively adored the house in Peckham and spent virtually every spare moment, which admittedly was rather infrequent, on tending the home, keeping the place spotless and always adding delightful touches with delicately made soft furnishings. She took special pride, too, in the small back yard, tending the little collection of plants to be sure that there was almost always something in flower with which to decorate their special front room – their very own parlour, even if it was so small that it would be barely recognised as such by most of the stall's audiences each evening. That didn't matter to Nellie – to her it was their home. By contrast, she loved the wide-open spaces of Greenwich Park and had almost forgotten her earliest feelings that any place south of the river was foreign territory. Now it was the other side of the Thames, the very north bank of her birth, other than the Strand and the Savoy, which seemed to her now as the foreign field that must not only be forgotten but also ignored. But above all, Nellie relished beyond words her marriage, her Tom.

"You've a good one there," Florrie Parker would so often say to her. It was all that she could do to hold back her tears of joy at the remark that she so appreciated to hear. She would merely smile and then bury her head once again in her work so as to avoid her embarrassment.

But the comment was all so true and she so realised it, blessing more and more each day that she had by then, for nearly seven years, been able to spend all the working day with her husband as well as the precious, but very little, free time together. Not only that, she really loved the work in the theatre, even surprising herself just how much she had grown to appreciate so much the work of Gilbert and Sullivan, to acknowledge their obvious universal appeal, simply to be proud of the part she effectively contributed to it. She felt delighted to be able to fully share her Tom's very earliest and continuing enthusiasm with the work which was now as much her own as his as well.

Nellie's happiness was equally reciprocated for Tom. For him, every day was like a happy dream, a perfect dream from which he so often felt he would need to pinch himself to make sure it was all for real. His happiness began from the time that they got up and breakfasted together until they lay in bed together once again at the end of the day, cuddling close to each other as they reviewed all the events of the day before falling happily into slumber, almost reasonably without a care in the world. As much as being at work, he appreciated every moment he and Nellie could savour at home in Peckham. Together, they took delight as they tidied their precious house before they set off, husband and wife, for the short walk to the station and the other part of their equally satisfying daily life. He treasured being a couple on the train to Blackfriars, especially when so many of their fellow passengers were travelling alone and very obviously leading quite separate family lives. His joy remained as next they walked from the station towards the theatre, each step taking them ever nearer to their beloved Savoy.

Just as Nellie was respected for her work, then so too was Tom who, in the same way, had more and more responsibility thrust upon him by his ever grateful boss, Fred Dean. Each working day then was always the same, a quick social hello with the stage manager, with other company members, be it one of the long serving principals like Mr. George Grossmith or the most junior stage hand, then onto the immediate tasks of making the stage ready perhaps for yet another rehearsal that Mr. Gilbert was always demanding to keep the performances, not to say the singers too, at their peak. It was a known fact within the company that Sir Arthur considered Mr. Gilbert's over extensive rehearsal methods to waste time through their indulgence. Tom and Fred Dean did not agree and both felt it was the only way to achieve a dedicated perfection and fully supported the work even when it invariably meant extra duties. With a growing sense of self-satisfaction, he was being left to get on with all manner of stage management, usually later to be congratulated by an ever-grateful Fred Dean more than once during the day.

"You're part of the brickwork, the very foundations here, Tom, my lad," Fred often used to say to him, a very reference to the fact that Tom had by then almost 17 years of company experience. "There's little that you don't know about the stage, our productions, I can always leave everything to you to get on with and I'll see a job well done – not only me, but Mr. Gilbert himself realises that too!"

"Right you are, Mr. Dean." That, as always, was Tom's standard reply, an answer even in it's brevity that was truly meant and equally happily received.

Tom and Nellie Dobb's bliss was one of perfect harmony and one both noted and respected by all in the company at the Savoy. It was, however, something that wasn't so evident in all of the company and it especially wasn't something then too evident either in the lives of the most important people associated with the theatre - Sir Arthur, Mr. Gilbert or Mr. D'Oyly Carte themselves.

187

The main issue of concern stemmed from something that no less a person than Queen Victoria herself had said to Sir Arthur Sullivan, that he should write a grand opera and that he would "do it so well". Richard D'Oyly Carte had never forgotten what he took as a royal command and felt that it was his duty to ensure that the composer did as he had been so regally requested. It quickly became common knowledge amongst all of the company at the Savoy that Mr. D'Oyly Carte was even planning to build a brand new theatre, The Royal English Opera House, on a site in London at the junction of Shaftsbury Avenue with Cambridge Circus. Sir Arthur was immediately excited about the prospect and saw it as a way of concentrating on what he described as "proper music", even more likely as a reason to turn his back upon the Savoy and his lighter work there. As a kind of appeasement to his writer colleague, then already of 17 years partnership, Sir Arthur invited Mr. Gilbert to write the words of the grand opera. Mr. Gilbert, though, was having none of it, replying negatively that he thought "we should be risking everything in writing more seriously still".

Sir Arthur wasn't dissuaded and took up Mr. Gilbert's suggestion that he should get "a serious librettist" with whom to collaborate on a grand opera. That he did by working immediately with Julian Sturgis.

Of more concern, though, to Mr. Gilbert was Sir Arthur's refusal to write another comic opera with him, at the same time, replying that "it is not too much to say that it's distasteful to me".

As a virtual beacon of all information, a correspondent to the company at the Savoy at large, Fred Dean relayed on a daily basis this and all of the news that he had gleaned about the developing discussions, not to say potential confrontations. One day, he was quick to inform everybody that he had learnt that Mr. Gilbert had said that he didn't believe in "Carte's new theatre", that "the site is not popular and cannot become popular for some years to come".

"It's all becoming almost something like a storyline from one of the earlier comic operas, except now it is our own management who are the main players!" Fred Dean observed rather wryly.

"Mr. Dean, I'm not too worried about any of this as I once was," Tom said to his stage manager one day. "Now that we have already 10 very successful and very popular Gilbert and Sullivan operas, even if there was never another new piece, then I am sure that Mr. D'Oyly Carte would want us to continue here at the Savoy with a constant programme of revivals."

"I'd say that you are absolutely right, Tom," Fred Dean answered, with a very obvious sense of relief as a result of Tom's words. "But I still think it is a shame if this proven partnership doesn't still go on for more and more," he emphasised, adding "our public want it after all!"

"We'll see, but do you know what I think?" Tom ventured.

"Tell me," Fred Dean replied, scratching his head and running his finger around the collar of his shirt as if he still felt somehow troubled.

"Well, Mr. Dean, we've seen it before, Sir Arthur saying he wanted to do something more serious than the comic operas, getting into despair with Mr. Gilbert's storyline, then the two of them, well they sort it out, get back together and, what next – a new piece – with all the gaiety and melodious music as before!" Tom declared with a rather theatrical flourish of his hands.

"Time will tell, time will tell," Fred Dean answered as he set off to the back of the stalls, there to turn round and be sure that all was well with the stage setting. It was very much a routine for him that was more force of habit than a necessity. He knew that Tom would have done it to perfection but in a situation in which he felt less than comfortable, it was a kind of personal solace to retreat to the empty stalls.

Nellie joined with her husband in feeling little concern about what might or might not be going on between the composer, writer and theatre owner. With the current Savoy production and numerous touring productions, she had more than enough to concern her with making sure all costumes were spic and span for all the ongoing performances.

"We've got our work to do, like you say, Tom, more than enough and I agrees with yer, it's 'append before, if this present opera finishes, then we'll 'ave another production of one of them previous pieces!" Nellie declared with reason.

"That's it, love, after all, we can always bring back 'The Mikado', Tom replied with a smile, recalling the command from the gallery at the end of the first night of 'Ruddigore'.

Whilst there was no doubt that 'Yeomen of the Guard' was going to be a greater success than 'Ruddigore', it was also evident to all in the company that the new opera was not going to be another 'Mikado' either. The general feeling that the public wanted their Gilbert and Sullivan operas to be of a more amusing genre could not be ignored, something very much observed by Mr. Gilbert as he was quick to inform Sir Arthur.

"Tom," Fred Dean called out. "Listen here, Tom, Mr. Gilbert has told me about the correspondence that he has had with Sir Arthur. In it he said, just a minute, I've made a note about it here," Fred continued whilst digging in his pockets to retrieve his precious note book, 'his bible' as he told everybody. "Yes, I've got it – Mr Gilbert says 'the success of 'Yeomen', which is a step in the direction of serious opera, has not been so convincing as to warrant us in assuming that the public want something more earnest still'. Then Sir Arthur, here is his reply – 'I confess that the indifference of the public to 'Yeomen of the Guard' has disappointed me greatly'. Apparently," Fred continued, "he then went on to stress that any return to their former style of pieces is something that he could not do. So there we have it, it looks very much to me that we are having another possible standoff between the writer and composer! Then, if that's not enough, we also have Mr. D'Oyly Carte becoming more interested in his new grand opera theatre development." Fred Dean also then threw up his hands before, once again, heading for the sanctuary that the back of the stalls offered him.

Unfortunately, the growing dissent between writer and composer also had a salutary effect on the singers, if not affecting the stage members in the same way. Some of the principals wanted to leave the company whilst others were demanding more money. That even Mr. George Grossmith should want to leave after so long was a shock at first to both Tom and Nellie until Tom thought more about it and reasoned to his wife: "It's a shame, of course, but I believe the operas are bigger than any of us, bigger than the singers, and that if one principal leaves, if several leave in reason, then others will fill the shoes, so to speak. It's Mr. Gilbert's words and Sir Arthur's music that really matters."

Nellie agreed with Tom and although she didn't tell him, she felt really both surprised and with a degree of admiration that her husband thought so clearly and responsibly about the issue.

With the summer of 1889, 'Yeomen' continued to play to good houses and Sir Arthur Sullivan went away to France for a holiday, but not before further acrimonious exchanges of correspondence between him and Mr. Gilbert. Fred Dean, as always, got to hear all about it and was swift to tell Tom who, in perfect grapevine fashion, quickly related everything to Nellie, plus, naturally, Florrie Parker who just as much relied upon him for the flow of information from the stage area to the wardrobe department.

"What's this that you have got to tell us now?" Florrie Parker asked one afternoon as Tom once more came into the wardrobe room, this time a little more red in the face than was usual. Nellie put down the costume on which she was working for a moment to listen.

"It's getting really bad this time between Mr. Gilbert and Sir Arthur," Tom began, as both ladies looked directly at him, shaking their heads. "Apparently, Mr. Gilbert had said to Sir Arthur that a librettist of grand opera is always swamped by the composer to which Sir Arthur replied that it was exactly what had happened to him, vice-versa, in all the comic operas!"

"That sounds like a right proper argument blowing up, if you asks me!" Nellie replied to which Florrie Parker nodded her agreement.

"It gets worse," Tom continued, "Mr. Dean told me that Mr. Gilbert replied directly to Sir Arthur. I've got it written down here." Tom produced, with a flourish, the prized piece of paper where he had, newspaper reporter-like, copied down what Fred Dean had told him. He continued, reading from the paper with a furrowed brow. "Mr. Gilbert, well he says 'if you really are under the astounding impression that you have been effacing yourself during the last years, there is certainly no modus vivendi to be found that shall be satisfactory to both of us. You are adept in

191

your profession and I am adept in mine. If we meet, it must be as master and master not as master and servant'." Tom stopped for breath before he carried on to wryly comment "Well, if that hasn't put the cat amongst the pigeons then I don't know what will!"

"Cor blimey!" Nellie exclaimed.

"I couldn't put it better myself!" Florrie Parker added, as she supportively patted Nellie on the back.

Having delivered his news, Tom once again took leave of his wife and Miss Parker to return to the stage area, only to be met by a very excited Fred Dean.

"Tom, Tom, about what I told you earlier – there's more!" he declared.

"What next, Mr, Dean?" Tom asked.

"Now, Sir Arthur has written to Mr. D'Oyly Carte – I've just been to his office and he has told me all about it!"

Tom waited a moment whilst the stage manager paused, like to take breath before going on to deliver what was obviously going to be even more crucial information.

"Well, actually, Sir Arthur has seen some reason in all of this – in his letter he kind of indicated that if the pair worked together in the future as 'master and master', like Mr. Gilbert put it, then the way forward could be a lot smoother and many of the past difficulties of the relationship could be removed. To me, that sounds some good news, that he may be prepared, they both may be prepared, to carry on in some way."

"There you are Mr. Dean, it's like I said, we've seen it all before, and, for what it's worth, my money is on a new piece being written – just you mark my words," Tom added in an unusually, for him, authoritative way, to which the stage manager reciprocated with a smile and gentle affirmative nod of his head. Nellie, who was passing by the stage area at the time, had cause for the second time in a short while to feel a sense of admiration, not to say also to feel proud, at her husband's very obviously growing stature within his chosen world of the theatre.

Tom's prosaic words seemed to be not only well-intentioned but also an amazingly accurate vision of what was happening. Even though there was an obvious estrangement between the writer and composer, there was also little doubt that they each respected each other. Tom learnt through his usual source, his erstwhile stage manager, Fred Dean, that Mr. Gilbert had next written to Sir Arthur and had said: "You say that our operas are Gilbert's pieces with music added by you. You grievously reflect upon yourself and the noble art of which you are so eminent a professor." Then later, he was to write again to the composer to add "You are the greatest English musician of our age – a man whose genius is a proverb wherever the English tongue is spoken".

"What did I tell you, Mr. Dean!" Simply, Tom could not resist the temptation to add the immediate weight to his earlier comments with the stage manager.

"Right you are, Tom," Fred replied, "and you must remind me the next time that I could save myself some sleepless nights if I listened more intently to you in the first place," he added with a wry smile.

As they chatted on the train home that evening, Tom predicted to Nellie that "before the year is out, I wouldn't be at all surprised if we will have a brand new Gilbert and Sullivan comic opera here at the Savoy". With an obvious degree of respect, Nellie nodded contentedly to her husband before the motion of the train lulled her into a dozing sleep. Some hundred miles away from South London, as if in support of Tom's foresight, at the same time, Sir Arthur was enjoying a holiday then in Venice, where he was unwittingly immersing himself in what would be the scene of his next comic opera work with Mr. Gilbert.

Tom's prophecy became reality when on 9 May 1889, Mr. Gilbert and Sir Arthur shook hands in the presence of Mr. D'Oyly Carte to, as Fred Dean succinctly put it, "bury the hatchet". Plans for a new comic opera began immediately although Sir Arthur insisted than in the new piece his "music must be more prominent".

As Mr. Gilbert began to write the new piece, he immediately informed Fred Dean of some very significant changes that would be included. Naturally, Tom was soon aware as the stage manager confided in him with all the news – 'gossip' would be too crude a word – emanating from the writer.

"What with all the ruckus caused here in the company with so many of the singers either wanting to leave or demanding more money, Mr. Gilbert has vowed that in the new piece he wants to break away from the stock parts of the past, where a character from a previous opera, and with a same principal singer in mind, is rewritten, although in different guise, in the new opera," Fred declared.

"That should prove rather interesting," Tom commented, realising to himself that there were certain to be more ructions amongst the singers when word got out. "But in many ways I agree with it," Tom added. "I say again that it is the words and the music that are both responsible for the success of the operas, not the singers that are alone responsible for it."

"You better not let them here you say that!" Fred Dean replied, pointing his hand in the direction of the stage wings and the dressing rooms beyond. "But, maybe, well more than that, it is right what you say!

"It's no more than talking amongst ourselves, Mr. Dean," Tom affirmed, "but

I just wonder, if you know, what exactly Mr. Gilbert may have in mind?"

"This time, he tells me, the opera will not have any principal parts as such, no character will stand out more prominently than another!" Fred answered.

"The Earl, the Marquis, and the Dook,
The Groom, the Butler and the Cook,
The Aristocrat who banks with Coutts,
The Aristocrat who cleans the boots,
The Noble Lord who rules the State,
The Noble Lord who scrubs the grate,
The Lord High Bishop orthodox,
The Lord High Vagabond in the stocks –

Sing high, sing low,
Wherever they go,
They all shall equal be!"

Much later when Tom heard one of the songs from Act One of the new opera in early rehearsal, he reflected upon his earlier conversation, what the stage manager had told him, and soon realised how true to his word Mr. Gilbert intended to be with the new opera. The contents of the song made him smile to himself, more so when he thought how it would be received by the folk in the gallery!

A joyous air of anticipation once again descended upon the whole company at the Savoy with the news of the early preparations of the new piece. By the summer of 1889, Gilbert had the libretto ready whilst, as usual, Sir Arthur worked unhurriedly on the music, more so then as he was also working on the music for his grand opera which he was to call 'Ivanhoe'.

"Well, Tom, it really is so different this time between the two of them, Mr. Gilbert and Sir Arthur, I mean," Fred Dean declared. Tom, as always keen to glean any pieces of information that he could, stopped his work and turned towards the stage manager.

"What's happened now then?" he asked.

"Well, it is that Mr. Gilbert is anxious not to upset Sir Arthur and he tells me that when he sends him some more of the libretto for the new piece, he asks if it will do and if it won't then to send it back and he'll try again. Now that's a real about turn in things, if you ask me!" Fred Dean answered, his voice rising a discernable few octaves in sheer amazement, almost disbelief, at the news that he had just imparted to an equally startled Tom.

"Oh goodness, indeed, whatever will be happening next!" Tom exclaimed. "Let's hope that Sir Arthur doesn't take him too much at his word otherwise there's not likely to be another opera after all!"

"I don't think there'll be too much fear of that," the stage manager replied. "I think in their own way now they kind of respect each other and neither will want to put a foot wrong." He then thought for a moment before adding "but we shall see".

"until it is ascertained which of you is king, I have arranged that you will reign jointly…"

"As one individual?"

"Something like that!"

Bernard Lockett

The dialogue from the new opera was expression of evidence of the equality and new strength within the partnership of composer and writer. The significance certainly was not lost to all at the Savoy, Tom and Fred Dean especially, as early rehearsals got under way at the theatre.

When it became known that the new opera was to be set in Venice and that Gilbert had taken as a theme Venetians as red-hot republicans, everyone at the Savoy knew that once more the opera would be poking fun at politicians, that the writer was back upon his hallowed territory. As Fred Dean told them all: "Seemingly, it's what our audiences want and this time, well they're going to get it again!"

"Lord Chancellors were cheap as sprats,
And Bishops in their shovel hats
Were plentiful as tabby cats –
In point of fact too many
Ambassadors cropped up like hay,
Prime Ministers and such as they
Grew like asparagus in May,
And Dukes were three a penny."

"In short, whoever you may be,
To this conclusion you'll agree,
When every one is somebodee,
Then no one's anybody!"

"We're back on solid ground, so to speak now, love," Tom told Nellie as they excitedly talked about all that they so far knew about the new piece. "That'll please all the faithful audiences!" Tom spoke the words with a straight face just as if he had originated the idea!

"Expect it will," Nellie acknowledged. "And Miss Parker has already told me about some of the costumes, for the boatmen...."

"Gondoliers, that's what they are called," Tom interrupted. "In fact, so they tell me, the rumour is that's what the new opera is to be called too, although we won't know for sure until much nearer opening night!"

"So it is, I couldn't remember the name, something foreign, that's all I know!" Nellie declared before continuing. "Anyway, there'll be some lovely costumes for us to do, also for the ladies, then the heralds, pages, not to say for the Kings of the Court and a character called Grand Inquisitor. I'm looking very much forward to the work and there's only one thing that worries me…!"

"What's that, love?" Tom asked, his expression suddenly looking rather pained with concern for his wife's feelings.

"That's whether the stage crew will be up to making a good enough set for all the lovely costumes to appear on!" Nellie rocked with laughter as she watched Tom's face, then to see him respond with a broad grin and a laugh that was more like a yell of delight. "Got you there, didn't I just!" she exclaimed

By the late autumn of 1889, word spread throughout the Savoy that the first night for the new opera was expected to take place before the coming Christmas. There was much to be done for the whole company. Because some of the earlier principals had already left, some new cast members had to be recruited for the coming piece. Mr. Gilbert had been true to his word in not creating any special leading role in the new opera but rather a larger cast of more equal performers. That in itself gave Fred Dean and Tom much extra work as the new singers had to be extensively coached as to what was expected of them at the Savoy. As always, Mr. Gilbert was very much on hand to direct, and the two listened with half an ear and smiled to each other as they overheard the writer:

"Have you ever acted?" they heard him ask of one potential singer.

"No," came the startled reply.

"So much the better for you, you've nothing to unlearn!" They heard Mr. Gilbert say to the nervous applicant.

They both knew though, and were more than used to, Mr. Gilbert's methods, in fact they respected him, especially in his disciplined coaching of the singers. Tom and Fred Dean nodded their own agreement towards each other as they so often heard him say: "Exact diction, every word to be heard at the back of the house – whether spoken or sung". And when Mr. Gilbert was not at the theatre himself, both Fred and Tom, exactly as the perfectly drilled team that they were, became for the writer the most perfect exponents of what the he decreed and expected. At least then, Fred Dean had the perfect excuse to wander to his favourite place at the back of the stalls, doing as Mr. Gilbert instructed, there to listen to the performers and to be sure that everything could be seen and heard. Fred was at his happiest there, almost in his perfect element, and it was in similar fashion, too, that Tom, when he was either left in charge or merely to help his stage manager, often wandered to stand at the back of the theatre for the same reasons. It was almost as if as Sir Arthur and Mr. Gilbert were together in a perfect partnership, then so too were both Fred and Tom, brought together in their collective work at the Savoy.

"Will we make it, Mr. Dean?" Tom asked his stage manager anxiously, as it was still evident that although most of the libretto and stage directions were complete, some of the music remained unwritten.

"I expect so, Tom me lad," Fred replied. "We're all used to this by now and Sir Arthur will deliver, even if we have only a few hours – sorry, I should say days – to get the finished score completed. It'll all come together as a comic opera masterpiece, of that I have no concerns and neither should you Tom – you've been in at this from the beginning and know how it all goes!" Fred's statement was made more as a gesture to reassure rather than one in which he implicitly believed this time.

"You're right, as always," Tom observed, "as you say, I should know but I don't know why I always get so worried!" Tom's reply, though, was also made just to support the stage manager rather than a genuinely held belief that all was so set fair.

"Take a pair of sparkling eyes,
Hidden, ever and anon,
In a merciful eclipse –
Do not heed their mild surprise –
Having passed the Rubicon."

And:

"There lived a King, as I've been told,
In the wonder-working days of old,
When hearts were twice as good as gold,
And twenty times as mellow."

Two songs from Act Two for which Sir Arthur finally completed the music in just one evening's hard work. Even though neither Fred Dean, nor Tom, dared to either admit or to say so to each other, they were this time even more scared and hugely concerned than usual whether all would be ready in time for the planned first night of 7 December 1889. What was more this time, and to make matters worse, Fred Dean knew that Mr. D'Oyly Carte was even contemplating postponing the first night, something that they had never done before in the continuous 14 years of the operas. Sir Arthur, though, would have no such talk.

"It ain't 'alf good that us wardrobe folk, as lowly as we are, never keep you lot waiting!" Nellie observed to her husband, continuing "'cause if we did there wouldn't 'alf be 'ell to pay and I would knows it!"

Tom realised that he didn't need her reassurance but nevertheless asked of Nellie if all was indeed ready. He got his reply and made a very swift ducking down to the stage to miss his wife's fist, directed to him in jest – well, at least that was what he told himself as he returned to the side of the stage laughing.

"And whilst you are here, what do you think of the setting for Act One – it's the Piazzetta in Venice," Tom declared.

"Oh, is that it," Nellie replied, "it looks more like the Isle of Dogs to me!" She laughed aloud as by then it was her turn to scamper to avoid a direct body hit.

"What are you two up to now?" a laughing Fred Dean asked, in perfect good humour, as he came out from the wings. "You two pull each others' legs so much that I would think that by now you would both be over eight feet tall!"

"My wife, Mr. Dean, thinks our set looks like the Isle of Dogs!" Tom declared and was pleased to see how the comment made his stage manager almost collapse to the stage himself in a riotous attack of laughter.

"Oh dear, oh dear, can you imagine just what Mr. Gilbert would think if he had the same idea of all of our efforts and work on the set! Well, I know what would happen -it'll be forever with one of the secondary touring companies for you, and me, Tom me lad, putting up unsubstantial and rocking scenery in far flung theatres the length and breadth of the land!" Fred Dean concluded, referring to what most at the Savoy most hated the very idea of – to be 'exiled' to one of Mr. D'Oyly Carte's touring companies. The startled look on Tom's face was immediately too much for the stage manager as, still almost helpless with laughter, tears flowing down his face, his stomach heaving as he desperately tried to control himself, he sought support from a side wall of the much talked about piazza. Fortunately for all concerned, it easily bore his weight. Still laughing, he finally managed to say a few more words to Nellie, just as she began to make her way once more back to the wardrobe room. "I would like to make a similar joke to you, Nellie, about your costumes, but in all honesty, I can't – they're simply always too good and it would do your work no justice at all if I did so!"

"Oh, Mr. Dean," Nellie replied, "don't fink that I was in any way casting ursper . . ."

"Aspersions!" Tom interrupted, jumping gallantly, even in jest, to his wife's verbal rescue.

"Yer, like Tom says, I wasn't wanting to say anyfink nasty about the stage work," Nellie concluded with a degree of embarrassment lest her joking may have been taken the wrong way.

"I believe you, thousands wouldn't," Fred Dean declared, still laughing heartily as the three finally broke up to carry on with their various duties amongst the hustle and bustle of the pace of final preparations.

Tom and Nellie smiled to each other, Tom giving his wife a knowing wink that she happily reciprocated. As she went away upstairs, Nellie reflected on what would have happened to her those years before, still embedded in her subconscious, when she had worked in the dress factory. Joke, there would have been no joke, she thought to herself – in fact, if anybody would have dared laugh, they would have paid for it through a deduction with their wages – or more likely, shown the door with their 'cards' as a memento of the occasion! The immediate episode down on the stage meant so much to her and she realised just how much her life in the theatre had brought to her so very much happiness and contentment.

Just five days before the opening night, Sir Arthur had his first orchestral rehearsal and only then did he and Mr. Gilbert finally decide upon the title for the new piece – 'The Gondoliers' – just as Tom had somehow earlier anticipated by way of a rumour.

As they heard the opening music in rehearsal for Act One, Fred Dean soon took the opportunity of commenting to Tom "Well, it looks this time that Sir Arthur has got his own way – this is the first piece where after the overture, there is, by my reckoning, some 20 minutes of continuous music unbroken by any spoken dialogue whatsoever!"

"And lovely, most beautiful music it is too," Tom replied. "After 'Yeomen', you can see that the style is truly back to the old, tuneful and immensely joyous. Oh not that the music in 'Yeomen' wasn't melodious, 'cause it was, very much so, but this sounds, as I say, like of old. And another thing – the audience will like once again to have a rousing opening chorus!"

"List and learn, ye dainty roses,
Roses white and roses red,
Why we bind you into posies
Ere your morning bloom has fled."

Standing in the wings, taking the chance for the occasional peek through to the auditorium, Tom could see that the usual glittering and cream of society first night audience seated in the stalls were entranced by the beginning of the opera. Fred Dean spotted it too and took a brief opportunity to say to Tom "That's what they all like, the tuneful and bouncing opening chorus, this opera is sure to be a success!"

Loud cheers coming too from the gallery told them that the faithful supporters of Gilbert and Sullivan from the least well off classes were as equally happy with the new work. A sense of relief spread through the whole working stage area of the theatre, a good feeling picked up too by the singers who were very obviously thrilled with the reception that each and every one of them received as individually and in chorus they performed their roles to a delighted audience. The happy tone was well and truly set for the whole evening:

"Once more gondolieri,
Both skilful and wary,
Free from this quandary
Contented are we.
From Royalty flying,
Our gondolas plying,
And merrily crying
Our 'preme', 'stali!'"

Tom took Fred Dean's thumped sign to lower the curtain at the end of Act Two, the end of the opera itself, to such a crescendo of cheering from the audience that the sounds were deafening to all of those on and around the stage. The cheering not only continued but, if at all possible, got even louder when Sir Arthur Sullivan and Mr. Gilbert joined each other on stage for their customary curtain calls. So many times did Tom take the stage manager's instruction to raise and lower the curtain that he felt his arms would freeze in one position through sheer tiredness. By then, Nellie had joined him and, seeing his obvious weariness, even helped him as he negotiated the pulleys to work the mighty curtains.

"I don't 'ave to ask 'ow it went," Nellie said, tears of unrestrained joy flowing down her face, overcome at the response coming from across the theatre. Overcome too that even after seven years in the theatre, she still found it hard to believe, or accept, her own very important role in yet another very obvious success at the Savoy. Tom so often told her, as did her own boss, the wardrobe mistress Florrie Parker, that they were all together as part of the team and that what they achieved was never down to no single person.

"It's glittering, glittering – a first night up amongst the very best of them," Tom exclaimed. He didn't feel in the least bit ashamed that for a brief moment, with a free hand, he too had to wipe from his cheeks similar emotional tears to those his wife was experiencing. "Oh, I know how much you felt for 'Yeomen', and I agree, the music was very good and a human story too, but it's so obvious that this gaiety is what our audiences want from their Gilbert and Sullivan operas. Listen to them, Nellie, listen how they scream and cheer!"

"I can 'ear, Tom – so can the whole theatre, not to say all the Strand, not to say probably all over London an' all!"

The enthusiasm voiced by the whole theatre so vociferously on the opening night was carried through the immediate following days by the critics from the press in equally positive esteem. In their customary way, hidebound as they had become in all respectable ways of the life in the theatre, as if too with a sense of superstition, the company gathered on stage and listened both quietly and attentively as Fred Dean, holding his time honoured centre ground, read a selection.

"Ladies and gentlemen, I've got two articles here that you'll be delighted to hear," Fred Dean began. "The first is from the 'Daily Telegraph' and says that 'The Gondoliers conveys an impression of having been written con amore'." A wave of polite clapping burst out around the stage as Fred Dean held up his hand, to continue: "There's more – here 'The Graphic' says, and I'll read it – 'the composer has borrowed from France the stately gavotte, from Spain the Andalusian cachucha, from Italy the saltarello and the tarantella, and from Venice itself the Venetian barcarolle'."

The assembled company once again indicated their very obvious pleasure with the news given to them and once again Fred Dean clapped his hands together indicating that he still hadn't finished.

"Indeed I am pleased to say that there is even more! Sir Arthur and Mr. Gilbert have asked that I make you aware of an exchange of correspondence that they have had between themselves." Fred Dean cleared his throat, an obvious indication, Tom thought, that something very significant was about to be imparted. "Firstly," the stage manager continued, "Mr Gilbert has written to Sir Arthur: 'I must thank you for the magnificent work you have put into the piece. It gives you the chance of shining into the 20th Century with reflected light'. Then, there is more!" Fred Dean was repeating himself and he made a great stage play of shuffling his papers before he continued. "Sir Arthur has replied thus: 'Don't talk of reflected light. In such a perfect book as the Gondoliers, you shine with an individual brilliance which no other writer can hope to attain'. So be it, ladies and gentlemen, I think that in that exchange of wonderful correspondence, we have it all, a perfect comment upon the musical and writing partnership of these two gentlemen and who we, as a company can be justifiably proud to interpret and perform the wonderful works on their, and of course Mr. D'Oyly Carte's, behalf!"

Fred Dean smiled and wiped his brow to shouts of "bravo" from all on the stage, Tom and Nellie included, neither of whom even bothered to attempt to wipe the tears of joy flowing down their faces from what they had just heard.

Chapter 15
"Here's a pretty mess!"

Tom and Nellie's joy on stage as they heard about the critical reception of the new opera, 'Gondoliers', could not have been in more contrast to that which Rupert Moore felt at the Adelphi Theatre, forward in time by 92 years and just over two months. Rupert's downcast feelings, though, were symbolic for the whole audience in the theatre that night, including his grandmother, Alice Harding. Together they had all enjoyed and were, as one, shouting "encore" and "more", stamped their feet and made their hands sore once more from clapping as the excerpts from 'The Gondoliers' came to an all too soon end. The performance by the D'Oyly Carte Opera Company had in every way been as brilliant, as vivid and as close to perfection then as Rupert had considered it to have been in all the years that he had been attending performances, disguising how the singers themselves must have felt on such an emotionally charged evening. Alice thought the same and her own experiences were even so much greater, with the benefit of some 50 years more of experiencing Gilbert and Sullivan, than her grandson's. But that night all was so much tinged with an ever growing sadness, then soon verging on a growing sense of desperation, especially as far as Rupert was concerned.

In his anguish, Rupert felt not only selfishly for himself, but for his grandmother too and he also felt that so many of those sitting around him and throughout the theatre must have had similar sad feelings. In his state of ever saddening reflections, the gathering pace with which the evening was progressing made him all the more introverted within his thoughts that he barely any longer cared too much about what others might be thinking or feeling, preferring to concentrate much more on his own very real and very hurtful plight. He fully realised, completely undramatically, that it was nothing less than his very wellbeing that was at stake. During the whole, by then already rather long, evening, he had fidgeted in his seat many times but now, with so much of the excerpts having already been given, even that movement became somehow more hazardous and uncomfortable. He felt as if his trousers were somehow becoming glued to the fabrics of the seat, so much so that he found it increasingly hard to alter his position and grew even more distressed as the result.

"All right, love?" his grandmother said to him, taking the time to speak whilst there was so much noise and commotion coming from within the auditorium. As soon as she had uttered the words, she immediately regretted it, realising that of course her grandson wasn't in any way "all right" and for reasons that she fully understood. She coughed into her handkerchief as a polite way in which to try to distract from her inappropriate question, hoping that perhaps Rupert at least hadn't heard her question. She saw that he continued to look towards the stage, somewhat bemused and extremely red in the face. She felt sorry for him but also very relieved that he so obviously had not heard her question. Quickly she put her handkerchief, once more neatly folded, by the side of her bag, ready for what she foresaw as probably the need for its camouflaging use once again before long. "That was good, the excerpts from 'Gondoliers' – I did so enjoy it," she said, quickly changing the subject to her very obvious relief.

"I'm glad you liked it," Rupert replied, "of course, I did too. It's such a joyous opera and it's always been my favour..." Rupert stopped himself but neither he nor his grandmother laughed. The time for laughter was becoming very inappropriate and Alice didn't want to add further to her grandson's obvious woes.

"Despite everything, I thought the songs came over even more with a real verve and vigour, the expressions just as happy and just as beautiful as if…" For one moment, Rupert gulped at the significance of what was in his mind, something that somehow he could hardly bring himself to say in words. But he continued "as if it was nothing more than another happy performance that everybody has enjoyed during the 90-odd years' productions of this opera".

"That's the way it is – the show must go on and that's the theatre for you," his grandmother answered, herself also in a deep thought and equal sense of reflection. "You don't need me to remind you, love, that I was just 13 months old when 'The Gondoliers' was first performed and one of my father's favourite songs, one that he frequently sung around the piano at home, was 'Sparkling Eyes', from this very opera. So you can see, it means very much to me too, you see."

"I know that Nan," Rupert replied, "but you know what it is now – we're coming more to the end of the evening, more than three-quarters gone, very much more, yet still nothing is being said about the future! Now I am really beginning to fear the very worst because I believe that if there had been something positive to say, then it wouldn't be at the end when we've all been put through so much agony and those fears already spoiling our evening. I really am losing all hope!" Rupert sighed, his face becoming even redder with his last statement, his hands the more clammy and the seat the more uncomfortable for him as he expressed his heartfelt alarms. The very significance and depth of his statement made him gulp as if the oxygen in the highly charged theatre was insufficient for him.

"There, there, love," Alice intervened, "I know how you're feeling, how we all are feeling." Alice's arm pointed around the whole theatre, or at least to the areas that they could see from their own seats. "Throughout all the years of Gilbert and Sullivan, right from the time they were first being written, there's often been upsets, even some disputes between them both, writer and composer, as you know, yet it always came out all right in the end – it's what the audiences wanted just as much then as they do now! And that's how I'm sure, or should say, hoping that it will be this time as true as well. Just think, love, again you don't need me to tell you, but through thick and thin for now over 107 years the company have been continually performing the works, both near and far, through good times as well as bad, in the years of peace and prosperity and then in the dark years of two world wars. Given that as a pedigree, then there should be every reason to carry on now!"

Alice felt exhausted after her impassioned speech but the smile that immediately appeared on her grandson's face, his very obvious sense of relief at her words of support, made her feel pleased that she had made the effort.

"I just hope that you are right, Nan," Rupert replied. "Goodness only knows it's what we all want, what we are all hoping for." He looked down at his hands as he uttered the words, realising that his fingers were crossed on both hands as if in engendered solidarity with his remarks.

"Come on love," Alice commanded, "let's enjoy what remains of the evening and who knows what then may happen at the final curtain – whilst there's life there is always hope!"

"Like I said, and say again, I just hope that you are right," Rupert sighed. He appreciated his grandmother's efforts to cheer him up even though he was far from convinced that anything would be said by the end of the evening to make him happy and stave off the growing fears that he felt so increasingly in the pit of his stomach.

For the moment, though, any further thoughts or discussions were once more suspended by the darkening again of the house lights and the familiar view of the conductor's back as he raised his baton to signal the start of the next piece.

* * * *

Tom, Nellie and indeed the whole D'Oyly Carte Company felt an overwhelming sense of euphoria as 'The Gondoliers' settled in to what was very obviously going to be a lengthy run at the Savoy. It was with a sense, too, of almost relaxed contentment in which all got on with their work, be it the stage scenery and props for Tom or the clothing, wigs and dresses for Nellie and the wardrobe department, as much as for the singers and musicians themselves. The fact, too, that Mr. Gilbert had left for a cruise to India and that Sir Arthur was travelling around southern Europe meant that although Mr. D'Oyly Carte remained in charge in London, Fred Dean, and therefore with much delegated to Tom too, together were managing the round of rehearsals to keep everybody on their toes just as Mr. Gilbert wished and had instructed. The very fact that they were also left to get on with it emphasised and made them realise just how esteemed they indeed were within the company, for which they all felt extremely good and happy as a result.

The long run for which the opera was so obviously destined was not reflected by any lack of work for all at the Savoy. With an envied theatrical standard to be maintained, there was incessant review and instruction to ensure that each night the audience were presented with a performance as fresh and as authentic as if it had been the very first night. Nothing less was demanded by Mr. Gilbert and, in the same way, the work ethos was instilled in all within the company. For them, Tom and Fred Dean included, anything else would have been a failing, letting down not only themselves but the company, not to say Sir Arthur and Mr. Gilbert.

And so it was too in the wardrobe department. The frequent cleaning and pressing of every item of clothing, be it for the chorus or the very much-expanded range of solo singers that Mr. Gilbert had written into 'The Gondoliers'. Florrie Parker, exactly like Fred Dean, was well versed in Mr. Gilbert's requirements and just as the stage manager knew that he could rely upon and trust Tom in every way, then so too could the wardrobe mistress with Nellie. Always it was a job well done with vigorous attention to every detail so that for each performance when the audience gasped and clapped their obvious approval of all the beautiful costumes, it was as if too everything was fresh and pristine, just like the first night.

The very happy atmosphere amongst all those working at the Savoy came very much from the respect that each and everyone of them felt for Gilbert and Sullivan and which as thorough professionals they all wanted to cherish. As Tom so often said to Nellie, "It's not like work at all, it's more like doing something that you love, like a favourite hobby, every day of your working life".

"Course it is Tom, and even more for you when you've 'ardly known anyfink other than 'featre work all yer working life," Nellie would usually reply. But she could, at the same time, never resist the temptation to add "Lucky you, you've never 'ad the 'orrible experiences of working in a clothing factory in them years before all of this. I 'ave and so for me the life 'ere is even betterer!"

The pleasant demeanour felt by all the company members was not though felt by Mr. Gilbert when he finally returned to London from his trip. A number of large expenses had been run up at the theatre, mainly by what Mr. D'Oyly Carte had controlled during the writer and composer's absence. "Keep your head down, Tom," Fred Dean advised, "I think that the roof is about to blow now that Mr. Gilbert's back!"

"Not because of anything that we've done, though, is it Mr. Dean?" Tom asked anxiously, even though he knew well within his heart that they had done all that was expected of them.

"No, No, not at all, Tom me lad," the stage manager replied. "As I understand it, Mr. D'Oyly Carte has told them that the preliminary expenses for the new opera have amounted to £4,500."

"Is that so very much?" Tom asked. "I know that it sounds a life's fortune to me but I don't know how really to compare such things as this," he added, honestly.

"Well, all I can say is that it is a good deal more than has ever been spent in the past and that's where the problem lies!" Fred Dean advised. "When Mr. Gilbert asked of Mr. D'Oyly Carte how the money had been spent, he was told that it had been on the costumes. Well that's natural, they are all very lovely and that's the work done so well by Miss Parker and your Nellie!"

Tom nodded his agreement.

"But that's not really it," Fred continued, "there's £460 spent for the stage gondola, the one that we faithfully push on and retrieve from the set several times per night," he smiled. "What's really set the cat amongst the pigeons, though, is that £500 has been spent on new carpets for the front of house and it's that which most irks Mr. Gilbert. I say he has a point too and that's mainly what is making him feel that some kind of financial controls are lacking on the part of the theatre management!"

"Oh dear," Tom replied, his short answer very much showing that despite his years of work in the theatre, his place in stage crafting was very much the ideal one for him and there were no aspirations to advance to theatrical management, the skills for which, despite by then his almost 20 years in the theatre, still remained very much of a mystery to him.

Nevertheless, the discussion about such higher matters didn't distract from his everyday enjoyment of his work, nor did it matter either to Nellie. And that was because Tom didn't tell her, accepting that he had such a small grasp of the issue that he felt unable for once to discuss it or pass the information on. Similarly, Florrie Parker worked happily in her world of clothes racks, needles, cottons, hats and delicate fabrics, always making sure that she simply did not get involved in anything else at all, whatever was going on around, as long as her world was not affected. So often news that she dismissively put down as nothing more than gossip came her way and she let it easily flow over her. As long as the work of her own department was accepted, not only that but favourably received, then that was all that mattered to her. If Miss Parker was happy then Nellie was happy too and the perfect arrangement of their own very special partnership worked equally both ways.

A few days later, as soon as he had heard further news, Fred Dean immediately passed it over to Tom who was spending some time painting the gondola and making sure all was smooth for the evening's performance. Thus it was always the way with Fred, although as a longstanding stage manager, he still felt far happier discussing, or rather telling, things with Tom than he did entering into any such conversations with the theatre management.

"There's more!" he declared to a startled Tom, up to that moment so very intent upon his work. Because Tom only briefly looked up and didn't say anything other than mouth a kind of "oh", Fred immediately continued. "Mr. Gilbert has demanded from Mr. D'Oyly Carte that a new management agreement be drawn up. To that he agreed but told Mr. Gilbert that the rent for the Savoy Theatre should be £5,000 per year, that's £1,000 more than now!"

"That's a lot isn't it Mr. Dean," Tom replied.

"It is indeed and Mr. Gilbert told him that he was not satisfied to which Mr. D'Oyly Carte replied and said that if he was unhappy with the arrangement, then he mustn't write any more pieces for the Savoy!"

If Tom hadn't been listening too intently up to then, the statement that he had just heard from his stage manager made him immediately stop his work on the gondola. He put his paintbrush and pot down carefully in the corner of the stage and looked up at Fred Dean, an expression of very real concern and anguish upon his face. "Is it now as serious as this?" he asked.

"Yes, I'm afraid it really is," Fred replied. "And what is more, this time it seems very entrenched even though I've also heard that Sir Arthur is anxious to try and calm things down, to become a kind of mediator."

This time, Tom decided that it all sounded far too serious and far too significant for them all. As a result, he didn't hold back from telling Nellie who listened very intently as he related all that he had heard.

"Cor blimey!" Nellie exclaimed, "but then I almost says 'so what' 'cause there are 11 full length operas now. You're 45 this year, I'm only three years behind yer, so even if the worst came to the very worst, mefinks that even if there was never any new opera then there's more than enough to be revived for a long time to come. 'Mikado' ran well over 600 performances and 'Gondoliers' looks like being set for a similar success, so I reckons there'll be more than enough for you and me to be getting on with for a long time to come!"

"Do you really think so?" Tom asked, more for reassurance than because his wife could possibly have any kind of psychic powers.

"Yes, Tom, I do. In any case, you know how it is as soon as something is revived, new stage sets are called for, new costumes, there's always plenty of work for the likes of us to be getting on with. We ain't so young any more and really I am not at all worried!" Nellie declared.

Tom thought for a moment before he replied. "I suppose that you are right and they've patched things up before and maybe it will be the same now – who knows – we'll no doubt find out before too long," he declared.

But the argument did not go away so easily. Next Tom heard from Fred Dean, always the conveyor of every morsel of information. He told him that Mr. Gilbert had met again with the theatre manager and declared "You are making too much money out of my brains", before storming out from the meeting with a very theatrical huff and puff.

"The trouble is," Fred Dean continued, "Mr. Gilbert is that kind of man who fights first and then asks the questions afterwards. In fact, what Mr. Gilbert said about the price of the carpet for the theatre…"

"That it all cost £500, you mean, Mr. Dean," Tom interjected, desperately trying to keep up with and also remember the flow of information of the situation.

"That's the one," Fred replied. "Well, it wasn't £500 at all, it was just £140 and I understand that Mr. D'Oyly Carte had pointed that out to him fair and square, also suggesting to Mr. Gilbert that his letters are inaccurate and that it probably shows that he has never properly examined the accounts in the first place!"

"Now, that is a turn-up," Tom observed. "What, then, do you think will happen next then Mr. Dean?"

"Lord only knows!" the stage manager replied. "Just let's think ourselves lucky that 'The Gondoliers' is proving to be so very popular and we can get on with it whilst they," Fred cast his eyes and pointed his hand in the direction of the theatre's office, "fight it out amongst themselves!"

And "fight it out amongst themselves" was exactly what the writer, composer and theatre manager carried on to do.

The company at the Savoy could do nothing but look on as bystanders as the battles raged. Next Tom heard from Fred Dean that Mr. D'Oyly Carte had accused Mr. Gilbert that he had been left to run things, "working like a slave", whilst the writer had

213

taken a holiday to India. Then they all heard how the theatre manager's wife, Helen D'Oyly Carte, had tried to step in as peacemaker, pointing out to the writer that they had paid for the building of the new theatre in 1881 and had kept it in good order ever since, not ever letting it "looking like some neglected provincial theatre" and that "no theatre in London has been kept so bright and clean as the Savoy and for so small a cost".

If there was any kind of reassurance for the company at the time of the to-ing and fro-ing quarrelling, it was that at first Mr. Gilbert had declared that he had no dispute with Sir Arthur although he accepted that a coolness had developed between them both as a result of the argument with Richard D'Oyly Carte. But even that stand-off position was rather set to decline and it was a very concerned Fred Dean who gathered not just Tom, but indeed all the stage crew as well as Florrie Parker and Nellie, together on the quiet morning stage.

"Ladies and gentlemen," Fred began, "I felt it only right that I should tell you that the recent difficulties between the partners here at the Savoy, about which we have all been only too well aware, have now become even more difficult." As discernable gasps were uttered from all gathered around him, Fred held up his hand to indicate that he wanted to continue. "Now with Mr. D'Oyly Carte already working on the new theatre for Sir Arthur's grand opera, I am afraid to have to now tell you that Mr. Gilbert has written to Sir Arthur to say that he considers the 'time for putting an end to our partnership has at last arrived'."

This time the response from those on stage, the highly charged and discernable "No's", meant that for some moments Fred could not continue. Tom and Nellie immediately put their arms around each other to offer joint support and most others were doing exactly the same in a very obvious display of genuine distress. They were not alone in showing their emotions at what they had heard, in spite of their earlier more positive thoughts and statements. Questions like "what now?", "where do we go from here?" and "what about to-night's performance?" were directed to the embattled Fred Dean from all areas of the stage.

Fred held up his hands in very heavy despair. "Ladies and gentlemen, please. There is absolutely no question about tonight's performance nor, indeed, as I believe, any of the future performances for this current opera. We have full houses not just now but booked into the future so whatever may happen, these will most definitely go ahead, as too all the dates for the touring company! The row concerns finances between the composer, writer and theatrical management and... well... it's in everyone's interest that it be sorted out. But I wanted you to know the position and to hear it from us here in the theatre rather than having to listen to what will undoubtedly be outside rumour – and that a'plenty!"

By the time that Tom and Nellie travelled home together on the train to Peckham that evening, further developments had occurred that completely filled their minds, thoroughly eclipsing the uplifting feelings they had both experienced once again during that evening's magical performance of 'Gondoliers' received, as always, by a widely enthusiastic house.

"So, do you mean that now Mr. Gilbert has actually issued a writ against Mr. D'Oyly Carte for the payment of profits from the present opera," Nellie asked of her husband, an incredulous look across her face.

"That's what I've heard, of course Mr. Dean told me," Tom advised.

"Blimey!" Nellie exclaimed. "Do you know what, Tom?". Her husband looked quizzically, so she continued before he had time to even reply. "Methinks that this is just like one of them far-fetched plots what Mr. Gilbert is always wanting to write for one of the new operas and Sir Arthur refuses to even consider!"

Not for the first time in their marriage, already of more than 20 years, Tom once again could not cease to be amazed at the clarity and obvious depth to Nellie's thoughts. Not for the first time, either, he acknowledged, but unchivalrously only to himself, that he could never have possibly reached the same kind of conclusion. For all of that, he looked very lovingly, even more appreciatively, towards her as she continued.

"And that is why, and I've said it before and no doubt will say it many times again, whilst I've got breath in my increasingly old body, this is probably no more than another lot of 'ot air between the likes of them all. It'll blow over, you marks my words, and they're all get on again together as right as rain. Mr. Gilbert, well he'll get over it, cool down a bit, he's had 'is puff, and then once they all simmer down, it'll be back to the old ways – of course, that is until the next time. They've all made too much money from the partnership for any single one of them to want it to end!"

"We've all made money out of the partnership," Tom quietly added, still in a state of awe at the vision of his wife's statements.

"True, true, Tom but you and me 'ardly 'alf in the same way as them three – but I know what you mean," Nellie added. "Anyway, we'll see 'ow it all goes and, for now, we've got plenty to be getting on with what with all the costumes required for the 'Gondoliers' touring company."

"And don't I know that," Tom added, "getting a gondola that will work right night after night in all manner of theatres up and down the land is about as nerve wracking for me as the gallery scene in 'Ruddigore'."

"Which went alright night after night, 'ere there and everywhere!" Nellie interjected, to which Tom nodded. "Well, there's you 'ave it Tom, this er all go just as right as well in the end!"

Tom relaxed a little for the remaining moments until the train pulled into Peckham station and he and Nellie alighted and so began the short walk home. The next day, back at the Savoy, one of Nellie's predictions apparently came very remarkably true when they all heard that Mr. Gilbert had, indeed, calmed down and, as Fred Dean put it, had written to Helen D'Oyly Carte in "an overture of reconciliation". There was more that they heard later. The full letter had gone on to say: "I cannot believe that you and your husband can be anxious to maintain the unhappy relations that now exist between us". Fred Dean told then further, quietly as if the information should someway be in confidence although so many knew about it that it was impossible, that Mr. Gilbert had even admitted that his notorious carpet statements had been made in anger.

"What did I tell yer!" Nellie exclaimed, "it's all the stuff of the plot of the next opera, nothing more, nothing less!"

Some, though, felt far less about the whole situation, Sir Arthur, for one. He let it be known that he felt "physically and mentally ill over the wretched business" for which his chosen antidote was to get on with the composing of his grand opera – 'Ivanhoe'. The first night was set to be on 31 January 1891.

Nobody of the Savoy company was involved with the grand opera work; they were all still too heavily involved in the highly successful nightly performances of 'Gondoliers', but nevertheless all took a deal of interest in the goings on. "It's like something happening within our family," was the once more very perceptive way that Nellie put it to Tom.

They learnt that the opera, 'Ivanhoe', had been cast with the finest English singers that Mr. D'Oyly Carte could engage, plus a large chorus and orchestra of 63 musicians, everything on a much grander and larger scale than any of the comic operas at the Savoy.

"I appreciate the news but I must say that the one thing that attracted me in the first place to Gilbert and Sullivan 20 years ago was the very idea of establishing English comic opera," Tom declared to Fred Dean in one of their usual on stage conversations during their busy working day. "And that's how it still remains, grand opera is not for me and I am happy here!"

"I think I agree with you there, too," Fred replied. "But they tell me the new theatre is splendidly equipped and that interests me. No doubt they will let us enjoy some improvements here too when they see how things work out at the new place!"

Tom felt rather strange as they prepared for that evening's performance of 'Gondoliers' at the Savoy on Saturday 31 January, knowing that less than a mile away in Cambridge Circus, a new opera by Sir Arthur was itself being performed for the first time that night. "It's all rather odd, us being here, but Sir Arthur working on his new opera some place else and us not being part of it," he sighed to Nellie. "I can see it all in my mind's eye, Sir Arthur entering the pit, bowing to the audience with his so familiar monocled expression, I can hear the cheers, sense the excited atmosphere, the usual glittering occasion of the first night Audience – Mr. Dean has told me that the Prince of Wales and the Duke of Edinburgh are to be in the audience – it'll be a real gala night!"

"So what," Nellie answered, "we've 'ad plenty enough of them gala nights 'ere and we'll 'ave more yet, so I says let them 'ave their grand opera gala and I'm 'appy enough with what we've got 'ere at the Savoy!"

"Oh, I know that, love," Tom quickly interjected lest his wife should think that his loyalties were already lying elsewhere, like the time all those years ago when he first left the music hall for the new works. "No, I'm with you on what you say, and comic opera, these Gilbert and Sullivan works, these are my true likings and I wouldn't want to be with the grand opera. No, it's just me thinking that after 20 years, how strange it is not being involved with one of Sir Arthur's First Nights."

"Listen, Tom, Sir Arthur 'as written 'undreds of pieces of music, nothing whatever to do with Mr. Gilbert or what we do 'ere at the Savoy and as I sees it, then tonight is no different to that!" Nellie reasoned.

"Yes, as always, I suppose you are right," Tom answered, realising only too well how correct the statement was and it wasn't worth continuing the discussion.

That evening's performance at the Savoy was as enchanting and delightful as any of the preceding performances of 'Gondoliers'. The audience clapped and shouted their enthusiastic delight and the final chorus seemed once again to sum up exactly how both performers and audience felt:

"So good-bye, cachucha, fandango, bolero –
We'll dance a farewell to that measure –
Old Xeres, adieu – Manzanilla – Montero –
We leave you with feelings of pleasure!"

The curtain fell at the Savoy only for Tom to be instructed, just as on other evenings, to raise and lower it several times in reply to the audience's vociferous demands for numerous curtain calls. It hardly seemed to him, or any at the Savoy, that any special event could possibly be occurring in another theatre on the same evening. By the following Monday, though, Tom was anxious to hear from Fred Dean how all had gone with 'Ivanhoe' at the English Grand Opera Theatre.

"They tell me that it all went very well, a real success," Fred advised. "But Mr. Gilbert wasn't there, oh, he was invited, of course, but he declined to go. Anyway, the papers were enthusiastic so I'm sure that Sir Arthur will have another well deserved and much applauded composition." Some weeks later, Fred was able to add: "Tom, Mr. Gilbert has told me that he has been to see the new opera."

"Did he enjoy it?" Tom asked of his stage manager.

"Apparently, yes he did," Fred Dean replied. "In reality, he told me that he wrote to Sir Arthur pointing out whilst he was quite unable to appreciate high-class music and expected to be bored, the fact that he wasn't meant that it was the highest compliment that he could ever pay to a grand opera. So, yes, I suppose that you can say, Tom me lad, he enjoyed it!"

Soon, though, all at the Savoy were aware that 'Ivanhoe' was not in any way to be held in the same public esteem nor destined to capture the success of what they regarded as their own comic operas. Whilst it did run for 155 continuous performances, they quickly acknowledged as no mean feat for a grand opera, it did not establish Sir Arthur as a composer of grand opera. There was to be no follow-up and worse still for Mr. Richard D'Oyly Carte, his new Grand Opera Theatre proved to be a professional miscalculation. When 'Ivanhoe' closed, the theatre manager mounted performances of a French light opera – 'La Basoche' by Messager – as a stop-gap but it was not a success either. Later he gave up on the new theatre completely and the building became 'Palace Music Hall', which, for Tom, was a most ironic happening.

"Thankfully, you never got yerself off to working for the new grand opera and stayed 'ere instead!" Nellie observed when they heard the news. "If yer 'ad, then life for you, me old Tom, would 'ave gone full circle and yer would 'ave been back in the music 'all again!"

Tom replied with just a weak smile although inwardly he felt so very relieved that he remained with the Savoy company where, despite all that had happened over the turn of the decade

219

into the 1890's, their performances of Gilbert and Sullivan operas continued from strength to strength.

At the Adelphi Theatre in 1982, there was no mention, nor indeed any thoughts of 'Ivanhoe' It was as if the opera had never existed and, in any case, Rupert and his fellow audience members had far too much else on their minds to even cast the work a single thought.

Chapter 16

"Then one of us will be a Queen, And sit on a golden throne"

"Well, Tom me lad, now we do really have a job to do, not just you and me, but your Nellie and Miss Parker too!" Fred Dean called to Tom as soon as he had arrived to work and walked on to the stage one Monday morning well over a year into the run of 'Gondoliers'. Even though the past year had been very upsetting and difficult with all the arguments at the Savoy, lately life had been much calmer and everybody had got back into their usual confident, yet relaxed, frame of work. Now Tom realised from the very flushed and ruddy look of his stage manager's face that there must indeed be something highly significant and very important that he was about to learn. He immediately felt another sense of foreboding as a result.

"Don't look so worried, me old Tom," Fred declared, immediately realising why his assistant looked so nervous and so quickly made to address the situation. "It's no more of the troublesome news – in fact, it couldn't be more the opposite!" Tom's expression changed to one of relief although he still looked expectant as to what he might about be told. "This is very special news," the stage manager continued. "Mr. D'Oyly Carte himself has just told me that the company has been commanded to perform at Windsor Castle, no less!"

"At Windsor Castle! You mean, Mr. Dean, where the Queen…" Tom looked startled and his mouth gaped open as he ran out of words.

"The very same!" Fred replied, his head bowing as if in a ready salute. "Yes, Her Majesty Queen Victoria has requested that we mount a full performance of 'Gondoliers' at Windsor Castle. In fact, 'requested' is my word; the citation has been received and says that Her Majesty has ordered a 'Command Performance of a comic opera by the D'Oyly Carte Company'. It will be the very first time that any theatrical company has received any Command to Windsor since the death of the Prince Albert, and that will be 30 years ago by the end of this year. So there you have it, a most glorious occasion bestowed upon us and there you have the reason for my saying to you that we really do have a job to do!"

Tom gathered his thoughts for a moment, neither wanting to say something stupid nor to take so much time before replying lest the stage manager thought that he must be equally stupid. Just a few seconds elapsed therefore before Tom finally made a brief comment. "That'll be an honour, Mr. Dean, for all of us, the whole company, not to say for Sir Arthur and Mr. Gilbert!"

"Very much so, especially after all the difficulties of the past year," Fred Dean replied. "It's an incredible and prestigious honour for each and everyone of us! And do you know what is ironical in all of this request?" The stage manager immediately continued without Tom having even the briefest chance to ask what. "Well, Her Majesty The Queen herself had suggested to Sir Arthur in the first place that he should write a grand opera, which, of course, by royal command if you like, he really did. And now Her Majesty will be seeing 'Gondoliers' but she never did see 'Ivanhoe' and will be most unlikely to now that it isn't even being performed any more!"

"Fancy that," was Tom's less than measured reply, although in his thoughts he very much took in all that the stage manager was telling him.

"Anyway, there's much work to be done because we've to build the stage and the set at the castle, in fact the whole lot, and no doubt we will have to make several adjustments because the stage area will not be any thing like what we have here, let alone the equipment. Then, all the costumes will have to be taken over, it's going to be a massive task and we simply dare not let there be anything to go wrong – this will be probably the most important performance with which any of us have ever been, or likely to be, involved!"

"Right you are, Mr. Dean." Tom thought for a few seconds and realised that whilst he had taken in the news, he very much hadn't considered the extreme momentous nature of what was going to happen. But he realised that there was immediately something that he very much wanted to do. "Can I run upstairs and tell Nellie, Mr. Dean?"

"Of course you can, Tom me lad. In fact, I'll come with you and do everything proper and tell Florrie Parker myself at the same time, so we can all begin to think together of all this news entails!" Fred Dean answered, still muttering to himself about the enormity of the job in hand.

The brief task of climbing the stairs gave Tom sufficient time to gather his thoughts and he was ready to deliver the news to a startled Nellie, who was busily preparing a set of costumes for the coming evening's performance. She looked up, slightly startled as her husband and Fred Dean rushed into the room. Fred immediately went over to Florrie. Both the wardrobe mistress and her assistant had enough experience of all the dramatic news and gossip over the past months and both, in unison, wondered what on earth was then happening, so much so that Miss Parker spoke for both of them by saying: "Goodness, for what do we have the honour, gentlemen?" Tom left it to his boss to speak with the wardrobe mistress and turned immediately to his wife.

"We're to work with the touring company!" Tom declared very cheekily to a quickly reddening Nellie.

"Oh, gaud, what the 'ell do yer mean?" his wife replied, dropping the costume on which she was working to the floor, so much was her sense of shock.

"Like I say, we are to go away from the Savoy, both of us, and help mount a touring production of 'Gondoliers' – I've just been told!" Tom couldn't resist the temptation to jokingly tease his wife who, because she saw Fred Dean in the room also talking quietly to Miss Parker, could only believe there was truth in what her husband was telling her.

"Oh, Tom, no surely not – you know it's somefink what I 'ave always dreaded, being away from our 'ome and being on the go from one 'featre to another, day in day out, week in week out – oh, I know that we'll be together, but to be away from our 'ome for gaud knows 'ow long – that's really 'orrible! Besides, what will they do 'ere, what will Miss Parker do if I am not 'ere to 'elp 'er!"

Nellie's words came thick and fast and Tom saw that his wife was becoming really and most genuinely distressed. He felt both angry and despicable with himself for teasing her so and immediately sought to put her out of her misery, but not before one more short further tease. "Don't get upset, love, it is only going to be just for one town, then we'll back to the Savoy".

"Oh – one town you say – oh, well then, that ain't so bad I suppose, I'll be able to put up with that, you'll be with me and well, I'll just 'ave to get on with it, there probably ain't no other way! One town only, where is that then, Tom?" she asked, already calming down.

"Windsor," Tom answered.

"Windsor!" Nellie exclaimed. "I don't fink we've ever 'ad a touring company go there and I've always supposed that the 'featre ain't big enough, so 'ow comes we're going there now?"

"It's not the theatre we are going to – it's the castle!" Tom declared. His wife's mouth dropped in sheer amazement at what she had heard.

"Windsor Castle! You don't mean the place where Her Majesty is!" Under the circumstance she felt it was perfectly right and proper that she should remember to sound her 'h's'!

"The very same, my love!" Tom replied.

"Cor blimey – oh gaud, I mean, please excuse me your Majesty," Nellie flutteringly declared, her head bowing and her body curtseying with respect as she spoke. By then, Florrie Parker, almost with as much nervous disposition as Nellie, and Fred Dean had come across the room to join Tom and Nellie.

"So, Tom has no doubt told you my dear," the wardrobe mistress said, rather quickly gathering her prim composure, to which Nellie merely nodded her reply. "Well, it's an enormous honour for the whole company," she stated most satisfyingly, mirroring the sentiments that Fred Dean had earlier expressed. "It will mean some very special preparations for the costumes for that night!" Again Nellie just nodded, as Miss Parker still continued. "But that's really no problem for you, and us here, because for every night's performance we, especially you, my dear, always ensure that everything looks just like new!" Again, Nellie said nothing but simply smiled by way of her reply.

"But it's not like that for us," Fred Dean intervened, ensuring to assert the difficulties that they would be facing. "For Tom and me, it'll be a real major undertaking – building not only the set but first of all having to build a stage to put the set on!"

"Well, that will be different!" Florrie Parker observed, with a self-effacing smile.

"It's more than that!" the stage manager replied, still very conscious of the enormity of the tasks ahead. "It's the biggest thing that we've ever been asked to do. Tom and I will need to start thinking about it right now. Apparently we're to mount the production in the Waterloo Gallery at the castle, stage, side and front curtains, orchestra space, dressing room space – oh seating of course – the lot!" he declared, his arms throwing wide across the room.

"Oh, you'll do it, both of you, completely within your stride, I've no doubts about that!" Florrie Parker supportively declared to which Fred Dean responded with a discernable contented purr. Tom nodded as well and Nellie backed up her husband with a helpful pat on the back.

With the performance at Windsor Castle set for 6 March 1891, and the 'Gondoliers' continuing to play to capacity houses each night at the Savoy, not to say also by the touring company up and down the length and breadth of the country night after night as well, the early weeks of the year were a blur of activity for everybody, weeks too filled with excited anticipation. Fred Dean visited the castle on several occasions and reported back instructions to Tom who busied himself on stage at the Savoy in making things ready.

"If the gondola must move smoothly on any one night, then the night at Windsor must be that one!" an increasingly nervous Fred Dean declared to Tom.

"That'll be fine, Mr. Dean, we've hardly ever stuck yet, well 'hardly ever'," Tom added with a smile. He couldn't resist adding "It's just a pity that Her Majesty hasn't ordered a performance of 'Ruddigore' so we would be building the gallery scene for the Castle!"

Fred laughed, holding his stomach in his mirth. "That's a good idea, Tom – but then, I suppose they've got enough galleries in Windsor Castle that we wouldn't have to build a set!"

"Bet the pictures there probably don't move though, the ghosts wouldn't be able to walk out Mr. Dean," Tom quickly replied, "so that wouldn't do either!"

Tom's last remark was too much for the stage manager who then had to quickly leave the stage in a fit of coughing and spluttering. But Tom's remarks were just the tonic that he needed to calm him down and it wasn't long before once again they were both engaged in their preparatory tasks.

Just a couple of days before the appointed performance, it was time for Tom and Nellie to pack their cases and shut the door to the little, but extremely precious to them, home in Peckham. They had barely ever left the place overnight before and had made sure to ask their kind and friendly neighbour to look in to see that all was well. Although rather modest by nature, for once they also couldn't resist explaining why they were having to go away either!

Nellie felt sad as they walked the familiar steps to the station and couldn't resist frequently looking behind her just to see their home was alright for yet another time before they left for the few days away. Tom hugged his wife as they walked and again reassured her everything would be fine to which she responded with a weak smile. By the time they got to Blackfriars she felt better and was even beginning to look forward to what she increasingly saw as an exciting adventure. Because they didn't walk the usual route to the Savoy but, with Tom guiding with his arm around her, instead took an Underground train, dirty and steamy, to Paddington, she soon realised that it was no ordinary day. Later, as the train steamed across the bridge over the River Thames and into the station at Windsor, she thought for a moment of the many occasions in the summer when she and Tom had been with the rest of the company in the very same area on the traditional riverboat picnics. But a dreary and cold day in March soon shook any such summery thoughts from her memory and as the train finally came to a steamy and spluttering stop in Windsor station, Nellie knew that this was a different occasion altogether.

"Come on, my love," Tom said kindly as he offered her his arm as she got out of the train. "Mr. Dean has said we should go to our boarding house first, to leave our bags and collect ourselves, before we then go up to the castle. I've got our passes here to show at the gate," he declared proudly, looking for what must have been the 20th time that day at the embossed passes with the names 'Mr. Thomas & Mrs Nellie Dobbs, D'Oyly Carte Company' clearly shown.

Tom and Nellie spent only a few moments at the boarding house that Mr. D'Oyly Carte had booked for them, neither wanting to waste what they felt to be company time. A few others from the company were also to be staying in the same place but would not be arriving until the day of the performance itself, with even more spread around several similar small establishments around the town. Tom and Nellie very much respected the fact that they represented almost the company's advance party of members and the comforting feeling of obvious seniority and importance that implied. With a very quick wash and brush up, an increasingly nervous Tom and Nellie made their way to the gates of Windsor Castle itself, there to be quickly admitted without question as Tom, in the most gentleman-about-town way that he could muster, held up their passes for inspection. A quick salute from the guard, something that Nellie could scarcely believe was for them, more like, she thought, a scene from one of their very own Savoy operas, and they were soon in the castle itself. It was as much as either of them could do to follow the man who they thought must have been one of the castle's footmen, along many various passages, both daring hardly to take in what they saw around them, not to notice the paintings nor furnishings, until they finally entered a huge room, then a scene of frantic hustle and bustle.

"This, this is the Victoria Gallery and you will find your company colleagues towards the stage area," the footman declared, bowing ever so slightly as he took his leave of the startled pair. "Thank you very much, I'm sure." Nellie, at least, had the foresight and collected herself quickly enough to make a hushed reply. Tom, on the other hand, felt once more too overwhelmed.

"There you both are!" Fred Dean's words soon roused Tom from his stupor. "Welcome to the Windsor Empire!" he went on in a very hushed tone. Nellie fought to hold back her giggles. "Anyway, we're making progress and will do more than ever now you are both here. Tom, I'll leave it to you to get the gondola up and running in the first instance; Nellie, the baskets with the costumes for the First Act are over there by the side of the orchestra area," he directed, his arms opening and one hand pointing to the direction of the forlorn looking clothes baskets.

"Right you are, Mr. Dean, I best set to then," Nellie replied.

"That's my girl, I'll leave you to it until Miss Parker arrives later," an obviously satisfied stage manager answered. "Right, Tom me lad, I'll leave you to get on with your work and I'll try and tackle what we want to do with the orchestra area!"

"Very good, Mr. Dean." Tom and Nellie blew a kiss to each other and immediately immersed themselves with the work in hand. Within moments, both were almost unaware of the location in which they found themselves and felt almost as if they were back at the Savoy and preparing just for another of the already many performances of 'Gondoliers'. Nellie soon thought to herself that it was all as Fred Dean had said – "the Windsor Empire" after all!

They all had a most effective couple of days of hard work at the castle, retiring each evening late, overly tired, to the boarding house, instantly falling asleep only to get up early again the following morning, to quickly wash and dress, but being sure to take time to have a substantial breakfast, to set them up for the day ahead. More than any one thing else, that was something which Nellie most appreciated.

"Oh, Tom, I feels like a Queen meself, having a breakfast like this prepared and laid in front of me – no cooking, no washing up, just being waited on! Then no beds to make, no cleaning of the 'ouse to do, just get ourselves out the door when we're ready!" Nellie sighed as she reflected on what she had just said.

"Well, my love, you are a queen, to me anyway!" Tom answered, at the same time giving his wife a loving hug. "And who knows, perhaps one day we're be able to take a little holiday ourselves, by the seaside perhaps, in a place like this – not for a couple of days, maybe a week!"

"Who knows, maybe one day," Nellie spoke casting her eyes down to the floor. "It's funny, but when we 'ad to come away, I thought that I would 'ate being away from our 'ouse, and of course I like being at 'ome, but I realise that just for a few days, then it's all rather nice after all!"

"It's all a nice change," Tom declared, rather too modestly. "But now, well it's time to get back to the castle and to get on with our day!" In all his life, Tom could never have made before such a nonchalant statement, so inappropriate for the circumstances, but Nellie's own head was in too much of a whirl to notice. They were both soon out of the front door and wrapping up against the cold March winds, walked the few steps through the steadily awakening town of Windsor and to the entrance of the castle, then once again to the Waterloo Gallery, by then looking very much ready for an opera performance.

On the morning of 6 March, Fred Dean did something that he did virtually every day of his working life – that was to walk to the back of the auditorium, there to turn and look at the stage to see that all was well. This time, though, he stood at the back of the Waterloo Gallery and not the Savoy Theatre. Now it was portraits that lined the wall, there was no dress circle or gallery above his head, instead a chandeliered ceiling. Flowers and plants adorned the area separating the orchestra from the audience. As for the stage itself, it looked so much smaller than what he was used to at the Savoy, but the side curtains and front main stage curtain looked suitably regal for the important occasion.

He signalled to Tom who then from the small space they had in the wings, so much less than they were ever used to, somehow managed to make the gondola glide effortlessly on and off the set. Fred nodded his satisfaction, stood a moment longer to once again take everything in, then walked slowly back to the stage area itself.

"That's absolutely fine, Tom me lad," he declared with a very obvious sense of approval.

"Right you are, Mr. Dean," Tom replied, just as if it were all no more than just another day.

Later, as they were joined in the gallery by the whole company, the singers and musicians, a full scale dress rehearsal took place. Most satisfyingly it went without a hitch, so much so that Fred Dean realised there was no need for any further run through, with the performers having time to relax before the most important evening. Tom and Nellie, Fred Dean and Florrie Parker had no such luxury as the stage team again and again made certain that the set was in order whilst the wardrobe pair checked, brushed and re-pressed the costumes. But everything was already most spic and span and the further nervous energy was hardly required.

Slightly before nine that evening, the company received the much anticipated signal that Her Majesty Queen Victoria, the Princes and Princesses of the Royal Family, Ladies and Gentlemen of the Household and their guests were about to make their way into the Waterloo Gallery. A respectful hush descended upon the whole company, Tom, in the tiny area that they had as the wings, held Nellie's hand, both resisted for the moment any temptation to peek through the curtains. Some polite clapping greeted the conductor, for that evening the D'Oyly Carte Company's Francois Cellier, something of a surprise to most of the company that Sir Arthur himself, nor indeed Mr. Gilbert, were present on the evening. As if in any normal theatre and equally as if for any of the many by then thousands of performances of a Gilbert and Sullivan opera, silence descended throughout the auditorium as the overture began. The very special performance of 'Gondoliers' was underway.

Once during the evening, Nellie did get a chance for a very quick peek through to the audience and let out a very hushed, but equally deeply reverenced gasp, as she clearly saw Queen Victoria, a very small, squat figure dressed in black, sitting with her family in the front row. She noticed that Her Majesty held a copy of the opera's libretto in her gloved hand and also that she was both studying it, then next glancing to the stage, whilst at the very same moment she was very clearly seen to be beating time. Quietly Nellie indicated in her much-practised stage whisper to Tom, who merely nodded, got on with his work in hand and made no attempt to look himself, very much as if he didn't want to be reminded of the importance of the occasion and all that was entailed. For Tom, it was better for him that he just kept his mind on the job in hand, just as if he was back at the Savoy – the night was still too young with time enough for something to go wrong!

"Rising early in the morning,
We proceed to light the fire,
Then our Majesty adorning
In its workaday attire,
We embark without delay
On the duties of the day."

"First, we polish off some batches
Of political despatches,
And foreign politicians circumvent;
Then, if business isn't heavy,
We may hold a Royal levee,
Or ratify some Acts of Parliament."

The song of 'Guiseppe Palmieri', himself a Gondolier but also in the story perhaps to become the 'King of Barataria', had that evening, more than ever, a very special potency that was not lost on any of the performers. The company were very relieved when it became obvious that no offence had been taken by any in their revered audience.

231

Fred Dean and Tom were especially pleased that the performance had so far gone without a problem even though as the finale itself approached, both had the same thought on their minds – would the temporary stage hold up at the very end when there would be around 80 singers, principals and chorus together on the stage. Nervously, Fred asked Tom once more to take a quick check beneath the structure, neither realising the possibility of catastrophe, after which he reported back that all seemed to be well.

And so at nearly 11.30 in the evening the performance came to a close. Whilst it was not the usual highly boisterous clapping and cheering coming from the audience that they were always so used to at the Savoy, nor with the customary shouts from the gallery, which didn't exist there anyway, it was nevertheless, respectful enough. The conductor joined the performers on stage to take a very deep and highly reverent bow to Her Majesty The Queen and the special audience. Much to everybody's surprise, the whole company was then invited into the Drawing Room for a reception. For Tom and Nellie, the situation was so totally one of awe, that they could scarcely believe where they were, nor what was really happening to them. They both stood very much to the back of the room and only once, just in fact as the queen was leaving the room after only a short while, did they both catch a glimpse of their most important Gilbert and Sullivan opera guest ever.

"Pinch me, Tom, pinch me, this ain't surely actually 'appening to me, is it!" Nellie exclaimed.

"Course it is, luv," Tom replied, forgetting himself with the overawing sense of the occasion and reverting to his mispronunciation of his term of endearment for the first time in a long while.

"I'll remember this to me dying day," Nellie continued, "my Tom and me, 'ere in the Drawing Room at Windsor Castle, in the same room as Her Majesty', Nellie made an extra special attempt once more with her 'h's'. "Not only that, but with a plate in me one 'and", soon forgetting herself once more, "and a glass of refreshment in the other!"

"It is very special – in fact you can almost say that it is by 'Royal Appointment!'" Tom quipped. As he said it, and before Nellie had time to respond, they were then joined by an equally overawed Fred Dean with Florrie Parker beside him.

"It went so very well," Fred declared, "thanks to you for all that you did!" Florrie nodded her agreement to which Tom and Nellie responded with an embarrassed half smile. "Mr. D'Oyly Carte has told me that Her Majesty enjoyed the performance very much, she says that she found Sir Arthur's music charming and Mr. Gilbert's dialogue very witty. And, Tom me lad, Her Majesty commented to Mr. D'Oyly Carte that she found the settings to be very lovely!" A broad, satisfying smile spread across the stage manager's face before, turning to both Florrie and Nellie, he concluded by saying "and, ladies, a special mention was made was made by Her Majesty that she found the dresses 'very gay and smart'. So there we have it, a most successful evening and one that will no doubt be seen as the most important evening for the D'Oyly Carte Company!"

"So far," Tom added with a smile.

"Well, perhaps, who knows," Fred Dean added, clapping his assistant on the back. "Well, we best be away now, try to get some sleep before we get off back to London tomorrow and the Savoy – who knows what everybody's been up to there whilst we've been away!"

For Tom and Nellie, sleep was completely out of the question, no matter how tired they were. They lay in bed in the Windsor boarding house, their minds filled with the events of the day and what they had experienced less than a mile away on the other side of the town.

"Who would 'ave thought it!" Nellie exclaimed as she lay in Tom's arms. "Nellie Dobbs with 'er 'usband, Tom, taking refreshments in the same room as 'er Majesty, not to say mounting the production in the castle itself! 'ow it's all been possible, I 'ardly knows and I says it before and no doubt will say it again, I almost feels like it's a scene from one of our operas!"

"For once, my love, the words of the opera were right for you," Tom replied. "Well, almost, one of us 'will be a queen'. More than that, you, dear Nellie, you are always my queen!"

233

With that, they both managed at least to have some rest even if the sleep evaded them both but at least they were a happy, if very tired, pair that made their way back to London the next day after they had overseen the clearing up of the set at the castle.

Tom and Nellie, and the whole D'Oyly Carte Company, lived in the reflected glory of their Command Performance for a long time beyond the evening itself. The event caused widespread interest not only in Britain, with an even greater clamouring for seats to see the opera, but in America as well – not to say how several neighbours in a street in Peckham heard everything in remarkable detail! A week afterwards, when once again everybody was gathered on stage at the Savoy in preparation for a usual performance of 'Gondoliers', even this time in a more mundane setting than what they had enjoyed days before, Fred Dean took the opportunity of reading from a copy of 'The Era', for 14 March.

"The paper here reports of a conversation that our Mr. D'Oyly Carte had with Her Majesty in which the Queen asked, as she was closely following the libretto during the performance, what were the meanings of the interpolations which she had noticed. Mr. D'Oyly Carte told Her Majesty that these were 'gags' to which the Queen replied that she thought 'gags were things that were put by authority into people's mouths'. Here's the best bit though," Fred Dean laughed, as he continued. "Mr. D'Oyly Carte, well he replied 'These gags, your Majesty, are things that people put into their own mouths without authority!' So you can see just how much Her Majesty concentrated on the performance and all in all what a successful evening it all was." The conclusion of the stage manager's speech was met with an outbreak of spontaneous and well-meant clapping from all around the stage.

For the rest of that spring and into early summer 'The Gondoliers' continued it's successful run, finally to close on 20 June 1891 after an initial run of 554 performances, second only in popularity to 'Mikado'. Instead of any immediate revival of an earlier Gilbert and Sullivan opera, for the first time in its history, the Savoy staged a comic opera not by the famous composer and writer. 'The Nautch Girl', by George Dance and Edward

Solomon, was, though, successfully received mainly because the Savoy, and Mr. D'Oyly Carte as its manager, had a faithful and devoted public. For most in the Company it didn't seem right at all and many did not feel at ease with the production, just accepting it as continuity of work for which they were all thankful. Tom and Nellie, though, by late summer, soon had their minds directed fully to their beloved operas once more.

They learnt that the Queen had been so pleased with 'Gondoliers' that she had requested a further Command Performance. This time it was 'The Mikado' that was to be performed and the location to be Balmoral Castle. As Mr. D'Oyly Carte had decided to send one of the touring companies, that would then be playing in Aberdeen, to perform, it was decreed that just a couple from the Savoy itself would need to go. And that couple were Tom to oversee the stage and Nellie likewise for the costumes, in support of the touring company. Their responsibility of virtually being in charge, and as representatives of the London company, overawed them both almost as much as once again, in less than six months, being involved in mounting a performance for Queen Victoria. Inwardly, and privately admitting to each other, they both felt immensely proud that the two of them were both held in such high regard by the company that they were being entrusted with such an important mission.

"I ain't even been further north than Tottenham before, let alone all the way up there!" Nellie exclaimed as Tom pointed out the location of Royal Deeside on a map held in his hand.

"Well, it's certainly a lot further north than Islington, I grant you that!" Tom laughed.

This time, Nellie didn't even feel such pangs of sadness as she and Tom, then with an even bigger bag to carry with all their things for over a week away, what with all the travelling involved, closed the front door on their home in Peckham. Their ever friendly neighbour had joked that she felt "honoured to be living next door to the likes of them that frequent Royal Circles!" Nellie laughed at the comment but how proud she felt how her life, and Tom's too, had become as a result of their work at the Savoy. She could hardly bear to think how it would all have been had she remained at the dress factory and then it would be Tom, alone, off to Windsor and Balmoral – and her in Shoreditch! How grateful she felt once again that then, over 10 years before, she had taken up Tom's advice and joined him at the theatre.

The journey north was both long and very tiring although they both spent much of the time preparing their work, with Tom going over and over again the stage instructions, Nellie re-reading her costume notes or doing some needlework and enjoying the passing scene from the train window. Any sense of alarm they had at being so far from home was quelled by their being together. Even when they finally arrived at Aberdeen, a city looking so different and populated by people who spoke a language almost un-understandable to them, they once more took comfort from each other. Soon, though, both felt very much at home when they met up with the D'Oyly Carte touring company, many of whom they knew from their years at the Savoy. As they spent a couple of days in Aberdeen, mostly all the time at the theatre, it was almost impossible for them to know where they were – another theatre, another performance although neither for once had any immediate work to do, rather to just see all that was going on.

"This is really the very first time that we've seen an opera together, like part of an audience really, since you first took me to the Savoy – and 'Patience' – 10 years ago!" Nellie exclaimed. Tom nodded his head in agreement, although he could hardly believe that such time had elapsed. "I like the 'Mikado'," Nellie added, "even more so when I sees it at leisure."

"Me too," Tom added, "but I like them all and I don't think that I could ever say which is the best for me. What do you say, love?"

"Don't know, really – but them earlier ones, when I wasn't with you, well I've only seen them in revival and that don't somehow feel the same. I've been involved in everything since 'Iolanthe' so they all feel very much one of me own even in a revival," Nellie responded. "I am glad to say, and feel, that there really is a part of me in all of this!"

"Glad to hear it – and that's why they are so very good!" Tom smiled and held Nellie's hand ever tightly. "It's been a good production tonight, just as well performed and looking as good as it did at the Savoy. I'm sure it will be fit for the Queen!"

On 4 September 1891, Tom and Nellie joined the rest of the touring company members in taking the train from Aberdeen to Ballater. Although there was much chatting amongst them all during the journey, Nellie especially felt overawed by the beautiful scenery that they passed through, seeing the distant Grampian Mountains seeming ever to be closing in around, as if to enfold, them. She found the whole situation so totally bemusing.

"It's a kind of purple 'ue, 'ain't it Tom," she exclaimed, pointing her hand to the distant vista, rousing for a moment from her deep thoughts.

"It's early heather," Tom advised, looking for the moment very knowledgeable.

"'ow the 'ell do yer know that?" a startled Nellie asked. "You're no more a country bumpkin than I am!"

Tom smiled. "I read it in this book," he confessed and immediately felt a strong nudge in his ribs.

They all got out of the train at Ballater Station and were met by a string of coaches and wagonettes to be conveyed to Balmoral Castle. It was a beautiful day and Nellie felt that her eyes were surely going to pop from her head when the turrets of the castle came into view, in the perfect and tranquil setting of the Scottish mountains. "Oh, Tom," she sighed as they alighted in the courtyard of Balmoral Castle.

The company were shown into a large room that had been set aside for their performance. Tom, to Nellie's proud amazement, very much in command, immediately took charge of the preparations for the stage setting whilst she opened the baskets to lay out the costumes, fans and wigs, all in perfect and pristine order.

"It just seems like yesterday when we were 'andling all these fans, Japanese masks, robes," she reflected.

"Six years ago now, the first night," Tom replied, "time goes by so very fast!"

"Even more so when we play such places as Windsor Castle and Balmoral!" Nellie exclaimed, hardly being able to believe what she was saying. "All I know, it ain't the Strand!"

Any further exchanges were curtailed as Tom helped to direct the first rehearsal, so well that the rehearsal became the only one needed. In the evening, the performance was given very successfully and received with as much acclaim as 'Gondoliers' had been at Windsor. Afterwards the whole company, of course including Tom and Nellie, were presented to Her Majesty The Queen. That occasion was all such a blur for them that although they felt so supremely happy, neither could take in the event nor hardly remember what was happening to them. Deep down they were so satisfied that for their work, the evening had gone so well. In the end, it was after midnight when the company gathered once again in the courtyard of Balmoral Castle, this time to take their leave.

Nobody quite knew how it happened but in the light of the flaming torches in the courtyard, the company as one, with Tom and Nellie close to the end of the second row, stood and sang the National Anthem. As they did so, Queen Victoria came out on to the balcony and waved them farewell.

Sitting once again in the coach, Nellie had tears in her eyes, teeming right down her face. She snuggled up to Tom and said nothing. Tom didn't speak either. He too was crying with both the sheer emotion of the occasion and with relief that the night, really in both his and Nellie's charge, had gone so very well. Their sense of euphoria lasted not just for the remainder of the journey back to Aberdeen, but all the rest of that night, indeed for all the long journey back south to London.

When they returned to work at the Savoy, just a couple of days later, everybody there had already heard the news of the successful Command Performance given at Balmoral. Tom and Nellie were treated like returning heroes.

"Well done, Tom me lad and Nellie me girl," Fred Dean exclaimed as the two came into the theatre. He gave Tom a bear-like hug, but not before first giving Nellie a kiss on each cheek. Florrie Parker made a similar embrace of them both and their magic moment became all the more special when, on the stage manager's signal, one of the bell boys came in with a huge bunch of flowers.

"For you, my dear," Fred Dean said, handing the bouquet to a very startled, and for the moment highly embarrassed, Nellie.

"Thank you, thank you very much I'm sure," she somehow managed to reply.

"Yes, indeed, thank you so much, Mr. Dean," Tom added, shaking the stage manager firmly by the hand.

"Not at all, not at all," Fred replied. "It's our appreciation, Mr. D'Oyly Carte, Miss Parker here, and, of course me, for all that you have done, not only just for Balmoral, but for all the time!"

The continuing sense of happiness, a kind of autumn gold during the remaining months of 1891, was made the more so for the whole company by the news that the music publisher, Tom Chappell, had stepped in as peacemaker between Sir Arthur, Mr. Gilbert and Mr. D'Oyly Carte. Fred Dean told Tom that Mr. Gilbert had stated that he was "quite ready to let bygones be bygones" and that Sir Arthur had responded by saying "let us meet and shake hands". All at the Savoy were overjoyed when they learnt that on 12 October 1891, the composer and writer had met for two hours, and especially that Sir Arthur had declared that "a cobbler should stick to his last".

There was an immediate excited anticipation from all in the D'Oyly Carte Company of there soon being another new Gilbert and Sullivan opera.

* * * *

For any chance of a similar feeling of euphoria for the audience at the Adelphi Theatre over 90 years later on the night of 27 February 1982, Rupert Moore could only wish in his wildest dreams.

As the evening wore on, becoming more ominously close to what would soon have to be its end, Rupert sank further and further into the innermost depth of his increasingly negative thoughts. Time and time that night, he wished how much better it would have been for him to be born a hundred years earlier, to be amongst those he considered lucky enough to be around at the very start of the Gilbert and Sullivan partnership. For him, at that very moment, any thought of all the glorious performances and special occasions, like the Command Performances at Windsor Castle and Balmoral, and all else in the long 107-year history of the D'Oyly Carte Opera Company, palled into insignificance when compared to what might happen to the Company that very evening.

He shook at the enormity of his thoughts but somehow tried to concentrate on what was about to be performed again on the stage in front of him. He glanced to his grandmother sitting beside him and noticed that she too was very much deep in thoughts, even though her eyes were also cast towards the stage. The pair both continued to look ahead but for that moment it seemed as if neither were fully concentrating on what was happening.

Chapter 17
"Oh, admirable art!
Oh, neatly-planned intention!"

Late summer, 1892, and a picture of late Victorian elegance generally throughout the country, felt as much by Tom and Nellie as they strolled, arm in arm, through Greenwich Park, reflecting most happily upon both their lives and their years of work at the Savoy. It hardly seemed possible to them that by then a combined total of over 30 years between them had been spent in the world of Gilbert and Sullivan. Both considered it to be a very respectable and wonderful milestone, one that had given them so much that was good in their lives and for which they were so thankful. The summer's outing in the park seemed for them both as a time of worthy celebration of all that it had meant. As if to even more pleasantly mark the occasion, in the distance, the familiar music being played by a band on the park's bandstand, a selection from 'Iolanthe', seemed to emphasise just how good it had all been and would, they earnestly hoped, continue to be.

They looked a perfectly respectable pair, Tom in his smart blazer and boater, Nellie in her floral dress, matching hat and parasol, almost gliding through the rest of the thronging people, those too equally enjoying a Sunday in the park. Whilst they acknowledged with a respectful bow or smile some of the people who passed by, mostly known through frequenting the same place on so many numerous and similar occasions, they otherwise were there only for each other. The loving looks and glances between them said it all. Soon they decided to lay a blanket upon the grass, being sure not to be too far away from the bandstand, there to sit and enjoy the picnic that Nellie had prepared in a beautiful wicker basket, itself reminiscent of one of their annual company river picnics that continued to be held in a sense of happy tradition.

"Happy, love?" Tom asked, in similar vein with the same question he had posed so many thousands of times during their lives together.

"'Course, Tom." Nellie's reply was equally predictable but none the less well meant for that.

"You know, love, what would have happened in our lives if you had never taken that courageous step to leave the dress factory and come and work with me in the theatre?" Tom said softly.

"I often thinks like that meself, Tom," Nellie replied, whilst at the same time she undid the serviette and handed Tom a piece of large and succulent pork pie. "To begin with, I very much doubts that we would have been sitting here in this park, no, instead we would have been over there!" Her head nodded in the direction across the River Thames and to the area of Shoreditch beyond, out of sight, on the north bank that a long time ago by then used to be their home territory. "We would 'ave been more struggling to make ends meet, I would have been 'orribly miserable, even ill with them working conditions in the old factory, and you – well, I suppose that you would 'ave been at the 'featre, course you would, but…"

"But without you beside me everyday, not as happy nor as contented as I am, and have been for all the years," Tom concluded, gallantly.

"Thank you for saying that," Nellie replied. "But it's all true and I sort of give thanks in me prayers every night, that had it not been for Sir Arthur and Mr. Gilbert, even Mr. D'Oyly Carte 'imself, and of course your persistence in wanting to get involved in the new works all them years ago, there would 'ave been none of this – therefore, it's as much down to you, as anyone else, Tom me lad!" she exclaimed, mimicking the stage manager by her last statement.

Tom appreciated the joke, but even more appreciated hearing Nellie's words and he gave her, yet again, a loving hug. For some moments they ate their picnic in silence but none the less pleasurably for that. In the distance, the band continued their playing and as one Tom and Nellie found themselves singing along together to the Peer's Chorus from 'Iolanthe'.

"Tantantara! Tzing! Boom!" they both cried with laughter whilst at the same time they beat their knives on the plates.

"My well-loved Lord and Guardian dear,

You summoned me, and I am here," Nellie sang to a delighted Tom, who responded:

"Oh, rapture, how beautiful!

How gentle – how dutiful"

"And that, my dear, says it all for us. Sir Arthur's music, Mr. Gilbert's words but, most important, you and me!" Tom said sincerely.

"Oh, Tom," Nellie replied, tears welling up in her eyes.

A few moments later they cleared up their picnic things and put everything neatly away in the basket. They then enjoyed a few more minutes walking in the park before reaching the gates where, as a kind of indulgence to their more secured working status, they took a cab home to Peckham, rather than having to walk through the suburban streets. Once at home, they took equal delight in making preparations for work the next day, assuring them once again just how completely satisfying that their lives really were.

Since there had been no new Gilbert and Sullivan opera at the Savoy since 'The Gondoliers' had finished over a year before, and by then having had the chance to calm down from the euphoria of having been involved in mounting two Command Performances for Her Majesty Queen Victoria, their work had been mainly concentrated on the costumes and sets for the touring company and in preparation for revivals. It all meant for a far less frantic and therefore much calmer atmosphere that they at first appreciated, giving them both time to really get involved once again and to re-acquaint themselves with some of the earlier works. All nice enough but for Tom, especially, he found that he was growing increasingly anxious for the chance once again to begin work on a new opera with all the patent thrills and excitement which it would bring and in which he realised he revelled. Somehow, he felt sure that it would soon come from the writer and composer.

"Have you heard anything yet about any possible new piece?" was a question that Tom would pose to Fred Dean almost as matter of habit every Monday morning when he began work at the Savoy.

"No, not yet Tom" became the standard reply from the stage manager at first, until by the late autumn, there came a change. "Tom, I have heard a whisper, well more than that really, I do believe that Mr. Gilbert does now have an outline plot for the next opera," Fred declared, obviously with as much pleasure at delivering the news as Tom felt in hearing it.

"I've been expecting that!" Tom replied nonchalantly although internally his stomach was twisting with excitement and he could barely wait for the moment to slip away quickly upstairs to report to Nellie.

Soon there was more news, this time more detail that Fred Dean was able to pass on to the thrilled Tom.

"Right you are, Tom me lad – I've now been given some outline detail for the new piece! I believe that Mr. Gilbert has once again set out a plot where he will, in his own special way, make fun of the various British institutions that he sees as part of his world – that's likely to include British business methods, the party political system, the Army services, the Law!"

"That all sounds Gilbertian enough for a start!" Tom replied, laughing at the very thought of how once again an opera was set, as so often with the most successful ones of the past, to expose vagaries of the society. "Some of the best operas, not to say also the most successful ones like 'HMS Pinafore', 'Iolanthe', 'Mikado', not to say the recent 'Gondoliers', well they've all been taking a Gilbertian view of society and everybody seems to like them the more for that!"

"You're a perceptive chap aren't you Tom?" Fred Dean replied, although without a trace of cynicism.

"No, Mr. Dean, no not really, but I just listen to what I hear and try to think it out a little for myself as well," Tom replied modestly, with his face reddening from the observation that the stage manager had made.

"Well, no doubt we'll learn more about it but maybe not for a while yet," Fred Dean advised. "They tell me that Sir Arthur is not at all well and he's taken himself off to the French Riviera, probably even for the whole winter, to try to restore his health. But Mr. Gilbert has given him the outline plot, written, they tell me, on 37 pages of an exercise book – Sir Arthur has it packed in his bags! Time will tell, Tom, time will tell!"

"So it will, so it will," Tom sighed, admitting to himself that he felt a little deflated that although there was a real prospect of a new piece, there would be nothing coming too soon.

By January of the New Year, 1893, coming soon to the fourth year without there having been any new Gilbert and Sullivan opera, with the theatre-going public voicing frequent alarming thoughts that there might never be another new opera, word finally got to the Savoy that Mr. Gilbert had travelled out to the South of France to meet with Sir Arthur. Further news soon filtered through and this time it was a very excited, also obviously much relieved, Fred Dean who greeted Tom with the customary Monday morning exchange.

"Right you are, have I got news for you!" he exclaimed. "The new piece, well there's sure to be some veritable stage work for us to do!"

"That sounds most intriguing," Tom replied, trying to appear both measured and calm although internally he felt anything but at the news that he had both longed for and much anticipated!

"Well, to begin with, this time we are going to have a completely new setting to anything that we've ever had before – a glamorous South Sea Island, no less. If you ask me, it seems that all that Mediterranean air and sea have truly got to them both!" Fred Dean declared, his face already displaying a very ruddy complexion.

"Dear me, dear me, I can see what you mean about the prospects for the stage work," Tom replied. "For the moment I can hardly conjure up in my mind exactly how that would be as

245

a setting apart from blue skies, sea and sunshine and, erm, there are some special trees aren't there, Mr. Dean?"

Yes, Tom, palm trees or some such like," the stage manager replied, "but we'll need to wait a bit until we know exactly what Mr. Gilbert wants and has in his mind."

"Do we have any details yet about the likely characters or the plot for all of this?" Tom asked.

"Yes, Tom me lad, I have some outline," Fred Dean replied, pulling some papers from his jacket's inside pocket, the package clearly indicating that it was more than just "some outline". "Here we have it – the people of the island are the subjects of their king, King Paramount, who wants to reform his country into a kind of Utopia, modelled on England! He has sent his daughter, the Princess Zara, to be educated in England at Girton College, who afterwards returns to the island with her six imported 'Flowers of Progress', six Englishmen who will then set examples to the islanders as to how to live!" Fred Dean wiped his brow and took a deep breath before he continued:

"The first of the Englishmen is 'Lord Dramaleigh, a Lord Chamberlain, then 'Captain Fitzbattleaxe' of the First Life Guards, next 'Captain Sir Edward Corcoran, K.C.B.' of the Royal Navy…"

"What, never!' You mean, 'Captain Corcoran' from 'Pinafore'?" Tom interrupted, smiling as he recalled one of the earliest operas.

"The very same, although now he has apparently abandoned sail for steam as the plot goes!" Fred Dean affirmed. "Now, where have I got to?"

"Three, so far, at least that's what I believe," Tom advised.

"Yes, yes, that's it there are three more characters still," Fred continued. "Next we will have 'Mr. Goldbury', a so-called company promoter, then 'Sir Bailey Barre, Q.C., M.P.', politician and lawyer, then lastly we will have 'Mr. Blushington' of the county council that Mr. Gilbert says is Britain's latest 'toy' that needs to be included!"

Tom scratched his head as he tried desperately to take in all the information that he was being given. "Goodness, this all sounds as if it is going to be very complicated to set," he answered.

"I agree with that!" the stage manager answered. "It seems to me that Mr. Gilbert is making sure that we now make up for all the past four years of revivals by giving us all something more complex with which to get involved. It'll be a colourful stage and your Nellie, and Miss Parker, well they'll be kept just as busy as well if you ask me – it's a big cast this time!"

Fred Dean's thoughts were immediately reciprocated when within only a few moments Tom had rushed upstairs to pass on the news to his wife and an equally inquisitive wardrobe mistress.

"You mean, grass skirts and all that kind of fing!" Nellie exclaimed. "I ain't so sure that I likes the sound of that!"

"No, no I don't think so, well not at least from the first news that Mr. Dean has received. But I don't know really, but I do know that it will be a large and varied cast – the king and his court, then the so called 'Flowers of Progress', the men's chorus of first lifeguardsmen, the princesses and the maidens…"

"This, indeed, should all prove to be very interesting, very interesting," Florrie Parker interrupted with her usual measured reply. "Of course, it's very early days yet and no doubt we will, as always, be receiving very detailed instructions before too long – it wouldn't be the Savoy if we didn't – nothing ever is going to be left to chance! We'll be more than capable, won't we, my dear?" she concluded, turning to Nellie whilst, at the same time, giving her a comforting pat on the back.

"Oh sure, sure we will an' all that, Miss Parker," Nellie replied, adding "it'll be nice, though, like my Tom feels too, to be starting on the work for a new piece once again after all them revivals – we all look forward to the work!" Nellie's words spoke for all of them as in their time honoured fashion they all once again dispersed to get on with their immediate daily tasks.

As Fred Dean so very neatly put it, the coming weeks soon put some further "meat on the bones" as they received further plot and character details as work progressed on the new piece. Very obviously, and exactly as they first thought, Mr. Gilbert was using endless opportunities to poke fun and to take a stab at various British authorities. The writer let it slip to Fred Dean that many of the new characterisations had been drawn from the very guests who had been frequenting his summer garden parties during the previous year since he had moved to his new home at Grim's Dyke, near Harrow in Middlesex.

As usual, Richard D'Oyly Carte was desperate for the new opera to be completed and mounted at the theatre as soon as was possible, even more urgently given the length of time since 'Gondoliers' and for what he saw as the obvious need for another success for the Savoy. He very naturally wanted, too, for the previous, and very much proven, magic of the Gilbert and Sullivan partnership to be cast again, for what he saw, for what he equally believed that the public equally saw, as their resurrected genius.

Fred Dean was told that Sir Arthur had returned to England from the South of France in March. The stage manager was much amused to learn that the composer had written to the writer, agreeing to come to a meeting to progress work on the new opera, saying: "I assume that you are not averse to standing a bit of bread and cheese and a drop of beer to a poor working man wots been out of work for some years?"

"Sir Arthur must be feeling better," Tom observed to his stage manager on hearing the news, "especially so when he is being so humorous to Mr. Gilbert!"

"It makes me even more happy to see that they seem to have patched up the past differences between them, even that Sir Arthur would seem to especially realise just how much they depend equally upon each other for both their future work and successes," Fred Dean declared, not even bothering to hide what was his very obvious delight.

"And I'm pleased too," Tom smiled, supportively.

"There's something else, too," Fred continued, "Mr. D'Oyly Carte has asked that the new opera be ready for a first night this coming October – so that will set our minds to all that has to be done!"

"Is it possible?" Tom asked.

"Possible, yes, I don't see why not, just as long as Sir Arthur's health keeps improving," Fred replied.

Both the writer and composer carried on their work diligently during the whole of that long and very hot summer, 1893, even though again Mr. Gilbert was suffering from gout and, for once, the roles were reversed with Sullivan completing the music first and Gilbert next adding the libretto. As Fred Dean succinctly observed, "In their 22 years, THAT was very much a first!"

With the final completion of Act Two, the overall plot became very much clearer. The whole company had a further read through on stage, Tom with his worthy notebook in his hand into which he feverishly scribbled directions in readiness to prepare the set.

"So, ladies and gentlemen, there we have it," Fred Dean declared as he put the manuscript down. "Just to be sure, and it's a lot to take in, this one, on a first reading, I think far more complicated plot than anything that has gone before, I'll summarise Act Two." He once again coughed, cleared his throat and began. "The six 'Imported Flowers of Progress' have completed their work with the South Seas Island Society being reorganised and reformed on an English basis. In fact, they have done so well that all the laws are perfect and all lawyers are out of work; the jails are let as model lodgings for the working classes! All the neighbouring nations have disarmed and war is impossible."

A respectable laughter rang from all those gathered on stage to Fred Dean's summary of the plot. He held up his hand in mock authority. "Ah, but there's more!" he indicated and the assembled company once again became respectfully quiet.

"I'll continue. But the islanders rebel against their new found Utopia and the king's daughter, Princess Zara, suddenly remembers that she has forgotten something, the most important element of all! I'll read this directly from the script, just in case I forget something, or worse still, don't fully understand it myself!" the stage manager quipped. Once again he cleared his throat as if to underline the importance of what he was to say. "When asked what it is that she has forgotten, the princess then replies: 'Government by Party! Introduce that great and glorious element – at once the bulwark and foundation of England's greatness – and all will be well! No political measures will endure, because one Party will assuredly undo all that the other Party has done; and whilst grouse is to be shot, and foxes worried to death, the legislative action of the country will be at a standstill!' So, ladies and gentlemen, with that the king decides to adopt government by party and that his country will then no longer be a 'Monarchy Limited' but a 'Limited Monarchy'. I do hope that you all understand that because I don't much feel for the moment to go through it all again!" Fred Dean wiped his brow, very much delighted that his speech was over.

Those on stage smiled and nodded. Tom, for one, looked rather severe and found it hard to join in with many who were laughing and commenting amongst themselves about what they saw as the obvious topicality of the plot. For Tom it would take several read-throughs and rehearsals more before he fully understood and began to warm to the new piece that he still regarded as thoroughly over-complicated. Nellie didn't even bother to begin to understand the significance of it all although she took unequivocal delight at the costume requirements.

"Miss Parker," she declared, "is it really so that the budget is £3,500 for the dresses?" to which the wardrobe mistress nodded her agreement. "That's a lot of money," Nellie exclaimed, her eyes wide open as if to emphasise the enormity of it all, a sum that she could only just about manage to comprehend as being possible.

"There's more, my Dear," Florrie answered. "Mrs. Helen D'Oyly Carte has estimated an expenditure of ten shillings for each pair of shoes, then the army costume for Captain Fitzbattleaxe at one hundred guineas." At that, Nellie's eyes open even wider but she made no comment as the wardrobe mistress continued. "Then we have the court uniforms for 18 chorus gentlemen to cost £720. The ladies will all have jewellery, gloves, stockings, shoes, underskirts, 28 sets of costumes in all, and that'll be another £420. And if all that's not enough, there's also to be some sketches done by the artist, Percy Anderson. Overall, it's an enormous and lavish expense this time but I know we'll all make it look very lovely indeed," she concluded.

"Right you are, Miss Parker, I'll… erm, we're do's our best," Nellie answered.

"As always, dear, as always," Florrie Parker smiled.

This time it was Sir Arthur who became alarmed at the mounting costs for the new opera. Fred Dean heard that after he had complained to Mr. Gilbert, the writer had replied that he agreed and felt that the "expense of the production should be curtailed if this could be done without cramping the piece".

"Have they agreed to cut down then?" Tom asked.

"They have – then they have not," Fred Dean replied. "Mr Gilbert has said to Sir Arthur that they cannot expect any of the cast to appear naked, so good uniforms must cost £50 apiece!"

"Thankfully for that!" Tom commented, "wouldn't leave much for my Nellie and Miss Parker to do if that was to happen, eh Mr. Dean!"

"Not with a needle, in any case," the stage manager replied with a wink and a laugh.

If a deal of money was being spent for the costumes, then it became soon evident to both Tom and Fred Dean that the lavish sets with a budget of £1,500 would also be the most expensive ever staged for a Gilbert and Sullivan opera. For Act One they created a so-called 'Utopian Palm Grove' but it was for Act Two that time and time again, Tom and Fred Dean each spent endless moments at the back of the theatre to look back to the stage at what they saw as their best work ever, the throne room in King Paramount's Palace.

"Oh, Tom, ain't that just lovely," Nellie purred, much to Tom's delight, when he first guided her to the back of the theatre to reveal his work. "Without any doubt, that's truly the very best yet, you must be proud, Mr. Dean, both of yer – and if you ain't then I knows that I am!"

"We are pleased," Tom replied in such a sense of false modesty that Nellie couldn't resist to lovingly punch him in the back.

"What's it with yer 'we are pleased'!" she mimicked. "I should bloomin' well say you should both be pleased! What guidelines did Mr. Gilbert give you to work on the throne room scene, or 'ave you been copying from your mind what we saw at Windsor and Balmoral!"

"Actually you are not far wrong there my love, Mr. Gilbert made it quite clear what he wanted," Tom advised. "We were told that he wanted us to reproduce the ceremony of one of Queen Victoria's 'drawing room' receptions."

"Well, it's very beautiful and I'm sure it will be well received on opening night!"

"Along with your costumes," Tom quickly added. "They are so very special this time too!"

"Enough money's been spent on them, that they should be the best," Nellie claimed. "Cor blimey, I only wish I 'ad 'alf the amount of what one of the dresses cost to spend on me 'ole wardrobe!"

Tom wasn't sure how to take his wife's last comment so he did as he always did when he didn't know how to deal with a situation – say nothing and look down to the stage as if in deep thought. Nellie let it pass too.

The opening night for the new opera, by then entitled 'Utopia Limited', was set for 7 October, 1893 and so the early weeks of the autumn were once again a scene of the frantic activity at the Savoy which those like Fred Dean, Tom, Nellie and Miss Parker had become so used to and were led to expect. Further alarm and a growing sense of unease, in view of recent money conflicts at the theatre, was felt by all when it was revealed that the production costs were finally almost £500 over budget so that the opera had cost over one-third more than any of the others to stage.

"It'll be alright as long as it's a success," Fred Dean observed to Tom. "Visually, dramatically and musically it should be, but... well, somehow I've got my worries!"

"What's that exactly, Mr. Dean?" Tom enquired.

"I'm just a little fearful that Mr. Gilbert may have gone a little bit too far this time with some of the barely thinly-veiled comments against the establishment," Fred replied.

"We've had it before, what about 'Iolanthe'!" Tom reasoned. "Often, it's what our audiences like."

"True, true – well at least they did but we're 11 years further on now since that very obvious political piece, then in 'Mikado' such comment was more disguised. There's no doubting in my mind that people think differently to what they did. We'll see though. I say again, I just hope for Mr. D'Oyly Carte's sake as much as anybody that it's another Savoy success. Ever since his disastrous English Grand Opera House venture, he must be wanting some good news!" Fred Dean declared. Tom nodded in agreement.

The night of 7 October for Tom and Nellie as much as all in the D'Oyly Carte Company was just like old times; once again a Gilbert and Sullivan first night. Even though so many of the original Savoy performers had moved on to other productions, there were still several of the regulars remaining in the company, such as Mr. Rutland Barrington and Miss Rosina Brandram, both of whom Tom was as much used to helping with the stage directions as Nellie was to designing and helping fit the costumes. Appearing in the new opera, too, was Mr. W.H. Denny, who had become firmly established in the company since the first production of 'Yeomen of the Guard' some five years previously. So for all of them it was much a theatrical family of which they all felt so much to be a part and in support for each other. Therefore, it was with a special care that night that Tom assisted on stage and Nellie in the wardrobe department helped one of the company's newest members, Mr. Walter Passmore, playing the role of 'Tarara', the Public Exploder at the Court of King Paramount. He was about to appear for the very first time in one of the opera's comedy roles so well created over the years by George Grossmith and who had left the company before 'Gondoliers', by then some four years ago. With all that had gone before, much rested on the new singer's shoulders, facing a Savoy audience brought up in the faithful tradition of past performers and the whole company felt in support of him.

For Tom, it was also a momentous evening in its own personal way. Although he felt almost alarmed to admit it, but it was then 22 years since his association with the very first production of 'Thespis' and for the past 18 years, ever since 'Trial by Jury', the company had been his life for his every working breath as he had played his role in the creation of English comic opera. Nellie stood beside him in the wings as the final preparations for the performance were made. The growing excited sounds from the auditorium, the social chatting and niceties from those in the stalls and circle, the chorus singing from the past operas boisterously given by the faithful patrons of the gallery, all added to the occasion that all in the company loved and cherished of old.

"Ain't it wonderful to be experiencing this all over again," Nellie declared, linking her left arm through Tom's. "I still feels a tingle at all of this and it's only been 11 years for me – it's even more exciting for you when you were 'ere at the beginning, part of the very furniture that you are!"

"It wasn't here, it was at the old Gaiety Theatre," Tom replied, needlessly curt and rather over pompous for the moment.

"All right, clever 'ead, I knows that well enough," Nellie answered, just a bit crestfallen at her husband's insensitiveness but she let it pass, realising that a first night was an enormous pressure for him. "Whatever, wherever, it's been a very long time for both of us and all I says it is perfect magic to experience this sense of occasion all over again!"

"Of course, my love, that's absolutely right," Tom replied, regaining his sense of correctness. "Oh, sorry, I didn't mean to be sharp earlier," he quickly added. Nellie smiled and he felt much relieved that the situation had been recovered by his added well-included remark!

The familiar signal that the whole company had been waiting for, denoting that the performance was about to start, was given by Fred Dean, in just the same way that he had given it countless times before and an immediate hush fell upon those gathered in and around the stage area. Next, in an equally satisfying and commanding way, Sir Arthur Sullivan entered the orchestra pit to be greeted by the usual thunderous applause. With his raised baton, the magic spell of a new Gilbert and Sullivan opera was cast upon the whole expectant audience. The overture began – 'Utopia Limited' was launched.

"In lazy languor – motionless,
We lie and dream of nothingness;
For visions come
From Poppydom
Direct at our command."

The opening chorus was immediately well received by a delighted audience, intrigued at the South Seas setting before them. There was discernable excitement at the entry of the guards, with members of the King's Court, to a typically popular rousing chorus of a Gilbert and Sullivan opera:

"O make way for the Wise Men!
They are prizemen –
Double-first in the world's university!"

The audience listened intently as King Paramount sang:

"A king of autocratic power we –
A despot whose tyrannic will is law –
Whose rule is paramount o'er land and sea."

There was little doubt to the company that the entry of the six so-called 'Flowers of Progress', "imported from England", caused the most stir in the audience so far that evening, nothing more so than when one of them was revealed as none other than 'Captain Corcoran'. The faithful in the theatre quickly realised what they saw as a restoration of none other than a favourite character from 'HMS Pinafore', beloved by many of them as the most popular first real success of the series of operas. Intently they listened as the captain sang:

"Though we're no longer hearts of oak,
Yet we can steer and we can stoke,
And thanks to coal, and thanks to coke,
We never run a ship ashore!"

"What never?"
- "No never!"
- "What never?"
- "Hardly ever!"

Cheers rung out through the whole theatre there and then, especially from the gallery, as the audience enthused to once again hear the well-known refrain from 'Pinafore' so well resurrected in the new opera. Later, during the interval, as Tom helped in the preparation of the stage for the magnificent set of Act Two, he heard the familiar strains of "What never? – well, hardly ever!" coming as a boisterous roar from the galleryites, so very vocally enjoying their evening.

"It sounds as if they all like it," Nellie observed, laughing, as she placed some costumes for the coming second Act in the wings.

"It's wonderful to hear it, love," Tom agreed. Pressure and the demands of the immediate work for both of them meant there was little time for any further comment even though they could relish the sounds around them.

At the start of Act Two, Fred Dean and Tom were especially heartened to hear the audience's applause and obvious appreciation of the stage setting as the curtain rose on the palace's throne room, the setting that they had all worked so diligently upon.

Later, 'King Paramount' sang:

"This ceremonial our wish displays
To copy all Great Britain's courtly ways."

The company noticed that the song was immediately greeted with applause and much laughter from those in the gallery but noticeably more coolly received from the stalls and circle. Fred Dean, standing near Tom in the wings, visibly sighed and took a sharp intake of breath at the response, next frowned slightly and shook his head towards Tom, almost as if to say "I was worried about this all along". Further on in the Act, the song from one of the 'Flowers of Progress', Mr. Goldbury, the company promoter, was much more enthusiastically received and this time by the whole house:

"Go search the world and search the sea,
Then come you home and sing with me
There's no such gold and no such pearl
As a bright and beautiful English girl!"

And so to the final chorus:

"There's a little group of isles beyond the wave."

The first night of the first new Gilbert and Sullivan opera in four years came to an end and the curtain came down to deafening applause from an excited audience, grateful in the extreme that they had been given another new opera by their celebrated and much loved writer and composer. Nellie stood as always beside Tom in the wings as, just like in all the previous glorious times, Sir Arthur once again joined Mr. Gilbert to take their bow together on stage. But there was a difference this time, one that Nellie noted far more perceptively than Tom – Sir Arthur looked so frail whilst Mr. Gilbert who used to stand so straight, now hobbled with a stick because of his gout.

Whether the audience felt the same, it was impossible to tell from their response. They cheered, they clapped, they called out, shouted for "more" and when Sir Arthur and Mr. Gilbert turned to each other and shook hands, visibly united as composer and writer once more, the roar of applause became even more deafening. Several curtain calls were taken before Fred Dean gave the sign to Tom to bring the curtain down for the last time that evening.

It was just like it had always been, just as if it was once again after the first performance of 'Iolanthe' or 'Mikado', or any of the operas that had gone before except with the possible initial reception of 'Ruddigore'. Cast and stage members, very much relieved, circulated at the back of house, all shaking hands and with a renewed feeling of elation that the Gilbert and Sullivan magic had once again been achieved. All in the company talked excitedly and happily as the stage area was cleared and costumes were again put back on racks in readiness for the following day's performance. At the stage door, as groups exchanged final words before they made their various ways home, it was still with a sense of elation for the experience of the evening. For Tom and Nellie there was only one way in which to end the evening – by once again sharing a cab ride home to Peckham with Fred

Dean and Florrie Parker, just as they had done on so many first nights before. Even though for them, it was no longer something as special as it had been 10 years before, now they all took cab rides more as a matter of course, they all nevertheless took great delight from enjoying their special tradition once again as a meaningful and respected conclusion to the evening.

As another tradition, one that was just as equally anticipated, within several days of the first night, many of the company gathered on stage to hear Fred Dean report upon the theatre critics' reviews of the new opera.

"Ladies and gentlemen," Fred Dean began, "the 'Morning Standard' has declared, I have a copy here, 'a more complete success has never been achieved in comic opera even at the Savoy'. Next, I have the 'Saturday Review', from 19 October, and a notice written by the playwright, Bernard Shaw. It's a long review but importantly it includes comments like 'the pictorial treatment of the fabrics and colours on the stage' – before I go further, this is the moment for Tom and me, Miss Parker and Nellie to take their respective bows," the beaming stage manager declared. The company responded with clapping and shouts of "bravo" all around. Both Tom and Nellie noticeably flushed and nervously looked down to the stage and were grateful when Fred Dean finally continued.

"It then goes on to say 'the cultivation and intelligence of the choristers, the quality of the orchestra, and the degree of artistic good breeding, so to speak, expected from the principals,' and concludes 'how great an advance has been made by Mr. D'Oyly Carte in organising and harmonizing that complex co-operation of artists of all kinds which goes to make up a satisfactory operatic performance'. Ladies and gentlemen, with that, I suggest, we can all take a bow!"

Tom, Nellie, Fred Dean and Florrie Parker, and various members of the whole D'Oyly Carte Company talked cheerfully amongst themselves at the conclusion of the stage manager's speech. They all felt elated at what to them appeared to be another Savoy success, even though the new opera was the most complex, the most expensive to stage and with a requirement for an extensive range of multi-tasked principal singers.

Fred Dean's earliest fears that with the subject matter, perhaps Mr. Gilbert had gone a little too far in his parody of society seemed a perfectly valid prediction when in the weeks following the first performance, demand for the higher priced stalls and circle seats was noticeably less than for the gallery.

"This is not going to be another 'Gondoliers', let alone 'Mikado'," the stage manager very rightly commented to Tom.

* * * *

At least one thing was sure in Rupert Moore's mind as he listened to the selection of songs from 'Utopia Limited' at the Adelphi Theatre on that night of 27 February 1982. There was never any question that he would ever say that this particular opera was "his favourite"! He realised that it was no particular slight upon the opera but more the fact that even for such an enthusiast as he undoubtedly was, the opportunities of seeing the opera had been very few indeed. There had hardly been any performances given and the few that were in recent years always coincided with times when, to his great regret, commitments kept him from the theatre. He had had to content himself with the recordings but it was not for him the same. Yes, he admitted that much of the music and libretto were recognisable as his beloved Gilbert and Sullivan but the simple fact was he hardly knew the opera sufficiently well.

But by that stage of the evening, such a revelation and realisation was the very least of the thoughts in his highly troubled mind. There wasn't so much of the evening left any more and with the gathering pace, even less time for his much awaited and highly anticipated announcement that the D'Oyly Carte Opera Company would be saved to continue to perform the repertory of Gilbert and Sullivan operas that they had so effectively done so for 107 years.

As he sat introverted within his thoughts, only being half aware of the cheers and clapping going on around him as at least the rest of the audience showed their very obvious appreciation of the opera, it was once again the reasoned comments of his grandmother sitting beside him that gave Rupert the restored hope that he craved.

"After all, love, there would hardly be any announcement about the future of the Company being made in the middle of a selection from the operas! More likely at the end," Alice Harding tried to reassure. She didn't necessarily believe it but she wanted to ease the obvious burden that her grandson felt.

"I hope you are right, I hope you are right," Rupert replied.

Chapter 18

"Oh, the man who can rule a theatrical crew Can govern this tuppenny State!"

As the early days of the new year, 1894, were reached it soon became apparent that after the immediate excitement following the opening of 'Utopia Limited', there was not going to be another Gilbert and Sullivan success such as 'Mikado' or 'Gondoliers', either at the Savoy or with the D'Oyly Carte Company's touring productions. Fred Dean called across the stage one morning to Tom and said as much:

"Mr. D'Oyly Carte has told me that he's already advised Mr. Gilbert that the new opera, already in its third month, is not drawing enough at the box office to imply that we are in for a long run!"

"The audiences each night seem happy enough," Tom reasoned, "and I thought that maybe once the piece settles down, and word gets around, then the forward bookings would quickly improve as a result."

"In his heart, Mr. D'Oyly Carte doesn't think so," Fred replied. "What he, Mr. D'Oyly Carte I mean, believes is that what people want now is simply 'fun', not to have to think about anything, not to have a too complicated plot. In two words, to 'enjoy' and be 'entertained'!"

"I suppose that he's right," Tom answered, "after all, we've had enough really wonderful entertaining pieces here at the Savoy, all to the most enormous acclaim, to prove that point very well enough – so why not so again!"

"The world's a different place now," Fred Dean reasoned, adding to his own argument without really listening to what Tom had said. "Others have even copied in various ways the original successes of Sir Arthur Sullivan and Mr. Gilbert. We're not alone any more. There are musical shows spreading out all over London, not like the bad old days of the vulgar music hall, but quality pieces, well produced and well performed, very much like our own here. There's much more now for the theatre-goer to spend their hard-earned money on, to the point of being almost inundated with choice."

"You are sounding very down about it all, Mr. Dean, it's surely not anything like as bad as that," Tom exclaimed.

"Maybe, maybe not." Fred Dean, in very deep thought, looked down to the stage for some moments before he continued. "But there's no doubt times have changed. We've, you and me, not just us but of course Miss Parker, even your Nellie, have all been here now for so long and to us it's like the same as it always was. But just you think Tom, since we first began in 1871, that's well over 20 years ago and some of our audiences in those days aren't even around any more – others, the new ones growing up, they've got to be attracted as well."

"But younger people have taken their place and those people are every bit as enthusiastic for the operas, more so really, then the audiences that were there before them. For these younger people, they've been brought up to the operas, seen them when they were young, heard and sung to the music in their own homes! That new audience is there and ready for us – at least that's how I see it!" Tom affirmed.

"Oh, you're right, you're right," Fred nodded. "And yes, what we have all been involved in here is nothing short of a theatrical change over the past 20-odd years. But Mr. D'Oyly Carte as a respected theatrical manager knows the situation and I tend to agree with his thoughts that people want pure entertainment – they want another 'Mikado' and I think they find 'Utopia

Limited' just a bit too demanding. Oh, I know that Mr. Gilbert has always directed his wit against many in the previous operas but I think it was more veiled then than in this new opera. Here, I wonder whether it's all not just a bit too much really with the very obvious comments pointed at our own society."

"I know, you have always reasoned like that," Tom replied. "Nellie and me, we notice ourselves, of course you do too Mr. Dean, how the people in the stalls and circle are somewhat uncomfortable with some of the dialogue in the new opera. But those in the gallery – well they like to hear the more farcical comments about those in authority and laugh aloud. You hear it yourself, don't you Mr. Dean?"

"Course I do, Tom, but just you remember one important thing." Fred Dean, although he spoke kindly to Tom, his face showed that a look of concern. "Those in the gallery don't pay our wages alone or keep the theatre in profit – for that we need, more than that, it's essential for a full house of the people in the stalls and circle paying for the top price seats! That's when Mr. D'Oyly Carte is happy and when he is, then we are all happy as a result!"

"Yes, I see that too, now you come to mention it," Tom answered, himself by then very much in thought. After a few moments, he continued. "What you are saying really, it's just like after the first night of 'Ruddigore', you remember the shouts from the gallery of 'Bring back the Mikado', or something like that!"

"You're right there, Tom me lad," Fred Dean smiled as he patted his trusted assistant on the back, "that's what we really need, another 'Mikado'."

Upstairs in the wardrobe department of the Savoy Theatre, Florrie Parker and Nellie were in a similar reflective mood as they worked in preparation for the continuing performances of 'Utopia Limited'. The extensive costume requirements for the new opera, plus the very large cast of both principals and chorus, ensured that the two wardrobe ladies had always plenty of work to do. Their efforts were tirelessly to have everything always looking clean, tidy, and generally as spic and span as it did, to everybody's critical acclaim, on the first night. The work received their usual dedicated care and attention even though there was the highly disturbing and nagging thought forever in their minds that the already expensive budget for the costumes had been in any case exceeded. Repair and mend had to be the order as any replacement costumes could not be afforded.

"You know of course, my dear, without me having to keep saying, that this time we must make do with delicate repairs rather than replacing any items of the costumes for this opera," Florrie Parker reminded Nellie.

"Yes, Miss Parker, I do and I always remember that you can be sure," Nellie reassured as she continued working industriously with an almost 'hot' needle in her hand as a result.

"I should have known that without even asking! Sorry, my dear, you must forgive me," the wardrobe mistress sighed.

"Fink nothing of it, Miss Parker," Nellie replied. Realising her wardrobe mistress' obvious concerns, she quickly added: "We knows and understands each other well enough not to take umbrage at anyfink like that!"

"Thank you, dear." Florrie Parker thought for some moments and so the only thing to break the silence in the wardrobe room was the barely discernable sound of needles with cotton piercing pieces of fabric. "There is something that I feel that I must say though," she later continued and Nellie, quizzically as well as alarmed, looked towards her boss. "No. No, it's nothing towards you my dear," Florrie quickly said when she saw Nellie's worried expression. "It's just that I somehow do not feel so much at ease with this new opera, it doesn't in any way feel the same way to me as all the previous pieces. Oh, I know that it seems to be playing well enough each night and we hear that the audiences appear to like it, but to me it's simply not the same as before."

"My Tom tells me, or at least he has heard it from Mr. Dean, that the forward bookings are less than Mr. D'Oyly Carte would like them to be." Nellie passed on the gossip with a sense of authority as she felt, very much liking to be in the centre of things at the Savoy.

"So I believe, so I believe," Florrie Parker replied. "What mainly causes my concerns comes from the enormous expense which 'Utopia Limited' has cost to mount in the first place and what I see, perhaps because I am far too set in my ways, as a very unnecessary extravagance. Nothing was spared this time! Think of all the costumes that we have mainly because it's such a huge cast and, not only that, many of the clothes, not to say shoes and all accoutrements, all cost us dear as well!"

"True, Miss Parker, but fink about 'Mikado', 'ow expensive all them Japanese silks were and them fancy 'eadgear and fans," Nellie reasoned.

"I grant you that," Florrie Parker replied, "but that's where I see the difference! 'The Mikado', 'Gondoliers' too, were all so joyous, all so well received by delighted audiences and because of that they played for many, many performances. The costumes have lasted to be used again and again, both here at the Savoy and for the touring companies as well so that it was always money well spent." Nellie nodded as the wardrobe mistress continued. "But even that, those costumes never cost so much as these in the first place. I simply do not see that for all the money spent on them, the opera will last in the public's affections long enough for it to have been worthwhile!"

"But it's alright though, ain't it Miss Parker?" Nellie asked, looking concerned as she glanced up from the attentive work with which she was involved. "You ain't 'finking that somefink awful is going to 'appen to all of us 'ere or anyfink, are yer miss?"

"No, no, of course not," Florrie immediately reassured Nellie when she saw how alarmed that she looked. "Please excuse me, my dear, but I suppose that it's nothing more than I am just a bit older, if not more wiser, than I once was, nothing else, and it's been now many years of work here with the company at the start and later here at the Savoy. I always hark back within my mind to the beginning, all the sense of the new that we then all experienced. I just want there to be another 'Mikado'," she sighed. "But don't you worry, like I say, it's just me getting a bit more old!"

"You ain't old, Miss Parker," Nellie exclaimed. "Them words, that's for my Tom to be saying 'cause next year, the poor old so.., soul, I mean, well 'e'll be turning 50!"

"Careful, dear, Florrie laughed, "age is not for discussion here, only by Mr. Gilbert who began all those years ago with his reference to the 'elderly, ugly daughter' in 'Trial by Jury'!"

Nellie laughed as well before she looked towards the wardrobe mistress, with a twinkle in her eye, she sang:

"Silvered is the raven hair,
Spreading is the parting straight."

Then:

"Fading is the taper waist,
Shapeless grows the shapely limb."

"Lady Jane from 'Patience', Nellie," Florrie Parker declared, laughing until tears rolled down her face. "How lovely, my dear, well perhaps you are right, neither of us are quite yet like 'Lady Jane'. But, fancy you remembering that just now, it must be over 12 years ago and ..." she thought, "but you were not even with me then were you my dear?"

"No, I wasn't, true," Nellie replied, "but 'Patience' 'as always been special for me 'cause it was the very first of all the operas what I saw when Tom took me to the new Savoy Theatre just after it 'ad been opened, autumn 1881 it was and I remember it as if only yesterday!"

"Of course you do my dear, I can see that well enough, it meant a lot to you didn't it?"

"It did that, Miss Parker," Nellie answered, "it was probably the most important fing what ever 'appened to me, as far as me working life was concerned, 'cause it made me give up me working in the dress factory and come 'ere to the Savoy! And I don't ever regret it one moment and, well whatever happens to this 'ere 'Utopia Limited', then mefinks what we 'ave all got 'ere is so special, so bloomin – oops, sorry Miss Parker – so really marvellous and I knows that it will continue and I've been proud to be a part of it – with you, of course, and 'ere to be working with you, Miss Parker! Long may it all continue, that's what I say!"

"That was so beautifully and sincerely said, thank you my dear." Florrie Parker smiled and extended her hand affectionately towards Nellie. Both thought for a few moments before Nellie said: "Well, on with it then, what say you Miss Parker?"

"Yes, indeed, Nellie dear, as you say, 'on with it'."

Given all the various thoughts and misgivings that the company had, it came as no surprise to anyone at the Savoy when 'Utopia Limited' finally finished its run during the summer, 1894. It closed after an initial run of 245 performances, not a disaster by any means but nevertheless poor in comparison with any of the previous operas, except for 'Thespis' that hardly anybody thought about any more. With the closure, Gilbert and Sullivan had nothing new ready to take its place so Mr. D'Oyly Carte did something in the circumstances that he always did best – mount a revival. The whole company were delighted to learn that 'The Mikado' was to be once again performed at the Savoy.

Within a few days of the opening night of the revival, a delighted Fred Dean said to Tom as they cleared the stage after the performance "there you are Tom, me lad, what did I tell you?"

"Tell me, Mr. Dean?" Tom replied, as he moved a basket of costumes to a side of the wings in readiness for Nellie when she came down later.

"Yes, Tom. This is exactly what the public want – fun and entertainment," Fred continued. "See how they go wild again about 'Mikado'. It's 'House-Full' notices already. Mr. D'Oyly Carte says the advance bookings are as healthy now as when the piece was new! It's like a renewed success at the theatre!"

"I am very pleased for it and, if you don't mind my saying," Tom at first hesitated until he saw Fred Dean nod. "Well, it's like we talked about before and it does show, as I sort of believed, that there is as much a new audience for the operas as there was when they were first produced."

"Grant that you are right, yes, Tom, like you said," Fred Dean acknowledged. He smiled to himself as he realised how Tom had summoned up the courage to make his point. "I am so glad you've been proved right, Tom!"

The work devoted by the company to the revival of 'Mikado' was every way as much as it had been for the original production. Tom, with Fred Dean, ensured that Mr. Gilbert's stage instructions were followed precisely and, not only that but Mr. Gilbert himself frequently called in to the Savoy to control that all was to his liking with the revival, just as much as he had done for the first performances.

"Tom, Mr. Gilbert has written to Mr. D'Oyly Carte to say that he noticed that one of the singers was away from the theatre last Tuesday night ill," Fred Dean advised.

"Yes, I remember that, we had the understudy in her place," Tom replied.

"Well, unfortunately for the lady, Mr. Gilbert said he was at a ball at the Albert Hall on the same night – and met the lady there. Very obviously not too ill for the ball but too ill for the theatre!" the stage manager answered.

"Oh, dear!" Tom exclaimed. "Not so good for the lady, then."

"No, not at all. In fact Mr. Gilbert has said that the unfortunate lady must be dismissed and no doubt that will be exactly what Mr. D'Oyly Carte will do – like as in 'Pinafore', we run a tight ship here!" the stage manager replied. "Now, about something else, Tom," he began to continue.

Tom immediately felt a sense of unease as they had just been talking about personnel matters within the company and wondered if it was now his own turn for some kind of reprimand, although he could think of no specific reason why.

"Miss Bond, as you know, is in the revival of Mikado," Fred Dean began. Tom's face, at hearing the start of the conversation, lapsed into an uncontrolled smile, relieved that there was no trouble directed at him. "Miss Bond," the stage manager continued, "she has asked Mr. Gilbert if she could be given a new song in 'The Mikado'."

"Has Mr. Gilbert agreed, Mr. Dean," Tom asked. "The opera is pretty extensive already, I don't see any slowing within the plot and I reckon that it would maybe interrupt the smooth flowing of the piece."

"No, he hasn't, he most probably thinks the same as you have just said. But what else that he said is most interesting," Fred began to indicate. "Apparently, Mr. Gilbert said he was loath to ask Sir Arthur to compose any new song because it would cause a delay to the new piece that they are considering!"

Tom's eyes lit up. A new piece, Mr. Dean, do you mean to say that it looks as if we will get another new opera for the Savoy?"

"From what he indicated, it would appear so, Tom," Fred Dean replied, "although, I certainly haven't heard anything more definite yet!"

When they had their lunch break, Tom naturally told Nellie who, in turn, passed on the information to Miss Parker the moment she got back to the wardrobe room.

"I suppose that the news doesn't altogether come as a surprise," was Florrie Parker's reasoned reply. "With 'The Mikado' doing so well here once again, I do not myself see the need for any particular rush, but then, I'm not the writer or composer!"

It was especially satisfying to both Tom and Nellie that 'The Mikado' played so successfully throughout 1895. As Nellie said to her husband, "ain't it a real fitting tribute to your 50th birthday!" Indeed, it was special for him and helped to make it a very happy year for the both of them. Nothing much different happened in their lives, which were content enough for them in any case. What they did do were happy routines, enjoying some happy times together in their small home in Peckham, which increasingly became more like their own "little palace", as Nellie put it. Then they extra specially enjoyed their summer outings to the parks and countryside, even taking the train to the sea at Brighton for a day. One routine that became especially significant that anniversary year too was the annual D'Oyly Carte Company summer picnic on the River Thames, an occasion when for once both Tom and Nellie allowed more than one extra glass of champagne to pass their lips. It was in every way a good year for them, one equally matched by some much less demanding working times at the theatre as a result of the successful 'Mikado' revival.

By the autumn of 1885, still with 'The Mikado' continuing to play to full houses at the Savoy, Fred Dean was able to finally confirm to Tom that a new Gilbert and Sullivan piece was being written and that it was planned to open in about March of the following year. "It'll be the 13th of the full lengths operas, some achievement when you think about it, and all within 25 years," Fred Dean declared with both a sense of very obvious pride and satisfaction.

"But, if you forget about 'Thespis', then 'Sorcerer' was the first full length piece in 1877, so another way of saying it, is 12 operas in only 19 years!" Tom declared, with a broad smile beaming across his face.

"Yee Gods!" Fred exclaimed, "'O Mount Vesuvius, here we are in arithmetic', to quote the line from 'Gondoliers'!" he laughed.

"Just a thought," Tom replied, reddening with embarrassment.

"And a worthy one too, Tom me lad. But what ever way that you look at it, it's a highly impressive record and we've all been a vital part of it together!" the stage manager affirmed as he pulled a sheet of notes from his pocket.

"Well, the new piece, Tom, I've got some outline details here. Be a good lad, perhaps you would run along and bring Miss Parker and your Nellie down to the stage so we can go through things together!" Fred Dean exclaimed. Tom didn't have to be asked twice for any excuse to go upstairs to see Nellie and he left the stage within seconds, to be back down again only moments later with his wife and the wardrobe mistress dutifully in tow.

"Right you are, ladies, Tom," Fred Dean began. "Here we have the outline details for the new opera! The plot concerns a theatrical company visiting a country called 'The Grand Duchy of Pfennig Halbpfennig'. Mr. Gilbert has said it's a sort of Gilbertian Ruritania! There, the theatrical manager conspires to depose the grand duke and to put himself in his place! Then follows some usual Gilbertian confusion with a duel played by cards instead of with weapons. Nothing gets resolved other than a general pairing off of couples from the grand duke's side and from members of the theatrical company!"

Fred Dean was for the moment interrupted by some uneasy shuffling by Florrie Parker. He looked over to her, as he continued. "Yes, Florrie, I think that I know what's going on in your mind!"

"I am sure that you do, Fred, but it already sounds to me as if it is to be about as far fetched as 'Utopia Limited' – and we all know what happened to that. Anything that is too complicated, almost implausible, then our audiences did not like it!" the wardrobe mistress answered, with an almost dispirited sigh.

"I understand your reservations," Fred Dean replied. "But anyway, let's see, with tuneful music and some general gaiety all may very well be for the good. I'll continue. Tom, we'll have two acts this time, the first is to be a town square – oh, the town is to be called 'Speiseaal'," he added. "The second act is to be a hall in the Grand Ducal Palace, so that should allow our creativeness, me thinks!"

"Sounds very much so, Mr. Dean," Tom indicated. "We've had palace halls before, and I like the idea of a town square, that should be interesting, like the village scene in 'Ruddigore'!"

"Right you are Tom, but do not start getting any ideas that we should copy the gallery scene from that opera as well," Fred Dean laughed as he recalled the troubles they had both experienced in that past production. Tom smiled.

"Now, ladies," Fred Dean continued, turning to Florrie Parker and Nellie, "the range of costumes. Well there's the grand duke himself, the courtiers, princesses, another prince, various members of the theatrical company… "

"Well, that at least should be easy, the theatrical company, I mean," Florrie Parker interrupted, "we can just take a look around our colleagues here at the Savoy!" she laughed.

"Not as easy as that," Fred smiled, "to begin with, Mr. Gilbert has set the date of the piece as 1750!"

"Of course, there's always a catch, we should have realised that, Nellie," Florrie sighed yet again, looking towards her assistant who immediately supported her with a quiet "right you are, Miss Parker".

When it was finally announced that the new opera would have its first night on 7 March 1896, it was also said that the name would be 'The Grand Duke', not very much of a surprise to anybody on stage at the Savoy listening when Fred Dean had given the initial run through. It was once again like the cherished old times at the Savoy with all the work and preparations needed for the new opera. Miss Parker and Nellie had their costumes to prepare whilst Mr. Dean and Tom had the sets and stage effects to arrange. Once more, too, Mr. Gilbert was just as meticulous with the latest piece as he had been those 25 years before with 'Thespis', indeed with all the operas of the series.

"Twenty-five years, can it really be?" was a question that Fred Dean frequently asked of Tom in the early days of 1896 and the planned first night for 'The Grand Duke' of 7 March loomed.

"I know, Mr. Dean, it seems like only yesterday!" was Tom's reply each and every time that the question was posed.

The difficulty of accepting the time span was all the more relevant for those at the Savoy, especially when many had remained as a team with the D'Oyly Carte Company throughout, and not just Sir Arthur, Mr. Gilbert and Mr. D'Oyly Carte themselves. Some of the original young bell boys were now valued stage hands, perhaps even one day in the future to move on up to Tom's own position. And Tom? Of course, in one part of his mind, he would have liked to maybe himself become stage manager at some time, but within that thought he could scarcely bring himself to think of a life at the Savoy without Fred Dean who, in any case, was only a couple of years older than Tom. On consideration, Tom was more than happy for the working positions to remain as they were. In the wardrobe department, the scene was exactly the same for Nellie and Miss Parker. Nellie had absolutely no desire to step into the wardrobe mistress' shoes and wanted nothing more than to remain as the twosome, very much part of the most effective team.

The 'family' wasn't just the backstage workers either. Many of the cast had been in the operas and with the company for many years, some beginning in the chorus before rising to minor roles then next as principals. So it was that for the coming new opera, it was still that Tom found himself offering stage directions and Nellie preparing costumes for Mr. Rutland Barrington who first appeared in 'Sorcerer' 19 years before. Miss Rosina Brandram was to be 'Baroness Von Krakenfeldt' in 'The Grand Duke' and she had first come to the Savoy for 'Princess Ida' in 1884. It felt so good, in a comforting kind of way, for both Tom and Nellie to be working amongst those that they knew so well and within a feeling of mutual respect that grew up around them all. Then, if one of the singers was reasonably new, like Mr. Walter Passmore who was to be 'Rudolph', the 'Grand Duke' himself, in the new opera, then it was as if the person was likened to a re-incarnation of a more famous predecessor, in this case, Mr. George Grossmith, and would be recognised as such within the company.

Such a comforting sense of tradition purveyed throughout at the Savoy. It was the same for the first night itself and Tom felt it so easily could have been for anything that had gone before, be it, by example, for 'Iolanthe' in 1882 or 'Yeomen of the Guard' in 1888 as the normal excited anticipation from the whole audience was felt by all those backstage in the closing minutes before the start of 'The Grand Duke'. Tom noticed that Mr. Gilbert was just as nervous as usual, Sir Arthur Sullivan not nearly so much so as he talked to members of the orchestra and wished a kind "good luck" to many of the singers so equally well known to him. Nellie, with Miss Parker, as always both felt an immense sense of both pride and satisfaction that the costumes which they had so perfectly created, all looked so pristine and exquisite as the singers stood, some rather nervously, in the wings awaiting the overture first and then the curtain rise.

It was for the whole company so perfectly natural and just so as it had all been for the many years before, the first night was again the usual social and glittering occasion in the theatre which they had all become used to. Then, as Sir Arthur entered the orchestra pit to the usual tumultuous applause, Tom really had to pinch himself to be sure that it wasn't once again some 19 years earlier, or many other intervening years ever since.

"Won't it be a pretty wedding?
Will not Lisa look delightful?
Smiles and tears in plenty shedding –
Which in brides of course is rightful"

With the first chorus well received, the audience settled down for their evening. Tom felt the evening was going rather successfully with both the libretto and music seeming to be appreciated as the audience listened with their usual high degree

273

of intensity. The performance of Mr. Passmore as 'Rudolph, the Grand Duke' and his song:

"When you find you're a broken-down critter,
Who is all of a trimmle and twitter,
With your palate unpleasantly bitter,
As if you'd just eaten a pill."

It met with cheers and rapturous applause, so much so that Tom really felt it was like old times.

At the end of the evening, there was little doubting that the audience were thrilled and greeted the appearance of Sir Arthur and Mr. Gilbert on stage at curtain call in their usual and time honoured way, ecstatically and with a genuine sense of both adoration and appreciation for all that the composer and writer had done so well in their partnership over the years.

In keeping with tradition, there could have been no other way to end the evening than for Tom and Nellie to have their customary cab ride home with Fred Dean and Nellie Parker. The foursome talked together of the evening, about the performance, the reception, their thoughts and most of all about the old times that always seemed so especially relevant and overwhelming on such occasions. Collectively, just before they finally reached Peckham, Fred Dean summed up the evening virtually on the quartet's behalf.

"We'll see, but as we have all said, 'The Grand Duke' went well enough, especially as far as the singing, the staging and, of course the wonderful costumes!" Florrie Parker and Nellie each made a responsive bow at that point, before Fred continued. "The audience seemed to appreciate it, but, and here we all seem to think the same, it is not on the top of any of our lists, or anywhere near it, as one of our favourite of all the pieces!" he declared to which the other three responded with agreeing nods.

One further tradition had still to be performed, that of Fred Dean gathering his colleagues on stage, there to read out some press criticisms for the new opera. Therefore, just a few days from the opening night, he took his opportunity once more, this time rather more noticeably subdued than at any time previously. "Ladies and gentlemen, I think that you should hear what the 'Times' has had to say about the new opera." Once again, as so many times before, the stage manager rather dramatically cleared his throat. "They say, and I now quote, 'The Grand Duke is not by any means another 'Mikado', and, although it is far from being the least attractive of the series, signs are not wanting that the rich vein which the collaborators and their various followers have worked for so many years is at last dangerously near exhaustion'. And that, ladies and gentlemen, was their comment," Fred Dean concluded seriously, his eyes cast down towards the stage.

The whole company gathered there on the stage, stood in silence at what they had heard, many too copying the stage manager's stance with their heads hung and their eyes fixed at some imaginary spot on the stage which for the moment gave them all a degree of comfort.

But for once in the quarter century partnership of the composer and writer, there was no such comfort and after only 123 performances, 'The Grand Duke' closed, the shortest run of any Gilbert and Sullivan opera since the very first, 'Thespis'. And unlike Tom, hardly anybody ever talked about that piece, which would prove to be exactly the same destiny for 'The Grand Duke' as well.

* * * *

The disappointment felt by Tom, Nellie, their colleagues and the whole D'Oyly Carte company at the Savoy in 1896 barely stood comparison with the shattered feelings felt by Rupert Moore, his grandmother Alice Harding or indeed the whole audience just across the road at the Adelphi Theatre, albeit 86 years later as the curtain came down after the final song from the small selection given of 'The Grand Duke'. Nobody in the theatre that night needed the programme notes to know that in any case the excerpts just played came from the very last of the Gilbert and Sullivan operas – there was nothing left to be performed. On top of their own sombre thoughts at that moment, what the members of the D'Oyly Carte Opera Company itself must have thought at the same time, nobody in the theatre that night could dare guess. The sight of the closed curtain upon the stage said it all, a symbol not just of a conclusion to a performance but perhaps of something even more graver.

Within his depressive thoughts though, Rupert still somehow remained optimistic, an optimism fuelled by the fact that the bright spot lights still played upon the closed curtain. "Surely that means there's more to come, most likely the long-awaited announcement of the company's financial reprieve," he declared, his face ever more flushed and his hands running with sweat as he grabbed the side of his seat in ever hopeful anticipation, hardly diminished even in that situation of the 'eleventh hour'.

"Maybe, let's hope so!" Alice replied, herself dabbing the corner of her eye with her handkerchief. "There's always hope," she began to continue, but her words were immediately stopped by the dimming of the house lights, just slightly, but more importantly, the raising of the stage curtain once again.

Chapter 19

"The sun, whose rays
Are all ablaze
With ever-living glory"

"It don't surprise me that 'The Grand Duke' closed and after only 123 performances," Nellie reflected to Tom as they were both engaged backstage at the Savoy, packing away props and costumes for the failed new opera. "I never really took to it much meself, the music wasn't so memorable for me and the plot, well it was kind of plain stupid!"

"A hundred and twenty-three continuous performances of one opera is not altogether a bad record, although I grant you that it's only a fraction of what we've achieved in all the past works, other than for the very first," Tom declared. "I don't know if 'Grand Duke' was as bad as all that, given very often the plots themselves don't stand up to much close scrutiny," he continued. "But, yes, I agree, it didn't have any of the obvious appeal or the delightful satire of any of the earlier pieces up to 'Gondoliers'. At least with 'Utopia Limited' there was more in the way of Mr. Gilbert taking a coy observation of the official systems. Besides too, the stage setting was much more exotic and the audiences liked the South Seas theme!"

"What yer mean is that your trying for me acknowledgements for all yer fancy stage sets and 'andicrafts, that's what it is, ain't it Tom!" Nellie laughed.

"No, not really," Tom said, casting his eyes towards the floor with an air of modest embarrassment. "But really, love, I suppose really that times out there have changed and maybe it's not the same audiences any more. After all, 20-odd years is a long time and people's attitudes change, so maybe that's what more than likely has occurred."

"Well, Tom, I ain't so sure that you are right about that either!" Nellie declared. "Look what has 'appened now that we've doing another revival of 'The Mikado'. It's playing to capacity 'ouses with as much cheering and 'appy applause as for the last time it was staged and just as much as when it was first done over ten years ago! It's coming over as fresh as a daisy to new and old audiences alike – they adore the work and it's being received just as well as any time before. That's exactly what our public really wants – all the fun, the gaiety, the 'appy music is back in the 'featre 'ere now just like before – and not just 'ere either, on the streets and in all the parks as well, music from 'Mikado' being played all the time. You know and must see and 'ear that yerself!" Tom nodded, as his wife, very much in full spate, continued: "No, mefinks, and I ain't no musician or writer, but I finks it more a case of both Sir Arthur and Mr Gilbert just ain't the same no more and then, why should they be, they've done well and given us all such great work over the years. Besides, they neither of them ain't so young now, nor are you and me either come to that, so it's natural all of us appreciate the chance to slow down a bit. You see, it's like what yer Mr. Dean said when he read out that newspaper critic after the first night…"

"What was that?" Tom asked, rather without consideration, as he obviously knew perfectly well the message. In as far as the theatre was concerned, and especially the Savoy, he had a virtual encyclopaedic mind.

"Don't be silly, love!" Nellie chastised, "yer remember well enough! The paper said as much that maybe both the musician and writer are near exhausted, or somefink like that!"

"Yes." That was all Tom felt for saying as in an air of very obvious despondency he busied himself with the work in hand, barely saying more than a brief comment about a work matter to his wife. The sullen air, though, was broken just a few minutes later when a very excited Fred Dean came rushing to the wings, obviously from the direction of Mr. D'Oyly Carte's office.

"Tom, me lad," he called. His time-honoured expression reserved for moments of good news immediately revived Tom's spirits as he looked up towards the approaching stage manager. "Tom, oh sorry, good day to you, me dear," Fred Dean first politely acknowledging Nellie's presence. "Listen both of you, some good news. I've just come from Mr. D'Oyly Carte's office and he told me that we are going to mount a revival of 'The Yeomen of the Guard' next at the Savoy, after the present run of 'Mikado'!"

"That's good to know," Tom was first to exclaim and before he could say more, Nellie intervened.

"Oh, Mr. Dean, that's one of me all time favourites!" she said, "so very 'uman and a 'eart feeling story line – I'm sure our audiences now will love it every bit as much as earlier."

"Yes, yes, very true my dear," Fred Dean acknowledged. "But especially for us Tom, you and me, there's some extra special good news. Mr. Gilbert himself is to design a new set for Act Two, a view of Tower Wharf without the Tower of London background. It'll be like us working on a new opera piece altogether!"

Tom immediately revived. "That really is exciting, Mr. Dean," he replied, "I'll very much look forward to working on that, indeed I will."

"There you are Tom, what did I tell yer!" Nellie declared as Fred Dean left them a moment later. "Whatever may 'ave 'appened with 'The Grand Duke', and even if there ain't no more new pieces, the revivals will continue to be like new opportunities for all of us to enjoy – we in the company whether at the Savoy or on tour and all the audiences too! Anyway, enough of all this talk, I've got me Japanese gowns and fans to clean up, mend and repair, make ready for to-night's 'Mikado' – all as spotless just as if it was the First Night all over again. Nothing but the best will do for the D'Oyly Carte company or their audiences!"

"Just as you say, love, just as you say," Tom smiled with a very much lighter heart. He gave Nellie an appreciative kiss peck on her cheek as she set off once again back towards the wardrobe room, there to be sure to be first to convey the news about the revival of 'Yeomen' on to Miss Parker. The conversations, though, had revived Tom's spirits considerably and he especially realised the truth in what both Nellie had said, and Fred Dean had indicated, that whatever was to happen as far as any new operas might be concerned, there seemed a surety that a repertory of Gilbert and Sullivan revivals would be established both at the Savoy and for the touring companies, most probably into the immediate future too. He settled down once again to his work, much more contented as any fears not just about his and Nellie's working future, but also the future for his beloved operas, were dispelled. Totally relaxed once more, he was soon humming from 'The Mikado' – 'The sun whose rays'.

As Nellie had observed, 'The Mikado's' popularity ensured that the opera continued to play for several more months and with it, the endless and dedicated cleaning and repairs to the fans and costumes by the for always bustling Florrie Parker and Nellie. Still the opera was as thrilling and captivating to audiences, whether old or new, night after night. And not just the audiences either as both Tom and Nellie's love of the opera never tired. More, it became not only renewed but even stronger. Each night Nellie was in the wings at the end of Act One, in readiness to prepare for the change over of costumes. Always she revelled to hear the closing chorus of 'Ye torrents roar' as much she did to hear the beginning of Act Two, the opening ladies chorus of 'Braid the raven hair'. If she could, she always stayed just a few extra moments to be sure to hear 'Yum-Yum' sing 'The sun, whose rays' which always had the same emotional effect on her. She lightly dabbed her eyes as she made her way back to the wardrobe room, saying the same thing to Tom if they met in the wings – "Oh, ain't it all so very lovely!" – which he acknowledged each time with the same appreciative smile and nod of agreement.

There was no doubting of the appeal of 'The Mikado' whether at the Savoy or in the countless performances that continued to go on up and down the country with the touring companies and abroad too. Tom and Nellie's heads were filled so happily with the melodies night after night and they talked of the evening performance as they made their way home to Peckham with as much enthusiasm as they had done on the first night. The only difference was that they sat in the train rather than within the luxury of their traditional first night cab.

It was well into 1897 before work began in earnest for the revival of 'Yeomen'. Mr. Gilbert was just as much on hand at the Savoy to direct the work, especially with the new setting for Act Two upon which Fred Dean and Tom quickly prepared the set to precisely the writer's instructions, just as they had done on every previous occasion over the past 26 years. Fred and Tom frequently smiled to each other as they between them continued to appreciate the writer's still very obvious dedication and enthusiasm to ensure that everything would be just right and as he intended in every way, just as much for the revival as for the original production.

"And that, Tom me lad, is exactly as it should be, now and always, if the works are to continue to be presented in a meaningful and proper way," the stage manager observed.

"Right you are, Mr. Dean," Tom replied in agreement. Nothing had changed in their own relationship either!

On the opening night of the opera's revival, 'Yeomen' was received so enthusiastically by the audience that it was almost hard not to believe that the whole company had somehow been transported back nine years to the very first night. For the revival, Mr. Henry Lytton, who had just been promoted from the touring company to London, played the leading role of 'Jack Point', the character who was the sad jester, at the Savoy for the first time. He conveyed an even more poignant conclusion to the opera by very obviously dying, rather then collapsing, as the curtain fell.

Nellie found that interpretation especially moving and she never missed an evening to witness the scene at the end of Act Two. "Why do you put yourself through so much tearful unhappiness each night by being here at the end?" Tom said to his wife as she stood either sobbing or at the very least dabbing her eyes and blowing into the handkerchief that she always had ready in her hand.

"Oh, you!" she exclaimed, "where'e yer 'eart – it ain't un'appiness, it's deeper and all that – it's all so very 'uman, likes I always say, and it melts me 'eart no matter ow many times I see and listen to it! Mr. Lytton does it so well and it all only goes to prove me points – that these operas will go on and on, then with new singers sometimes with very slightly different interpretations but always so well observed and vivid. It's so wonderful, Tom!"

"I know, love, you are right, and I didn't mean to tease," Tom replied quietly and with affection. "You know that Mr. Gilbert has been so impressed with Mr. Lytton's playing of the character that he's even agreed to change part of the last verse of the final song from 'who laughed aloud' to 'who dropped a tear'."

Nellie gave a sharp intake of breath. "I 'eard, and that's really beautiful, Miss Parker finks so too! Not only that, Tom, do you see 'ow Mr. Lytton kisses the 'em of 'Elsie's' dress as he falls down." Tom nodded. "Miss Parker 'as told me to be sure that the dress is prepared for that very fing each night. Now and every time I do it, I fink of the ending! I've always liked 'Yeomen' and now I finks I like it even the better!" Nellie exclaimed.

"Yes, yes, it's easy to see why," Tom replied. "And how the bookings are for the revival, then I don't think that you are the only one who likes it either! Mr. Dean says we should be in for a long run!"

"There you are – what did I tell 'yer! Oh Tom, me'gaud, I won't 'arf need a good supply of 'andkerchiefs then, won't I!" Nellie answered but not before she was sure to be out of reach of Tom's approaching hand in a friendly gesture.

The revival of 'Yeomen of the Guard' ran for over six months at the Savoy and the opera's popularity was equally as great elsewhere in the country with performances continuing to be given by the touring company. And for the touring company, it wasn't just 'Yeomen' that they were performing because they continued to include all of the operas in their repertory, with a constant demand upon the resources of Tom for stage settings and Nellie for the costumes, as they criss-crossed the country from one town's theatre to another. All in all, it seemed not only a most fitting tribute to the Diamond Jubilee of Her Majesty, Queen Victoria, but also to the enduring works of Gilbert and Sullivan.

Then, back in London at the Savoy, once the revival of 'Yeomen' was drawing to a close, Fred Dean was quick to tell Tom that following would be some further performances of 'Mikado' again and that come the new year, 1898, there would then be a revival of 'Gondoliers'. Tom couldn't but help feeling that it was all becoming just as Nellie had correctly predicted, the ongoing and continuing performances of the Gilbert and Sullivan repertory seemed assured to keep them all in active employment for time enough even without there being any new operas forthcoming. He did, however, broach the subject one morning with Mr. Dean as the two of them grappled with a very effective looking granite slab that represented an impressive part of the Tower of London.

"Mr Dean, do you think that Sir Arthur and Mr. Gilbert are planning another piece?" Tom asked.

"I haven't heard if they are and somehow, well I do have my doubts and, what is more, I believe that Mr. D'Oyly Carte even thinks in the same way as I do as well – and he must know more about these matters than any of us do!" the stage manager replied.

"But you haven't heard one way or the other, not for sure, have you Mr. Dean?" Tom continued to press for information.

"No, no that's true, I haven't," came the reply. "It's more like a hunch, a kind of feeling that we all have, more like that neither the will nor the inclination to do another opera is not so much there anymore for either of them. Sir Arthur has been travelling abroad, to the south of France and to Switzerland for his health. As for Mr. Gilbert, well he's very much around as well you know and he tells me that he spends a good deal of his time visiting many theatres here in London. Some say, or so I have heard, that it is more like Mr. Gilbert reliving his past, rekindling his memories. But I think that it's more likely, as well we know, that he has a true love of the theatre and likes nothing more than to see what's going on!"

Tom nodded but as he saw that the stage manager had more to say, he decided to say nothing further for the moment.

Fred Dean laughed before he continued: "It was funny, the other day, Tom, when he called in to us here at the Savoy, Mr. Gilbert told me that he has been seeing some pretty atrocious performances in other theatres. So much so, he told me, that at one theatre an actor had asked him about his own performance and Mr. Gilbert replied 'My dear chap! Good isn't the word!'. As we all know, Mr. Gilbert has a subtle and very sharp wit! I'm just glad that it wasn't a conversation made here and about this company's work," Fred Dean concluded, smiling to himself.

Tom smiled too as he thought about the conversation as so very typical of the writer. Mr. Gilbert's avid attention to every detail of any production and the way that individual singers performed was legendary at the Savoy and was something that both he and Fred Dean strongly respected.

"It's always been like that with Mr. Gilbert," Tom said, smiling in appreciation of the thought. "What he has done for the Savoy operas is proof enough and, well, if there will not be any more then so be it, I suppose." A sad look of resignation spread across Tom's face that Fred Dean pretended not to notice but instead continued by answering just the first of Tom's statements.

"It has, Tom, yes you are right and none of us would have been here, still where we are to-day after now well over 25 years, if that wasn't the case either. It's that very intensive direction towards both the performers and stage management, ensuring that everything remains as intended from the very beginning of it all by both composer and writer, here and wherever the D'Oyly Carte Company perform night after night. It is that which has kept the productions to be always in their prime," Fred Dean said as Tom, yet again nodded, in complete agreement. "But there is something that Mr. D'Oyly Carte has just told me – Sir Arthur will be here at the Savoy for the last night of the present revival of 'Yeomen'."

"And Mr. Gilbert too?" Tom enquired.

"No, well not as far as we've heard," Fred replied. "And that's why I've my feelings that as more as like for like, I think that there may be no more new operas!" He thought for a moment before visibly cheering up and smiling, he concluded: "But, Tom me lad, we've more than enough for us to do here well into our old age with the various revivals and touring productions, them all as popular as ever, with that I've got no doubts!"

"That's very good to know, Mr. Dean," Tom answered, reciprocating the smile that still remained on the stage manager's face.

Indeed, as Fred Dean had indicated, Sir Arthur Sullivan was present in the theatre on the last night of 'Yeomen'. Tom and Nellie felt very pleased and happy to see him again although both noticed that he had become even more frail. Then, when they saw the composer on several occasions during the evening, both in the auditorium itself and back stage as well, often he appeared to be set very deep in a kind of melancholy thoughts.

"Poor chap, he must be finking of all them past glorious first nights, what was the special social occasions for 'im in those days," Nellie commented, with a small tear in the corner of her eye.

"Suppose so, love, but it's good to see him back, nevertheless," Tom replied in a rather matter of fact fashion, belying Tom's own concerns which he resisted by a swift dismissal of the subject.

"It's more a pity that Mr. Gilbert wasn't 'ere as well with 'im – that would 'ave been really nice to see them together. Even coming to the stage for the final curtain, that would have been really special. The whole 'ouse would have erupted, and the roof blown off on to the Strand if that 'ad 'appened!" said Nellie.

"Yes, love, I agree with you – that would have been nice but somehow it's not to be for this time," Tom answered, admitting to himself his sadness that such an appearance had not taken place.

"Perhaps, never again, who knows!" Nellie declared as she walked away and back to the wardrobe room with another basket of costumes to be put away, leaving Tom to reflect, for that moment, rather sadly, on the inevitability of it all.

After the performance, as Tom and Fred Dean were both on stage clearing props away, Fred gave Tom a friendly pat on the shoulder. "You'll be very pleased to know as we all are that Sir Arthur liked the performance, he told Mr. D'Oyly Carte as much

Bernard Lockett

– in fact, he made some detailed criticisms about not only the stage sets but the singers too!" Tom looked for the moment alarmed and the stage manager immediately smiled. "No, it's nothing to worry about," he assured, "they were positive comments, more that he appreciated it all and said as much!"

"Oh, that's good then, isn't it Mr. Dean," Tom replied.

"It is, it is." Fred Dean paused and thought for a moment. "Tom, I asked Mr. D'Oyly Carte once again if he had any idea, or had heard, whether there may be a new opera coming given that he had the chance of speaking with Sir Arthur here this evening. But there is no word and, like we've said ourselves, we all really think it's now unlikely." Tom just silently listened. "But, like we also say, there's another show to prepare for here at the Savoy, so it's away from the Tower of London and back to Japan!"

"Indeed it is, Mr. Dean. Somehow, the revivals mean more stage work than when we had lengthy runs of the original productions!"

"True, true, you're right there Tom and in a few months, I reckon sometime in the new year, in fact, we're back to Italy again!" Fred laughed, before looking a little more serious, he continued. "Tom, there is something – because there isn't any prospect of any new operas, it maybe that occasionally there may be some other performances here at the Savoy, not Gilbert and Sullivan at all and not even given by the D'Oyly Carte company either. Occasionally, when that happens, it would mean that you and me, your Nellie and Miss Parker too, may need to go off to help out with the increasing tours that the company is undertaking around the country – and beyond – who knows! Would this be in order for you? I ask because it's always been something we've all tried to avoid except for those memorable Command Performances!"

"Why, of course, Mr. Dean," Tom replied, "especially when you say that Nellie and I can go together, it's not something that either of us would like to do willingly on our own, especially after all of this time being together!" Fred Dean nodded his agreement as Tom continued. "Yes, I understand, respect what you say too, but we do work in different circumstances now that the works are more established and no prospect for any new operas!"

Tom and Nellie talked about the events of the evening a good deal as they made their way home. In the first place, they both exchanged the news about the possibility of them both working with the touring companies when there were some gaps in the programme at the Savoy. Both accepted the idea without too much difficulty and the reassurance they had both received from their respective bosses, Fred Dean and Florrie Parker, that they could be together not only softened any misgivings that they may have had, but the prospects of some occasional trips around the country rather thrilled them. What, though, was of more immediate concern to them both were the repercussions from the last night performance of 'Yeomen'.

Seeing Sir Arthur once again at the Savoy, even without Mr. Gilbert, had brought back so many memories to the both of them of the earlier glory days, the fabulous excitements of the many first nights and the thrills of launching any of the series of the new operas. It was, too, a very personal reflection for them, especially what the years with the D'Oyly Carte Company had meant and which had given so much to their own lives. So great was their own involvement, that such issues were inseparable, as if they were all entwined as one within the web of theatre and personal life.

"You are sad ain't you Tom?" Nellie asked as she leant her arm around Tom as they sat in the train for yet another totally familiar journey from Blackfriars to Peckham. That virtual daily train trip itself had become just as much a regular fixture within their lives as home and work.

"A bit, yes love," Tom confessed.

"Methinks, it's more than a bit," Nellie challenged. Tom looked towards her for a few seconds before he even began to think about an answer.

"What it is love," Tom began at last, "it somehow seemed very poignant tonight that Sir Arthur should be at the theatre for the last night of a revival. To me that sort of said it all – you know, in comparison to all the first nights that we have both experienced over the years!"

287

"I sees and understands that," Nellie replied, "but Tom, it don't mean it's the end – not by any means! That's something what you must see for yerself as much without me telling yer! 'cause it ain't like one of the past first nights, that I grant yer, but on the other 'and it's not an end either, certainly not to the operas themselves, so I don't sees it as any reason to be too sad!"

"I know that you are right there, of course we all hope, rather, I should say believe, it is not the end overall but then what I find so very saddening is that it is most likely the end as far as any new pieces may be concerned. That has always been the excitement as we prepare for the new opera, the first stage designs, set-up and then re-planning, getting everything right, you having all of the costumes to do. Then when everything was prepared, before the first night, it was always to see the magnificence of it all and knowing through our eyes it was something that no audience had ever yet seen. That was the sense of fulfilment and excited anticipation and if there is not ever another new Gilbert and Sullivan opera then there will never be that experience again. To me that's very much an end of an era and an end of a very important part of my life, since 1871 beginning with 'Thespis' – 26 years – and that's a very long time," Tom lamented.

Nellie thought for the moment, fully realising the depth and obvious importance of what Tom had just said. Quietly, she began to say: "It's been your life Tom, and in that it is all to your credit as much as to anyone else in the company. It was you what took yerself off to Mr. Gilbert all them years ago when you wanted to better not only yerself but also our little family from what yer saw, and rightly so as it turned out, as the 'orrors of working in the music 'all! Not only that either, you saw the 'featre as the place for me to work and through you I got out of the wretched dress factory and to a new working life what I never believed possible. Respectability is what you achieved for both of us in our working life and I'm more than indebted to yer for that – more then yer ever possibly know!"

Tom looked affectionately to his wife but she held her hand up kindly. "I ain't finished yet Tom!" she continued. "Whilst I'm at it, there's somefink else that I wants to say 'ere and now too – is all down to you with yer work an' all that we were able to better ourselves 'ere in Peckham with our little 'ouse, away from the dust and muck of Shoreditch! So, as yer boss would say, 'Tom me lad', there ain't 'alf a lot what we've to be grateful for to Sir Arthur, Mr. Gilbert and Mr. D'Oyly Carte – and that's all before the 'whole musical world states their claim!"

"Thank you for saying so, love," Tom answered almost inaudibly and really quite inadequately, especially in view of the depth, sincerity and sense of Nellie's speech. In any case, his words, short as they were, became drowned by the noise of the clattering of the train along the track and the screeching of breaks signalling the approach of Peckham station. He felt glad that the need to gather themselves together and collect their belongings in readiness to alight from the train gave him a few moments to consider before he made any more comments. In any case, it was Nellie who continued the conversation.

"I means what I say, all of it," she said with the same depth of meaning to her voice as earlier, this time as they walked out of the station, arm in arm, along the familiar streets for the short journey home. "But also, you must now start to look at 'fings about our 'featre work differently too. What we've all done so 'ard to achieve is now all set up, yes true, but what our tasks are now is to make sure that in the work which we are entrusted to do, we do our bit to be certain that the operas all continue. And that means in the way that they were always intended to be! You for them stage settings, me for the costumes, oh together with Mr. Dean and Miss Parker, of course! Nothing less than to preserve and make it so that in the years ahead they are kept as bright and fresh for the 'undreds of thousands of new audiences to see the performances not just 'ere in London, but throughout the country and all over the world an' all. And it is for our company, the D'Oyly Carte Company to be the custodian of all that so we makes it our aim we both do our part towards that an' all! When we do that – and we will – then you and me can reflect truly on an even more wonderful, more magnificent achievement!"

Tom lovingly looked at his wife, not for the first time in a sense of almost marvel and unwarranted disbelief at the depth and considered meaning of her words. He squeezed her hand, held her even more tightly and once again said, simply "thank you". Two words only, but so very much sincerely meant and a statement of such deeply true bonding and love.

"Just you remember what I've said and don't get yerself depressed anymore!" Nellie emphasised. "We've all of us got a lot work still to do in the featre, wherever the featre may be, and all of that so do what we all can to keep the performances going. I've got no doubts that we will succeed an' succeed well an' all. Do you know what, Tom?"

"What's that, love?" Tom asked, his mind still rather too loaded to be able to make too much other comment.

"Well, I reckons that Gilbert and Sullivan operas will be around much longer then you and me, the company, too, building on all the foundation work what we've all done – so much will be the real lasting achievement for all of our work together over the years and you alone before that!" she declared. As she, almost theatrically herself, finished her statement, they reached their own front door and Tom, for one, was especially glad to be nearing the sanctuary of their own home and for some moments of quiet reflection upon all that had been so sincerely said by Nellie that evening.

In silence, coming from them both because of being in deep thoughts rather than from any degree of unhappiness nor anger, they hung their coats and in a twosome in a perfectly disciplined and managed way, as much at home as in the theatre, they prepared a late supper and a hot drink before finally getting ready for bed. But Tom didn't sleep much that night, his mind was too full and racing as he mulled over their evening – the events at the theatre and more so their conversation on the way home which had meant so very much to him. Once again, and not for the first time in his already rather long working life, he felt that he had a clearer perspective of the way ahead for them in the theatre and how best to deal with it in the changed circumstances which were then inevitable.

"Thank you for what you said last night." They were the first words that Tom spoke as soon as he realised that Nellie was stirring beside him for the start of a new day. "I've thought of little else all night, about everything really," he added, "and not only do I deeply appreciate all that you have said, but I've also done a deal of reflective talking to myself as well!"

"That must have been rather interestin'," Nellie sighed, sleepily, as she roused from what for her had been a perfectly adequate and restful night. "I 'ope you got yerself some reasonable answers!"

"Oh yes, I did love, very much so," Tom replied. "And do you know – thanks to listening to you, I realise as you pointed out, now is the time to be enjoying the work in a different way. It's as you say, to develop upon what we have already got, what's there for us here and now and for me to spend less time moping as to whether there may be any new operas coming. It is really so, as you have pointed out, our future doesn't now depend on any new works maybe coming, not now that there are already a full repertory of established and successful pieces! More important, as you say, our future depends on the ongoing performances and success of the already popular pieces!"

"You're right in most of what you say there, Tom, but wrong in the use of one of them words – 'moping'!" Nellie declared, by then fully awake. "It's not less time moping, for you, me, any of us in the company, it's no time moping at all! We've all got too much to be grateful for, too much to do, so we 'ave no moping and no time for it anyway!"

"Right you are, Dear," Tom quickly replied, "'moping' is not the word to be considered at all, that I do honestly agree!" In that it was a statement that he then believed in sincerely. So much so, he was in a far more light-hearted spirit as he washed and dressed ready for the new day and then, as a special treat, prepared a breakfast of ham and eggs for them both.

"Cor, blimey!" she declared, "you are better, and that's what I like, Tom me lad," adding with a laugh. "What with everything else, I now will really be well set up for the day!"

By the time that they had both once again reached the Savoy, the light-hearted feelings had been well maintained not only throughout their journey but also continued throughout the day. For the first time in weeks, Tom didn't even ask Fred Dean if there was any news of any possible new pieces coming from Sir Arthur and Mr. Gilbert. He realised that there was plenty else of work to do in the theatre and most satisfyingly so!

Chapter 20

"Welcome joy, adieu to sadness!
As Aurora gilds the day"

"Tom, Tom, oh, and good morning to you me'dear," Fred Dean called as soon as Tom and Nellie had once again arrived backstage at the Savoy. "Mr. D'Oyly Carte has told me for sure that 'Gondoliers' is to be revived but it will be for later in 1898. So that will mean now for all of us a spell of work with the touring companies – it's what we expected anyway!"

"Right you are, Mr. Dean." Tom replied for both of them and did so with a light heart and ready smile. "We're both ready for it and, what's more, rather excited about the experiences too!" Nellie, by his side, nodded politely.

"Glad to hear it," the stage manager replied. "It will probably do all of us the world of good to have some meanderings around the country, just to see what's going on here and there – to see for our selves rather than always relying on what they tell us, to be sure that standards are maintained just as Mr. D'Oyly Carte would want them to be, not to say by Mr. Gilbert and Sir Arthur as well! Although, all the touring companies have it well instilled into them what is expected and as to the very high demands of performance so I for one don't expect to find much amiss!"

"I'm sure that will be the case," Tom agreed. "Anyway, the work will keep us more than busy until such times as Mr. D'Oyly

292

Carte is ready for the revival here." Tom's words were spoken more in the sense of a kind of back-up assurance for himself even though his previous fears had been by then overcome. Nevertheless, Tom couldn't help but feel happily relieved by his stage manager's nod of agreement.

As they walked away, Tom lovingly nudged Nellie. "There you are my love, some travelling for you, in this your 50th birthday year – you can't say that we're not recognising it in a very special way!"

"Don't rub it in, 'cause if you do, I'll remind you that you're three years older than me anyway!" Nellie replied with a laugh. That cheerful exchange very much set the tone for both of them, not just for that day but well into the future too in a spirit of genuine contentment and happiness in both their working and personal worlds.

Just days after Fred Dean's announcement, the company working as always in its customary precise and efficient way, Tom and Nellie closed up their treasured home in Peckham, leaving the key with their worthy neighbour who never failed to be impressed, almost in awe, of their respected theatre lives. First, they travelled by the train as usual to Blackfriars but then instead of following their well-trodden steps to the Savoy, headed by bus to Euston. There was to be no travelling on the Underground trains anymore for Nellie who, as she put it quite firmly to Tom, said: "I'm 'appy enough to 'ave some new experiences but I draws a line on that!" Once at Euston, they took the train to Manchester. They both enjoyed the train journey and especially took delight in viewing the kaleidoscope of villages, countryside, canals, the bigger towns and cities that they passed through and for which Tom especially avidly, in a kind of boyish enthusiasm that belittled his age, traced from the map that was never far from his hand.

"That's the Grand Union Canal over there," he declared to Nellie, pointing to the busy scene of barges, lock gates and a bright lock-keeper's house beyond the train's window. Nellie gave a brief nod of acknowledgement in return. It wasn't that she was uninterested because she liked to look out of the window at the passing scene, but more with a sense of detachment than

Tom, preferring to concentrate her mind to her needlework in a relaxing kind of way. "Soon it will be Rugby and then travelling along the Trent Valley," Tom continued to which Nellie continued to respond with a nodded smile as her fingers busily worked with her delicate task.

Once they arrived in Manchester, and after having checked in to the guest house which already had quite a few other company members staying, they next made their way to the theatre. In barely a few moments of handshakes and acknowledgements to various colleagues, both Tom and Nellie set to their work and after only a handful of minutes had passed, they scarcely knew that they were a couple of hundred miles away from home. For them, it was that they were completely immersed in a familiar theatre scene and the well-drilled ritual of preparing for another Gilbert and Sullivan performance. It was almost that the town's location was of no significance, the sights of which they were almost hardly ever aware. The reality was that the 'Mikado's' Japan was the same, be it in Manchester, London or wherever and that was what mattered most to all in the company, Tom and Nellie included.

The one difference that they both felt and fully realised, though, was that their roles were of a more supervisory nature than at the Savoy. The touring company had its own team of stage crew and wardrobe assistants to which Tom and Nellie had more to check that all was well, offer advice and guidance if they saw the need for it. The role was not especially well suited for either of them, they both preferring to be directed, or rather to be left to get on with their work, rather than themselves doing the directing or, worst of all, actually telling. "You're the real stage manager here, you know, Tom me lad," Nellie exclaimed to a startled Tom who then took just a few seconds to reply. "Well, if that's the case, then you're the Miss Parker!" But the truth was that neither much liked the inference and therefore neither joked about nor laboured the point any further.

"If, perhaps, I may suggest," was the usual way in which Tom would broach the subject to one of the stage crew. For Nellie, it would be "that look's pretty nice, love, but maybe, erm, ain't it, wouldn't it be perhaps a little bit better if you were to sew that dress there", pointing to the spot, needle in hand only immediately to do it herself when her colleague had turned away. Later, Nellie would say, as a kind of stressed re-assurance "Thanks, love, that's all a very fine bit of work what you 'ave done and will look a perfect picture on stage tonight!"

Generally, it was both a very happy but very hard working atmosphere. At the Savoy, Tom and Nellie were both used to long runs of the same opera but with the touring company life was very much different. There, it was a strenuously hard repertory that they presented with several of the operas being performed in each town. In some instances, the sets were a little less complex than for the Savoy, especially so when the stage working area was often much less. But smaller stages created just as many problems as large complicated sets and there was no easy medium either way short of adapting every piece of scenery for the vagaries of individual theatres.

For the costumes, there was very rarely any such luxury of saving. The range of uniforms, robes, suites and dresses was equally elaborate as for the London performances but with the added problems of coping with the huge wardrobe for the several operas being performed. Stage wings were often barely adequate for storage and there was a constant bustle of movement between the theatre and some back street temporary storage that had been found for the time that the company was in town. Whatever, it meant only one thing – a deal of work and running around.

"C'or blimey, I ain't 'alf tired," Nellie bemoaned to Tom one evening as they made their way back to the guest house. "Some special 50th birthday travelling year, as yer so delicately put it, this is all turning out to be! Oh, me feet, they're bloomin' killin' me," she continued, "if you asks me, we don't know just how good we 'ave it back 'ome at the Savoy as compared to all these poor souls what work with the touring company!"

"It is hard, I agree, more so when you realise that most of them are touring for sometimes as much as 50 weeks in any one year, never more than a week or two at the most in the same town, always different guest houses or grim flats – it's anything but easy!" Tom answered. "You can't help but admire their enthusiasm or the dedication to the works of Gilbert and Sullivan – real D'Oyly Carte ambassadors, that's what these folk are, really so!" Nellie nodded, as Tom continued. "And that's why any one of them always see it as valued and recognised promotion when they are sometimes offered the chance to come to the Savoy! I am amazed at the sheer professionalism of them all, how they mount such good performances every night, as fresh and as clear as if it was for the very first performance of a London first night years ago. This is our first town – just imagine how it's going to be when we pack everything away here at the end of next week, move away over the Sunday and ready to set up in Birmingham on the Monday!"

"Don't remind me!" Nellie replied, "I think that by very soon I'll be waiting for the call from the Savoy that they are ready to mount 'Gondolier's' – with that we can 'ead 'ome again – and I can put me feet up!"

"I agree with that well enough," Tom assured. "But there's something happening before that which lays very heavy on my mind!" Nellie looked quizzically towards Tom, who was heavily frowning as he continued. "What I mean, is a couple of performances of 'Ruddigore'!"

Nellie laughed aloud. "Ah, Tom me lad, your favourite gallery scene to set up and make 'appen!"

"Yes, I thought that you would well remember that!" Tom replied. "As you often remind me, I'm three years older than you as it is but after overseeing 'Ruddigore' a few times in various theatres, then I think that I will be about 10 times older than you! But, honestly, I do admire them, the way they work so hard, night after night, and often with the different operas. We just don't, or haven't, realised just how much easier that we've had it!"

Despite Tom's misgivings, 'Ruddigore' went off without a hitch, the Manchester audience very obviously appreciating the infamous gallery scene with a barely concealed collective intake of breath as the 'ghosts' stepped down from the picture frames in the gallery. As the scene later operated successfully in reverse, it was then Tom's sigh of relief that broke the silence backstage.

In repertory, there was never any time to relax after one successful show. If Friday night was 'Ruddigore' then Saturday became fairyland and Westminster for 'Iolanthe' and whilst the following Sunday for once was not a so called "changeover" day to the next theatre, like most in the company Tom and Nellie were too tired to even begin to think about much personal exploration of Manchester. Tom had initially an idea that it would be nice for both of them to take a day out to the Lake District but he didn't even resist when Nellie said, very firmly, "no, maybe not this time!" But they did enjoy the chance to relax and to talk socially with their fellow company members, relive the old times and collective experiences of so many performances, before it was once again the start of the week and the stage at the Manchester theatre to be transformed to the 'Exterior of Castle Bunthorne' in readiness for that evening's performance of 'Patience'.

The Manchester season flew by until they reached the final Saturday and the closing performance that for that visit was to be the double bill of 'Trial by Jury' and 'Pirates of Penzance'.

"Two operas, two varying sets of costumes and we're to be out of 'ere by first thing on Sunday," Nellie bemoaned, to which Tom could only agree about the sheer amount of work needed.

In a well-disciplined way, everything was, of course, done in time and in a tired sort of haze they bade farewell to Manchester on the Sunday morning and joined their colleagues on the train to Birmingham. This time, though, Tom did not give Nellie a running commentary about the places that they were passing through on the train – he was spending the time dozing, unlike many of the company who were enjoying their Sunday travelling ritual with chatting and social niceties. As Nellie said to him later, in a kind of reproach, "You'll, erm both of us, we'll jolly need next time to be a bit more awake and join in with the others less they think we are the stuck up ones from London!"

In Birmingham, they opened with 'Mikado', the set and costumes having arrived earlier from Manchester. And so it continued for their two-week season in the city, varying each day from stage settings of the Tower of London, through Venice, via 'Castle Adamant' of 'Princess Ida', to the 'Quarter Deck of 'HMS Pinafore', off Portsmouth', once again to Cornwall for 'Pirates', not forgetting Tom's 'favourite' gallery setting for 'Ruddigore' and performances of both 'Iolanthe' and 'Patience'. If all that wasn't enough work, there also was included a brief return to the South Seas for 'Utopia Limited'. Tom was especially pleased for the opportunity once again to stage that opera, the stage setting for which he always saw as a particular fine achievement of his already long career.

Over the weeks, Tom and Nellie's knowledge of their own country became ever wider as Birmingham became next Leeds that in a fortnight was turned into Newcastle, across once again to the North West, where at last Tom and Nellie finally had the chance of a brief visit one Sunday to the Lakes, before they both travelled nearer home to be with the company in both Oxford and Brighton. During this time, Tom and Nellie became more aware of the routine and looked upon the Sunday changeover days with the company together for the train journey as something of a respected highlight of the week. They no longer did the indecent thing of snoozing on the journey. Instead, they relaxed in the spirit of conversation and friendship with their fellow company members.

It was a tradition for the journey that all would be sure to dress in their Sunday finery – the ladies in their best dresses and fine coats with matching gloves and hats; the men in either a best suit or a blazer with coat and hat. Many would bring with them some fine food as a picnic that would be handed around and shared so that the whole company enjoyed a veritable feast.

"It's just like our annual river picnic on the Thames!" Nellie remarked to Tom one Sunday on the long and rather complicated journey south once again as they made their way to Oxford. "Except this is different 'cause this 'appens every Sunday when we're on a changeover – and that's nice, very nice indeed!" she added. Tom happily agreed with her and admitted that he really looked forward to the occasions just as much as well.

That Tom had by then been involved in the operas for 27 years, he was held in a combined sense of both awe and esteem by many in the touring company, even looked up to, especially as Fred Dean wasn't even there with them. It was, as Nellie was prone to joke with him, a kind of "Elder-Statesmen, kind of authorative role what they see you as!" But he appreciated the thought and, more than that, revelled in reflecting upon his experiences of all the early preparations and rehearsals, the glorious first nights plus all of the original and revived performances with which he had been involved over the years. Without pushing himself, he was nevertheless quick to take up his reflections when questions were asked in the carriage and he appreciated too that Nellie, as proper that it was, would join with him in their combined recollections.

"Mr. Gilbert, he always has been very precise with what he wants, the every stage direction and movement as well as how the words are both sung and spoken, with very clear diction at all times – to be heard at the back of the 'gods' as much as in the front stalls! We were always told by Mr. Gilbert that he had seen too many plays badly rehearsed and under-dressed and that he would never allow that for his works! In the same way, it was just so too with Sir Arthur, how the music be played, the number of musicians needed to ensure the quality of performance, for the right tone and pitch. And there was never any deviation. If, very occasionally there was, Mr. Gilbert or Mr. D'Oyly Carte would soon get to hear of it and matters would need to be quickly corrected – or else!" Tom commented to his attentive colleagues, respectfully listening to his every word.

"But surely, there must be sometimes when changes be allowed because our audience's attitudes may themselves change so that what was right for the 1870's may not be the case for the 1890's – or rather, that maybe is how I see it," said a recently recruited new member of the gentlemen's chorus to Tom on the Sunday morning train trip to Oxford.

"No, I do not think that you are completely right there," Tom replied, kindly and re-assuring with a warm smile. "True, there are instances where a small change may be necessary by way of a different interpretation, but never to detract from the overall value of the piece. For example, Mr. Gilbert himself agreed when Mr. Lytton wanted the character 'Jack Point' in 'Yeomen' to appear to collapse and die at the end of the opera, something that never happened in the original. That was a very real and

299

accepted change, including a change to one line of the song, which many of our audiences have found to benefit the opera."

"It's all so 'eartwarming, always such a very 'uman piece and more so now," Nellie interjected to which Tom and many in the carriage nodded their agreement.

"What Nellie says is so true for that particular work," Tom emphasised. He continued. "With some of the others, 'Ruddigore' for example, we made some changes even after the first night and what you perform now is not precisely as was the very first performance – but they were amendments agreed and made by both Sir Arthur and Mr. Gilbert. Believe me, over the whole repertoire of the years, changes are very, very few and that, I say again, is precisely how I think it should be!" Tom paused once again and returned a kind smile to those around him who all continued to listen intensely and make nods of approval.

"But for the operas to be a true Gilbert and Sullivan performance, then in my mind it should be so that they are played now, and continue to be played, in exactly the way that the composer and writer intended and instructed." Tom paused for a moment and noticed, with considerable relief, that his colleague was nodding with a sense of understanding agreement. "The fact is, old chap," Tom carried on, "that the value of the work lies in the brilliance in which they were first written, Sir Arthur's melodious music, Mr. Gilbert's crisp and meaningful dialogue, plus the absolute brilliant characterisations. So much so, I would go as far as to say, and my dear Nellie would surely agree with me," he added, looking to her for support that she immediately reciprocated. "There you are," Tom acknowledged, "it really is so in our view that if you have virtual perfection, as we have with these operas themselves, that the good must not, should not, be tampered with!"

"Not to say about the excellent sets and costumes an' all," Nellie added, not with any sense of self-promotion but because she realised the real worth and value they had all achieved in the line of productions.

"Yes, exactly as Nellie says," Tom picked up his wife's comments. "That's very important too, because never has any expense been spared in the productions for stage design nor for costumes – only the very best and top quality would ever do! With all these ingredients together giving a first class and quality performance, one in which the audience very obviously delights, then there is hardly a need to even begin to consider changes as such or just for the sake of it. Mr. Gilbert's humour is equally as valuable now as are his weighted means of poking fun at society and institutions as when first written – I am sure that will continue to be the case as well, hopefully even beyond our time to the future century!"

"I think I can see that Mr. Dobbs," the new chorister replied, reddening a little from what he realised was a succinct but worthwhile valued response from Tom, so passionately delivered.

For a moment, Tom could barely react to being called by his surname and by that style. It made him feel a somehow out of place senior, rather older than he felt himself to be, and it took a few seconds to collect his thoughts. Nellie noticed and quickly guessed what he must be feeling and gave him a friendly and supportive nudge in his side.

"In all of this, though, I don't see it that our duty is to preserve a kind of museum piece, no, not at all and I wouldn't see that to be right either," Tom declared. "Yes, there will, I see, be some changes in text in time to reflect what may be more relevant at a different time and in a different town, maybe," he continued. "We have this already in 'Mikado' with 'Ko-Ko's' 'Little-list' song. You maybe have noticed that yourself?"

"I hadn't really appreciated it to be honest, Mr. Dobbs," the chorister replied.

"Oh yes, yes indeed," Tom answered. "One or two lines have been changed and Mr. Gilbert agrees to that – to make the song's contents more valid to the moment – that's keeping it respectfully fresh!"

"That's interesting to know."

"And there are other changes – but overall, relatively minor," Tom continued. "But that's fine, it's not interfering with the piece as such. I just say again, what we have with the Gilbert and Sullivan operas are exquisite pieces of Victorian musical theatre, epitomes of English comic opera and with them will be what I, we, all of us hope, will surely be a lasting work for the theatre for now and, again, hopefully, years to come. I would go as far as to say that the children who we see on the streets now should be our audiences for the future, especially as many of their parents will be playing the music on the piano at home for them to learn and appreciate already!" Tom paused once again, cleared his throat and thought for a moment before he continued to what he realised was almost a devoted audience attentive to his every word. He hoped that it wasn't because that within a moving train, it was a captive audience without any alternative other than to listen! But he felt, and welcomed, Nellie's very obvious support and so once again took up his address.

"I must say, as no doubt you will have heard so many say and to which I whole-heartedly concur, that the collaboration of Sir Arthur Sullivan with Mr. Gilbert has been the most remarkable and most successful in British musical theatre. It has introduced English comic opera. Mr. Dean, my stage manager at the Savoy, once told me, quite recently, in fact, something that sums this achievement up. He said that Gilbert and Sullivan have, through their operas, rescued popular musical entertainment from the 'vulgar fooleries of burlesque', the 'smell of orange peel and lamp oil', like the old music hall!" Tom added, as much to give weight to his own thoughts as well. Tom, by then was in almost unstoppable mode as he continued. "But there is one important thing more as well," Tom stated as his audience's collective response was an inquisitive look awaiting the ready answer. Tom then gave it to them without question. "This is that none of it would have been possible without the involvement, virtually from the beginning, of the founder of our company, Mr. Richard D'Oyly Carte!"

The collective sounds of "hear-hear" reverberated around the carriage which Tom and Nellie together acknowledged with an agreeable smile. Perhaps it really was so that after so many years in the theatre they were just as much the successful partnership as the composer and writer!

"So, to conclude, I would just like to add," Tom began, "that it was the vision, the diplomacy, the business acumen if you like, of Mr. D'Oyly Carte that ensured the success of the Gilbert and

Sullivan partnership, importantly that they remained together over the years to give us 12 regularly played, full length operas – plus 'Trial by Jury' and that's not to mention 'Thespis'!" Tom laughed, before he once again carried on. "That was before the time of most of you! Remember, too, that it was Mr. D'Oyly Carte's vision of building the Savoy Theatre for the operas which ensured that our London audiences had probably the finest theatre in the land, if not all of Europe, in which to come to and enjoy the performances, not to say way back in 1881, the first theatre to have electricity and with it, all the improved conditions for both audiences and performers which that entailed!"

By then, the young chorister who had first posed the original question had with unfounded embarrassment retreated within himself. Nellie sought to reassure him, put her arms around him and said: "There you are, love, now you 'ave it, and straight from the 'orses mouth!"

"Thank you, Mrs. Dobbs, and Mr. Dobbs too, very much so. Of course, I do appreciate all that you have most kindly told to me and have found it very, very interesting, a fine insight into all that has gone before with the operas," the chorister answered, quietly although sincerely.

"That is the tradition that we have all striven to build up and what we hope may be a lasting Gilbert, Sullivan and D'Oyly Carte legacy," Tom concluded the discussion with a warm and kind smile that seemed to be appreciated and acknowledged by all assembled in the railway carriage. The discussion had certainly made the journey pass quickly and all could hardly believe when just a few moments later they heard the guard call out "Next stop will be Oxford".

It was spring and Oxford was a happy week for Tom and Nellie. Just once they had time to walk by the river and the sight of the Thames reminded them of the treasured annual picnics that they enjoyed with their fellow company members every year, although further downstream from that spot. The week was good, too, because of the successful performances given – four of the operas in the six nights and all without any hitches. Before the passing of time had seemed hardly possible, it was Sunday once again. This time, the train that they took, because they were moving to Brighton for the next week, meant that they all travelled via London and Tom and Nellie had the chance for a brief visit home to Peckham to make sure all was well.

Brighton was equally successful but because they gave six different operas over the six nights, there was hardly time for more than a very swift breath of sea air as they walked between their guesthouse and the theatre. "We'll come again, later in the year for at least a long weekend," Tom said reassuringly to Nellie who replied, "That will be nice, sure it will!"

Before the week was out at Brighton, the expected call for Tom and Nellie to return to London and to the Savoy was received – the revival of 'Gondoliers' was imminent. Tom would be in charge of the stage management as Fred Dean had travelled to South Africa to be with the D'Oyly Carte Company that was performing several of the operas there, including 'Mikado', 'Yeomen', 'Utopia', 'Grand Duke' and also 'Gondoliers'.

"C'or ain't it fine for 'im – we gets the likes of Birmingham and Manchester whilst he gets South Africa!" Nellie wryly observed.

"Well, he is the boss," Tom replied, "but, who knows, some time later, maybe after 'Gondoliers' and some other important revival, perhaps it will be our turn for somewhere more exotic!"

All the preparation work for the revival at the Savoy went with ease and Tom felt no hint of earlier self-consciousness, felt on the recent tour, at being the boss. Tom was considered to be reasonably firm but fair by those around him who all respected his knowledge and dedication coming from his years with the company. All the team worked diligently as a result. At the same time, Nellie was busy with all the costumes and although Florrie Parker was 'boss', she was left to get on with it as very much her own work. Before many days had passed, both Tom and Nellie were thoroughly happy to be back in their accustomed routine, especially to be home to their cherished house once again, so much so that any nurtured thoughts of envy towards Fred Dean soon disappeared.

A delighted audience just as enthusiastically received the revival of 'Gondoliers' at the Savoy in 1898 in much the same way as for the first night nine years earlier. Tom felt proud of his work and was especially pleased with himself when Fred Dean returned from South Africa a few weeks into the run to exclaim: "Very well done, Tom me lad – I couldn't have done better myself!"

There was only one possible response that Tom could give. "Right you are, Mr. Dean" – and he didn't fail on that occasion either!

Both Sir Arthur and Mr. Gilbert took a very keen interest in the revival and called into the Savoy, separately, on several occasions to cast their respective eyes on what was happening and to be sure that all was well. One morning, Fred Dean called over to Tom. "Here, Tom, Sir Arthur was in the theatre last night and Mr. D'Oyly Carte has told me of a most amusing incident!"

"What was that, Mr. Dean?" Tom asked.

"Why, Sir Arthur was standing at the back of the crowded pit, enjoying the opera he was! After a moment, a stranger touched him on his arm and apparently he said to him: 'Excuse me, sir, but I paid my money to hear Sullivan's charming opera, not your confounded humming!' I think that somehow Sir Arthur found it all more than somewhat amusing!" Fred Dean concluded.

"I can just imagine that, and probably even if the stranger had recognised Sir Arthur, it was probably the very last place, at the back of the pit, where he would have expected to meet the composer!" Tom concurred, laughing at the thought at what he had just heard. "And of Mr. Gilbert, has he been making any comments about our recent performances?"

"Yes, Tom, there was something the other day," Fred Dean replied. "Apparently, Mr. Gilbert, too, had been at the back of the pit on another night and he sent a note to Mr. D'Oyly Carte saying that he considered one of the gentlemen of the chorus to be garishly over-acting! He made it known that if he does it again, then he must be placed in the back row of the chorus! The gentleman concerned has been told – and he won't be doing it again!"

"It's good to know that even after all these years that Mr. Gilbert is still taking a very keen interest in the productions, as always, really," Tom commented.

"Yes, very much so," the stage manager replied, "and long may it continue, that's what I say because, next to the excellence of the operas themselves, it is one of the main reasons of our continuing success!" Tom nodded in agreement, before Fred continued. "So Tom, whatever we do, we must be sure to avoid being at the back of the pit when a performance is on – you'll never know who you will meet!" Tom, once again, laughed at the very thought of it all.

'The Gondoliers' continued to play to packed houses and to charm audiences, both old and new, much to the delight of all in the company who felt they could all once again comfortably relax into their precise, but less pressured, daily routine. For Tom and Nellie that meant some Sundays at home to their great delight, especially with their many picnics in Greenwich Park on summery days, often accompanied there by a distant band playing some very familiar melodies from the operas. That only added to their pleasure and sense of general wellbeing.

Later in the same year, just after he and Nellie had taken their much promised long weekend visit to Brighton, in a rare absence from the theatre for either of them, as a happy occasion to mark Nellie's 50th birthday, Tom next heard that following 'Gondoliers' there would be a revival of 'The Sorcerer'. That would be special for Nellie too because it represented the last for her of the early operas that previously she had only before been briefly involved with at an earlier short revival. She felt it very fitting that such a milestone for her would be reached in her own special birthday year. Then, when it was announced that the opening performance at the Savoy would be on 17 November 1898, exactly 21 years to the very day of the first night, the sense of excitement felt by them both and all within the D'Oyly Carte Company became very sustained indeed.

"This atmosphere is just like it used to be when we had any one of the original first nights!" Tom exclaimed as Nellie came down to the stage area for further discussions about the costume requirements. "The whole place is in a sense of thrill, a kind of very excited anticipation!"

"I've noticed it meself – I said it to Miss Parker an' all – methinks it must be something other than just the revival that's put such a spirit into the air! 'Ave you 'eard anything Tom?" Nellie asked.

"Well, of course it's very special that the opening should be on the significant 21st anniversary of the very first night. But more, true, there has been a rumour that Sir Arthur himself will conduct on the opening night and if that's so, well maybe Mr. Gilbert will be in the house as well," Tom declared, barely able to contain his own sense of thrill at the significance of such a possible event.

"And that would be really just like the old times," Nellie replied, she too smiling to herself at the very thought of it. "I really 'ope so, it would be so lovely to see the two of them on stage together again!"

"The two of whom on stage, dear?" It was Florrie Parker that came over to Tom and Nellie. Nellie immediately told the wardrobe mistress what Tom had said. "I agree," Florrie Parker replied, "that, indeed, would be something so very nice to happen – to see them both back here at the Savoy!"

Fred Dean, from the side of the stage, overhearing the conversation, simply called out "Me too – I agree with all the thoughts the three of you are expressing. Let us all will it to happen that way!"

"Well, goodness me, if it's not our explorer back from the jungle!" Florrie laughed, even though she had seen Fred many times since his return. "My Nellie, with her husband, get to visit the far reaches of this country and..." She stopped herself from saying something else but then continued. "I stay here to supervise the main wardrobe whilst you see half of the world!"

"There you go again!" Fred Dean laughed, as he came forward to the centre stage, "it'll be your turn another time, that's if you want it that way," he assured.

"Sometime, who knows, but not for the moment" Florrie replied, very quietly, with her head bowed down towards the stage. Nellie went over to her boss and gave her a hug, knowing only to well that Miss Parker's sister, Lillian, was not so very well and that Miss Parker would not want to leave her alone in the house they shared in Peckham, not far from where Tom and Nellie lived, in any case. "Thank you, Nellie," the wardrobe mistress said softly and very appreciatively, acknowledging the gesture.

"Of course, my dear," Fred said softly. "But whilst you are all here, I may as well mention something that Miss Parker and I have already talked about, eh?" Florrie nodded. "Right, Tom and Nellie, it's time for you to know that we, Mr. D'Oyly Carte and all of us here, want you both to go over to America and Canada next year to spend a bit of time with our company there, to do like you have done so well with the touring company here, have a look what's going on, oversee and make sure all is well! Is that something which will be in order for you?"

"Mr. Dean," Tom began, looking towards Nellie who was by then quite overcome, but managed to mouth a soft "yes". "I think that I can say for both of us that we would be extremely honoured to do just that!" Tom spoke with a dry mouth that belied his excitement but was unable to say anymore. His racing and positively feeling mind more than made up for his speech.

"Right you both are then, that's fixed!" Fred Dean replied. "We can sort out the exact timing later, to be definitely in the next year, 1899, though. However, since I've already been told we are going to be mounting a revival of 'HMS Pinafore' in the new year, we'll need to work around that because you'll both too valuable to be away from the Savoy for that! Then after all of that, we'll have to talk between ourselves about some similar visits that will be needed to both Australia and New Zealand, so ladies and one gentleman, there's more than enough work for all of us to be getting on with, here and over there, well into the future!" Fred smiled cheerily to those around him.

Tom and Nellie left the stage as if walking on air and talked of little else than their impending trip and what they both gratefully saw as the fine acknowledgement to them both for all their collective work with the company. Shortly, the impending opening of 'Sorcerer' soon concentrated their minds on their immediate jobs on hand although their forward thoughts were very much focused too, first on the coming year, then all that was likely to be for their future work in the theatre.

The rumour of Sir Arthur Sullivan conducting on the opening night of the revival of 'Sorcerer' was quickly confirmed as true, a dream fulfilled for all in the company. On the night of 17 November, Tom and Nellie had to both pinch themselves otherwise they would have both thought that they had been transported back in some way many years to one of the many glorious first nights they had both so happily experienced in the past. Again they were aware of the excited anticipation of the audience, as barely concealed and excited murmurings wafted from the theatre and through the brilliantly lit house stage curtain to the stage itself. Once more, a peek from the side of the stage revealed many of the audience sat in the stalls and dressed in all their finery, their jewellery sparkling as if to add a greater sense of magic to the evening, as the house lights reflected the gems. Then, to complete the valued memories, it seemed that the whole of the gallery were once again singing vigorously and enthusiastically the choruses from their beloved Gilbert and Sullivan operas, then with an even greater repertory from which to choose from all the pieces.

"Nothing ain't changed at all, in all of the years, 'as it Tom?" a delighted Nellie stated, barely bothering to restrain the tears of joy on her face.

"No, my love, it hasn't – proof enough, if any were needed, that the allure of Gilbert and Sullivan is as much with us now as it was 21 years ago!" Tom replied proudly.

"And as it will be henceforward 21, 51 years... whatever number of years from now, that's what I finks!" Nellie exclaimed.

"Who knows, maybe it will, we can only hope that not just Sir Arthur and Mr. Gilbert, most importantly naturally, but all of our efforts within the company in this very real and warranted development of the English music theatre, will maybe have established something that will still be around – and thoroughly enjoyed, by thousands here, there and everywhere – long after we've gone!" Tom spoke from his heart, just for a brief second somewhat sadly, as he thought of the depth of the words he had just spoken. Quickly he revived to conclude: "But more than anything, this night is dedicated to you, my Nellie, as much as everything because without you here with me, none of these theatrical experiences, these evenings, all now so very happy and treasured, would have been anything without you by my side!"

"Oh, Tom, you... " Nellie cried, as once more not even bothering to wipe her eyes, she ran off further backstage to compose herself for a moment. She took control of herself before coming again to the stage and to Tom, turning to him to say: "My love, you couldn't 'ave said anyfing more perfect to make my birthday year any more lovely or special!" She kissed him on his cheek as the sound of the orchestra tuning in the pit signalled that the start of the performance was imminent. In the state of true professionals as they both were, their personal moment was over and each got willingly, but ever so happily, on with their respective duties, contentment etched upon both their faces.

As Sir Arthur Sullivan entered the orchestra pit, Tom and Nellie looked once again towards each other but neither this time made any comment about how the roof of the Savoy was likely to blow away, so great were the shouts and screams, the applause from the audience that greeted their sight of the revered composer. They had said that about the roof enough many times before and both merely took delight in the fact that nothing in all the years had changed.

Everyone in the company gave a dedicated and first-rate performance for the revived 'Sorcerer', as perfect in every way as it had been ever since the first night. The audience cheered, the encores were continually demanded and enthusiastically received. As the final curtain came, Nellie stood once more beside Tom, Florrie Parker with Fred Dean, all eagerly anticipating the reception that would come from the delighted audience. It was an absolute crescendo, even more rousing than in the past, if that was possible. Then, when the moment came that nobody had dared believed would happen – Sir Arthur Sullivan and Mr. Gilbert – joining the rest of the company on stage to take a curtain call, that was the time when Nellie could not resist saying to Tom "Now the roof really will be blown away!" For once, the remark was more than relevant.

The fact that neither Sir Arthur nor Mr. Gilbert spoke any words either publicly or even to each other, seemed hardly to matter.

It was all just enough that they were there, standing together again on the Savoy stage which was important. Even Tom, by then, had tears in his eyes as he shouted himself hoarse and, with Nellie, indeed the whole company, clapping vigorously from the sides of the stage or anywhere in the Savoy in which they found themselves.

The ovation lasted several minutes until finally Fred Dean, aware through years of experience of both Sir Arthur and Mr. Gilbert's wishes, gave Tom the signal to lower the curtain. Still the house clapped and cheered but both Sir Arthur and Mr. Gilbert had left the stage – there was to be no encore of that appearance.

"Oh joy! Oh joy,
The charm works well,
And all are now united."

Tom sung the words from 'Sorcerer' as he, with Fred Dean, cleared away the stage after the performers had left.

"Do you think so, Tom me lad?" Fred Dean asked.

"Oh, Mr. Dean, I don't mean that I'm expecting a new opera from Sir Arthur and Mr. Gilbert. I'm adjusted to the thought that it is now most unlikely. No, it's more that I felt so pleased, so nostalgic from all the years, just for seeing them together again and it's something that I will never forget," Tom assured. "Those two gentlemen have meant so very, very much to me – then, of course, Mr. D'Oyly Carte too, for all of my working life since 1871," Tom continued, "and one more, too, as much as anyone – you, Mr. Dean, all of you I owe my most sincere thanks."

"Thank you, Tom me lad, for what you say," Fred replied. "We've all been together a very long time and, hopefully, for very many more years to come as we work continually on all of the revivals, which seemed to be as popular as ever! Yes, we are a good team and for my part, I have always been grateful to have you faithfully by my side through it all!"

By then Tom felt exceedingly embarrassed. He held his head to conceal the tears he felt upon his cheeks and mumbled a barely audible "Thank you for saying so, too, Mr. Dean." He tried desperately to regain his composure and thought it best to once more repeat "I'll not forget the pleasure of seeing Sir Arthur and Mr. Gilbert on that stage once again!"

"Neither will I, neither will I," Fred Dean replied.

They completed their tasks on stage without saying anything further until Fred Dean, looking in one of the programmes for the evening, read it for a moment before he turned to Tom. "Here, Tom, read this, it just about says it all – for all of us!"

Tom took the copy. By then, too, Nellie, together with Florrie Parker, had joined them and so Tom read aloud:

"This is what the programme note says: 'It is also the twenty-first anniversary of the commencement of the successful continuous Series of Operas by W.S. Gilbert and Arthur Sullivan produced under the management of R. D'Oyly Carte, of which operas over six thousand performances have been given in London and probably between twenty thousand and thirty thousand, under Mr. Carte's direction, in the provinces; besides the many thousands of performances, authorised and unauthorised, in many parts of the world'. That's it," Tom concluded quietly.

For some moments there was not a sound on the stage as all four stood deep in thought. It was Fred Dean who finally broke the silence. "That is some record of which we can all, all of us here and wherever in various theatres up and down the country and overseas wherever the D'Oyly Carte Company performs, can be justifiably proud!" His comment was met by a quite but well meant "hear-hear" from the other three of the quartet on the stage.

"Right!" Fred Dean continued, "ladies and one gentleman, there is only one possible way in which we can end this evening – our traditional 'first night' cab ride home!" His words were met by a soft cheer and within a few moments, after they had collected their coats, Fred Dean, Florrie Parker, Tom and Nellie were once more outside the stage door of the Savoy and waiting to board a cab.

All were talking excitedly, reminiscing not only about the evening but also about the countless many other such evenings that they had all experienced in their collective many years of working with the D'Oyly Carte Company. After a moment of mellowed silence, with all in deep reflection in their thoughts, Fred Dean broke into song, from 'Ruddigore', which Florrie Parker, Tom and Nellie were more than happy to join in:

"In all London city,
There's no one so witty –
I've thought so again and again."

Just as the impromptu chorus finished, a cab drew up and the foursome happily climbed in. Then, before the cab drove away from the Savoy, towards the Strand, Fred Dean took a bottle of champagne and some glasses from the bag that he had so carefully been clutching since they had left the theatre.

"Ladies and one gentleman," Fred laughed, "a toast to you all, but especially also to Sir Arthur Sullivan, Mr. Gilbert and to Mr. D'Oyly Carte!"

"To Sir Arthur Sullivan, Mr. Gilbert, Mr. D'Oyly Carte and, most importantly too, to the whole D'Oyly Carte Company and long may it continue!" Tom, Nellie and Florrie Parker replied as one, collectively.

Chapter 21
"Heavy the heart that hopes but vainly"

Rupert Moore stared, almost dumbstruck even if not impolitely open mouthed, towards the stage at the Adelphi Theatre on that dramatic and highly charged night of Saturday 27 February 1982. For once he didn't even look towards his grandmother, sitting beside him in the stalls. His eyes, just like 'Robin Oakapple' from 'Ruddigore' were "fully open to my awful situation". But then, Rupert's eyes and ears were only for the stage ahead.

Following the excerpts from 'The Grand Duke' with which he had barely registered, through both a lesser knowledge of the opera, something for which he hardly dared admit to himself, but more because he knew it was the very last of the operas and therefore a sure finale of the evening. His stare, frozen and statue-like, was transfixed on the stage. Before him the whole D'Oyly Carte Opera Company were assembled and in fine voice immediately launched into a rousing chorus. Then, he could scarcely believe what he was hearing as they sung from 'Gondoliers', with such thrill and enthusiasm, as if without a care in the world:

"So good-bye, cachucha, fandango, bolero –
We'll dance a farewell to that measure –
Old Xeres, adieu – Manzanilla – Montero –
We leave you with feelings of pleasure!"

314

"Feelings of pleasure." The words rang round and round inside Rupert's head. What "feelings of pleasure"? What exactly did the words mean in this very context? An instant moment of sure hope mingled just as quickly with another moment of inward and deep devastating despair. He thought further. How could there be anything at all appropriate in such words, especially when there had been no statement made or even the slightest indication even hinted that there would be some kind of reprieve for the company, even at such an eleventh hour. Unless! Unless – it must certainly be so – the positive announcement was just about to be made! Surely that was the craved-for answer, it was all building up to such a spectacular climax that would be all the better received because of the pure drama! Of course, Rupert told himself, that was it! All his fears, the bad feelings of not only the immediate past minutes, also throughout the evening but equally of the preceding weeks before when rumours of the company's demise had abounded, all was surely to be then set to rights with the imminent and much-anticipated announcement. You fool! Rupert scolded himself – you fool, letting all this time being spoilt for you when you should have realised that all would be well in the end!

For a moment only, just a handful of seconds in reality, Rupert allowed his reasoning to settle his thoughts and his mind, to live in a self-induced and therefore very happy make believe. Quickly, his memory recalled the words from 'The Mikado', spoken by 'Nanki-Poo', on learning that he was to be beheaded in a month and desperate therefore for an extension of time in the same way as Rupert himself felt:

"These divisions of time are purely arbitrary..."

"We'll call each second a minute, each minute an hour – each hour a day – and each day a year."

The thoughts so expressed in those lines gave Rupert a much-needed respite, also they came with a very comforting solace – he was so desperate for a lengthening of time, no matter by whatever means. But in the reality of the moment, the seconds were nothing longer than a sixtieth of a minute and they elapsed just as quickly as such. The time void was no more.

Next, in an evening charged with so much significance, the stage there before him, although still brightly lit, was suddenly empty of people and props. The whole company had vanished. Then, within seconds, all the lights extinguished except for one main spotlight trained towards the back of the stage. A hush fell upon the whole house, so much so that it would have been possible to hear the proverbial pin drop. This is it, Rupert muttered to himself, still desperately in a state of self-convincement that all would be well. For the moment, instantly relieved, he allowed himself, for a fraction of second and for the first time in a while, a swift look towards his grandmother. But she was herself equally transfixed, her own eyes trained upon the stage and purposefully not daring to look towards Rupert. He noticed that Alice had her hands firmly clasped, resting on her lap, quite still, her expression one of steely determination. Rupert's spirits remained momentarily upbeat.

Then, before them all, on the bare stage with that one single and most over whelming powerful spotlight, stood Kenneth Sandford, a leading singer of the D'Oyly Carte Opera Company, himself a custodian of the 'Pooh-Bah' bass baritone roles for 25 years. Rupert, together with the whole audience, cheered vigorously, not only because the singer was a much respected and fine performer, but also in anticipation of – what? He wasn't sure, other than the enormously desired positive outcome.

From the paper in his hand, the singer read out details of the negative report about the company from the Arts Council, a report that was an effective nail in the coffin. There was to be no financial support forthcoming as there was to be for so many other musical and drama institutions in the country. There was to be no funding made available for the company to continue to perform and with it the cold words conveyed the horrible inevitability of it all. That was well and truly it. The scarce and harsh words, so straightforwardly and factually delivered, immediately removed any lingering hopes that Rupert, his grandmother Alice and indeed the whole audience that night at the Adelphi Theatre, held for a reprieve.

With the end of the announcement, the spotlight symbolically faded to a stage then in a total blackout. It was the end in every cold and conceivable way and one obviously without hope of a favourable alternative.

The whole audience gave a collective, sharp intake of breath after which a few seconds of total silence before emotions erupted in a spate of barely restrained sobs coming from all parts of the house – from the stalls, the circle, from the gallery, from people standing along the sides of the house, from everywhere. It was no exaggeration to say that it seemed that the theatre was a virtual pool of tears.

Alice looked towards Rupert. His face was ashen, his hands gripping the arms of his seat, his knuckles turning from an unnatural beetroot red to an equally unnatural pale and life-expired white with the pressure. She put her hand to his arm in a small but heartfelt aim to comfort but was unable to utter any word of comfort as she too struggled to fight back the tears as she vainly tried to deal with the lump of sadness she felt so strongly in her throat.

In a flash of a handful of seconds, Rupert saw in his mind a kaleidoscope of all his D'Oyly Carte years, a personal tally of more than a quarter of a century. Of his numerous visits to see performances both in London and around the country, of all the highs – there were no lows. He remembered his thrills always of the fine stage settings, the brilliant costumes, the astutely observed character interpretations, always the fine singing from both chorus and principals – the 'stars' to him and countless audiences. He thought of the sometimes negative comments given by some critics whom he regarded as snooty and unnecessarily highbrow. The ones who said the company was old-fashioned and who by so declaring failed to recognise that they were merely upholding and preserving all that both Gilbert and Sullivan wanted and had originally directed as the right way for their operas to be performed. It was how it should be – not quaint museum pieces but an upheld tradition. Oh, there had been some minor changes to the performances made over the years, perhaps for a topical reflection, but always delicately done and within the accepted spirit of the operas.

Rupert thought further for a brief moment. Changes, yes, there were a few he admitted as he recollected his personal repertory of performances. And, naturally, there had been many instances of re-staging, new sets and costumes, but always very properly done and strictly to the ideas laid down from the beginning and therefore so in keeping with the original pieces. Perfection is not there to be tampered with! Rupert felt very satisfied with that thought.

And if that was so wrong, then how had the company managed to survive 107 years, celebrated their own centenary year just seven years previously, always managing to operate under the D'Oyly Carte family management and until then financially self-supporting. During all that time, they had performed continually, night after night, both at home and abroad and had always delighted their audiences of countless hundred of thousands over all the years, even right up to that very last night! Quickly he recalled, his Gilbert and Sullivan encyclopaedic memory then working in overdrive, that for a short time around 1910-18, the company had not appeared in London and had just toured the country but their return to a London season in 1919 was a triumph. That was how it had been ever since. It was the financial pressures of the 1980's that now caused this problem and the company needed grants, just like other similar opera companies, to help their continued performances. If only I could be such a benefactor, Rupert thought in earnest!

But! Of course there should be such a triumph return again and again! Then, if it didn't, why should such loyal and devoted audiences be robbed of the entertainment that they so valued? Why should the country be robbed of the tradition of such a special triumph of the English musical theatre – their very own, home-grown, comic operas!

Rupert's swift and meandering thoughts were interrupted by the pending activities once again before him on the stage.

The stage curtain fell, yet still the audience's reaction was a very strange mix of cries, sobs, yet cheers and clapping as well. It seemed that collectively, no single person there had any idea as to how to behave. Rupert realised that he had probably not been alone within the audience in thinking that even at the eleventh hour, there would somehow be a much wished for and desperately wanted happy ending. But. Once again that evening there was that very huge word – 'But'.

Rupert's thoughts were once again interrupted by all the powerful spotlights again trained on the mighty stage curtain that once more began, ever so slowly, to rise. Vainly he squinted by bending down to try to see what the curtain that was lifting so desperately slowly would reveal. He saw at first nobody's feet and then with a few more areas of revealed stage, no sign of life at all. The lifting of the curtain seemed then to gather speed and finally the whole aperture of the stage area was revealed. It was completely and utterly empty. Rupert and Alice, as one with the whole puzzled audience, continued to clap and cheer. For what? Rupert wondered.

Then, the curtain once again lowered, yet still the audience applauded, cheered, sobbed and clapped in a cacophony of various sounds. Within seconds, the curtain again lifted and again the stage was revealed to be completely empty when after only a few seconds the curtain again came down. It remained down for maybe a minute or more although by then Rupert had lost any sense of real time let alone any make-believe time. Once more the curtain lifted and as it rose, ominously, the stage lights were slowly extinguished until for what was very obviously a final time, the curtain fell, closing off the darkened stage. As it did so, the spotlights trained upon the stage were also dimmed as the main house lights of the theatre came on in their place.

It was over.

Of that there was no doubt. Rupert, Alice, the whole audience in the Adelphi Theatre on that Saturday night, 27 February, 1982, had all been witness to the very last performance of the D'Oyly Carte Opera Company after 107 years in existence and 107 years of dedicated performances of the works of Gilbert and Sullivan. The very company that had been all together on stage barely minutes before, the whole company that had rounded off the evening with a rousing, cheerful chorus from 'Gondoliers' would perform as that company no more.

Rupert's mind was flooded once more with so many thoughts going back to his very first visit to see a D'Oyly Carte performance some 25 years before. He turned to his grandmother, sitting very

319

quietly beside him and dabbing her eyes delicately with a no longer perfectly spotless white handkerchief. The sight of his grandmother made him realise that whereas his own memories were of just a quarter of a century, then her own were well over three times as long. On this very last night, Alice, born in the very same year that 'Yeomen of the Guard' had first opened, was a living embodiment of the time when the D'Oyly Carte Company were enjoying their very own first score years and here she was a witness and a presence at their demise. The horrible significance of it all was almost too much for him – it was so much an end of an era, a most glorious era.

Worse than all of that – frighteningly – Rupert realised that the end of this era, so much linked with his grandmother, emphasised too her own mortality. It was a stark and horrible thought, as much as he tried to dismiss it from his mind, something that he had to bear. As if to seek a much-needed and immediate sign of reassurance, Rupert reached out to his grandmother and clasped both her hands warmly within his own hands in a firm and loving grasp.

"Oh, Nan," were the only words he said.

"I know, I know," was all that Alice immediately said in reply.

Rupert, looking around in the auditorium, realised that most of the audience were still sitting in their seats, like them, hardly seeming to take in the situation or know what then precisely to do. Then, he noticed with a horrible start, that the theatre staff had opened all the doors to the street, and were standing by the doors very much in readiness to usher the audience from the auditorium. A cold blast of air from the February street beyond whistled through the numerous doors then opened and into the warm theatre. Very slowly, and very gradually, a few members of the audience rose from their seats and again, zombie-like, made their way to the opened doors and to what seemed to be the uninviting street and world beyond. A world beyond which was harsh and in no way akin to the cosy, warm and make-believe magical world of the theatre.

The significance was not lost on Robert, even through his distress. That world out there was the world that had signalled the end of his beloved D'Oyly Carte Opera Company, the world of the Arts Council, of mean finances, a world which simply did not understand. To Rupert, it was the outside world that seemed to be unbothered about a great musical theatrical tradition that had lasted so long, delighted countless hundred of thousands of people of all ages and on all continents of the world and which was now so unceremoniously and unemotionally dumped by the faceless powers who controlled finances for the arts.

For that immediate moment, Rupert was in no mood to begin to consider the very many organisations who in his mind were of dubious worth and equally lacking in performance appeal, but that had received grants and funds from that villain of the day, the Arts Council. They were now there to survive and continue their performances – but 'his' company wasn't!

In a kind of daze, Rupert turned to his grandmother and said "I suppose it is time to go!" Even in Rupert's state of dull reality, he had finally realised the inevitable and that there was nothing to be gained by staying any longer.

"If we may wait just a moment," Alice replied, "I would like to come to and, in any case, we are not alone and many are still here, sat in their seats." Rupert said nothing but did think that like him, his grandmother was probably wanting to savour every possible moment of the evening, no matter how cruel the very end had turned out to be.

Rupert noted that many people were huddled talking amongst themselves, some making contacts with small groups, all devotees with the same experiences and sharing the same horrible and wrenching moments in the best way that they knew how. Was it by blocking out the reality of the event, perhaps by reminiscing about all the better times, of which there were an uncountable many? Perhaps, talking of all the performances over the years that they had so obviously always enjoyed or loved?

Talking perhaps about many of the past performers, talking of the long history of the company, talking about Sir Arthur Sullivan and Sir William Gilbert, or rather more likely 'Mr' Gilbert since the writer had not received his own knighthood until 1907 and 11 years after the last opera had been written? Whatever was being talked about, there was no doubting that it was all then in an overriding sense of dull and utter sadness because of what had just occurred.

He stared around once more. He realised that a small handful of those he saw were also of his grandmother's age, also with memories surely from the very earliest years. How they must feel too! Rupert felt choked at the very thought.

Rupert and Alice were not alone. But there was no comfort to be gained from joint adversity.

Neither felt like making much conversation with either of their seated near neighbours other than to say almost banal generalities like "terrible, isn't it", "what a crying shame" or "we can't simply take it in!"

"Right, love," Alice, said, "I think, that if it's alright with you of course, I'm ready to go now."

"As you say, Nan," Rupert replied, as he got up from his seat and supported his grandmother under her arm as she slowly raised herself from the seat that had been her virtual home for over four hours, so long had the evening been. "All right, Nan?" he asked, caringly.

"I will be," Alice, replied, "just let me get the feeling back to my legs for a moment, I've been sitting for so long that I have almost taken root to the spot!"

"I expect you wish that you had, taken root to this very spot, I mean," Rupert answered in somewhat of a daze. "That this could somehow now be the very start of the evening which could end in a totally different way to how this has now turned out to be!"

"Maybe that's right too," Alice answered, "but one thing that I've learnt in my long life is that life does, and must, move on, and it's the same with all of this – at least that's how I see it, but we can talk about it all later. Now, let's savour the last moments of the evening and being here in this theatre for this special last night!" Alice looked around her, almost in a serene way, glancing first around the stalls, then upwards to the circle and distant gallery before fixing her eyes once again to the stage area, then so quiet and deride of activity. She sighed. She looked again until a hint of an almost quietly satisfied smile spread across her face. It was a slight smile that said whatever the unfortunate outcome of the evening, Alice felt proud that she was able to have been part of it. Perhaps, also, in acknowledging her own age, it was also with a sense of immense satisfaction that she felt in being able to be there at all. Whatever, she felt for that one more moment to take in everything.

They both stood, silently, for a few more moments before Alice nodded and nudged her grandson as if to indicate "I'm ready". With that, the pair made their way to the nearest door, there joining the by then many tens of people that had finally decided that there was nothing more to be gained by staying in the theatre any longer. A highly subdued hue seemed to hang over everybody, all clutching their prized programmes, evidence of what had turned out to be a momentous evening, clutching equally too their memories. As a mass, all made their way to the street which was for many of them, as a result of how the evening had ended, the most unwelcoming, harsh world beyond their theatrical world of make-believe.

Rupert, and Alice, looked back to the stage area just one more time before they passed through the doors and to the corridor leading to the foyer. Nothing good was revealed from that glance, just the mighty stage curtain closed and with just minimal footlights hovering above a sadly vacated, therefore very forlorn, orchestra pit. Even the rapidly emptying auditorium seemed to cast a more ghostly, unreal glow over the place, the sounds of hushed voices then reverberating in the cavernous space.

When they reached the theatre's foyer, by contrast, they noticed the bright lights of the television cameras that were trained on the audience, by then streaming out of the theatre. Cameras so obviously wanting to pry on the moment of grief, Rupert thought, unfoundedly and mischievously, rather than accepting that they were there to record a moment of theatrical history. Rupert noticed that reporters had stopped quite a few people and were engaged in a variety of interviews.

"If they stop us, we'll walk on!" he declared to Alice in a curt and abrasive way.

"Well, I for one, don't want to speak to anybody, not after what they've done this evening!" his grandmother declared, her spirit immediately recovering as a result of the adversity. "If I speak to anyone, I would give him or her truly what for!" she fervently declared.

Gathering their things, Rupert and Alice made their way through the crowds thronging the foyer, through the exit doors and on to the street where many people were milling around, blankly staring back to the theatre that they had just vacated. There they joined the masses, the late Saturday night bustle of that street, with its excited crowds making their way from other venues, all laughing, thrilled and talking about what they had been seeing or doing. For all of those people it was obvious that they had enjoyed a satisfying evening. Rupert told himself that was something he must not grudge, but their very obvious happiness seemed in horrible contrast to how Rupert and Alice, or anybody coming out of the Adelphi, all thought and felt. For them, especially for Rupert, the evening could not be remembered in the same positive way.

They were standing on the Strand once more. It was the street that held such significance in the long history of Gilbert and Sullivan and D'Oyly Carte. Barely a hundred yards away, around the corner, was Southampton Street, the very birthplace of W.S. Gilbert. Slightly further away, on the opposite side of the Strand, most importantly, was the Savoy Theatre itself, still standing although rebuilt and modernised since the original theatre from the 1880's. It was the street that had witnessed the very best of D'Oyly Carte times. First, the glorious first nights, then later with the return visits by the D'Oyly Carte Opera Company to their Savoy home over many wonderful occasions. Rupert had heard about these so many times from his grandmother, like their triumphal seasons there in the years between the wars, then for the Festival of Britain in 1951. In the later years, Rupert had of course been to the Savoy and he was there with Alice for several performances during the company's own centenary just seven years previously. In his thoughts, Rupert felt thankful that there had been no predictions at that time of just how few years the company had left to perform.

Now it seemed to Rupert as a particularly cruel twist of fate that the same street had then witnessed the very last night too. Although he hadn't thought about it before, it then occurred to

Rupert that he should have recognised it as a possible bad omen that the latest London season had been at the Adelphi. The Savoy Theatre had been already booked with another long-running production so 'his' company performed instead across the road. "I don't know though," Rupert finally thought to himself, "perhaps it was right that after all the Savoy hadn't been witness to the end of it all – that would have been too cruel!" He thought of the Savoy as the virtual shrine, the real home of Gilbert and Sullivan, the very name 'Savoy operas' summed it all up. Yes, it was right, Rupert avowed, that this last night had been across the street and that the Savoy itself could remain untainted!

Rupert blinked uncontrollably at the thoughts upon the words "end of it all" and the associations of the area flooded his very troubled mind. He wondered if the old bricks of the Savoy theatre could talk, what would they be saying and thinking about the evening that had just occurred across the road at the Adelphi? The very gruesome idea sent a ghost-like shiver down his back and was something that made his overall being immediately feel even worse.

Rupert said nothing to his grandmother. But he looked around him again. It was all there, would always be there as testimony to the great partnership and theatrical manager. But what was the use of all of that without the rightful opera company being left to perform the works. Rupert gave a deep sigh to the thoughts before, remembering his responsibilities, he offered his hand to his grandmother to guide her through the crowds, across the busy Strand and back to their car parked across the road, within sight of the theatre.

Returning to the sanctuary of the car gave Rupert a haven, much needed, in which to retreat. It was a place where, with Alice, their thoughts of the momentous evening could somehow be collected and even, perhaps, where they could try to come to terms with all that had happened. Once they were safely in the car, immediately and quickly coffee was poured from the flask and sandwiches handed around. Initially, they ate and sipped the coffee in silence. Rupert found it amazing, given all that had occurred, that he felt any hunger at all but it was so – in fact he felt strangely ravenous. Rationally, he should hardly have been surprised at all given that it had been over five hours ago since they had eaten when they first arrived in the Strand.

Alice was first to speak. "I don't know really what I was expecting to happen but, if I am truthful, then I suppose that I am not surprised that it should have all come to this!"

"Oh, really," Rupert's reply came in an almost non-committal, absent-minded kind of way as if he was not fully aware of what his grandmother had said. The truth was that he was very much deep in a kind of melancholy thought.

"Why I am not surprised," Alice continued, "is that there are always so many moves afoot in these so called modern times to make changes to anything that is seen as old--fashioned, especially anything regarded as proper from another era. That's despised because of its age rather than any thought given to the quality and traditions! What, oh what, is ever going to become of this world!"

"And that's what you think this is all about?" Rupert asked, still not fully concentrating on what was being said.

"Yes, I suppose that I do," his grandmother replied. "It's exactly the same with traditional opera performances. How often do you see them well done now, in the way that they once were! Oh, I grant you at least they are still being performed although hideously modernised by many of the other, so called, quality opera companies. And those companies, nevertheless, can only carry on with the financial support which they receive in a big way from outside sources, the council or whatever."

"Arts Council," Rupert interjected.

"Yes, yes of course that's what I mean!" Alice seemed a trifle irritated by Rupert's interjection and for a moment lost her train of thought. She realised that it was already near midnight and it had been a long and emotional evening. Also, she wanted to avoid any kind of lengthy dialogue with Rupert about the rights and wrongs of financial supports and subsidies to musical companies – the thoughts of first the drive home and then further thoughts of getting tucked up in bed were, to her, of more natural and imminent appeal. However, it was not in her nature to give in to circumstances and stoically she decided to continue the discussion.

"Anyway, Rupert, Arts Council or whatever, we all know what we were hoping for, but what's done is for the moment done and you and me can do nothing about it," Alice insisted.

"But it's so unfair!" Rupert replied. "Gilbert and Sullivan is part of our heritage and has a right to be performed just as much as any other kind of musical theatre. It is a terrible loss to countless future generations that, unlike me, will never have the benefit of growing up and seeing the operas as a natural part of their culture!"

"Nobody is saying anything about banning Gilbert and Sullivan – that would never do!" Alice exclaimed. "What has happened this evening is the end of the original D'Oyly Carte Opera Company, bad enough and sad as it is, after over a hundred years of dedicated performances, but it's not the end of Gilbert and Sullivan – that can never happen!"

"I understand what you are saying. But nobody can perform it like the Carte," Rupert muttered in a crestfallen and subdued reply.

"Thanks!" Alice half-laughed, "what about me and my family and our evenings of yesteryear, gatherering around our piano – you never got to hear those 'fine' renderings and if you had, then you wouldn't think as you do!" Alice laughed again, not to be difficult but she was trying to lighten her grandson's feelings; also wanting him to realise how she saw a future for the works no matter what.

"I don't know about that," Rupert replied, still hurting and not really taking in so much of what was being said. He thought for some moments before continuing. "One thing that I do know is that the whole of the Gilbert and Sullivan history would never have been so successful if it hadn't been for the D'Oyly Carte Opera Company, never!" he emphasised.

"That's very true, of course I fully agree to that," Alice replied. "We all realise that had it not been for Mr. Richard D'Oyly Carte in the first place as the original theatre manager, then the whole history may very well have been different or, even, not happened at all. Look, love, all I'm saying is that there have been, no doubt will continue to be, masses of performances given of Gilbert and

Sullivan, here and the world over. It is not the end of the operas and that's something you must accept."

Rupert listened to his grandmother. Inwardly, he respected what she was saying but his whole being at that moment was not really willing to accept any good from the situation. He merely nodded, in a non-committal kind of way, and let Alice continue her conversation without comment.

"Besides, who knows, perhaps one day, not too long away either, the D'Oyly Carte will rise again, like a phoenix from the ashes, so to speak. You see, however things look bad for the moment, that may not always be the case and anything can happen,"

Alice concluded, finally taking the chance to finish the half-eaten sandwich that she had held so delicately for some moments.

Alice's words lightened Rupert's feelings a lot. Finally, and amazingly even with a half-smile, he looked towards his grandmother. "Do you honestly think it is possible?" he asked.

"Of course, I do," Alice replied. "I wouldn't have said it otherwise! And why I say so," she continued, "is because when I was in my twenties, after 1911 when Gilbert died, there were no D'Oyly Carte performances in London for eight years. I remember that time so well and my mother and father spoke so often about it. Then, in 1919, the company made a return to London and the season was nothing short of a triumph – it was at the old Princes Theatre, at the top of Shaftsbury Avenue, and I remember it so well – I was there!"

Rupert smiled towards his grandmother before a frown covered his face, almost as if he felt guilty about allowing himself to smile in the first place. "But Nan, that was different, the company were still around then even if not appearing in London, they continued to tour throughout the country, their performances were alive!. Now, it's not like that, no, no, not at all!"

"No, I grant you that, but all that I'm trying to point out, love, is that it hasn't always been so rosy in the past and then things got better," Alice reasoned. "Likewise, why not at least try to believe that the same can happen now – that's what I do – and so should you!" Alice's statement came over as real command and

Rupert therefore listened with thought to what his grandmother was saying.

"I suppose so," Rupert replied, rather reluctantly. "I do remember reading how the D'Oyly Carte got what we would call now 'rave reviews' when they had their 1926 London season, how the lasting appeal of Gilbert and Sullivan was stronger than ever. And it will be again!" Rupert virtually shouted and thumped the car's dashboard. He quietened down for a moment before continuing. "Who knows – but it is a crying shame that it all has had to come to this, it's so unfair and I'll never be able to enjoy the operas in the same way if it is not given by D'Oyly Carte! I have seen some other versions, not many I grant you, and they've mostly been hideously updated, cheap jokes, rotten staging, poor music – simply not the same. So be it if there must be updates, modernised versions, everyone to their own, but that was somehow passable when there was always the proper D'Oyly Carte version as well – now, it's most likely that will be no more! It really is the surviving of the tradition, the tried and tested, that's the real point of it all!"

"I know, I understand too," Alice replied, very much realising that much of what Rupert said was right. She realised too that many of her efforts to try to cheer her grandson up were very much counter-productive, therefore useless. She thought for a moment before she continued. "All in all, love, I agree with you, there's not anything that can be said to butter-up what has happened. It's awful what they've done, allowed to happen, to the D'Oyly Carte."

Rupert nodded intently. His grandmother then continued. "I suppose that I am somehow blessedly grateful to have been here tonight, to be in the audience and reliving so much of my own treasured past, when it's all meant so very much to me even it does seem to be a closing of a chapter. What a happy chapter though – almost since I was a babe in arms and weaned on the music! But it's a sad, sad end. I dread to think what my own parents would have said if they had been around to witness this night – they would have found it so very impossible, very hard!"

329

Rupert looked towards his grandmother. "I am sure that's very true too. There's not much really to say other than what we have said, and felt so deeply, already," he replied.

"One thing to say, though, Rupert, well two things really," Alice began. "First, we've got a good collection of D'Oyly Carte records, nothing can take that away. Through those the company lives on – in our house!" Rupert nodded as his grandmother continued. "Then we have our belief that maybe, just maybe, some time ahead then there may be a revival – I hope so and I also hope that I may, god willing, still be around to see it!" Rupert was about to say something. Alice held his hand, kindly, then continued. "There's a third thing to say – we have both got our wonderful memories of countless performances, many more, very many more for me than you, I grant, and they will always be with us!"

"That's true," Rupert answered, more quietly as with his constant thoughts, his spirits became again deflated.

"And I give the most grateful thanks to Gilbert, Sullivan and to the D'Oyly Carte Opera Company for the years and years of happiness that they have given to me – and that's something that simply cannot ever be taken away – and neither should you lose that either!" Alice said.

"Oh, of course, I never shall either and, do you know what Nan?" Rupert asked as his grandmother indicated for him to continue. "What it is Nan, I do believe in what you say and that before too long, then maybe we shall once again see the likes of the company, maybe even a new D'Oyly Carte, with all the traditions, the performances once again resurrected and presented in the way that both Gilbert and Sullivan intended! Yes, from adversity, that's what I fervently hope and believe in!" As soon as the words were out, Rupert wondered whether he did believe in anything that he had been saying – but why not to keep the pretence for at least a few moments!

"Amen to that," Alice replied, "Oh sorry, I don't mean to sound sacrilegious, but you do understand me and know exactly what I mean."

"Of course, Nan, I do," Rupert replied. "I am glad that we have talked things through before we begin the drive and I know that you must be tired – it's been a long night without any of this!"

"It has indeed, but, yes, it was best we talked here so that you can concentrate on the drive," Alice replied, kindly.

"Nan, if it's alright with you, there is one thing that I would just like to do before we set off – it'll only take a couple of minutes, but I shall have to leave you in the car, that's if you don't mind," Rupert asked.

"No, no I'll be fine – after all, nobody's likely to want to run off with a very old lady are they!" Rupert and Alice both laughed at her words, the first time that Rupert had felt like laughing for some time. "What is it, I suppose you want to go back to the stage door for a moment, is that it?" Alice asked, before she added: "If so, it may not be a very good idea. When you think how we are feeling, then what must the company members be feeling – for them it's worse and they are now out of work on top of everything! I don't think that you should go there, let them at least have some much deserved privacy."

"No, actually, it's not that. I agree it's not right to go over to the stage door and I won't. But, again, if I may, there is one thing I will do and I'll just be a moment, I promise," Rupert replied, not feeling for saying to his grandmother what was his intention. He got out of the car, looked around him for a moment, made sure that his grandmother was safe and well, then walked away from the Strand in the direction of the Embankment and the dark River Thames beyond.

As he walked, Rupert thought to himself of the words of one of the songs from 'Princess Ida':

"The world is but a broken toy,
Its pleasure hollow – false its joy,
Unreal its loveliest hue,
Alas!
Its pains alone are true,
Alas!
Its pains alone are true."

The pain that Rupert felt that moment was indeed "true".

Chapter 22

"Is life a boon?
If so, it must befall
That Death, whene'er he call
Must call too soon."

Rupert stood quietly at the gates of the closed Embankment Gardens, near the rear entrance of the Savoy Hotel. He could see, even in the dark but purely thanks to the lights from the busy Embankment, the statue of Sir Arthur Sullivan through the railings of the Gardens. He hadn't really thought, stupidly, that the gardens would be closed although the reality of it being nearly midnight should have made him at least aware that it would be the case. That night Rupert's mind was too weighed down by other matters for him to really think issues through properly. But, in the circumstances, the point where he stood was close enough to fulfil his wishes. Apart from the traffic noise coming from the Embankment, even that somehow muffled by the winter shrubs and trees, it was strangely quiet at that spot in a busy city, however otherwise late on a Saturday night that it by then was.

As he stood there, Rupert put his hands together, not as in a prayer, but more as a form of support as he leaned against the gate. This was the place for his virtual pilgrimage. Many

332

times he had visited Sir Arthur Sullivan's statue. It meant everything to him and especially the verse from 'Yeomen of the Guard', beginning "Is life a boon?". He found it so evocative, so very human and yet so entirely right and sympathetic as a memorial to the composer. He recalled from what he had read that when asked for a suitable epitaph to be engraved upon the memorial, Gilbert had suggested the verse as a fitting tribute to his composer collaborator. Rupert thought so too, although he admitted it sounded rather pompous of him to even try to offer a comment on such a matter.

Deep in thought and with a kind of reverence, Rupert mouthed his thanks through to the statue for so many years of pleasure brought not only to him, but also to his grandmother, her family and countless others by the composer's work with Gilbert. Rupert mouthed a hushed message – this is for Gilbert too, of course, but he had no statue in the same place. With that thought, Rupert stopped – perhaps there was, of course there must be somewhere, a statue for Gilbert but he didn't know where, something he immediately felt most guilty about. For the moment, then, his joint message would have to do in the circumstances. A few more seconds of quiet thoughts and that was it then. He felt that he had acted properly and with a dignity to the occasion. In that Rupert could take some comfort.

For his very special pilgrimage, Rupert was rather surprised that he should find himself alone at the Embankment Gardens' gates. Given the highly emotionally charged and significant evening that he and the audience at the Adelphi had experienced, he felt that there would be others, like him, who would somehow want to be there, to be quietly near that statue, in their thoughts for a few moments. He felt sure, that had she been able to undertake the walk, his grandmother would have done that although he purposefully hadn't mentioned to her what was on his mind and what he intended to do.

Rupert spent just a few more seconds there, as if glued to the spot, and he did not take his eyes away from Sir Arthur Sullivan's statue. He knew, though, that he must not be too long away from his grandmother and so, rather reluctantly at first, he turned round, ready to head back to the car. Slowly, he walked away from the Embankment Gardens. Purposefully, he walked away too from the bright lights and inviting entrance to the Savoy Hotel. He wondered if maybe there could have been a reception for the now defunct D'Oyly Carte Opera Company perhaps taking place in the hotel at that very moment. If so, then it was definitely something that Rupert did not wish to know about, nor be involved with in any way. To Rupert, receptions should only be in celebration of something joyous, never a wake.

To his troubled mind, the finale of 'Yeomen of the Guard' seemed a fitting memory to Rupert as he left the gardens:

"Oh, thoughtless crew!
Ye know not what ye do!
Attend to me, and shed a tear or two –
For I have a song to sing, O!"

The words of the song rang through his head as he began to retrace his steps, up the hill, to the Strand.

Rupert walked up Carting Lane, the mighty Savoy Hotel to his right that in the late hour as far as the external view was concerned, was already quietening down for the night, whatever might be going on in the luxurious interior. There was no activity in the less salubrious surroundings of the working areas of the hotel as he passed by, no delivery trucks, no laundry or garbage being collected. No hint of activity and all quiet indeed. Ahead of him further, again to his right, was the side and lower entrance of the Savoy Theatre, the other very special shrine on his agenda that he had the need to visit that night.

He paused at the site in deep thought. The area was dark and just like the Embankment Gardens a few moments earlier it was also quiet. The theatre's own performances for the evening had long finished and, very obviously, everybody had gone. Once again Rupert felt a degree of surprise that none of his fellow audience members of the Adelphi evening had come to the spot where he stood. Nevertheless, good, Rupert thought, I can linger here in peace. In the long history of the operas and the company, there was hardly a more significant place than this very one.

"Is life a boon? If so, it must befall That Death, whene'er he call Must call too soon."

That, for some minutes, is precisely what he did. Although the original, fine Victorian Savoy Theatre from the glorious Gilbert and Sullivan times had been closed in 1929 and what he saw before him was the building internally largely re-modelled and re-opened in 1930, when even the main entrance had been moved to the Strand. Some of the outer shell, though, was still the very original building. Staring at those hallowed walls meant absolutely everything for Rupert – it was still for him 'his' Savoy, the true and rightful home of 'his' operas. The plaque on the wall before him proudly confirmed the authenticity of the site, a sure memory that could never be erased no matter what! It was a place to which he could always return. That would not be taken from him!

His thoughts instantly swung back a hundred years to what it must have been like upon that very spot, the scene of all those triumphant first nights, for which he enviously craved. There and then, the very beginning of it all. He thought of the stream of cabs and carriages that would have been there for the fine audiences, those of the stalls and dress circle. He thought, too, of the happy working folk that would have been there, streaming to and from the gallery, all happily singing from their favourite Gilbert and Sullivan choruses.

"Their favourite" – the words stuck in his mind - what would they have been, Rupert wondered? How would those favourites have compared to his very own personal choice? And in any case, what for him were those real favourites! Rupert smiled to himself as he thought how his grandmother so often teased him on that very question!

How he wished it could have been possible for him, as if by some imaginary time machine, to be there about a hundred years before upon that very spot, to be a part for all of those glorious times for which he found so absorbing and dear. Then, he would have been at the start of the wonderful history rather than where he was now – at the end. He closed his eyes and tried so very hard to imagine how it would have been but in reality his mind was dulled through the sense of real shock as a result of the events earlier in the evening at the Adelphi. Still, he willed himself to visualise the past scene but the images eluded him.

Nothing. How cruel that was too, he felt, to miss out the sense even in his make believe.

"Kind sir, you cannot have the heart
Our lives to part
From those to whom an hour ago
We were united!"

The song from 'Gondoliers', which was humming around in his head, seemed to Rupert to perfectly sum up his troubled feelings as he moved along up the street a little further still. Next he was level with the darkened steps that climbed past the stage door of the Savoy Theatre, leading up to the front entrance of the Savoy Hotel itself. The stage door – what memories that could tell! Again, Rupert was deeply absorbed in his thoughts as he tried to summon up the sought-for images.

Suddenly, he felt a shiver and at the same moment became aware that, surely, somebody, even some persons, was nearby after all. He looked, immediately aroused from his soliloquy. Probably some people like him as he had expected, wanting to visit the scene too. Nothing. Yet still he felt a very strong presence. Rupert waited, his heart beating faster, pounding within his chest. So much he was anxious to be aware, to see what was about him, to be included and part of what was happening.

The sounds became clearer. Voices. Two couples. Each pair of a gentleman and lady. Rupert strained to try to hear what was being said. But – but as he looked there was nobody in sight. He closed his eyes, opened them and then blinked and again as he still heard the voices. Finally, they became clearer and the conversation then immediately audible.

"To Sir Arthur Sullivan, Mr. Gilbert, Mr. D'Oyly Carte and, most importantly too, to the whole D'Oyly Carte Company and long may it continue!"

In the darkness, Rupert once more blinked, desperate for an imagery of what was happening. Again, he looked around and, again, he saw nothing. Surely there was nobody in the street. Yet the voices were as clear as the night air. But the conversation somehow didn't sound right – more than that to Rupert it sounded false. Nobody that night would have referred to a 'Mr. Gilbert' and surely not either to a 'D'Oyly Carte Company', without including the word 'Opera', as the company was for so long known.

He looked about him again but no person was revealed and the street, the whole area, was rather eerily deserted. Rupert pulled his coat around him, looked up and down the street again; he looked up the empty steps that passed the Savoy stage door. But no, there was nothing and no one. Rupert was alone and he felt increasingly distressed by the situation so he hurried once again back up to the Strand, coming onto the street he realised directly opposite Southampton Street, Sir William Gilbert's birthplace, he thought to himself. That revelation made him think once again about the voices that he thought he had heard – no, he did hear – and that they had so definitely referred to "Mr. Gilbert". It just did not make any sense. Rupert again shivered before he next made his way quickly back to the car.

"There you are then, and not away too long, either," Alice said as he got back into the car. "And where did you go then?"

"I just popped down to the Embankment Gardens . . .," he began.

"Ah, yes, I thought so, to Sir Arthur's statue," Alice said, with an understanding smile spreading across her face.

"Yes, yes, that's right, Nan," Rupert replied.

"I thought that you might do that! In fact, I would have even probably come with you were it not for the walk back up the hill. I agree, it was a very nice and respectful thing of you to do," Alice spoke, sincerely.

"Thank you, Nan," Rupert began, "and be sure, what I did, I did for the both of us, for all your family, a collective thanks from all of us for everything!"

"I appreciate that very much," Alice answered, "very fitting, very fitting indeed. Were there many others there as well?"

"Strangely not," Rupert replied. "The gardens were closed but I stood by the gate, quite alone, it was a very moving moment. I came back past the Savoy Hotel and thought that there may even perhaps be a D'Oyly Carte reception going on, but I didn't want to hang around."

"So you saw nobody around at all then, neither at the gardens nor even going or coming?" Alice asked.

Rupert thought for a moment and wondered whether to tell his grandmother about the conversation he thought he had overheard between two couples as he stood by the theatre. He decided not to as he hadn't seen the people despite all of his efforts. "No," he said, "I didn't see anybody." It was not a lie; he had only heard something but not seen anything.

"So, my love, I suppose that is it then and we must now begin the drive home," his grandmother said, to which Rupert nodded his agreement. "Oh, one thing that comes to my mind – I suppose that it's just as well that the National Portrait Gallery is closed otherwise you would be wanting to go there as well – to stand before the two portraits of Gilbert and Sullivan, placed there side by side!" Alice smiled again as she made the statement which she realised had more than a hint of truth about it.

"You know me rather too well," Rupert acknowledged, to which Alice laughed further. "But, right you are, it's time to head home and tomorrow, or rather today," Rupert corrected as he looked at his watch, "we can relive the night, the good parts and recount all of our wonderful memories from all our Gilbert, Sullivan and D'Oyly Carte years!"

"We sure can, although I would think that would surely take longer than just one day!" Alice laughed. "Perhaps then you can then also tell me what was your favourite of all the operas!" Alice again laughed.

"Well, I think that I may be able to answer that . . ." Rupert began.

"Not now, love, I was just joking with you. In that respect you're very much alike me, it's very hard to have a favourite so let's just settle for the fact that they are all good!" Alice replied.

"Well, perhaps, but I don't know about 'Thespis'!"

"Away with you!" Alice teased. "Home, James, and don't spare the horses!"

Rupert was about to put the key into the car's ignition when he looked once more across the Strand and to the direction of the Adelphi Theatre where the house lights were still very much blazing forth. It was almost as if he wanted to delay any departure for as long as possible, but the site across the road really made him pause before he finally started the car.

"Look at that, Nan, it's just as if the show is still going on. Look at the brightly lit billboards, still announcing 'The D'Oyly Carte Opera Company in Gilbert and Sullivan Operas', as if there will be more performances on Monday, next week and beyond!" Rupert exclaimed.

"Perhaps it is more than a sign," Alice replied, "a signal of good portents that this will not be the end, of D'Oyly Carte rather, just the end of the beginning! Then, with surety, we can look forward to the next hundred years!"

"I like the sound of that phrase, well, both of the phrases," Rupert replied, picking up the salient point of what his grandmother had said. "Yes, the end of the beginning, then the next hundred years. Thank you, Nan, that was wonderful to hear."

With the particular phrase "end of the beginning" ringing contentedly in his ears, Rupert finally set the car in motion and edged out into the traffic flow moving westwards along the Strand. Even then, he realised that all was not yet over for the special evening, as he would need to make a turn around Trafalgar Square to come back eastwards along the Strand, passing the Adelphi once more, before finally heading on towards the City, the East End and the Southend arterial road home to Westcliff. As he negotiated the heavy traffic still thronging the Square, the thought of one more moment yet to savour filled him with an undiminished degree of excited anticipation. But excitement of what exactly, that he did not really consider!

They once again saw the Adelphi Theatre ahead of them and Rupert signalled to the left his intention to pull into the side of the road, just outside the door of the theatre. For that special night, Rupert was not in the least bothered about whatever mayhem he might cause to the London traffic!

"What are we stopping for?" Alice asked, perplexed at the thought of a further delay now that the journey home had finally begun.

"I just wanted to see if anything was happening!" Rupert answered.

"Well, I don't think so, not at this time of the night!" Alice replied. "As you can see, even the outside doors are now shut!"

"I just thought," Rupert answered, then crestfallen in the realisation that of course there was nothing new to be seen. "On we go then," he mumbled, the finality of it all sinking in with a horrible reality.

"As you are obviously in the mood for delay, just let's do one more thing then, something that now I'm rested a bit, I would very much like to do," Alice indicated, giving in once more to her grandson's whims. She even admitted to herself, too, that once seated in the car, and comfortable, then it did no harm to extend the evening and savour the moments whilst they were still there. Alice also realised that for her there would surely not be many more opportunities for "a night on the town", although she dare not say as much to Rupert.

"What's that?" Rupert asked, his spirits suddenly revived at the prospect of an unexpected addition to the programme.

"Please drive me into the courtyard of the Savoy Hotel – we can drive in and out there without bother – it will let me at least see what is the Savoy Theatre of today. I know it's not the original but nevertheless I've been going there to see D'Oyly Carte for well over 80 years – the old theatre as well as the present one. Will you do that for me, do you mind?" Alice asked.

"Of course not, Nan – it would be a pleasure!" Rupert enthusiastically replied as he switched the car's righthand signal on and pulled towards the centre of the Strand. There, in the middle of the road, he felt pleased that the traffic flow meant they had to wait some while in the sight of the Savoy. By contrast, in his rear view mirror, Rupert had sight of the Adelphi Theatre. For him, it was not really a perfect vista but it did say it all – the beginning and the end as one view.

"Are its palaces and pleasures
Fantasies that fade?
And the glory of its treasures
Shadow of a shade?"

"Is life a boon? If so, it must befall That Death, whene'er he call Must call too soon."

Rupert thought of the song from 'Mikado' as he continued to gaze through the mirror, until his grandmother spoke again.

"What I always think about," Alice began, whilst they waited, "is that in the days when the operas were written, at the time of the first nights, those in the D'Oyly Carte, could never have had any idea how their work would last, that the operas would still actually be being performed a hundred years later!"

"It is a thought, I agree," Rupert concurred whilst at the same time, seeing a break in the flow of the traffic, he finally drove into the forecourt of the Savoy Hotel. He pulled up by the darkened entrance of the Savoy Theatre.

"How wonderful if all those fine people working on the operas in the early days could only have had the perception of the enduring quality and success throughout the years, how happy they would have been!" Alice exclaimed.

"Perhaps they may have had an idea," Rupert quietly replied, as he looked from the car, through the closed doors of the darkened theatre.

"I wouldn't necessarily be sure about that," his grandmother answered. "I remember my father telling me that even though there were always wonderful reviews of the first nights, nobody then knew if it would last. And how could they? So often, people's desires change, there are passing whims and times change. What was good for the Victorian years may not have found a place later. But Gilbert and Sullivan did last, they have continued really to have stood the test of time!" Alice reflected in very deep thought for a moment before she finally continued. "No, I just think that it would have been so nice for those D'Oyly Carte pioneers to know that their work, their dedication to what was then the new form of English comic opera, went on and on over the years. Oh, I know that any such forward vision is impossible, none of us know what is waiting around the corner!"

Rupert nodded, happy in perfect agreement.

Alice continued. "We owe it all to those people – not just to Gilbert and Sullivan themselves, but to Mr. D'Oyly Carte, all the original singers and all the original stage people, for the wonderful sets, the costume and dressmakers for all the beautiful costumes, all of which we've seen copied until this very day.

All thanks to all the original theatre people that then did such wonderful initial work. I would like us to remember and to say a very big, most grateful, 'Thank you' to all of those people as we sit here tonight!"

It was obvious from the quiver in her voice that Alice felt quite moved by her own words and, with that, Rupert equally as well. They sat silently in the car for several minutes, both deeply thinking. It was fortunate that the driveway to and from the Savoy hotel was by that time of night so quiet, so much so that even the doorman didn't seem bothered by Rupert's car idling for so long.

Finally, Rupert broke the silence. "That was very lovely, what you said Nan. It is only right that we should give grateful thanks and acknowledgement to all of those in at the beginning. Without them, none of us would have the years of musical enjoyment that we, and you for so much longer than me, have experienced. Thanks to all indeed!"

"Right you are, Rupert" his grandmother replied. "I like to be here too because it is so atmospheric, so meaningful for me. All the years that I have been coming here to the Savoy for the operas, all the people whom I have been here with, my own parents, your grandfather, and with you, of course, too, Rupert, love. It all means so very, very much!" Alice continued deep in thought for a few moments. "But now I suppose that this is it and we must away!"

With that, Rupert once again put the car into forward gear and drove very slowly around the Savoy driveway, turning full circle past the hotel entrance, until the car was once more facing the Strand. This time, the Savoy Theatre was on Alice's side of the car and she wound down her window to take a closer look, as if to absorb more the atmosphere. Rupert stopped the car again for a minute and when it finally edged away, he felt pleased that the traffic flow that he had to cross was still so busy that they remained outside the theatre for a few more moments. His grandmother's wishes, not to say his own, could be fulfilled for a few minutes longer.

Alice was very deep in thought as she looked towards the Savoy Theatre. Then, just as Rupert saw a gap in the traffic and was about to move off, Alice laughed as she rewound her side window.

"What's that Nan?" Rupert asked.

"I was just laughing to myself at what I heard the four people over there by the theatre, two men and two ladies with them, saying," Alice replied. "Whatever you said about being alone for your walk, it was different now, people there and certainly showing that we are not the only devotees around!"

"I didn't hear, nor see them – what was it they said?" Rupert asked, taking his eye from the road momentarily.

"Oh, I heard them say – 'To Sir Arthur Sullivan, Mr. Gilbert, Mr. D'Oyly Carte and, most importantly too, to the whole D'Oyly Carte Company and long may it continue!' – amen to that, that's what I would add!" Alice said with sincerity.

Rupert froze as he heard the words and didn't even then try to take the space in the traffic flow that was there before him. "Is that what you really heard?" he asked of his grandmother.

"Absolutely, word by word," Alice replied. "I thought that it was strange because they referred to 'Mr' Gilbert, not Sir William, then they said 'Mr. D'Oyly Carte' and there hasn't been a 'Mr' at the helm of the company for many a long year! Strange, too, that they spoke of the 'D'Oyly Carte Company', the name it was often referred to colloquially when I was a child, even though the proper name was the same as now. They must have been oldies like me! In fact they almost looked Victorian, the ladies in their cloaks and big, flowery hats, very nice too!"

Rupert looked once more into his mirror. The drive way that went around the Savoy was empty, deserted of both pedestrians and vehicles.

"That was so wonderful to hear," Alice exclaimed, "it was just like the old times, even down to the beautiful clothes they were wearing. It brought back so many memories, good and happy memories! A perfect ending to this evening after all!"

Rupert, in a state of dazed confusion, finally drove away and into the Strand. The Savoy courtyard was once again empty.

The very same courtyard was also empty the moment after Tom, Nellie, Fred Dean and Florrie Parker finally set off home to

Peckham at the end of their own successful Gilbert and Sullivan and D'Oyly Carte evening at the Savoy Theatre.

"Live to love and love to live –
You will ripen at your ease,
Growing on the sunny side –
Fate has nothing more to give."

THE END.

Gilbert and Sullivan Operas - Chronology

Opening Nights:

Opera.	Theatre.	Date.	Initial Continuous Performances
'Thespis'	Gaiety Theatre, Corner Wellington Street/Catherine Street, London.	26 Dec. 1871	64
'Trial by Jury'	Royalty Theatre, Dean Street, Soho, London.	25 Mar. 1875	131
'The Sorcerer'	Opera Comique, Wych Street, near The Strand, London.	17 Nov. 1877	175
'HMS Pinafore'	"	25 May 1878	700
'The Pirates of Penzance'	Bijou Theatre, Paignton, Devon	30 Dec. 1879	
	Fifth Avenue Theatre, New York.	31 Dec 1879	
	Opera Comique, London.	3 Apr 1880	363
'Patience'	"	23 Apr 1881	578
	transferred to and opened Savoy Theatre, London.	10 Oct. 1881.	
'Iolanthe'	Savoy Theatre	25 Nov 1882	398
'Princess Ida'	Savoy Theatre	5 Jan 1884	246
'The Mikado'	Savoy Theatre	14 Mar 1885	672
'Ruddigore'	Savoy Theatre	22 Jan 1887	288

Opera.	Theatre.	Date.	Initial Continuous Performances
'The Yeomen of the Guard'	Savoy Theatre	3 Oct 1888	423
'The Gondoliers'	Savoy Theatre	7 Dec. 1889.	554
'Utopia Limited'	Savoy Theatre	7 Oct. 1893	245
'The Grand Duke'	Savoy Theatre	7 Mar. 1896	123

The Last Night of the original D'Oyly Carte Opera Company.
Adelphi Theatre,
The Strand,
London.   27 Feb. 1982

Bibliography

Gilbert and Sullivan Opera Quotations – from "The Savoy Operas" by W.S. Gilbert, St Martin's Library Edition

The Gilbert and Sullivan Companion by Leslie Ayre, W.H. Allen, 1972
The Gilbert & Sullivan Book by Leslie Baily, Spring Books, 1966